Blue Suede Darlin'

JULIET NORDEEN

ISBN-10: 0615750907
ISBN-13: 978-0615750903

For Chris
All my love

ACKNOWLEDGMENTS

Every writer says it, and I'm going to say it again: no book can be completed by just one person.

I would like to thank my beloved, Chris, for his support and energy. Without him this book would never have been completed...because I'd still be stuck to a CAD terminal, belly-aching about how badly I wanted to learn to be a writer. I also must thank my writers group, The Mixed Metaphors: Jessica and Anya and Eryn, for all of their hand-holding, steady encouragement, and ass-kicking hard work. You ladies have my undying affection. And to my first reader, Debbie, thank you for finding my glitches and preventing me from looking like a complete fool.

My beautiful cover image is the work of Andy Hartmark. Thanks, Andy, for allowing me to use it, and a special thanks to Cherry Dollface for brokering the arrangement.

And most of all, thank you Reader for taking this journey with me and Bailey. I'm currently working on the sequel. You can check up on my progress, or contact me, at www.JulietNordeen.com.

See you around The Bailey-verse!

1

After feeling like I'd been riding a rollercoaster through an earthquake for two and a half days, the inky Gulf waters finally settled down around our little wooden lifeboat. The calmer swells rocked us with a down-beat of gentle rollers topped off by a 4/4 tempo of lapping wavelets. The breeze that chilled the clammy skin of my bare shoulders drove the thick storm clouds eastward and the stars did their best to twinkle through the oppressively humid September air.

My four best friends slept, heads resting at awkward angles on each others' arms and torsos, trying to get comfortable in the little space the lifeboat allowed. I couldn't blame them. Since the rough seas calmed, I wished I could sleep, too.

But it was my turn to watch.

I scanned the horizon all around for the lights of fishing trawlers or the giant gouts of flame burning atop offshore drilling platforms. Between passes of the distant horizon I scanned the surface of the water closer to the boat, wary of fins. Occasionally I stretched out the kinks in my neck and glanced toward the stars, hoping to orient myself by a familiar constellation, but I couldn't find one.

Mostly I watched the four people I loved most in the world sleep. Exhausted, pruney, rain-sodden, and getting awfully close to that place where all hope for rescue and seeing dry land ever again is lost.

Even in their sleep, my bandmates kept a natural rhythm with each other. JoJo's un-lady-like, deep-throated snore set the bass line that Cooper's steady rhythm and Paulo's melodic snores riffed across, as if they were jamming on stage, rather than lost at sea. Maria—always the quiet one, unless she was pounding on the keys of her piano—held her snore-ful comments until the rare occasion when the other three fell silent, and then like Gracie Allen delivering the punch line to a perfectly-timed George Burns joke, she'd let out a snort from down deep in her gut and shift position.

I might have laughed if I could find something the least bit funny about being lost and adrift somewhere in the western reaches of the Gulf of Mexico in a twelve-foot lifeboat without food and nearly out of rainwater.

Then again, just smiling would've been bad for my dry, cracked, burning lips. What I wouldn't have given for a tube of cherry Chapstick to soothe them. I knew licking them each time they dried just made it worse, but I couldn't help myself.

And a toothbrush, I'd have killed for three minutes with a toothbrush. My tongue felt like it had gone-in-halfsies with my teeth for a set of custom-fit fuzzy slipcovers. Not pleasant.

But perhaps worst of all was the way the fabric of my favorite red polka-dot swing dress, stiff from soaking and drying and soaking and drying, chafed at my skin every time I moved. And it stunk—mildew, salt, too much time without a shower. I would have to throw it out if we ever got...home.

Being adrift sucked in every way, but it was less frightening than being sucked into the water in a capsizing boat.

Those ten minutes after a rogue wave had flipped-over our new record label's forty-foot yacht had been the most horrifying of my life. The three attempts it took Cooper to dive down and cut the lifeboat loose from the sinking behemoth had just about driven my heart out of my chest with panic. Three days of paddling the little boat with our hands, screaming out for help, and drinking rainwater squeezed from our clothes had forced me into a place of numbness where I stopped feeling much of anything.

Except love. And fear. Love and fear were all I had left.

I loved my bandmates; I called them my phamily—short for pseudo family. We'd been each others' rocks since I was fourteen years old, and I was scared to the depths of my soul that our final legacy on this planet would be a three paragraph article on the Austin Chronicle's news website with the headline: *Hometown Rockabilly Band Lost at Sea.* Billy's Asylum Rats—that up-and-coming, just-landed-a-recording-deal band of hep cats also known as me, JoJo, Cooper, Maria and Paulo—were as tight as friends and bandmates could be, and I hated this shitty situation and how helpless I was to do anything for them.

Lifting my watchful eyes again to the stars, I picked out the brightest one I could find. "I don't know if there's anyone out there listening, but we could really use some help," I said quietly.

"None of us is perfect," I told the sky. "We don't go to church or pay all of our taxes, and I think I might hold some record for time spent chasing carnal pleasure, but we rock hard, love deep and live big. That's got to count for something."

Maria snorted in her sleep and wriggled to find a more comfortable position resting on Cooper's shoulder. Her adjustment cascaded around the lifeboat—hand bumping hip shifting shoulder turning head—but they soon settled, each into a new, equally uncomfortable-looking position.

I needed to cry so badly. For them. For myself. Agony gripped every sorrow-expressing portion of my body—shoulders wanted to shake, throat wanted to cry, belly wanted to bawl—but I simply didn't have any more tears left to shed. I knew that meant I had lost all hope of being rescued.

"Please," I begged the sky. "Please, we're not done yet. I'll do anything to keep them safe."

When the brightest star in the sky started falling toward the rolling waters of the Gulf, I thought it was an illusion brought on by the upward roll of the lifeboat and the darkness surrounding us. But when the boat nosed down into the next trough and the star continued to drift lower, I knew something amazing was happening. My heart raced into my throat like the kids charging the dance floor at the start of one of our shows when Cooper lays down the first lines of *Blue Suede Shoes*.

Help was finally on the way. A rescue plane, or maybe better, a helicopter! I waved my arms, even though I knew they were too far away to see me.

The light blazed brighter and whiter as it grew closer to our little boat. I was about to reach over and shake Maria's shoulder to wake her so we could watch together, when I realized that the aircraft, whatever it was, couldn't hold altitude and was hurtling straight at us. A morbid part of my brain wondered if it would clobber the lifeboat as it splashed down into the Gulf. We could trade starving to death for getting pulverized.

The orb of light grew to about the size of a snare-drum skin held at arm's length and then silently, splashlessly, met the water and submerged into the black. I had a hard time guessing the distance between me and the point of impact in the darkness, but I saw the glow rise up under the surface of the water as it continued in our direction. In a few moments it closed the distance to the back of the lifeboat across which Paulo lay sleeping, and showed no signs of slowing. Acting on instinct I braced for an impact; one hand against the inside of the prow of the boat and the other clamped onto Maria's shoulder.

But no impact came; no splintering wood, drenching spray, or upended lifeboat. Instead I heard a small gurgle, like bubbles rising from an aquarium aerator, and then a gentle splash warned me something had breached the surface and was about to approach our little boat. I held my breath and attempted to look everywhere at once, trying to catch the first hint of any movement in the darkness. Fight-or-flight instincts primed my muscles with adrenaline; I was ready to pounce the length of the lifeboat if whatever was about to come out of the water made one wrong move toward Paulo.

One pale set of fingers, and then a second, rose up over the edge of the stern and then clamped on. The digits were long, though not inhumanly so, elegantly strong and tipped with manicured nails that reflected the silver of the starlight. Fingers became hands became wrists and forearms and then a full head of glossy, dark hair rose into view. A woman, maybe a few years older than me or Maria, pulled herself up on the edge of the boat until she could tuck both arms over the edge.

She was gorgeous—1940s Hollywood gorgeous—with ebony hair, milk-white skin, and light eyes in a shade of gray or blue that I couldn't make out in the darkness. She was bone dry and her make-up was perfect as if she hadn't just surfaced from the water, though I knew in my gut that she had. My sense about it was that she appeared that way for no other reason than *that's exactly how she wanted it*, as if a drowned-rat entrance to begin a rescue was both beneath her and impolite. She smiled at me in a way that filled her whole being with a glow and warmed me to the depths of my frightened soul. Hope flooded back into me so quickly that my toes tingled.

"Bailey Faye Michaels," she said, more as a statement to confirm my identity than a question.

I nodded because my mouth hung open too widely to form words.

She took in the state of my phamily—obviously knocked-out by exhaustion—the empty oar-locks of the lifeboat, and the expanse of dark water stretching to the horizon in every direction. "Oh, my. You do need some help. It's a good thing I've come."

Relief filled my body at her words, ushering the adrenaline out of my overly-tense muscles like a bouncer herding drunks after last call. I reached out to wake Maria, who was closest to me, hoping she could confirm whether I was hallucinating or if there really was a beautiful woman with a trillion-watt-smile hanging off the back of our lifeboat. But our visitor stopped me.

"Better to let them sleep," she said. Her voice carried a bell-like, soothing quality that made me wonder how I could have doubted my eyes. "They've had such a terrible few days."

Wasn't that the truth? I could shout three *Ooby Doobys* and a *Go, Cat Go!* in support of that little assessment of our recent events. The omniscient sympathy in her voice immediately made me certain that all I'd believed about Higher Powers my whole life was wrong and I was truly in the presence of a godlike being.

A goddess. There was a goddess hanging off the back of our boat in answer to my plea.

I forgot my manners and simply stared for minutes on end. Like a starlet addicted to the adoration of the paparazzi she absorbed my attention, apparently content to wait, bobbing up and down with the motion of the lifeboat.

My brain fought with itself. If she were a goddess, why would she arrive like that—splashing into the water and threatening to torpedo our little boat? Why not just appear, hovering in a glow of ethereal light? And what was she waiting for? Why didn't she just snap her fingers and teleport us all to the shore? Doubts of her divine power tickled my intuition and my mind came back to reality. I found my voice. "What are you?"

"I'm Laume." She pronounced it *l-oww-may*, with an Eastern European accent which would be all growly and clipped if she had been a man. On her it was intriguing; as different as you could get from a Texas drawl, but compelling in a similarly lazy way.

"Laume," I repeated, trying to get the unusual name to stick in my brain. "But, what are you?"

Laume tilted her head to the side and smiled at me like I was a puppy or particularly dim-witted child. "I'm here to help you."

She boosted herself higher on the back of the boat until her waist rested on its edge. Her long dark hair draped onto

Paulo's chest as she leaned forward, her gaze holding more intensity than I've felt from anyone since my dad found out I'd started a band with four other kids from the state mental hospital.

"That is if you still want my help," she said.

"Yes! Yes, please!" I put my hands to my face, surprised to feel cool tears on my cheeks; tears of hope. "I didn't know how we were going to survive this mess."

Laume relaxed, lowering her body back down until her arms rested easily on the edge of the boat and then she elegantly rested her chin on her arms. "I like your enthusiasm, little darlin', but perhaps it would be better if we discussed my price before you agreed?"

"Price?" I asked. Higher Powers put a price on rescue? I never heard of God charging to perform a miracle. Not that I wouldn't have given anything to get us all back to dry land, but I thought that was the kind of thing they did out of the goodness of their hearts, or to improve their reputations. How inhuman that felt, how not-divine.

"Yes, a price," Laume said, her smile becoming predatory. "A bargain, if you will. I have a task that your unique talents are perfectly suited for. In exchange, I will transport your friends to safety."

2

My unique talents?

A bargain?

A price and a task?

"What do you mean?" I asked, feeling like I'd fallen down some desperate, aquatic version of Alice's rabbit hole.

"First, we must agree to the bargain. You agree to help me and I will grant your wish."

"If I say yes, I won't have to kill anyone? Will I?" I asked.

Laume smiled in a wholesome way again. "Probably not."

I bit my lower lip. "I really don't have a choice."

"Of course you have a choice, silly girl," Laume said. "There's always a choice. It's only been three days, yes? You could wait another three or four sunsets for a boat to happen by before anyone dried up and died. Except for maybe this one," Laume nodded to Paulo lying beneath her.

Then a very odd sensation crept over my eyes, as if someone had blindfolded me with the softest, lightest silk in the world. I have no issue with kink, not among consenting adults, but what happened next was not something I would have agreed to experience had I known it was coming, and it scared me like nothing I'd ever faced. Instead of going dark, my vision began to lighten, fading up into what looked like a helicopter's view, time-lapse image of us in the lifeboat and the waters around it. The images flew so quickly that it took me a minute to understand that I wasn't seeing a replay of the last few days, but a preview of what we were in for.

Laume's version of *the Ghost of Christmas Future* was ugly. As she hinted, Paulo didn't make it to see another sunset. The worst part was watching the four of us argue—silently, of course, as this particular freak show had no audio or soundtrack—about whether to leave him lying in the back of the boat or lay him in the water and tie him to the boat. My stomach cramped watching Maria and Cooper get so pissed-off that they came to blows. Maria lost.

I wanted to vomit watching Cooper carefully pick Paulo up and lay him in the water where he bobbed, half surfaced-half submerged, with the setting sun finally giving his pale skin some color.

It was horrible.

We, the grown-up versions of the misfits from the juvenile ward at Texas State Hospital, were not prepared to deal with losing Paulo.

I bowed my head and brushed my hands at the mythical blindfold over my eyes, not that it helped. "Okay, okay. Just make it stop."

Laume purred her satisfaction. The vision stopped and I saw the darkness and the boat and Laume again.

"You must say *I agree.*"

"I don't know," I said. She had me at such a disadvantage. I did not want what I just saw to ever happen for real. If Paulo died, if any of us died in this godforsaken dingy, Billy's Asylum

Rats would be quitso for sure and I'm not sure any of the rest of us would really *make it*, even if we survived and got back to dry land.

The decision was too much for me to handle on my own. "I need to wake my friends and ask them for their help."

"It's not a difficult decision. Either you will help me so that I can help you and your friends. Or I'll just go and find someone else who can help."

"But..."

With that, Laume let go of the boat and dropped quickly out of my sight—bubbles gurgling to mark her submersion beneath the dark water.

The cynical side of me knew she was bluffing; Higher Power or not she answered my plea because she needed my help at least a fraction as much as we needed hers. I held tight to that cynicism as I waited to hear Laume surface again. And I waited. And waited. And the waves around the lifeboat stirred up a notch, like a song swinging into its bridge. And Paulo started to moan in his sleep—low, sad, distressed—his face so pale that it nearly glowed in the low ambient light of the stars. In my memory I saw his lifeless body floating, tied to the boat, and it was no easier to take as a memory than when Laume had given me the vision.

"Laume?" I asked the air. I stood up to see if she might be hovering just below the dark surface of the water at the back of the boat. There wasn't enough light to see clearly, but the shapes of the waves gave nothing away. "Come back."

Nothing.

My inner cynic started to panic.

"Laume!"

My shout caused Paulo's whimpers to grow louder, but none of the rest of them appeared to be disturbed by the desperation in my voice. They should have woken up but were as still as death. Death which might decide to come for Paulo first, but would get all of us sooner rather than later if we didn't get back to dry land, food and drinkable water.

Death that would surely come if Laume didn't come back to help us.

"Laume, please come back." I looked back up at the sky, tears clouding my eyes so that the stars streaked together. "I'm sorry. I'm sorry. Please. I need your help."

Without a splash or a sound, the lifeboat tilted a bit toward the stern and there was Laume, perfectly dry and perfectly pretty. "You must say I agree."

My tongue stuck to the top of my dried out mouth, trying to prevent me from making a huge mistake by agreeing to such a blind bargain, but I managed to peel it loose and say, "I agree."

She nodded to show that she'd heard me and lifeboat tipped toward its stern, plowing quickly through the water in the opposite direction of the skittering clouds.

Somehow, soundlessly and effortlessly, Laume pushed the little boat as smoothly as if it were being towed off the tail of a gigantic cruise ship. Compared to three days of hand-paddling and drifting with the wind and tide, it felt like the boat had suddenly grown jet packs. Miles zoomed by. I reached my hand over the side and felt the rush of warm water flow over it and knew that despite the unknowns, I'd made the right choice. The only possible choice.

Now I just needed to understand what I'd stupidly and blindly agreed to do. Just as I opened my mouth to ask, Laume said, "You do like children, I expect."

Children? What about me did she see as maternal? I doubt it was my carefully sculpted eyebrow arches or my waist-length platinum blonde hair. I'm sure it wasn't my skin-tight, red polka-dot swing dress that showed off my twenty-seven inch waist. And I'm convinced that it wasn't my tattoos—the leopard print full-arm sleeves, the blood-red heart over my breastbone, or the trail of stars running up the back of each leg—that made her think I had a soft-spot for ankle biters.

I'm the drummer of a 'billy band at night and a pastry chef before the sun comes up. My car, a chopped-and-channeled fifty-six Buick, doesn't have seat belts much less tethers for a damn baby seat. In fact, on the streets of Austin, most parents herded their children away from me when I walked down the sidewalks. And I'm talking about downtown Austin, home of everything weird.

I think there was enough moonlight that Laume could read the concern on my face.

"Oh dear. Not very fond of children," Laume said. "That might make this task a tad tricky for you, I'm afraid."

She was afraid? I hyperventilated as I envisioned her sending me on a trip to an African refugee camp to save hundreds of starving children or laying in for a stint as a kindergarten teacher with thirty munchkins underfoot. Or worse, I paled at the thought of magically becoming someone's evil step-mother.

"I really don't know anything about kids," I said.

"But you were one," Laume said. "Once upon a time."

A sarcastic laugh escaped me before I could stop it. Sure I had once been a small human, under the age of majority, too young to smoke or drink, legally. Not that any of that had ever made me a child. No, my father, who loved reminding me that he *raised me all by himself*, insisted that my behavior must, at all times, rise to his expectations of a young adult. And he enforced that mandate as soon as I was old enough to understand that my mother was years-gone and never coming back. I think I was three, maybe four. Took a lot of deprogramming at the Texas State Hospital during my teen years to get over that.

Thinking about my father and the couple of days at the hospital before I met Maria and JoJo made my scalp crawl in anger. "Could you fucking be less cryptic and just tell me what you want me to do?" I yelled.

Our speed dropped until the little boat flattened out and coasted to a stop in the dark water. Laume's eyes narrowed and I knew that had been exactly the wrong thing to say. She pursed her perfectly stained lips and considered me for a few moments over my sleeping friends before her face relaxed. "You are under a great deal of strain," she said. "I will forgive your slip in manners, this once."

I fought the urge to thank her as a subject thanks a queen's mercy, or to apologize like an employee caught with her hand in the register, but couldn't stop the urge to bow my head and Laume took that to mean whatever she needed from me and got the boat underway again.

"There is a girl, Hannah Faye Williams, she's in trouble and she needs your help. She also has daddy issues," Laume said, implying that she knew something—maybe everything—about my relationship with my father. "You will go to the northwest of your country, the city of Portland, and help her."

"Help her how?"

Laume raised her face to the sky as if to ask her fellow gods and goddesses why she'd been burdened with the stupidest human on the planet. When she met my eyes again she said, "I'm sure I have no clue what a child needs to grow up and become what you might call well-adjusted. I'm relying on you to figure that out."

"I'm not what most folks would consider well-adjusted." I was only good at three things in life; drums, pastry and sex. Well-adjusted people my age finished college, had babies and shopped for mortgages.

"Even so, you were a child whose mother was unavailable and whose father failed to live up to the role he took on for himself by engaging in coitus without the proper protection. I am confident you will know how to help. I would not have proposed our bargain otherwise."

"What kind of trouble is she in?" I asked.

"Dear Hannah Faye is in the worst kind of danger; she risks losing her soul. The government has taken her from her home and placed her in a vile place that threatens to quash the very essence of her being—as if she were some unwashed plebeian."

My imagination ran away with that thought. Not that I was a churchgoing, bible-thumper type myself, but suddenly my mind's eye spun images of ritual circles around raging bonfires and I feared that somewhere in the woods of Oregon a little girl was being forced into an arranged marriage with a man three times her age. It made perfect sense to me that a Higher Power might want to get involved with a situation like that. Hell, it might be worth a carefully aimed bullet or two if the circumstances went badly enough.

"Why this girl? Who is she?" I asked.

Laume smiled at me and gestured beyond the front of the lifeboat. "Look."

I spun my head around and saw something I'd been hungering after for three days: the lights of a fishing boat in the near distance. I'd been so caught up in Laume's description of my task that we'd gotten to within a couple hundred yards of it and I hadn't even heard the thrum of its engines. It looked like a shrimp boat; tall and wide with nets draping from large booms on both sides of the boat.

A cry escaped me and I turned to thank Laume with tears in my eyes. Satanists and creepy daddy-types be damned, I'd made the right choice and we were going to be safe. JoJo and Paulo and Maria and Cooper and me, we were going to survive. Billy's Asylum Rats would record and release music all over the internetz, we would play live again, and we would be whole.

"Thank you," I said.

Laume bowed her head to me. "Of course. We have a bargain."

"We do," I agreed.

I turned forward to watch the fishing boat grow from the size of a bathtub toy to its full hulking size, until I could smell the stench of its holds full of dead and dying sea critters. Gradually Laume's push on the back of the lifeboat fell off until we stopped within shouting distance of the shrimper.

"How do I explain..." I started to ask as I turned around to ask Laume what I could or should say to my phamily about how we'd been rescued. Only Laume no longer hung from the back of the lifeboat.

She was gone, just vanished, and so was my phamily. I was all alone.

3

In a night full of the Impossible, this bigger and greater Impossible smacked me across the face. Our little lifeboat, the one Cooper had nearly died retrieving from the sinking yacht, was empty but for me and a half-inch of dirty rainwater. Scared that somehow my phamily had fallen overboard, I scrambled from side to side along the length of the boat to search for them in the black water, stretching my arm down, again and again. I got all the way to the stern and found nothing but bathwater-warm, salt water. I took a second to look around and thought about it. I'd heard no splashes, seen no ripples, found no sign that anyone had been anywhere near the little lifeboat, except me. I was alone.

I slammed my hand against the hull of the boat, getting a wet thwack and a stinging palm for my trouble. The pain grounded my panic, like when someone asks you to pinch them, but my brain continued whirling in disbelief. Just when I thought things were headed in the right direction, Laume had vanished and taken my phamily with her. It was the only explanation.

"Laume!" I yelled at the sky. "You bitch. Where'd you go?"

I was angrier than I ever remembered being in my life, so much so that the lights on the fishing boat's deck took on a red tinge. That inhuman bitch had strong-armed me into blindly making an agreement and then she magically stole away into the darkness with the only part of my life that made any sense, my phamily.

Unless I had it wrong.

My skirt billowed around me as I plopped into the bottom of the boat, ignoring the dirty rainwater, and considered the possibility that everything I'd been through in the past three days had been a hallucination. A mad lie built to cope with losing Maria and JoJo and Cooper and Paulo in a horrible accident at sea.

Fixating on an empty oar lock, I tried to quiet the dervishes in my head so I could think.

I had no proof they'd survived the yacht going down, or been in the lifeboat at all. Starving and parched, it's possible I might have mixed some things up in my head; imagined our conversations, pretended we'd been together. I sure as hell couldn't say with any conviction that an evil, Higher Power had fallen from the sky as a ball of light, offered me a deal I couldn't refuse in exchange for rescue, propelled our little lifeboat miles and miles across the Gulf to one tiny little fishing boat, and then disappeared along with four adults—three of them bigger than her—when I turned my back on her for two seconds.

Even though I *felt* like it had all been real, I had nothing to show any of it had actually happened. That cold fact slammed around inside my brain, opening a crack into which Doubt invited itself to slither through and make itself at home—the first step down a familiar but unwelcome path toward some very bad times. The only two things left for me to cling to were a name, *Hannah Faye Williams* (strange, I realized, we had the same middle name), and a city, *Portland, Oregon* and I knew I couldn't have made either of those up.

No. No, I had not hallucinated the past three days. Hot anger born of self-doubt in my belly drove me to my feet to scream at the stars, "Laume, you dog-cold bitch! Come back. What the hell did you do with my phamily?"

My yelling attracted the attention of the men on the shrimp boat and a spotlight tracked across the water until it found me railing at the darkness like a lunatic in my little lifeboat. They followed me with the light as I fell back into their wake. A dozen men gathered along the aft railing, shouting in Spanish until the big boat's engines cut off. Ropes and flotation donuts flew through the air towards me as two men stripped down to their underwear and dove into the water.

As they swam toward me I felt torn between wanting them to hurry up and rescue me and not wanting to be saved without my phamily. How could I go home without them? How could I explain what happened? I didn't give a rat's ass about the record company's yacht; they could sue my ass and I'd work the rest of my life to cover the cost of replacing it. But how could I look Paulo's Mama or JoJo's sister in the eyes and tell them that all five of us had been just fine for three days and then the four of them disappeared minutes before we were to be rescued? I couldn't lie and say I had been the only survivor; I was a bad liar.

"*Then don't go home*," said a voice inside my head. At first I thought it was my chicken-shit inner nature looking for an easy way out, but then I realized it wasn't my voice. It was Laume's voice, talking to me from inside my own frickin' head.

Get out of my head!

"*Make me*," Laume said.

Not knowing how she'd gotten into my head in the first place—some Higher Power mumbo jumbo that was way above my pay grade—I knew that I was unlikely to just kick her out. I knew she knew it. As much as I hated the violation—my skin crawled from the thought of having another being inside the only private place I thought was guaranteed to me—I was powerless to stop it from happening.

If I couldn't fight it, my desperation drove me to try to make use of it. *What did you do with my phamily?* I asked, silently. *I want them back. Right. Goddamn. Now.*

The pity of having a conversation inside my head was the bone-deep knowledge that I couldn't hide the fear I felt. I was bluffing with my implied ultimatum. And I knew she knew that, too. She brushed me off, laughing right inside my brain, a sound more humiliating for its intimacy than any bully's taunts could ever be.

"I need your promise that you are not going home. That you will proceed directly to Portland to complete your task."

I have to go home first. I have to explain about...

"No, you don't. No one on that boat knows who you are or where you came from," Laume said, conveying absolute certainty. *"They haven't seen news coverage of your missing yacht. They have no idea that there were ever five miserable, half-drowned wretches aboard this lifeboat. As far as those fishermen are concerned they are about to rescue* una muchacha muy bonita. *You don't even have to speak with them, pretend you don't understand Spanish."*

Her brazen disrespect for my situation tied my brain in knots, I couldn't find a response that included anything but swear words. Laume mistook my inner silence for agreement.

"They will take you to shore; their vessel is ported out of a small village called Santa Teresa. You will ride with their daily catch to Ciudad Victoria and then take a bus north along the coast to Laredo, Texas. Your "lost" *passport will be waiting for you at the border."*

I knew she was full of shit because I'd never owned a passport.

You can stuff your bus trip and your fake passport up your skinny white ass, I yelled at Laume in my head, uncomfortable with being dictated to. *Where is my phamily? You said you'd get them to safety.*

"They're safe as moonbeams, little darlin', and will remain so as long as you execute your end of our bargain. It is in my best interest that you arrive in Portland, as quickly as possible, unencumbered by unnecessary concerns, so listen carefully. After crossing the border you will travel by bus again to Dallas, to the place where airships port, and there you will wait for further direction."

How do I know they are safe? Where did you take them?

"You'll have to trust me," Laume said in my head.

Screw that. There wasn't a molecule in my body that trusted Laume. She didn't even know airplanes and airports.

I don't. I don't have to and I don't want to. And I'm not going anywhere until I know they're okay. I thought this thought with all the conviction I could muster. Laume had to know I wasn't shitting her on this. If she wanted me to climb aboard some random Mexican fishing boat, much less run off to the woods to save a little girl named Hannah, she had to give me something to prove my bandmates were safe.

The two swimming fishermen had almost reached my little lifeboat and I knew something had to give, and soon. Laume's plan sounded well thought out, and given how easily she'd gotten the lifeboat to a rescue vessel I figured arranging a little ground transportation from the shore to Dallas and then on to Portland probably wouldn't be beyond her. But once I got onto that fishing boat I'd be stuck on her path, I could be in an even worse situation—if that were possible.

I wished I could at least talk to Maria about all of this. She was the steady one in the group, the one who always took care of us when we needed it or smacked us across the face with reality when our heads were too far up our own asses. Maria would know whether I could trust Laume at least enough to get onto the fishing boat, or whether I should tell her to kiss her own divine ass.

What do you say, Dolly? That's how I would ask Maria's opinion had she been there.

"*I think this babe's a schuckster, but don't let her rattle your cage little darlin'.*"

I startled. The voice in my head had changed, it sounded like Maria, not just her voice but that's exactly what I'd expect her to say: pragmatic, level-headed and direct. *Maria? Is that really you?*

"*It's me, kitty-cat.*"

You okay? Where are you? Are you all together? She said she's taken y'all somewhere safe. I wanted to believe that it really was Maria in my head and that she wasn't talking to me with a gun to her head, real or supernatural.

"This Faery Bitch might be lighting up the tilt sign with most of what she's dishing out, but for the moment we've got it made in the shade. Do what you gotta do, kitty-cat. Don't you worry about us."

That had to be Maria, and most of what she said made sense in a 'billy way. All except the part where she called Laume a Faery...that wasn't 'billy shorthand we tossed around in our circles.

What did you call her? I asked Maria in my thoughts.

"She's Faery, magic, not human...you know, Tinkerbell gone wild."

But she's so big.

"*That's enough*," Laume butted in to my mental conversation with Maria like she'd just taken her cell phone away. "*Your dog-paddling saviors have arrived. You have a job to do.*"

My heart ached at being allowed to talk to Maria and then having her yanked away like that. I believed in my gut that my phamily was alive, and not in danger, for the moment. I had to believe Maria would have found some way to signal me if that had been the case.

You'll keep them safe? I asked silently.

I heard, "G*et it done*," and then Laume's presence in my mind evaporated, too. Whatever magical connection we'd used to have that odd conversation had been severed. Violation ended.

I blinked my eyes and shook my head. Had I really just had a telepathic conversation with my Faery-napped best friend while floating in a lifeboat, awaiting rescue by a couple of Mexican fisherman? Was any of it real?

Assessing my new reality brought on a bloom of cold behind my breastbone, loneliness. For the last twelve years I'd always had at least one of Billy's Asylum Rats no further than a phone call away. Now it was just me and the crazy voices in my head.

I looked in the direction of the shrimp boat and was surprised to see a muscular young man with black hair and chocolate skin heave himself into the lifeboat, rocking it violently. He lay panting in the bottom of the boat as the searchlight did its best to stay on us. I hadn't heard his approach as he swam, nor his kick against the water to propel his body into the boat, not even his deep breaths as he lay a foot away from me in the bottom of the boat. The young man yelled—or at least his lips moved—as he gestured for the other man to swim over with the free end of the rope. But I couldn't hear his voice. Or the slosh of the water. Or the voices of the other men.

I couldn't hear anything.

After a day of Impossibility stacked upon Impossibility, it seemed a small thing to suddenly not be able to hear—but it was a huge thing. I'd never had trouble with my hearing in my entire life; for the drummer in a rock band, that said something.

As I opened my mouth to ask the universe *why the hell this was happening*, nothing came out. Not a peep, not a syllable. When I touched my throat with my hand I didn't feel any vibration, but I got a tickle on the inside like I'd swallowed a handful of junebugs. I started to cough and apparently that made a sound because the young fisherman looked at me with concern before turning his attention back to his buddy arriving with the rope.

I panicked.

After what I'd been through over the previous three days there shouldn't have been any adrenaline left to race through my body, but my heart pounded fiercely all the same. I couldn't hear and I couldn't speak. Why couldn't I hear? And what did that have to do with not being able to speak? Was this a spell Laume concocted to keep me from messing up her well-laid plan to get me to Portland? Was it punishment for my less-than-stellar manners? What kind of monster takes away a person's ability to communicate? And at a time like this?

Pulsating motion of the lifeboat broke through my panic and I realized the boys were pulling in the ropes, drawing us toward the hulking shrimper. We quickly fell into the shadow at the stern of the larger boat and a rope ladder unfurled. One of the young men held the lifeboat steady while the other held the rope ladder for me and motioned for me to climb. He smiled and nodded, looking serious and trustworthy, but I hesitated.

Crawling up that ladder and onto a strange boat under a usual rescue-scenario like this would be daunting. But not being able to communicate with my saviors made me feel awfully vulnerable as I counted the sixteen rope rungs between the lifeboat and the deck. Suddenly, having a less than perfect grasp of Spanish seemed like small potatoes, but it seemed I was out of options, no choice to get on the boat, take a step onto Laume's path.

I stood up in the lifeboat carefully, my footing as unstable as smooth leather-soled shoes on a freshly waxed dance floor, and reached between my legs to grab a handful of the back of my polka-dotted skirt. After I had it pulled through my legs and tucked it into the belt at the front of my dress, denying the boys a free peek while they held the ladder for me, I made my way up one shoddy rung at a time.

A frenzy of hands pulled me over the rail of the fishing boat and onto its rusty metal deck. The dozen faces that greeted me shared a sense of curiosity, and what came across in my silent world as a flurry of wordless teeth-gnashing as they said things I couldn't hear. Funny how it wasn't immediately clear to me whether they were happy or angry: their excited expressions could have been either—eyes wide, brows raised, lots of teeth needing orthodontia.

The one face I had no trouble reading was the one on the man standing next to a net full of wriggling shrimp that dripped seawater onto the deck. His arms-crossed demeanor, aggressive cigar puffing, and scrutinizing glare told me this was his boat, and he its captain. And the captain wasn't happy about his crew wasting time with the soggy blonde girl when they ought to have been hauling in nets.

After pulling a half-smoked cigar from between clenched teeth, the captain said something sharply that lit a fire under his crew. Most of them turned back to their duties immediately. The two who had swum out to get me petted my long hair and looked at me regretfully with their dark brown eyes before putting their clothes back on and joining their mates at the nets.

Fish out of water. That was me. I stood for the captain's inspection—flat-haired, mascara-streaked, swing dress still trussed up like pantaloons—and his predatory glare scared the crap out of me. It's not like me to cry in front of strangers, hell I hardly ever cry in front of my phamily except when too much tequila dredges up the past, but I was lost and alone and the pressure of the situation forced hot tears to dribble down my cheeks.

And that, apparently, did the trick.

In a blink the Captain's stern face melted into a soft-eyed smile and he stepped forward to take both my hands into his. He shouted something to someone over his shoulder, I couldn't say what or to whom, and guided me toward the cabin door. Afraid he wanted to take me down into the darkness of the trawler's belly, I resisted him until I saw a grandfatherly old man in a chef's coat and shorts come up from below with a steaming mug of coffee, a big bottle of water and a plate of tamales. The chef beckoned to me to sit on the worn wooden bench next to the door. When I hesitated, the captain demonstrated, patting the wood next to him.

I smiled at them, laughing for a brief moment at my own fear and stupidity, and untucked my skirt before settling next to the captain. I nodded inadequate thanks to the chef as he handed me the hot cup and plate and then set the bottle next to me. My stomach churned as I smelled the sweet corn masa of the tamales and I imagined what an unladylike rumble must have accompanied it. I grabbed the first tamale and demolished it between sips of the richest coffee I've ever tasted.

Six tamales, two cups of coffee and a liter of water later I felt like the hole in my belly that might never go away had finally been filled. But that one problem solved left too many others battling for space in my brain as I tried to figure out my next steps: my phamily, Laume, Hannah, communicating telepathically, and my unexplained problems hearing and speaking. No matter how hard I wrestled ideas in my mind I found no solutions and my head nodded drowsily, eyes drifted closed.

4

I woke up to the sun rising over the Gulf, drenching the back of the rusty, old shrimper in listless, orange light. Apparently as I slept, my back wedged against the cabin wall, someone had tucked a balled-up coat under my head and draped a roughly woven blanket over me. I lay still, taking stock of my situation.

Seven Mexican crewmen worked at three separate workstations at the back of the boat, chatting as they sorted through bins and bins of the night's catch. Their masculine tones provided a rhythm-line under frequent, sharp cries from the seagulls that dove from the boat's railings, chasing what the men tossed back into the sea.

My sleep-addled brain bounced through memories from the night before: Laume's star falling from the sky, being strong-armed into a blind bargain, elation at finally moving toward rescue only to be devastated by Laume's horrible magic trick: stealing my phamily. The violation at fighting with Laume inside my own head, and then the joy of getting a tiny connection with Maria—they were all alive, and in Maria's estimation they had safe-enough accommodations, albeit mysterious and provided by a Faery.

Laume was a Faery.

At that moment, I was so deep in contemplation about what the hell a Faery really was—Tinkerbell, on steroids and mushrooms was my best guess—that I nearly jumped out of my skin when the boat's air horn blasted three short toots, breaking through the quiet of the dawn.

I could hear!

I sat up. "Ooby Dooby?"

I could talk! I would have jumped off the bench in happy relief except my muscles and bones ached from sleeping in one position too long.

No one had heard me testing my voice, and I decided to continue to play deaf and dumb—I thought of it as D-n-D—as the growl of the engines changed and the boat pulled into its dilapidated dock. The return of my voice and hearing was the first stroke of luck in a day that turned out to be full of better fortune than the previous few had been. Not only did the captain arrange for me to travel with his daily catch to the city, but his girl at the docks was about my size (though less leggy) and she offered me less conspicuous traveling clothes: dun-colored cotton capris, a white cotton tank-top, and a pair of sandals. I gave her my dress in return, though its skirt would fall almost to her ankles.

Clean for the first time in four days, and wearing clean clothes, I joined two men in the cab of a pick-up that was nearly as old and rusty as the shrimper. I continued to play D-n-D for the trip into the city, Ciudad Victoria, with the truckload of shrimp. The two men treated me like the catch of the day until they realized I wasn't interested in them or their charming conversations. They gave up hitting on me to bicker amicably about something that sounded like well-covered territory. I was too overwhelmed, and grateful they let me rest my head on the window.

The scenery flying by the roadside struck me as a poorer version of the Texas coast I knew so well. I counted cows and children and ocotillo trees as I picked-out the occasional word from the men's' conversation—anything to keep from worrying about Maria and Paulo, JoJo and Cooper. That cold ball of loneliness still bloomed for them behind my breastbone, right next to my heart.

Before I hopped out of the truck at the bus station, my driver and his *amigo* pressed a small wad of wrinkled pesos into my hands for the bus. It wasn't in my nature to accept charity from such hard-working people—that stack of well-worn bills could feed a family for a week—but I realized that had the shoe been on the other foot I would have gotten a lot of happiness from helping a stranded person get home. After memorizing the company name stenciled on the side of the truck, I kissed them both on the cheek and ran for the bus with the "Laredo" sign in its windshield as a mechanic slammed its hood and the engine raged to life with a billow of black smoke.

The bus was chaos. Old women with chickens. Young mommas with uncontrollable toddlers. Drunken louts who snored more loudly asleep than they chattered when awake. Unlike the conversation in the truck between the driver and his buddy that soothed me, the roar of humanity inside the rickety old bus made me feel more isolated and invited my fears to clobber my wounded heart.

As I laid my head back and closed my eyes, my thoughts turned to my phamily. Where they were. How they must be feeling. Understanding that Laume was a Faery didn't really help me figure out how she'd taken them or what she might consider *safe as moonbeams.*

If only they were with me, stuffed into this noisy, deathtrap of a bus jouncing down the road. JoJo would probably befriend the old lady across the aisle, in minutes they'd be trading recipes for chicken molé. Cooper and Paulo would be hitting on the young, single girl in the back seat, competing to see which one of them could charm the pants off her the fastest. Maria and I would commiserate about the heat while we made up stories for everyone on the bus: that one's a drug mule with six hours left 'til his balloons bust, that one's headed north to work as a maid but one day she'll be the boss of her own company, the one in the front seat talking to the driver is a fallen priest trying to find his salvation through service to the less fortunate.

I miss you, Dolly, I thought.

And suddenly, as if it happened just because I wanted it to, Maria's voice filled my head again. *"We miss you too, kitty-kat."*

Maria?

"Why do you always doubt that it's me?"

I wanted to yell at her that two times does not make an always, and besides, I *didn't* know it was her.

What kind of car do I drive? I asked, testing to see if it was really Maria.

"The baddest-ass Buick hot-rod on the strip. Painted flat black and chopped so low that I mess up my beautiful 'do every time I get into the damned thing."

Maria. No doubt. I could imagine her fussing to get her hair under control after getting into the Buick, trying to pat it back into place as she looked in the mirror I added to the back of the sun visor just for her.

I need you guys to be okay. Please tell me what's going on.

"I was hoping you could tell us."

Where are you?

"It's either the Ritz-Carlton in Downtown Hell or David Copperfield's pad in Las Vegas."

What?

"This place gives me the willies, kitty-kat. Don't get me wrong, it's a nice place, for a frickin' jail. We got running water in the toilet and 20-year old HBO on the giant flat-screen, but there ain't no windows behind the curtains and none of the doors goes anyplace, they just open up on six other rooms that loop back around on each other."

You're trapped. But where?

"We don't know. That Faery Bitch shows up every once in a while with a platter of food and a jug of wine—just appears out of nowhere and disappears the same way. She won't answer any of our questions, but drops infuriating hints about a bargain she made with you to get us out of that damn lifeboat."

I took a second to tell Maria about the deal I'd made with Laume.

"Where are you now?" Maria asked.

Eastern coast of Mexico. Bus to Laredo.

"You going to do it? Heading for Portland to help that kid?"

Unless you guys can come up with a slick scheme to get out of there, I don't have much of a choice. I don't know how long it's going to take, though. All I've got is a name and a city. I don't even know if I can do anything for this girl without getting in trouble myself. From what I can tell, the kid's a minor.

"Don't you worry your pretty little head over us. We're okay here, for now."

Maria wasn't very convincing. I thought about the last time I'd seen them resting fitfully in the lifeboat, and then replayed the horrible vision that Laume planted in my head. My instincts said that everything wasn't as okay as Maria wanted me to believe.

Paulo okay?

"Hanging in there."

Don't sugar-coat it for me, Dolly. Is he okay, or isn't he?

"We got Paulo, you just go take care of that kid..."

I assumed Maria was going to say...*so we can all come home*, but before she got a chance the bus carrying me to Laredo hit a huge bump. I banged my head on the metal window frame and that dragged me back to reality. Suddenly my eyes, which had been filled with imaginings of my phamily in the hotel-room-from-hell, took in the chaotic happenings on the bus. But I couldn't hear the clucking of the chickens or the screams of the toddlers. It was like someone had flicked the switch and turned my hearing off again.

Damn.

An "*Ooby Dooby*" formed on my lips and died there, my voice had gone again, too.

Crap.

I punched the seatback in front of me and then immediately regretted it when I couldn't express apologies to the young momma and baby I'd disturbed.

Stupid me. I'd just assumed that waking up to the sound of the gulls on the back of the shrimper had meant one of my difficulties had gone away on its own. I wanted to believe that losing my hearing and my voice had been a temporary result of stress, or a punishment doled out by Laume. But if it were punishment, it just didn't make any sense for it to go out that way again. I hadn't even interacted with Laume, had no opportunity to give her attitude. How could I have pissed her off?

I was so tired of having questions without answers. Conundrums with nobody to guide me through them. If I could have sat down with Billy's Asylum Rats we could've figured this out before we finished our third pitcher of beer. It would be *mystery solved*, *answer deployed*, and *somebody order another one* because I'm going to kill off this pitcher to celebrate.

I couldn't even scream to vent my frustration. The only thing I could do to keep myself under control was practice my drum drills—palms playing paradiddles on my thighs—as the hours and the miles to Laredo rolled by.

I don't think there's ever been another person in the history of the world who was more alone than me in my silent little cocoon in that bus full of people.

5

It happened just the way Laume said it would. Truck to the city, overnight bus to the border (where I recovered my *lost* passport, driver's license, and a plane ticket from Dallas to Portland, Oregon) then another, nicer bus (Go Greyhound!) all the way to the Dallas-Fort Worth airport. I'm not sure the bus regularly stopped outside the American Airlines terminal, but on that day the driver rolled right up to Terminal A, just for me. I sensed Faery magic afoot in the driver's too-friendly-to-be-professional demeanor and the way the other riders didn't throw a fit for detouring so far from the bus station in downtown Ft. Worth.

But that wasn't the only magic along the way. When I woke up to the sunrise early that morning, scrunched up on the green vinyl seat of the Mexican bus, I could hear again, could speak, and was happy to be able to tell the *muchacho muy burracho* trying to get a glimpse down my blouse to get his tequila-stained breath out of my face. It was a good thing, made my interactions an hour later at the border go a hell of a lot more smoothly, but the pattern troubled me.

Best I could figure, my hearing and voice had gone out in reaction to communicating telepathically with Maria. Then it came back after I'd gotten some sleep. Healing while I dreamt, maybe? Sleep as a cosmic reset switch? I didn't feel certain about it, but the possibility was enough to keep me from connecting telepathically to Maria just because I was bored during my long hours on the bus.

The sun was setting as I climbed down the bus stairs at the departure level of the airport terminal—odd to have no purse, no luggage, just my ID and ticket which I'm sure were Faery-created, not the mundane kind—and passed through a crowd of people towing luggage and going about their usual days in usual ways. The big glass doors slid open, letting out a wash of cool air, and I started toward the AA counter to get my boarding pass. The line was ten deep, giving me plenty of time to think about going home instead of following Laume's instructions regarding a direct trip to Portland.

The departure board behind the counter showed a flight to Austin leaving every half-hour until midnight. Home. I was so close, but penniless and therefore powerless to get there. Or maybe not.

I had no money, but I had a ticket to Portland I could trade in on a ticket to Austin. But that wouldn't help with change fees. The airline would want money for that.

I just needed a little cash to get home.

To make it happen I'd have to get out of line and get to a payphone, call someone collect—someone who would know me well enough to help, but not so well they'd know I was supposed to still be lost at sea—and get them to wire some money for the ticket change fee. Once I got home I could clean up and pack some things, say a quick hello to my drums, give my neighbor a half-assed excuse why I'd continue to be gone for a while (hoping he'd be too chronically-baked to know anything about the yacht sinking), hit the bank to get some more cash and then take my Buick on a long-ass road trip. I'd get to Portland in a couple of days, on *my* terms, *my* path. Not Laume's.

Solid. Plan. Ready to implement. Go already.

I turned around to find that a dozen people had gotten in line behind me during the short time I'd been lost in my head strategizing. I pardon-me'd my way toward the back of the line, but the last person, a middle-aged man in a Cowboy's football jersey, deliberately stepped into my way and gave me a smile. "Where are you going, Bailey?"

Rattled, I looked at him. His face wasn't familiar to me; I didn't think we'd ever met. But that smile said he knew me and the predatory nature of it triggered a sense of recognition down deep in my subconscious that didn't quite make it up to the surface for me to understand. It just niggled me.

He tilted his head, a gesture way too feminine for a man of his age and obvious heterosexual bent. "Portland's waiting."

Laume. Only she knew where I was headed. Either this guy was an agent of hers (not likely given his ordinary-ness, he didn't shout Higher Power in any way) or she'd used some kind of Faery power to take him, possess him, to converse with me. The enormity of what that meant—that she was willing to track me and maybe even use an innocent person, a stranger, to force me into doing what she wanted—smacked me in the forehead. If Laume would sink to those tactics, what might she do to my phamily if I didn't behave?

My understanding of the bargain I'd made took a turn for the more-deadly-serious, vibrating up my spine like a minor chord from JoJo's stand-up bass and setting my arm hairs on end.

My brain served up two possible ways to tackle this unexpected roadblock. I could be up-front and deal with him/Laume, telling her I was going to go home to get some things—and then ride out her wrath, hoping it didn't make things too much worse. The other part of me warned that I'd be better off playing dumb: ignoring that he'd used my name (and assuming knew my destination because he'd caught a glimpse at my ticket), pretending he didn't have any connection to Laume, and then exclaiming an urgent need to use the ladies room.

I chose plan B, side-stepped him, and hustled down the terminal until I saw the universal stick-figure sign indicating my escape route. Not looking back, I dashed inside and took my time with things, trying to decide whether or not to continue with my plan to get back to Austin. When I came out—dancing around a little girl tottering in through the exit, staring wide-eyed at the tattoos on my bare arms—I saw him watching me from a gift shop across the aisle. I knew there was too much at risk to deviate from Laume's plan.

Damn. I missed home. Missed my clothes and make-up, my drum kit and nasty-ass hotrod. But I missed my phamily more, and I had to remind myself that they weren't at home and couldn't be until I completed my task. I couldn't stand for them to be hurt or lost forever because I selfishly needed my MAC fix and ten minutes banging on the skins before rodding my way out of town in a general westerly-then-northerly direction.

There was one choice left, the plane to Portland, and I resigned myself to it.

I got back in line at the ticket counter, picked-up my boarding pass, and saw the last of the guy in the Cowboy's jersey as I entered the jetway for the Portland-bound plane. I will never forget the way the slack look on his face contrasted with the watchful motion of his eyes—a shell of a man with a predator hiding inside, a Faery predator.

If there was one saving grace to all of it, it was my first-class seat. Apparently Faeries thought traveling in style was important. I agreed. Not so much for the comfort or the room or the included meal, but for the non-stop adult beverages. Three Johnny Walker doubles over ice soothed away all my anxiety as I stared out the window—lights, the only signs of life, sliding by below at hundreds of miles an hour.

No doubt, the guy in the airport had creeped me out. Every time I interacted with Laume I felt intimidated, violated and scared. She came and went as she pleased; taking anything she wanted with her. She ignored the human need for privacy inside one's own mind, dictating orders and laughing at helplessness. And then she had the balls to take over whole people and used them like zombies. Faery Bitch—Maria was right.

Whether it was the alcohol, my exhaustion, or just my subconscious talking to me, I didn't know, but I suddenly wondered why Laume had used the man at the airport at all. I understood why it would be a bad idea to suddenly appear in a crowd of people—poof! there's a gorgeous woman who wasn't there a moment ago—but why had she not just spoken with me telepathically like she had back in the little lifeboat?

Not that I knew a damn thing about Faeries or their magical powers, but it seemed like taking over a person's body and holding it in thrall for over an hour would take more energy and power than just talking to me inside my head. So why had she done it? What if the guy had been able to recover control of himself? I'd like to think he could have hurt her in some way.

I started comparing the situations in my mind and one thing made perfect sense. In the lifeboat I had been calling to her—pissed off and demanding to know what she'd done with my phamily. Since then I had assumed that she'd been the one to open up that telepathic link so we could communicate, and then held it open so I could also talk with Maria. But maybe that was wrong. After all, I had talked with Maria from the bus, too. Laume had had nothing to do with that. I'd done it all by myself.

Maybe the telepathic power wasn't Laume's? Maybe it was mine. If that was true, she couldn't have forced her way inside my head as I waited in line for my boarding pass. I hadn't wanted to talk to her then; I'd wanted to keep my Austin plan a secret from her.

I crossed my arms over my chest and gave myself a little hug. I wasn't powerless after all.

Telepathy. I had telepathy. I'd used it with a Faery and with my best friend. I felt an urge to prove it to myself, to reach out to Maria right that instant and confirm that I could do it anytime I wanted. But I also knew doing so would probably knock out my hearing and my voice until I had a chance to sleep it off—D-and-D: a price to pay for the privilege. I decided to wait until I had something more important to say than "Hi."

For an hour, or so, I daydreamed about who else I might be able to communicate with telepathically. The rest of my phamily? The flight attendant who was so generous with the Johnny Walker? The handsome single guy across the aisle who had almost as many tattoos as I did? The President? Carl Perkins or Elvis, dead in their graves? That one sent shivers up my spine. How cool it would be to be able to talk to the men who gave life and depth to the Rockabilly sound and wrote all the great songs.

Could I reach out to the late, great Roy Orbison, the most talented musician of all time, and do a mythical duet of *Ooby Dooby*—just me and him inside my brain? I'd take deaf and dumb to make that happen any day and twice on Sunday.

But not right then, I couldn't. I had a phamily to recover. A girl named Hannah Faye Williams waited just a couple hours flying-time away. She needed my help, and I had no idea how I was going to do that: I had no car, no money, no real clue what came next. Normally when I found myself feeling this way I'd call JoJo or Paulo, Cooper or Maria. One of them would certainly know what to do. Without my phamily I felt helpless.

I decided that if I didn't have a eureka moment by the time the plane touched down I would have to test my telepathy trick and *phone-a-friend* from the airport for some help.

6

It turns out I had not one eureka moment on the plane, but two. About 90 minutes before landing, the first strike hit: I'd been thinking that not having my bank card, or my smart phone, meant I had no way to get any money. But I finally realized there was an old-fashioned way get to my greenbacks: the two pieces of identification Laume had provided for me at the Mexican border would allow me to access my money if I just went in to the bank and talked to a real person. I was such a child of the new millennium.

Since it was a nationwide bank, there had to be at least one branch in Portland. I knew there wasn't a whole lot of money in my account, about $650, but that was better than nothing. Assuming I could find work—bakers were imminently employable—I'd be back on my feet shortly.

The second reason not to reach out through telepathy came thanks to my libido. I felt so good about figuring out how to get some cash (and thereby lunch, transportation and a roof over my head) that I fell into my old pattern of flirting with the cute guy across the aisle—who turned out to be a native Oregonian, named Brady, on his way home from a business trip. I started by complimenting his tattoos, bold tribal swirls up both arms, common ground to be sure, and the conversation quickly turned more personal. We found ourselves leaning across the aisle, getting in the flight attendant's way. I told him a little about my sudden, temporary relocation to Portland to help-out the estranged daughter of a friend of mine (a slight exaggeration) after losing my purse to a mugger in Mexico (an outright lie, unless the Gulf of Mexico could be considered "a Mexican"). He told me about his job as a copywriter for an ad agency and his English sheepdog named Chester.

By the time they collected empty glasses in preparation for landing, I'd arranged to get a ride from Brady to my bank, he knew of a branch near his office downtown, and landed a date with him for dinner. He knew a great spot where *the food was amazing and no one would bother us.*

I won't say I actually swooned thinking about what that might mean—a romantic dinner at his place, perhaps—but my body was absolutely thrumming with anticipation of the possibilities for dessert. Picking up a stranger on an airplane was the epitome of loose behavior, I know, but we were seated in first class and I hadn't had sex in sixteen days—a record for me since I was twenty. He looked like a nice guy and I had an itch that needed scratching, badly.

We flirted more as we waited for his bag to come around on the elevated, moving-sidewalk that passed for baggage claim in the tiny airport. His arms had that reptilian kind of muscle that was lean and tight and I wondered, as I traced the outline of one tattoo with my fingernail, what it might be like to feel them pinning me against the wall as he explored my throat with his lips and tongue. Delicious.

The cool morning air outside the terminal, where we waited for the bus that would take us to Brady's car, took the edge off the heat my body produced just from being so close to him. Ten of us, and everyone else's luggage, labored up the Red Shuttle stairs for the short drive to the long-term lot. It was a good thing we didn't have the bus to ourselves because the back seat gave good making-out motion every time it hit a bump.

Brady's car turned out to be a five year old Audi wagon which somehow managed not to come off as a grocery-getter. It was well-kept, but dusty from sitting in the lot. We climbed in and he quickly had us out of the lot and onto the freeway headed downtown. I was amazed at how green everything was, trees and grass and a million bushes that I'd never be able to name. By the end of the summer everything at home in Austin was dry as a crouton, covered in brown dust and ready to give up the ghost if the monsoons didn't come. There was moisture in the air here, but not the oppressive humidity I was used to; instead of carrying the tang of salt water it smelled sweet and alive.

Traffic was light, so was the conversation. Brady described the areas we passed through—East Portland, the Hollywood District, Lloyd Center—explaining which ones might be good for apartment hunting. Nothing looked much like Austin; I might as well have been in another country.

All too soon, after crossing a four-lane drawbridge, we pulled into a loading zone downtown and Brady shut off the car. I looked around and didn't see my bank. Wondering what I'd gotten myself into, I considered jumping out of the car, until he surprised the hell out of me.

"Why don't you keep my car for the day," he said as he laid his hand on my knee. "If you're hunting for a job and a cheap apartment you'll need to get around, and the nav system will help. You can come get me later."

"Seriously?" I'd met the guy two and a half hours before, just happened to sit across the aisle from him and admire his ink. This felt a little bit like the way the bus from Ciudad Victoria to Laredo had failed to start until the fish truck carrying me pulled into town. Or how the Greyhound driver delivered me right to Terminal A in Dallas. It stunk of Faery interference, Laume's interference.

"It's just going sit in the garage all day if you don't take it," he said, like it was completely reasonable to loan his $25,000 car to a stranger.

"You're just being a nice guy, that's all?"

"I have an ulterior motive," he said.

Of course he did.

"I want to make sure you don't stand me up for dinner," he said with a smile. "If you have my car you have to come back." His finger touched my cheek like I was made of porcelain and then trailed down my leopard-printed arm leaving goose bumps in its wake.

"Or you'll sick the cops on me?" I joked.

He smiled. "Something like that."

"I don't know," I said.

He looked at me with a puzzled expression.

I knew he might not tell me the truth, but I had to ask. "You didn't meet a gorgeous brunette with alabaster skin in the men's room at the airport who told you to be nice me?"

His puzzled look stayed. "Umm, nope."

"And you're feeling quite yourself. Mentally, I mean? No compulsion to do this?"

Brady looked at his crotch, looked back at me with a devilish smile and then raised three fingers on his right hand. "Scout's honor."

I had to smile at his boldness. I wanted to believe his Johnson and being a nice guy were all that motivated him. As JoJo would have said, *it looks like his elevator goes all the way to the top floor.* His eyes and face held complementary expressions, neither betrayed a vacancy I'd seen on the middle-aged guy at the Dallas airport. Maybe it was just a case of a nice guy helping out a girl he was attracted to in the hopes of getting somewhere, more quickly, after dinner.

I almost told him that he didn't have to bother. Once I had a shower, a change of decent clothes and my war paint on, I intended to show him how hot a night with me could get.

"Okay," I said, and he smiled.

We both got out of the car. He grabbed his computer bag and a jacket from the back seat. As we approached each other at the back of the car he reached out with his free arm and pulled me into a kiss, his head bowing to meet mine.

And *Ooby Dooby*, could that man deliver a kiss. It took me a moment to get over the surprise of his warm lips on mine, but I quickly gave in, closed my eyes and tilted my head a bit so I could show him a little taste of my best. The kiss only lasted a couple of seconds, but it filled my body with tingles. We had chemistry.

At exactly the right moment, he straightened up and we parted lips. I opened my eyes and saw a mixed-up smile on his face. "I'm sorry. I don't usually--"

It seemed inappropriate to tell him that *I did, sometimes, when I couldn't help myself.* I didn't want to scare him away—and not just because he was loaning me his car—so I said, "It was nice. Almost perfect."

"Almost?" Brady asked. "Why almost?"

"Because you have to go to work now," I said as I squeezed his hand and let it go. "And I have to get to the bank and find a job and a place to live and see if I can get some idea of where to find my friend's daughter."

I was shocked at how easily the partial-lie fit on the end of my to-do list. Laume was anything but a friend. Some part of me had apparently accepted that I wasn't going to see my phamily again until I fixed the Faery Bitch's little problem.

"Then I'll see you at six?" he asked. "Right here."

I nodded. He gave me a peck on the cheek and then I watched him walk up the block and disappear inside a tall glass door with a huge blue and green triangular logo painted on it. The view of him going was nearly as good as the one coming.

It turned out the loan of Brady's car was quite the gift for a new girl in town. Portland was not the grid-city Austin was. Not only was there a big, gorgeous river running smack down the middle of it with seven bridges to cross it, but the hills and the highways on the west side of the city forced the roads to veer off course or dead-end at the most peculiar times. With help from the built-in GPS I was able to mark the location of Brady's office (so I could go back to pick him up at six), find a bank branch, and six different bakeries within city limits.

Too bad I couldn't just plug *Hannah Faye Williams* into the car's little brain and track her down. But that'd be too easy.

After visiting the bank, I started my job hunt at the Lovejoy Bakery; it had a name that described how I felt about food in general and pastry in particular. The place was great, live-action cooking in an open kitchen. But they had no openings. The second shop, called The Pearl, hit me as too snooty for its own good. I was somewhat relieved to find they were fully staffed as well. It seemed the local economy wasn't digging out of The Great Recession as quickly as we were at home. I was about to leave, empty-handed, when one of the girls behind the counter gave me a lead for a commercial baker who was *always looking for slaves*—a place called The Rose City Oven.

Not in a situation to be picky about employment, I plugged the name into Brady's car and it took me back across the river to an industrial area with potholed streets and lots of homeless folks loitering on the sidewalk. Not willing to risk someone else's car in that neighborhood, I drove on until I found a busy hotel with a big parking lot. I left the Audi there and walked back six blocks.

The Rose City Oven was aptly named—the warehouse was shaped like one huge appliance, big enough to bake bread for an entire city. Its two-story, metal sliding door was open on the east side of the building and the exhaust heat of a full commercial kitchen blasted me in the face when I pushed through the translucent plastic curtains hanging in the opening (which I'm sure were intended to keep flying insects out, but really didn't do the trick).

The staff was mostly men, mostly Latin, and mostly clean aside from the occasional dusting of flour or smear of batter across white on white uniforms. Stainless steel prep tables, rolling racks (filled with cooling loaves and colorful pastry) and industrial vats of dry goods crowded the open floor in front of a bank of commercial ovens, with a whole corner devoted to a steam-proofer bigger than my bathroom back home.

To my right, the front corner had been walled in, an office with a wall of windows to keep an eye on the employees. Inside sat the fattest man I'd ever seen in real life, must've tipped the scales at over 350 pounds. His grizzly gray stubble did nothing to soften the sharp nose and chin that protruded from a doughy face. His heavy brow dwarfed dark eyes, making them look piggy.

He looked like a guy whose reputation included treating the help like slaves. But I could hack it. Since graduating from the culinary academy I'd met plenty like him. My experience was they were hard-asses who nobody liked, except on payday, because the checks always got cut on time. That's all I cared about, for the moment.

"What?" the fat man shouted at me through his open office door. His voice sounded higher-pitched than it ought to have been, given the volume of space he took up.

"Looking for a job," I said, as I walked that way.

"Circus doesn't come back to town until spring," he said, smiling briefly at his own joke. I assumed he was referring to my ink even though he wasn't looking at me.

"Good, I'm not fond of heights or things with big teeth."

My attempt at humor fell flat. I wasn't surprised, but I had to see if he was what he appeared to be. He grunted, still focusing on paperwork on the desk in front of him.

"Experience?"

I suddenly wished I'd taken the time to stop at a Kinko's to type up a resume. "Six years, including graduating the top of my class at Le Cordon Bleu."

That got his attention and he gave me an up-down appraisal. "Chef Walters likes you, eh?"

Not remembering a Walters on the staff at my school, I assumed there was another Le Cordon Bleu school nearby where most of his applicants came from. "I trained in Austin."

"Oh," he said, turning back to his paperwork. "You ain't some Prima Donna, an hour late every day, messing up production. Are you?"

After running the bakery back home for two years I understood what he was getting at. This was no showcase bakery like Lovejoy. It wasn't a neighborhood hangout like The Pearl. It was a third-world sweatshop. Dough in the oven. Bread on the rack. Pretty little pastries packed and ready to go when the customer called.

"Give me a week. You don't like my work, fire me."

"You look like a Prima Donna," he said, not letting go of the bone.

If I could have afforded to work for a week without pay I'd have offered that to convince him. As it was, I was starting to feel like negotiating with this guy was like negotiating with Laume—a no-win situation.

But, I'd learned something from Laume. "Your loss," I said and turned to go.

I got three steps away before he said, "Be here at 4 AM. Bring your own uniform."

I stopped, turned back and smiled. He'd given away just what kind of asshole he was: the kind with a gushy soft center. If you could dig down that far. "My name's Bailey. What do I call you?"

"Boss."

"Okay, Boss. See you tomorrow."

He grunted. But he raised an eyebrow; the second crack in his tough exterior showing—no need for telepathy to tell me that. Rather than try to break him the rest of the way open right then, I gave him the benefit of the doubt and left with every eye in the kitchen following me.

The clock in Brady's car said I had two hours before I needed to be downtown. The nav system said it would take 20 minutes to get back there in traffic. I either had time to look at a couple of apartments, or go shopping—a uniform for work, an outfit for dinner with Brady, and some much needed cosmetics—but not both.

It was presumptive as all hell, because I was basically homeless, but I decided to go shopping. If I crashed at Brady's, I could look at a bunch of places after my first day of work when I'd look all flour-y and exhausted like a hard-working prospective tenant should—not frumpy and wearing hand-me-downs from a Mexican boat captain's girlfriend.

It didn't seem like much of an assumption; not only had Brady said all the right things on the plane, he'd trusted me with his really nice car, all day. I felt safe taking the chance he'd offer me a place to sleep, wink-wink, then I could spend a little time taking care of myself instead of playing the what-disgustingness-is-hiding-under-that-fresh-coat-of-paint game with a couple of slum lords after work.

I poked a new search into the nav system—clothing stores.

Of all the places the Audi had gotten me to that day, the Buffalo Exchange was the suggestion that won it my everlasting devotion. I'd heard of the second-hand shop in other cities and was pleased but not surprised to find rack upon rack of vintage clothing that fit me to a T. Paisley printed pedal pushers, a red Cossack top, two pairs of shoes, and I even found a replacement for the swing dress I'd abandoned in Mexico, in red. The clerk pointed me toward a local overstock shop that sold cosmetics, cheap. I felt so good when I stopped at a gas station and (after giving myself a sponge bath in the bathroom) changed back into myself—a flattering dress, daring eyes, ass-lifting heels.

But I was sad, too. Looking at myself in the mirror reminded me that I was in a 'billy band and my bandmates—my phamily—were probably going stir-crazy in a posh Faery prison with no doors, no windows, no fresh air. I'd been assured they were safe, but nothing I'd done that day had gotten me closer to Hannah, or them closer to home.

I felt a compelling urge to check in with Maria using my telepathy. But the clock on the wall said I had enough time to buy a uniform for work and then maybe get the airport parking lot grime washed off Brady's car as a thank you before picking him up. No time for a nap to recover my hearing and voice after using my newfound gift. I cursed what I didn't fully understand and stuffed that urge down next to the cold thing that persisted in my chest. They got along well, my compulsion and my cold loneliness, it was like they hooked-up and made a baby named guilt.

Guilt that messed with my reflection in the mirror, kept me from looking myself in the eye. I turned away and stuffed my dirty clothes and sandals into a beaded shoulder bag I'd bought at the second-hand shop.

If I were a good friend I would have said *no thank you* to Brady's offers on the plane and headed straight for the nearest Public Library to start my search for Hannah. Instead, I'd gotten carried away by my libido, and procrastinated about the research I needed to do.

I should have gotten on it right then, but--

--but, crap. I had only flimsy excuses.

I promised myself that *no matter what happened* with Brady that night—that little stinker had been right, he had somehow known I would flake on our date if I didn't need to return his car—I'd find a cheap hotel to crash at so I was sure to be at the bakery on time for my shift. Afterwards I'd go straight to the library and get to work.

Yeah, sure, my Libido whispered in my ear as I left the gas station bathroom.

7

After hitting a uniform shop out on the west side to buy my baker's whites, I got back downtown to Brady's building with five minutes to spare. Traffic on the city streets was starting to turn from suits and sedans to shorts and pedal bikes. It was a gorgeous late summer evening and the natives didn't take it for granted.

I parked Brady's car in the same loading zone and got out to enjoy the fresh air. I waited, leaning on the back of his car, showing off my tanned legs in a skirt and bright red heels. Thinking back to our kiss earlier in the day was enough to send fantasies of him racing through my brain. I got lost in one that included a king-size bed in a penthouse loft when a sharp-fingered tap on my right shoulder startled me.

I turned to see Laume also leaning on the car in an identical dress and heels. Somehow, even without the bouffant hair and tattoos, she managed to pull-off the Rockabilly look better than I did. Until then nobody pulled off a tight-waisted swing dress like I could. Nobody.

Until Laume.

Damn.

And Brady was about to come out a door up the block with a big blue and green triangle on it. I wasn't fully aware of why, but I knew down deep in my belly that I did not want her standing there when Brady arrived. Did. Not. Want.

"Go away," I said, not thinking about my manners.

"Nice dress." She twirled in the street, forcing drivers to go around her. "I like the way it moves."

"Get out of the damn road."

Laume stopped spinning, but stood smack dab in the middle of the lane. She waved and smiled at the next car that detoured around her. "I'm in no danger here"—she stalked toward me with a wildcat's snarl on her lips—"unlike your friends."

"My phamily," I corrected her. If she was going to threaten me, I preferred that she do it right. "You said you'd keep them safe."

"As long as you uphold your end of the bargain." Laume held her hands palm-up and looked at the people around us. "And I don't see Hannah Faye, anywhere," she bent over to look into the car, and then straightened up with a mock look of concern on her face. "Is she hiding?"

I opened my mouth to speak, but she cut me off.

"I know; you haven't found her yet. That might be easier if you actually started looking, instead of shopping." Laume looked down at her copy of my dress. "It's not *that* nice a dress."

"I had important things to take care of," I said.

"More important than your family?"

It was as if she could look into my heart and see the guilt enveloping it. Like she'd taken the most painful of the words I said to myself and used them to lash at my soul. Of course none of what I'd done that day was more important than my phamily, but I had to get my feet on the ground. And although Laume had been all-sorts-of-helpful getting me to, and then onto, a Portland-bound plane, she'd been pretty damn light on the assistance meter since I'd ditched the watchful eye of the middle-aged man in the Cowboy's jersey back in Dallas.

"You could help me out here," I said. "I could get to work faster if you'd give me the money to rent a decent apartment and give me a car--"

"It appears you already have a conveyance," Laume said as she patted the roof of Brady's Audi. "It appears large enough for sleeping in. What more do you require?"

"It's not mine."

Laume pointed to the keys in my hand. "It is in your possession, it is yours."

"I have to return it."

"Why?" Laume asked.

Just then I spotted Brady coming out of his building. He hadn't noticed me yet because he was deep in conversation with two guys who I figured were coworkers by their matching computer bags and business casual dress. Laume followed my interest down the block and her predatory smile returned.

"The conveyance belongs to the handsome one in the middle?" Laume asked. "What is his name?"

"Noneya," I said. "As in none-ya-damn-business. And it's time for you to go." I did not want to try and explain her to Brady, or risk him developing a puppy-love-crush on her.

She waved a dismissal at him. "His face is far too fleshy, but that body might entertain me for an hour or two."

I grabbed Laume's arm to turn her away from him, divert her interest before she decided to ensnare him. Her skin was feverishly hot, like go directly to the emergency room, do not pass Go, do not collect $200 feverish. She immediately swiped my hand from her arm. "Do not presume--"

"Either help me, so I don't have to beg from strangers, or get the hell out of the way," I said. "You want this done. I want my phamily back. None of that's going to happen with you in my face."

Her gaze flipped back and forth between Brady and me. "Taking advantage of him bothers you," Laume said. "Interesting."

"It's not interesting. It's manners. Something you could use," I said.

That was not a smart thing to say and I wished immediately that I could take it back. But it was too late. Laume's brow knitted together over her lovely blue eyes. I expected her to lash out at me, but she didn't say anything. Her only response was to reach into the pocket of her skirt (funny, my dress hadn't come with pockets) and pull out a ring, a big, faceted ruby in an antique silver, filigree setting. Maria's great-grandmother's ring. In fourteen years I'd never seen Maria take it off. I gaped.

"You have a brash mouth for someone so beholden."

She held the ring up to a reflected ray of sunlight as if admiring its beauty, and then she just dropped it in the street. The ring bounced three times, its ting-tang-ting lost to the overlying sounds of the city, and then settled flat on the asphalt a few inches in front of her right foot. Before I could yell to stop her, Laume stepped on the ring and mashed it into the road as if she were stubbin' out a butt on the wood floor of a honky tonk.

Laume lifted her dainty little foot to reveal a splotch of silver and red dust embedded into the texture of the street. A treasured, hundred year-old heirloom reduced to sparkly grit in less than three seconds. Four generations of love and devotion, passed from mother to daughter to granddaughter squashed as a message to me. *What a bitch.*

I wanted to yell at her, but as she just demonstrated, she held all the cards.

"By this time tomorrow I expect you to have made measurable progress," Laume said. She turned and danced away in the road again, leaving me to stare at the ruins of Maria's ring. I got the implication. Loud. And. Clear.

A few seconds later Brady called out, "Hey there, beautiful."

I looked up to see his smiling face and immediately felt badly that I had tears in my eyes.

"Rough day?" he asked, holding himself back and giving me a little space.

I stepped into the gap between us and wrapped my arms around his hard body, the warmth of him reassuring me that goodness and generosity still existed in the world. "Just sad news from home," I said into his shoulder. I got a hold of myself, metaphorically, and plastered a fake smile on my face before stepping back.

"I got a job," I said. "Starts bright and early tomorrow morning."

"How early?" he asked.

"Baker's time. Four in the A-M. I guess that's a little more early than bright."

He looked a little disappointed. "Are we still on for dinner?"

"And dessert." I let my eyes—which were finally made up in signature Bailey-style with three elegant pearlescent pink shadows and black liner—explain that I was hungry for more than what might be served on a plate.

"Then we better get going," Brady said with a smile and escorted me to my car door.

Dinner didn't turn out to be at his place. Instead he drove to a parking spot on the street just a few blocks away and led me to another downtown parking area which had been turned into some kind of permanent food circus. Two dozen food trucks served up culinary choices from six continents in just one square block. Grilling sausages caught my nose's attention first—smoke and charcoal and sizzling pork—but Brady kept pulling me along past both windows of a cart advertising German cuisine.

Two stalls down we got in line for Vietnamese food at a little truck tagged with the name *Mai Pho.* I hesitated and explained that being from Texas meant I'd never been very curious about Asian food. He smiled and encouraged me to give it a chance. The tiny lady inside the truck multitasked between taking orders and cooking so it took several minutes to place our order. Brady pointed at the photos of the dishes and ordered three things: salad rolls to share, a noodle salad with fish sauce dressing and egg rolls for me, and a chicken stir-fry with lemongrass for him. It all sounded odd to my Texan taste buds, lacking beef and potatoes, but the steaming containers smelled like heaven when the bag came through the window.

There was no place to sit, apparently that was what Brady meant when he said no one would bother us, so we walked six blocks down to the waterfront. As we cleared the last block of buildings and the area opened up into a parkway of giant trees and well-manicured grass leading up to a paved walkway and steel railing at the river's edge.

The growing sound of a drum cadence reached my ears.

First, one drum, a low tom-tom, started a lively rhythm and then very quickly a dozen others took up the beat. Snare. Bongo. Bass. Kettle. The sounds of my heart.

I couldn't help smiling when a cow bell joined them. A cow bell!

I nearly dragged Brady across the street against traffic as I followed the surging beat. We turned left on the opposite sidewalk and then right as we came into a concrete amphitheater where a dozen counter-culture dudes sat cross-legged around their instruments in a rag-tag circle. They nodded and swayed in time with their own beat. I danced in place, unable to stop myself.

My enthusiasm might have initially startled Brady, but he smiled at me and then led me twenty feet further away to a cement picnic table halfway between the drums and the river.

We ate. We chatted. We watched the changing light of sunset reflect off the buildings across the river. My heart soared with the ever evolving cadences played by the drummers. Two drums, a snare and a bass, kept the beat steady while the others played fills and runs. I would have to come back once I'd bought myself a drum. I felt more alive than at any time since the yacht started to roll dangerously and take on water six days ago.

Six days. So much had happened. So much had changed. Never in a million years could I have predicted that I would be eating a fabulous noodle salad on the bank of a river in Oregon with a truly generous and sexy guy. If things had gone according to plan, my phamily and I would be finalizing our recording list and quitting our day jobs in Austin because Billy's Asylum Rats had finally *made it.* We'd worked so hard—toured and travelled, starved and struggled—and just when things were looking rosy, our dream got pulled out from under us.

"You keep getting that look," Brady said, pulling me from my thoughts.

"I'm sorry."

"It's okay," he said. "I just wish you'd tell me what's bothering you."

I shook my head. "Thanks, but you can't help."

"Try me," he dared.

Three options occurred to me. I could tell him something, everything or nothing. Nothing would shut communication down between us, and I needed him in more than one way. Telling him everything would scare the shit out of him—I know it would scare me if I wasn't living the insanity of it. I opted to give him a seriously abridged version of how I got stuck coming to Portland and chasing down this kid instead of heading into the recently reborn Sun Records studios in Memphis with my bandmates, like we were supposed to. I told him stories about JoJo and Cooper and Paulo and Maria. He laughed at all the right places.

"This Cooper guy, is he your boyfriend?" Brady asked.

I shook my head and ate the last bite of my salad roll. "Too much history for that to work. Ever."

"History?"

"We met at the Texas State Hospital, when I was fourteen," I said and spun my finger around my ear in the universal sign for crazy folks. Brady's brows scrunched up a bit the way people's eyebrows did when they think I could never possibly be the kind of person who got put in a mental institution—but I pushed through to explain before the reality of the statement could set it (I found it usually went better that way).

"That's how the band got started—*Billy's Asylum Rats*. Our bat-shit therapist insisted everyone had to participate in the dorkiest talent show ever produced. Crazy teenagers don't often have inborn talents, much less ones that get nurtured enough to be ready for primetime. The five of us got left in the dust when our fellow inmates picked teams, so we decided to show them all up. We picked out this really easy Rockabilly song, *Boppin' the Blues*, and practiced every minute of every day until the show. Maria knew a little piano. Cooper taught Paulo a couple of chords on the guitar so he could play rhythm, and JoJo figured out the standing bass. I took my frustrations out on the drums. And we won! Bragging rights and ten bucks each to spend at the commissary."

I took a deep breath. "It saved my life. All our lives."

"How?"

"When was the last time you talked to your parents?" I asked him.

"Sunday was Mom's birthday."

"Lunch and flowers?"

"Dinner and a kitten."

I took a deep breath. "Even if you added up all five of our lives, I'll bet you none of us has ever had dinner and a kitten with a parent in the same day. Once we found each other, and started playing music, those problems stopped being such a big deal. We've been together every day since then."

Brady thought quietly for a minute. "Sounds like you miss them."

I nodded. I missed them more than I could say without lyrics and a melody. If I didn't get my mind onto something else I was going to get really morose and ruin the whole evening. So I started stuffing our dinner containers into their plastic sack.

"And do you know the best thing in the whole world for curing loneliness?" I asked, standing up and giving him my best come-hither smile.

He didn't get up right away. "I don't want to take advantage of you."

I offered him my hand. "What if I want to take advantage of you?"

He hesitated.

"No strings. No expectations. I'm clean, get tested all the time. What do you say?" That was my best pitch. Usually it worked pretty quickly, but then again I usually laid it down on a guy when I was sweaty from playing two sets and an encore and he'd drunk enough beer to drown a small pig. It didn't sink in so easily with a sober Brady.

"Are you for real?" he asked.

"The realest thing you'll ever meet in a red, polka-dot swing dress." I swished my skirt, loving the free flowing sensation of fabric on my bare legs.

"I don't know," Brady said, still stalling.

"You must think an awful lot of your penis," I teased him. "You'll trust me alone with your car all day, but you won't let me take *you* home for a test drive?"

He actually laughed at that, and I knew I had him.

"No kinky stuff," he said. "Be nice."

I agreed.

He took my hand and led me to the car. The quiet tension of new lovers built between us as we drove, his place was ten minutes away. The elevator took a hundred and seventy-two seconds to get us to the eighth floor; I counted as a distraction technique. Thirty seconds after that we started to peel off clothes—his shirt went first and I traced his tattoos with my lips and tongue. Another minute later we got into his apartment and locked the door behind us.

Making love with Brady turned out to be better than nice. Much better. Who knows what they feed these northwestern kids while they're filling-out from boys into men, but I'll have to say, given the sample size I've experienced, not everything is bigger in Texas.

After, when I asked if he wanted me to go, he asked what time I needed to be up for work in the morning. After setting the alarm on his phone for 3:30 he shut off the light and pulled me to him, sweat cooling on our skin. I threw a leg over his and an arm over his chest.

"Hey, Bailey," he said.

"Yeah?"

"Thanks for getting my car washed." He kissed me on the forehead and then he was snoring inside two minutes. I guess I tuckered him out.

Orange lights from the streetlamps below threw a slanted, cross-hatched shadow pattern of the window panes on the ceiling. Lights in the buildings around us blinked out as the city went to sleep. But not me, I was miles from heading off to see the Sandman.

Though the evening, and the night, had been everything I'd needed to help me forget about the last six days, part of me knew I shouldn't still be in Brady's apartment. I'd said I wasn't going to stay, no matter what. Staying meant I wasn't doing everything possible to get my phamily home. I was in the arms of a new lover while they were in the clutches of someone who they mostly called Faery Bitch. Someone who would heartlessly take a family heirloom and grind it to bits in the street to make a point.

I looked at the clock, it was almost midnight. I figured that it was safe to use my telepathy to contact my phamily; I'd still have a little more than three hours to get to sleep before Brady's alarm went off for work. Enough time to reset my voice and hearing before the challenges of waking up in bed for the first time with a new lover, the first day on a new job, and hunting down little Hannah Faye.

Maria, are you there? I thought toward her and I felt a channel open between us.

8

B*ay?"* Maria's answer to my late-night, telepathic call came across fuzzy, muffled.

Did I wake you? I asked not knowing if there even was a time zone where they were, much less how it compared to mine.

"I wish," she said, "I've been drinking this sweet Faery wine, my seventh goddamn crystal chalice full, and I can't seem to get sleep enough to drunk."

I snorted at her unintentional joke. Maria was no lightweight. Italian heritage, she always said, wine in her sippy-cup. I'd seen her put Paulo and Cooper to shame a dozen times before any of us had reached legal age. But she was right, at some point in the night, without fail, everyone knew Maria would take one last sip and then it would be good-night-sweet-Dolly for at least ten hours.

I avoided the *are you okay* question; because I knew she wouldn't tell me the truth, at least not any more of it than her chasing a bender hadn't already said.

I'm so sorry she took your grandma's ring, I said.

"Right off my frickin' finger, this one right here."

I knew she was wagging her left pinky at me, the hand she plucked her bass with, and was too damn drunk to realize I couldn't see it.

"That's okay, though," Maria slurred. *"Joke's on her, dumb Faery. The ring only works if you're Italian, not if you're a dumb, ugly, mean Faery Bitch."*

I had no idea what Maria was talking about, but given how superstitious old Nana Venechi had been, I'm not surprised she told Maria the ring was something special when she'd passed it along years ago. Emphasis on the *it was,* but I decided to keep that to myself.

"I will not lay off the wine, and I ain't talking to you, anyway, I'm talking to Bay-Bay. No, I'm not *crazy.* I told you *I could talk to her in my head."* I'm sure that was meant for JoJo, but a drunk Maria didn't always keep her conversations in order, apparently not even the telepathic kind.

You need to get some sleep. I just wanted to check in and see if y'all were killing each other yet.

"Nope, no bloodshed, yet. But we're working on it."

I'm going to get you out of there. I'll find the girl tomorrow and start figuring out how to fix this family problem she's got.

"Yeah, you get right on that, because you're so damn good at fixing family troubles--"

That stung a little, even through the alcohol.

G'night, Maria. I'll be in touch as soon as I have news.

I pulled away from the communication without letting Maria finish. She could be a nasty drunk when she was pissed about something, and she had something worth being pissed about. We all did.

With my whole headspace back in Brady's apartment I felt the sadly-familiar sensation of not being able to hear after using my telepathy. I knew if I tried to roll over and sweet-talk Brady I'd get a similar result from my voice. Nada.

I didn't feel like talking, anyway. Being connected to an angry, drunk Maria had spoiled my blissful, after-sex mood.

If I'd learned nothing else from talking to her, I knew I didn't want to connect with anyone in my phamily again until I could report progress. I needed to be able to say I'd found Hannah and had some clue about how to put the girl's family back on track. For the moment it was still a mystery to me. How would I find her? What would I say when I did? Would my tattoos scare her off or make her more willing to confide in me?

Tomorrow loomed busy on my horizon. But first, some sleep. Time to rest. Time to reset.

And, I had to say, it felt good to stretch out and sleep in a real bed with a real pillow for the first time in a week—first it had been a tiny bunk on the yacht, then trying to get comfortable in the lifeboat, then the fishing boat's bench, the vinyl seat on the Mexican bus, and finally my first class flight to Portland. I looked forward to three silent hours, during which, for the first time in my life I wasn't worried about whether the new guy next to me snored or not. I was pretty sure I wouldn't make a sound.

I woke up to the same dark room with the same panels of orange streetlight lighting the ceiling. Brady's place. He shook me fiercely with a panicked look on his face.

I tried to say *okay, okay, I'm up*, but my voice wouldn't cooperate. And it wasn't just me being tired. No voice and I got the damned junebug tickle in my throat again when I tried. My ears weren't working yet either. Shit.

Brady's panic found its way into my heart, too.

I'd slept. Damnit, I'd fallen asleep and gotten three solid hours of rest. Why the hell had my hearing and voice not come back? That's how it had worked: I talked to Maria in my head and then I couldn't talk to or hear anyone in the real world until I fell asleep, rested, and woke up. My inner cynic had been afraid that the predictable little price for my invaluable little gift wouldn't stay predictable. And it hadn't.

There was no way for me to know how much more sleep I'd need to set things right. I'd gotten at least eight hours on the fishing boat the first time and at least six on the bus the second. But I had no time for that; I had to report for work in half an hour. I needed that job at the bakery.

I reached out a hand to calm Brady's flailing. It wasn't helping. And we couldn't both lose it. I pantomimed texting, as if I was holding a phone, and he got the hint that I needed something to type on. He handed me his phone with the notepad app up and running.

"Don't worry," I typed. "This happens sometimes. I'm OK."

He took the phone back. "What's wrong?"

"Can't hear. Can't talk. It's neurological, probably. Be better in a couple hours. Promise."

I handed back his phone and crossed my heart, hoping to hell I wasn't lying to him.

"What about work?" he typed.

Good question. Being deaf and dumb would usually be a show-stopper, but if there was one thing I could do without needing my voice, besides sex, it was baking. Bread was bread. Pastry was pastry. Every bakery had their own recipes to follow so they'd have to give me written directions. And it wasn't like the production floor at The Rose City Oven had been a particularly chatty place for folks who spoke English.

I had a good chance of pulling off a day at the bakery without being able to talk. The Boss himself had been a man of few words. I'd just do my best to try lip-reading what everyone was telling me, given the context, and make educated guesses when I was unsure. Worst case, if this D-n-D crap held on all day, I'd find a spot at the Library to catch a nap and hopefully that would reset me before I started my Hannah search in the afternoon.

I flashed Brady an OK sign and a smile to tell him that I figured everything would work out at the bakery. He looked doubtful, but I took his hand and lead him to the bathroom so he could sit, half awake leaning against the wall, and watch me take a quick shower. Fifteen minutes later, a bit of war paint on and looking like a ghost with platinum blonde hair, pale skin, and my new white-on-white uniform, I hopped into Brady's car for a ride to work.

Before he let me get out of the car he plastered a big kiss on my lips and typed on his phone, "My place again 2nite?"

I nodded, vigorously. Of course I'd be there—even if I'd had a place of my own to go to I'm sure I would have found my way back into his bed. But I had a lot to do after work, none of which I had time to explain on such a little keyboard, so I just typed "9:00" on his phone and then hauled ass down the block to get in the door by my 4 AM deadline. I hoped he was going to go home and get some more sleep before work, he looked exhausted.

Early morning chit-chat is taboo in most bakeries and The Rose City Oven looked to follow that pattern—lots of coffee, no inane chatter—so I followed the Boss from his office to the work area where he pointed at a big, brown dude for introductions and then handed me a laminated recipe page. He'd put me on baguettes. Basic bread. Hard to fuck up.

I could have made them in my sleep. (Too bad I couldn't sleep on the job, I might get my powers of communication back sooner but it would look especially bad on the first day.) And I got to measuring and mixing so he walked away without mentioning my lack of chattiness—I think. The recipe looked right. Flour, water, yeast, sugar. Mix, knead, proof, shape, rest. Bake, bake, bake, all day long.

Though I couldn't hear the music my Latin co-workers had picked to liven up their morning, I could tell it was something up-tempo by the way they all moved unconsciously in time with each other. I imagined guitars and horns and lots of snare work from the drums.

I made music for myself in my head. I wasn't much of a singer, not out loud—the band only permitted me to do backing vocals on a few songs—but I knew the Billy's Asylum Rats set list backwards and forward. Every note, every verse. As I worked, I imagined the songs to myself inside my head, just the way we played them on stage, using the down-beat as a tempo to finish-knead the dough and form the loaves.

If I took even a short break from singing to myself—*Bigelow 6-2000, Whistle Bait, School of Rock 'n Roll*, anything—I started to hear other voices fill the silence. Guilt and doubt sang duets for me. Negative, gloomy, morose crap from 90s grunge bands: *Dumb, Down in a Hole, Sour Girl.* Music I'd listened to before going to the Hospital as a suicidal teenager. Songs no righteous 'billy band would ever play.

About the time I reached the middle of our third set list, the one with lesser known hits like *Breathless* and *Ubangi Stomp*, I realized hints of daylight backlit the plastic curtains that hung in the main doorway. The light gradually grew warmer as pre-dawn meandered toward sunrise and mixed well with the yeasty smell of rising dough. Sunrises and bakers went together like racecar drivers and the half-way mark of a race—you'd better have gotten something done by that point or the rest of the day was going to be running your ass off trying to catch-up.

I had two racks of loaves baked and cooling, three more in the oven, six in the proofer behind that, and I was starting on dough for the next day's cinnamon rolls when the sounds of the bakery started to tickle my ears: giant mixers whirring, oven doors banging closed, the voices of my co-workers talking about a *beisbol* game and Spanish-language hip-hop coming out of the radio.

Ooby Dooby, I could hear again! I looked at the clock on the wall over the Boss's office; ten of seven in the morning. Was there something magical about that time? That didn't make any sense. If time had had any play in my resetting at all, I'd have had my hearing back not long after Brady had woken me up because sunrise on the eastern coast of Mexico, where I reset the last two times, had to have been hours ago.

Then it hit me. *Sunrise.* Both of the other times I'd woken up to find my hearing and voice recovered I'd seen the light from the rising sun: on the fishing boat and on the bus. Brady had woken me up before the sunrise. That's probably why I hadn't been able to hear or talk.

I didn't know if that was the truth, sunrise, or maybe it was the combination of sleep and a sunrise. Either way, I was closing in on how this new gift of mine worked, and that meant I could use it with fewer surprises the next time.

Being able to hear didn't change the job that much, but it did make ordering lunch from the Taco truck easier—what was it with Portland and portable restaurants? I got a couple of authentic tacos—shredded beef, cabbage and kick-ass salsa on doubled-layered soft corn tortillas—and sat with my co-workers at the tables outside, listening to them talk.

Most of them had family *back home.* For the first time in my life I understood how hard it must be to have to make that choice: leave everything you know and go someplace to do a job that you didn't really want to do to make sure your family (or in my case, phamily) got what they needed to survive and thrive. And in most cases there wasn't any other way to get it done.

Being without options sucked, especially when I didn't particularly have a plan, either.

At the end of our lunch break, the Boss came outside, stomped out really, carrying a slip of paper. He charged right at me and for a moment I was afraid he was going to fire my ass. Getting canned on the first day wouldn't be a record for me, but not making it through lunch would.

"I ain't your damn secretary," he said as he shoved the paper under my nose. "You tell that Loomie chick she can get you after 1:30 if she needs you again. Her emergencies ain't my problem. I don't care who she knows."

I almost warned him against antagonizing Laume—it was indeed her name on the paper along with another name tagged as something called *Guardian ad Litem*, a time (3:00 pm), and an address—but I doubted he'd *get the message.* He walked away before I could say thank you. The guys all looked at me with raised eyebrows.

When I showed the paper to my co-workers a few of them recognized the address on 2nd Street as the offices for the Department of Human Services.

"You got a kid in trouble?" the foreman, Miguel from San Salvador, asked me. "Don't let the boss find out, he don't like the state coming here."

"A kid?" I asked wondering how he'd worked that out from just an address.

"That's where my brother goes to visit his kid since the social worker took her away from her *madre loca*."

Suddenly Laume's note made sense: I had an appointment with someone in the child welfare system. A line on Hannah Faye? Of course, if she was in foster care she'd have some kind of state worker looking in on her. Some of the kids at the Texas State Hospital got visits from people like that if they'd been made wards of the state. Laume had apparently gotten the metaphorical stick out of her ass and helped me, putting me onto Hannah's trail.

I was both grateful that Laume had helped and astonished at when and how she chose to do it. Likely this 3:00 appointment would save me hours, or maybe days, of legwork—and that was good. But it meant I had about four hours to prepare to meet whatever a *Guardian ad Litem* was.

I made it through the whole day at the bakery, and didn't get fired once. I considered that a step up in my luck.

After work I changed into my pedal pushers and Cossack top, let my hair down, and with some help from my new co-workers, caught the correct bus across town. At 2:30 I found myself outside the Human Services office on 2nd Street, smack dab in the middle of downtown.

It was a busy place, people coming and going, the front door didn't stay closed for more than 30 seconds at a whack. It was pretty easy to tell the players. The social workers hurried along, oblivious to everything around them, glued to their smart phones. The best dressed—suits with ties, skirts on the ladies—walked smartly in groups with other suited folks, pegging them all as lawyers. Here and there a lone lawyer huddled in hushed conversations with members of the third group, the parents. The parents were pretty easy to recognize: mostly out of shape, under-dressed in terms of appropriate attire for a downtown office building, and far too many of them bore the scars of drug abuse. Meth, probably.

My time at the Hospital and out touring with Billy's Asylum Rats had put me in close contact with addicts of all kinds. Alcoholics I could take—had some family history there. Smokers I got used to at the hospital. (A lot of folks with mental health issues had substance abuse issues as well, and the hospital drew the line at tobacco and sugar. All else was officially shunned and driven underground.) On the road I'd seen far too many people hung up on meth, usually young girls, hooked and willing to do anything for their next fix. I hated that crap.

The place stunk of misery. I couldn't imagine a mind among them that I'd want to communicate with telepathically.

And that got me to thinking. I wondered, for the second time, if I could communicate with people other than Maria. Someone I didn't know, had never met? I itched to test my theory about the sunrise and stretch my telepathic muscles some more. But that would be a bad idea, unless I wanted to have an awkward meeting with the *Guardian ad Litem* and then frighten Brady with my D-n-D act again. But if I waited until the weekend, when I could sleep in past sunrise and give the whole resetting process a real test. That would be better. The possibilities tantalized me as my people watching continued.

At five minutes to 3:00 I entered the building, passed through a metal detector at the door and asked the front desk where I might find Kevin Butcher, the name from my appointment slip.

I got a visitor's badge and an escort up to the third floor where I got quite the surprise. Kevin wasn't the buttoned-down bureaucrat I'd been expecting, not like any Social Worker I'd ever met. Apparently *Guardian ad Litems* were a different breed altogether.

Kevin was a chubby white dude in glasses with a ready smile and long, curly hair worn in a ponytail. Sure, he had on the prerequisite button-down shirt and slacks, but his skull-themed tie and office full of signs declaring war on stupidity said he had intelligence and a sense of humor. I liked him instantly.

"You look just like your picture," Kevin said, extending his hand.

It wasn't every day I received such professional treatment from strangers and I appreciated it. His handshake was the professional two-pump sort that the A&R rep at Sun Records used after we'd signed our contract to seal our recording deal. I knew this guy had been around the block.

Lying on his desk was a manila folder with a black and white photo of me clipped to the front. The papers inside, all about me I guessed, stacked to a half inch or so, and I immediately wondered if my juvenile record was part of it.

"That's my file," I said, implying a question about how he'd gotten his hands on it.

"Yup," Kevin sat down at his desk and offered me the chair across from him. "Your CASA coordinator from Austin overnighted it to me when she recommended you for the Williams case."

Casa coordinator? *What the hell was that?* Casa was Spanish for house. But house coordinator? My landlord, maybe? But that dude wasn't Hispanic, and he'd never called my place a casa. I doubted that's what Kevin meant, so I played along to see if I could figure it out before I looked like an idiot.

Whatever a casa coordinator was and whatever story Kevin had swallowed along with that folder, the situation had Laume's stink all over it—like my forged passport and driver's license that had been so good I'd been able to cross the border, pass through TSA security and access my bank accounts. This was further proof of how good Laume was at creating official, human documents. I wondered if that was a Faery trait or something specific to my phamily's jailor. "She's a thorough one, she is," I agreed.

"I can't tell you how glad we are that you're here to help. We don't really have anyone in our CASA volunteer ranks with experience on these kinds of high-profile cases, with these kinds of kids. And, as you can guess, all the *Guardians ad Litem* in my office have caseloads up to their armpits."

Between Kevin's speech and the books on the shelf over his desk I started to put a picture together that CASA (not casa) was a type of job title for someone who volunteered with foster kids, but I wondered what made Hannah Faye a special case in Kevin's book. Laume, who was certainly *a special case* but not high-profile in any sense of the word, had never answered me when I asked why a Higher Power (who turned out to be a Faery) would be interested in a little human girl. I needed to fish more information out of Kevin, but I didn't want to blow the cover Laume had set up for me by asking stupid questions with obvious-to-those-who-should-know answers, so I played along.

"So this one's special-special, or just plain-old-special?"

"This one's more special than most of the celebrity cases we get. On the bright side, it's only one kid," Kevin said as he opened a drawer and fished out a brown file folder that had *Williams* hand-written on the outside in Sharpie.

"Hannah Faye, age 14. Like most kids with famous-but-absentee parents she's managed to get the attention of Law Enforcement about as often as her dad."

Kevin handed the file across the desk, it was thicker than the one he had on me. There was an inch of official-looking paper bound to the back half of the folder and the picture of a gorgeous young girl pinned to the opposite side. My first glimpse of Hannah. She was knock-out beautiful with brown hair, tanned skin, and brilliant blue eyes.

Very familiar blue eyes.

I'd seen them just the day before on the street.

That photo was the answer I'd been looking for, the puzzle piece that made the picture whole. No doubt in my mind, Hannah Faye was Laume's daughter. That's why Laume was involved. I didn't know how that was possible, Laume being a Faery and all—did that make Hannah half-Faery? But as obvious as the fire-crowned heart tattooed on my chest,

Hannah was Laume's kid—and that explained a whole lot about a whole lot.

I filed that tidbit away for later, to keep safe and then pull out when I needed leverage over Laume, because I was pretty sure she would have told me she was the kid's mom if she had wanted me to know.

"Who's the father?" I asked Kevin as I flipped through the file: pages and pages of legalese—court reports, judgments, CPS reports—enough to bore several people to sleep at once.

"Ryan Williams. Ex-ball player. You might have heard of him."

Of course I'd heard of him. Until a year ago he'd been the hottest player in major league baseball—the star catcher for the Oakland Athletics. His face had been all over the TV and the internetz, and not always for his sponsorships. He'd been a bad boy; in the good way and in the bad way, but mostly kept it on the edge of acceptable. If I'd ever met him in a bar I sure as hell would've tried to pick him up and take him home.

Ryan Williams had been Great, but then he'd gotten hurt during a game and lost his starting position, and then his contract. A while ago I saw a news report he'd gotten nailed with an intent-to-distribute quantity of cocaine—among other things, allegedly. He got arrested, and then disappeared from the public eye. I must have heard it happened in Portland, but it never stuck with me. And now I was going to get to meet him.

"These famous types get so pissed off when we hold them to the same parenting standards as everyone else," Kevin said. "They're so damned entitled. And most of them are shit parents, even when we're done with them."

I could tell from Kevin's tone that I was supposed to already agree with the sentiment. I hadn't ever thought about celebrity parents as a whole, but my own experience lined-up nicely with Kevin's cynical assessment.

My father, the great Chef Trevor Michaels, wasn't a capital-C celebrity of national standing like Ryan Williams, but certain circles worshipped him as though he carried a divine spark in his knife hand. During my childhood he travelled all the time to manage his restaurants in New York, Los Angeles, Honolulu and Las Vegas. I knew by the way he treated me that not only was I not on his life menu, but there wasn't even room for me on the chalkboard that listed his Specials of the Day. I'd like to say I'd dealt with it all, but some days that was truer than others. Thus, my Daddy issues. I no longer relished the idea of meeting Hannah's father.

"I made you an appointment to meet with the foster parents and Hannah at 6:00 at the foster home and then one to see Mr. Williams at his rehab facility at 7:00."

So much for avoiding my daddy issues, but at least there was going to be a face-to-face with Hannah in my day. Real progress. Something to telepath home about.

Kevin handed over two sheets of paper. One with the address for Terwilliger Recovery Center, the other with the name Nancy Carter, foster mom. Then he handed over a huge binder labeled *C.A.S.A: Court Appointed Special Advocates in Multnomah County*.

"I know the rules here are mostly the same as the program in Texas, but here's our playbook so you can see the differences."

I accepted the big binder—it weighed two pounds if it weighed an ounce—and stacked it underneath my two contact pages and Hannah's inch-thick folder. "Thanks," I said. If I were being honest I'd have said something like: *you think I don't need to read the whole thing, but I have no idea what I'm doing so I'd probably better*; or, *why is it so big;* or, *are we fixing a family or an airplane?*

"Your first court date is next Wednesday. I'm sorry to dump so much on you like this, but we'll need to file some kind of status update a couple of days before. Can you spend at least four hours with Hannah in the next four days so you can write that report and turn it in early on Monday?"

"Okay," I said. Four hours over the next four days would mean getting time with Hannah that evening, after work Friday and then again sometime during day Saturday or Sunday. Even without the report, I would be spending time with Hannah to figure out how to fix her family and get my phamily back. This hasty report would just help keep me from spending all weekend in bed with Brady. "My weekend just opened up."

"Great. Samples for how the judge likes her reports are in the appendix," Kevin said, pointing to the mammoth binder. "Stick pretty close to the format if you don't want extra-special attention from her or the lawyers."

Great. Judges and lawyers never liked me much anyway.

"Do you have a number where I can reach you in case something pops up?" Kevin asked.

I almost rattled off my cell number until I remembered my phone was sleeping with the fishes in a sunken yacht on the floor of the Gulf. "Can I call you later and give you a message number?" I asked, assuming Brady wouldn't mind if I shared his cell number this one time for emergencies.

"I can do one better," Kevin said with a knowing look. He spun around and dug into a filing cabinet behind his desk. Plastic clattered against metal for a few seconds and then he extracted a cell phone and charging cable. "It's not much, recycled by one of our volunteers, but it works and the program pays for 30 minutes a month," he said as he handed it to me.

I cradled the ancient Motorola flip phone as if it were a Grammy award for Best New Artist. I'd been out of contact with the world for a week—except for my telepathy, but that didn't really count. Even though the phone's case was dinged-up and the screen scratched, it felt good to be part of the world again, like I'd regrown a limb that had been lost in an accident. The little piece of electronics made me feel almost as capable as I had when I'd figured out that I had telepathy all on my own. Almost.

And Kevin wasn't done playing Santa Claus quite yet. He passed over a pair of badges: one with the photo from "my file" on it that gave me to access the building we were sitting in without passing through the metal detector every time, and the other was a pre-paid bus pass. "That'll get you on The MAX as well," he said.

I must've looked confused because he clarified that Portland had one of the best public transportation systems on the west coast, including a light-rail train that stretched from Hillsboro to Gresham. I assumed by the way he held out his arms that the train covered some outlandish distance. I smiled and nodded, glad to know I could get around without Brady's amazing little Audi.

I placed my badges and contact sheets inside Hannah's folder and then put it, the huge binder, and my new phone into my beaded shoulder bag. Slinging it over my shoulder gave me a sense of gravity about the whole situation that I hadn't really considered before: there really was a little girl in trouble. I'd been so focused on my own problem, on how much I missed my phamily, that I hadn't taken the time to be empathetic for Hannah. The bag full of reality swinging from my shoulder changed that for me.

"Any questions?" Kevin asked.

"What can you tell me about Hannah's foster family?"

After what Laume had said about them I prepared myself to hear that they were new foster parents and Kevin had never met them, or that he was sorry and it was the best the system could do for a kid her age, or that the state was looking for other possibilities for Hannah. But what he said surprised the hell out of me.

"The Carters? Man I love those people."

"Really? You know them?"

"I've had kids placed with them on and off for fifteen years. They're the best home we have for the real trouble cases. Nancy can work her way into even the most hardened of hearts. You're going to love them."

That didn't sound at all like *a vile place* where *people threatened to quash a child's soul.*

"They sound too perfect to be real," I said, hoping to fish out that these people hadn't always been the angels Kevin thought them to be.

"Maybe not perfect, but close enough."

That did not jive with what Laume had said. I didn't know if this was a case of smart people pulling the wool over the eyes of a public servant to get a big payday or if Laume had somehow gotten it completely wrong. My inner cynic leaned toward the former, because otherwise why would Laume have plucked my phamily from certain disaster to insert me into this mess? She certainly hadn't done it out of the selflessness.

I guessed I'd have to figure it out for myself. "I look forward to meeting them." Kevin missed the irony in my voice.

After another firm handshake I was out the door and looking for a local map because the bits and pieces of geography I'd remembered from running around in Brady's Audi the day before hadn't really stuck. I found a souvenir shop that sold metro maps a few blocks north and then my feet carried me ten blocks across town to this wonderful train called The MAX and my first meeting with Hannah Faye Williams.

It was about time.

9

Hannah's foster family lived in a western suburb of Portland called Beaverton. The MAX train picked me up downtown near the river (not too far from where Brady and I had eaten Vietnamese food and listened to the drum circle the night before) and trundled up the hill before cruising into a pitch-black, mile-long tunnel where my map showed it passing directly beneath a cemetery (spooky) and a zoo (fun).

Assuming I had at least 20 minutes to kill before the train reached my station, I thumbed through the giant notebook Kevin had given me that explained what I was supposed to do in my cover role as a CASA. From what I could tell in reading the first two pages, the job of a Special Advocate (the SA at the end of the name) was to act as a hybrid of Guardian Angel, Private Detective, and Guard Dog. Court Appointed (the CA at the beginning of the name) meant I had judge's orders authorizing access to anything and everything related to the ankle biter in question, Hannah Faye, and her parents. (Not that a judge's order would hold any weight with Laume.) In short I figured out that CASAs spoke up in court for kids in Foster Care so that they didn't get run over by the system.

Cool. I could do that for Hannah. Though I'd never been a Foster Child, I knew plenty about getting run over by the system.

I glanced quickly at the appendix that gave examples of the report I would have to write for the judge in a few days and discovered it required more concentration than I could muster. Thoughts of Hannah, finally so real and so close, filled my brain.

On the night Laume appeared at the back of the lifeboat, she had said that Hannah was in trouble, and her soul was in trouble too. Not that she had explained what she meant, another Faery thing, I'm sure. Laume also said Hannah had Daddy Issues, and now that I knew about Ryan Williams I started to understand why I might just be the perfect person to poke my nose into the situation.

I looked at the photo of Hannah in the file and wondered who she really was. Beautiful, sure, but that's what happened when pretty people got together, they made pretty babies. Hannah wore long, straight hair and oversized, trendy earrings which made her look much older than fourteen. (I'd have guessed at least sixteen; which could have been a blessing or a curse, depending on the circumstances.) The smile plastered on her face wasn't the kind that said she was happy; it said she would do what was expected of her, like smile for the camera, and not one bit more.

As I picked my way through Hannah's file I saw my teenage years reflected over and over again: picked-up for shoplifting, underage drinking, and joyriding. There were more incident reports than arrests, and more arrests than convictions. From what I could tell she'd never seen the inside of a juvie detention center, but she'd been assigned enough community service hours to clean out every roadside ditch in the city, twice. Before going into care she'd been bounced out of two different junior high schools. Reading between the lines I could guess at more trouble: age-inappropriate friendships and boyfriends, experimenting with drugs, and maybe even some attempts at running away.

As much as I hated to admit it, Laume had done something right by me, and by Hannah, when she inserted me into the situation as a CASA. Truly a brilliant move. I was a volunteer, for a state program, who had no responsibilities other than helping Hannah. It was my job to ask lots of questions—and if anyone gave me trouble I'd just explain that I had a report to write for a judge. I could go anywhere Hannah went, do anything Hannah did. That kind of access, some patience, and a little luck couldn't help but to speed up the process of understanding what the whole situation was really about. I'd fix things sooner. Get my phamily home sooner.

One thing I already understood before asking my first question: it couldn't be easy being Hannah, even if she didn't know her mother was a Faery. And from the court paperwork I figured it was unlikely Hannah had ever known her mother—those sections in the forms had all been filled in with "Jane Doe".

I'd just gotten to the part of the file that dealt with Hannah's dad, Ryan, when the train's overhead speaker called out my stop. I stuffed everything back in the folder and joined the herd of evening commuters getting off at a generic transit center behind an even more generic shopping mall. Looking like a total tourist, I unfolded my map and followed its directions northward toward the address where Hannah lived with her Foster Parents, Nancy and Mike Carter.

The first residential addresses I came across belonged to a park full of trailers; ugly, poorly maintained, sad. I walked along a line of mailboxes whose numbers grew and grew, but never reached the one written on the page from Kevin. I was surprised because the trailer park was exactly the kind of environment I'd been imagining Hannah Faye in.

I followed the sidewalk to the next property and found a multi-family housing campus, bigger and nicer than any I'd ever seen. I double-checked the address on my page against the sign at the entrance and, sure enough, my destination was somewhere inside.

The complex sprawled as far as I could see. Large clusters of two-story townhouse units and their parking areas broke up over ten acres of playgrounds, trees, and grass. Grass that would've cost a fortune to keep so soft and green through a Texas summer.

It took me fifteen minutes of wandering around to find the building with the right number, so I was late and slightly winded when I strode up the walk to their door. I was welcomed by a squat cubbyholed-rack painted bright blue and filled with shoes: everything from little pink tennis shoes that would just about fill the flat of my hand to a pair of men's basketball shoes I could stuff both feet into. A post-it note stuck over the doorbell said, "Knock please, Migraine On Board."

I liked the humor, but dreaded the idea of migraines. I'd had a couple of them after drinking too much cheap wine and I immediately felt sorry for whoever inside was suffering from them.

After tapping on the door a half-dozen times, quietly, I waited. Solid footsteps approached the other side of the door which opened to reveal a heavy-set man about my age wearing a Boston Red Sox t-shirt. He gave me a look, the look I get from people who don't have any tattoos and don't understand mine.

"Hi, I'm Bailey Michaels." I smiled to make myself less threatening. I'm told it works, sometimes.

He recognized my name and his face warmed like he'd stepped out from the shadow of a red velvet stage curtain and into the spotlight. "Bailey, come on in. Kevin said you were coming by tonight."

I followed him up a flight of stairs and into an apartment of quiet pandemonium. The tiny living room overflowed: two different TVs, two computer stations, toys, books, magazines. The furniture was overstuffed and mismatched. One wall had been dedicated as a type of shrine: before-and-after photos of at least twenty kids. The photos drew me in. Sadness turned to hope. Haunted smiles replaced by genuine happiness. Sunken cheeks filled until they dimpled with joy. Four of the wooden photo frames held only one picture each, the before shots. One of the four was a candid shot of Hannah.

"Four foster kids?" I asked Mike and wondered how big the townhouse was.

He smiled the kind of smile I expected Elvis Presley might wear if he'd still been around. "Just our two boys and two foster kids right now." He tapped Hannah's photo and one of a little girl about three years old. "The other two just went home last month. Been too busy to get their pictures put up yet. Takes a little time to be able to look at them again, you know?"

Chock up one point for Kevin's version of who these foster parents really were. Mike's words just didn't hit me as the kind of thing a guy would say if he was just in it for the money. His emotions felt sincere.

"Where is everyone?" I asked.

"Nancy's reading on the deck," he said, leading the way through the cluttered kitchen to a sliding glass door. "Taylor and Mikey, our two boys, took Cassie to the playground. Hannah's curled up in bed with a fierce migraine. Again."

"Migraines, plural? At fourteen?"

"And they usually happen about the same time she does something to get herself into trouble. Stuff that usually takes a couple of days to come to light." Mike shook his head as he opened the sliding glass door and stepped out onto a large, second floor deck. At the sound of the door his wife, Nancy, set down a book with a dragon on the cover and looked up with a smile.

Strike two against Laume's assessment. The woman sitting with her book and cup of coffee at a beat-up table amid a pile of coloring books and crayons could not be a perpetrator of anything vile, or threatening. Maybe she could be accused of perpetrating peanut-butter cookies, read-it-again bedtime stories and clean-behind-your-ears-please, but she couldn't be evil.

Nancy stood up and gave me a hug, welcoming me to her home.

It wasn't in my nature to be touchy-feely with strangers but I found myself hugging her back. She was warm, like JoJo, and squishy, like Maria, but shorter and more muscular than either of them. She smelled like vanilla perfume and fabric softener.

"Have a seat, Bailey," Nancy said. "We can let Hannah rest a while longer and get to know each other."

I sat across from Nancy with my back to the door and Mike sat next to her, alternately stacking coloring books and herding crayons.

"What do you do for a living, Bailey?" Mike asked.

"I'm a baker, and I play drums in a Rockabilly band."

"That explains the tattoos," Nancy said, but her voice did not ring with condescension. "That must've hurt." She pointed to the flaming heart and crown inked over my breast bone.

An odd sensation hit me, I felt compelled to tell her the complete and unvarnished truth about my tattoo. I wasn't ashamed of it, I liked it, but it covered up a scar I was embarrassed about. I'd just met this woman and I already wanted to divulge my painful story to her in the hopes that she could do or say something to make me feel better about myself.

"You must be an amazing foster mom," I said. "No wonder you have such a full wall."

Nancy didn't smile with pride like I expected. Instead her mouth pulled to one side and fell, like a soufflé that didn't quite make it out of the oven. "I wish I was having more success with Hannah."

Mike nodded. "She's a really sweet kid, and she gets along with everyone. But that's the problem."

"Why's that?" I asked.

"Because they say I don't think for myself," said a young, female voice from behind me. Hannah appeared in the doorway, the glass slider open just wide enough to show her face clearly. Her skin was flushed and she squinted, glassy eyed against the brightness of the day. Even so, she was stunning. Prettier than her photo. "Because no matter how hard I try, I can't learn the piano, I trip over my own feet when I play soccer, and I refuse to eat Brussels sprouts."

"Hannah, you know that's not how Papa-Mike and I feel about you. You sing like an angel," Nancy said. She had turned her whole body to face Hannah, like she was really paying attention to her foster daughter, but she didn't stand up and offer a hug like she had with me. My intuition said that was for Hannah's benefit. "Come meet, Bailey."

Hannah grudgingly stepped out through the door. "What're you supposed to be with those tattoos? Alien catwoman from another planet?"

"Hannah, your manners," Mike reminded.

"It's okay," I said. "Very few people recognize me in my human disguise."

Nancy got my attempt at a joke, and I caught a tiny turn at the corner of Hannah's mouth before she covered it up with an eye roll of teenaged proportions.

"Bailey's been assigned as your CASA. We talked about that," Mike said. I admired how level-headed he sounded without coming across as a patronizing ass. "Until the court okays you going home, she's going to keep us all honest."

"My dad's going to like her," Hannah said, turning around and going back inside.

Nancy mimed that she had no idea what Hannah meant. Mike's hands came together in a restless writhing on the table until Nancy reached over and settled them. "She's only been here three weeks."

"And she's been arrested for shoplifting, and suspended, and written up. It's those kids she hangs out with. We're trying to get her to find new friends, but..." Mike put his hands in his lap. "Sorry," he said to me. "I do my best to keep my frustration out of their way. But sometimes."

"I was like that when I was fourteen," I said. "Do you mind if I talk to her alone?"

Nancy pointed inside and then to her left. "Third door down the hall."

I left them sitting with their frustration and entered the apartment. Hannah's door had an American Idol sticker plastered across it and a sign with her name written in three colors of glitter. I added a third point to Kevin's side of the foster home assessment game. This place wasn't vile, and the Carter's weren't endangering Hannah's soul. I'd never had a door with my name tagged on it in glitter.

Knocking seemed appropriate. "Hannah. Let's talk."

"Whatever, fine."

Yes, this was a kid who would do what she had to do. But when I opened the door to a dark, cool room and a kid buried under her bedding, I got that impression again that she would only give the minimum.

I sat at the desk, the only other furniture in the purple-painted room besides a beautiful, full-size oak bed with a purple-and-tangerine quilt. I took a deep breath and tried to put myself in Hannah's position for a minute.

I'd dealt with something similar when I woke up in the mental ward of the Texas State Hospital. Being a suicider, they'd kept someone on me day and night until I finally admitted to my counselors that I just needed someone to pay attention to me, to my needs, for a goddamn minute every once in a while. My whole life had been about pleasing my dad, keeping out of his way, not messing up his precious schedule. All I wanted was for him to look at me and not see a reflection of himself mixed with a woman he hated more than he hated processed cheese spread.

Maybe that's why Hannah had said her father would like me, because everyone liked him so much, and then ignored her. Big-C celebrity or little-c celebrity, sometimes they loved the limelight more than their little girls.

"I'm not here for your dad," I said. Then I waited, watching the lump that was a fourteen year old girl trying to hide from a headache under a quilt. "I don't give a shit that he's famous."

"You're the first one. Ever," Hannah said from under the covers. "Or you're lying."

Ouch. No wonder Mike Carter had taken to wringing his hands.

"I doubt that Nancy and Mike would do anything differently with you if your dad was just an average Joe."

"Papa-Mike," Hannah said in contempt, "asked Dad to autograph a baseball the first time they met."

Scratch one point for me, and score one for Laume's vile-and-soul-threatening story. "I will not do that," I promised.

Hannah popped out from under her covers to glare at me. "Obviously you haven't met him yet."

"He's a ball player. A celebrity. Big deal. You meet one, you've met them all."

"Like you know any ball players."

"They came over to drink beer with my dad all the time."

That struck a chord with Hannah. "Who's your dad?"

"You wouldn't know him."

"You think I'm dumb."

I thought about that one for a second. My gut reaction was to say "no," but in truth, I thought every teenager was stupid to some degree. But not out of willful ignorance or lack of capability, most of them just hadn't pulled their noses out of their bellybuttons long enough to acknowledge there was a whole world outside their selfish little needs.

That made me look at Hannah a little closer. There she sat, head pounding from a migraine, and she was willing to stand up for herself and argue with me, a complete stranger. If I were her I'd be balled up on the floor, moaning for someone to please kill me before the headache got any worse. She didn't need to talk to me, but she was.

The least I could do was treat her with as much respect.

"His name is Trevor Michaels. He owns some five-star restaurants where he serves macaroni and cheese for $25 a plate to people who have more money than brains."

"Never heard of him. Sounds like an asshole."

I know she was trying to get my goat, and Bailey-before-treatment would have leapt to my father's defense for no reason other than he was the only parent I knew. Bailey-after-treatment had a slightly different opinion, less default and more realistic. "You're right. He is an asshole."

I think Hannah was about to bury herself back under her quilt but she stopped and looked at me. "You for real?"

"Realest thing you'll meet from Planet Catwoman."

Hannah actually smiled for a second before the migraine turned it into a wince. "Your tats are actually kinda cool."

"My tats are the ginchiest, 'cause I'm always the heppest cat in town."

"You talk funny. Are you British?"

"Silly chick-from-the-sticks, I am American. Texas born and raised, and 100% pure Rockabilly."

I don't think she picked up what I was laying down for her. She detoured the conversation. "You actually like my foster parents, don't you?"

"They're pretty damned earthbound."

"I hate them."

"Doesn't seem like there's much there to hate."

"They're so boring."

"Square," I said, teaching her the 'billy term. "My girls and I would call them squares, or cubies. But Mike and Nancy aren't so bad."

"They make me take piano lessons and I had to join the stupid soccer club."

"Oh, the horror," I said, covering my face with my hands in mock terror. Though, in truth, had I been forced into playing soccer as a teenager I probably would have broken both ankles just to get myself out of it.

"Sometimes I wish I would break an ankle, just so they'd let me quit."

A shiver rolled up my spine, like the kind I got when an amplifier squelched feedback during sound-check. For a second I wondered if Hannah had reached into my brain and stolen that little thought telepathically. I tapped my fingers on the desktop to make sure my hearing hadn't suddenly stopped working, and I heard my paradiddle plinks on the pressboard desktop just fine and breathed a sigh of relief. She hadn't been in my head.

"Why do you hate piano so much?" I asked. "Nancy said you sing."

Hannah gave me a shrug and half a smile that faded immediately. "I can sing anything the teacher gives me. But my fingers. I can't make them go where they're supposed to go. It's like they're made of slinkies."

Some kids I've known in my life, present company and phamily included, would say something like that just to get out of a difficult task. But Hannah really looked miffed that she couldn't play the piano. I felt bad for her.

"I'm in a class with five and six year olds," she said. "They're better than me. All of them."

"Did you explain that to your foster parents?"

Hannah gave me another of her heavily-accentuated eye rolls. "They tell me I have to stick with it. They say that I've got to learn that hard work pays off. My dad wasn't real good at teaching me persistence. If he wasn't good at something he'd just let it go. Except *he* was good at almost everything."

"Mike and Nancy want you to be well-rounded," I said, thinking of what Laume had said to me a couple of days before about my duties. I felt Hannah's frustration, though. In my experience, well-rounded wasn't all that and a bag of pork rinds. Given the chance, I wanted to be really good at a thing, to shine like a star. In truth, I wanted to be a little bit like my dad. But I was only ever good at drums, pastry and sex.

"Why do squares want other people to be well-rounded?" Hannah laughed at her own joke and then pressed a hand to each temple as if she were trying to keep her noggin from exploding.

Knowing how much her head hurt, and hoping to end our first meeting on a good note, I decided it was time to make my exit. I stood up. "I have an appointment with your dad in about an hour. Anything you'd like me to pass along?" I asked.

Hannah was quiet for long moments. I thought maybe the headache had gotten the best of her, but then she said, "Tell him I love him."

"Will do." I stepped to the door and opened it. "Feel better. I'll talk to Mike and Nancy about coming by tomorrow. I've got some stuff to talk to you about that will be easier when your head isn't splitting in two."

"Okay." Hannah crawled back under her quilt.

I closed the door, shutting the cool air in Hannah's dim room, and paused for a minute to think in the hallway. From the outside everything about the Carters and their home felt fine, just like Kevin said. But Hannah was unhappy, and she wasn't faking it, just like Laume said—but maybe not to such an extreme. My gut said there wasn't going to be an easy solution to this situation, not one that would be outlined in some manual, even if it weighed two pounds and was three inches thick.

My hopes for the quick return of my phamily started to fade, and I hadn't even met Ryan Williams yet.

10

When the Carters learned I was headed to visit Hannah's father, Nancy offered to save me the bus ride and drop me there on her way to the organic market. We talked about unimportant things during the five minute ride, but as Nancy pulled her minivan into the rehab facility her tone grew serious. "Watch yourself with Hannah's dad," she said.

"I'm pretty immune to celebrity."

Nancy thought for a moment before saying, "It isn't that so much as his sadness. It's like all the light has gone out for this guy and he's stumbling around in the darkness. Sometimes he's looking for help, other times I think he's trying to destroy himself."

It made sense for Ryan Williams to be lost. His career as a professional ball player had been taken away and much of his fame turned to notoriety. Drugs were a poor replacement for real dreams once you'd tasted them. No wonder his parental responsibilities had suffered.

"How much time have you spent with him?"

"Not much, maybe an hour. But Mike and I did a lot of research on him when Hannah moved in. We were trying to understand him so that we might help her figure it all out."

I appreciated Nancy's warning, but for me the dangers in meeting Ryan Williams were closer to my own past. Charming men attracted me like a fat kid to the fudge counter. I'd been programmed to worship them my whole life, and it took a great deal of conscious thought to keep myself in check around a charismatic man.

I thanked her again for the ride and stepped out under a large awning that covered the circular driveway. The building looked new-ish, and the landscaping immaculate. An Ooby for every Dooby, and all of them in the right place. That sense of order carried through inside the double sliding glass doors. The dozen chairs in the reception room were upholstered in a bold print that accentuated the carpet and the oil paintings on the wall. A desk as big as my Buick guarded the doorway leading back to the rest of the facility. Terwilliger Recovery Center, the facility name in two-foot tall stainless steel letters, dominated the back wall behind the desk.

The setting sun slanted in the front windows giving the room a sense of wellness that all that art and furniture couldn't quite manage without. Unfortunately, the sun never held still for long and the magic couldn't hold.

I gave my name to the receptionist who asked to verify it against my ID. I gave her my driver's license and my new identification card from Human Services. She asked me to wait and it took fifteen minutes for someone to come and get me. I took advantage and catnapped in the lobby. It had been a long day.

A nurse in sea-green scrubs finally came to get me, and he lectured me as we walked through halls flanked by doctor's offices and treatment rooms. "You have 30 minutes to visit. No physical contact is permitted with the patient. Cameras will monitor and record all activity. You are not allowed to give anything to the patient or receive anything from the patient."

The nurse stopped outside a door labeled Family Visit Room. "And, most importantly, please do not aggravate Mr. Williams."

I'd been nodding my head as he laid down the law. Everything else seemed reasonable for an in-patient care facility, but that last statement worried me. "Is he dangerous?"

"We've been cutting down his pain meds to facilitate his detox and he's not dealing with it."

With that, Nurse Rules-a-Lot swiped his badge and unlocked the visiting room. It was a small space, about the size of a large bedroom, furnished with an industrial couch, two chairs, and a coffee table. The opposite wall of the room had a brightly-painted mural, words of hope and encouragement. A tub of children's toys waited in the corner, jumbled but untouched.

Ryan Williams slouched in one of the two chairs, elbows propped on the chair's arms, head leaning forward on his hands. His right knee sported a shiny stainless-steel and black fabric brace—part creepy, part sympathy inducing, all high-tech. I stepped far enough inside the room that the door clicked shut behind me and I waited for him to acknowledge my presence.

He lifted his head as if it weighed a hundred pounds. His eyes looked right at me, but I wasn't sure he saw me clearly until he squinted and then tipped his head to one side. "They said you were here about my kid."

"I'm her CASA, Bailey." I knew I should walk in and sit down, but there was something in the casual grace of his body as he sat, the strength in his hands supporting his chin, the absolute perfection of him that tugged on me in a very dangerous way. I pulled an image of Hannah to mind. I was here to help her, and to help my phamily, not to continue my never-ending pursuit of carnal pleasure—no matter how tiger-like the man sitting before me was. "I just saw your daughter. She asked me to pass along a message."

Ryan's eyes lit up for a moment and then glazed over. "Let me guess, she said *fuck you.*"

"There was a *you* in it," I said. "But the sentiment was a whole lot sweeter than that."

I stood in silence as his head slowly bowed back to the position it had been in when I arrived, like he didn't care about his daughter at all. For the second time in a day I got a new sense of how serious, how hard, reuniting this family was going to be. Crap.

In ways he was just like my dad; he commanded a room, he made clothes look good—even hospital-issue baggy shorts and a long sleeved t-shirt—and silence seemed to be his friend, not his enemy. But unlike Dad, this guy lacked a spark that drove him to action. He was a shell of a man with nothing living inside, and I didn't think it was the injury to his knee. Not anymore.

"Do you want me to leave?" I asked.

It took a moment, but he shook his head. It was a sad, desperate motion. I felt that tug again and I let it draw me toward him, but I stopped at the far end of the couch and sat down. He looked up at me. "I won't bite you."

I slid down the couch to the middle cushion and stopped, not daring to get any closer.

"I'm here to help you get reunited with your daughter." I pulled Hannah's file out of my bag and flipped to the section on Ryan Williams. There was a plan, probably written by some social worker, a checklist of things Ryan needed to accomplish to prove himself a fit parent. Number one on the list: complete in-patient drug and alcohol rehabilitation at a certified facility.

"How much longer are you here for treatment?" I asked.

Ryan showed interest in the file I held open on my knees. Hannah's photo faced him from the inside cover. "Is that about her? Hannah?"

"I haven't read it all. But it looks like you're in here, too."

Ryan half stood and moved over to sit next to me on the couch, knee brace squeaking, so he could look at the file more closely. Delicately, he reached out and stroked his daughter's photo before turning his attention to the paperwork.

"What does it say about me?" Just like my dad, if it wasn't about him, it wouldn't hold his attention for more than two seconds.

I wanted to say, *it says you're an awful parent*, and then thought about what the nurse had said, *don't aggravate him*, and that took the wind out of my sails. "It says you both have some work to do to. The judge wants you to clean up your act."

He looked up from the file and stared directly into my eyes. For a second I saw raw anger, and I almost got up to leave the room, but then he inhaled deeply. He smiled and reached out to touch me.

His hand felt hot on my knee, even through the fabric of my pedal pushers. The light touch lingered, turned into a gentle caress, and then settled into a needful squeeze. His eyes, hazel with flecks of green, searched mine with energy unlike anything he'd displayed since I walked into the room. It was like he'd been sleeping and just woken up to the perfect sunrise.

He leaned forward and sniffed me. Actually sniffed me. I pulled away because I wanted more than anything to lean forward and draw in his smell as well. Elvis help me I wanted to do more than smell him, I wanted to taste his lips and feel the stubble of his crew cut beneath my fingertips.

"No contact with the patient, please," came a tinny, disembodied voice that sounded like Nurse Rules-a-Lot would if he'd been hit by a shrink-ray.

Ryan pulled his hand away, leaving cold tingles on my knee in its absence. I scooted a couple of inches away from him on the couch, about as far as I could bring myself to move.

"Thank you," said the tinny voice.

Rules. Goddamn rules. If I'd been visiting the rehab as a friend, not an official person with a judge's order, I would have stuck my middle finger up and flashed it around the room for the camera I couldn't quite find. How dare they spy on me while...

Whoa. Whoa! Wait! What was I doing? Where had that come from? And just like that Hannah's dad had gotten under my skin. I was definitely hot and bothered. *From a yearning look and a touch on my knee?*

I turned away from Ryan and took a deep breath. The breath brought me the strength to stand up and move to the other chair, opposite the couch, where the coffee table would help enforce the boundary between us.

Mr. Williams. I decided it would be better if I thought of him as Mr. Williams. Keep it professional.

"You don't have to sit way over there," Mr. Williams said, patting the sofa cushion. "We were just starting to get to know each other."

"Do you even care whether or not you get your daughter back?"

He scowled at me. A narcissist's reaction to losing focus, control, and attention. My dad pulled that stunt all the time with his business partners.

"Why the hell do you care?" Williams asked.

The truthful answer to that question would never fly; I was there to get my phamily back from Laume. I had no idea what his relationship with her had been like before or after Hannah's arrival, but given how much she'd already pushed my buttons I was pretty sure that topic would qualify as aggravating.

I could tell a half truth and say that I was trying to make up for the horrible relationship I experienced with my own dad, trying to prevent that hurt from touching Hannah—but there was too much baggage to have that conversation. I wasn't in the mood to have my life laid out for ridicule by a stranger.

Instead I went for the boring answer. "I'm a volunteer who just wants to see families kept together." Especially my phamily.

"Do-gooders make my balls itch." He sat back on the couch, crossed his arms over his chest, and crossed the opposite ankle up over his wounded knee.

Of all the things he could've said, he picked that. In a way it was perfect. It captured the attraction and repulsion I felt for him nicely. It was as if he couldn't decide whether he wanted me to come closer or go the hell away. Part of me toyed with the idea of offering to scratch him in his very private place, but the rest of me objected to be called a do-gooder. I wished I was free to speak. I wished I was free to leave. I hated being trapped in a situation with someone who roused my passion and then stomped on my feelings.

"I'm not here to rattle your cage, I'm here to help," I said. "If that makes you itch, maybe you should limp on down to the dispensary and get some hydrocortisone."

Like an earthquake getting worked up for the Big One, the shaking in Ryan's chest started with a small giggle and then grew into a full-blown belly laugh. He uncrossed his arms and legs and leaned forward, shaking his head. Eventually his laughter faded to a smile.

"I like you," he said.

"Hannah said you would."

"The way you look. The way you smell." He moved forward until his knee brace clanked against the coffee table. "Why did I have to meet you like this?"

I held up my hand, palm facing him. "It's not going to happen so you can just put it in neutral."

He set his hands on the coffee table and leaned over it so close I could smell barbeque sauce lingering on his breath. He whispered, "It'll take them three minutes to get someone in here at this time of night, five if I take you up against the door. I can do it. Don't let the knee fool you."

I suddenly wished that Cooper and Paulo were in the room to protect me. That was probably the most aggressive come-on I'd ever heard—the complete opposite of Brady's cocky little glance at his crotch the day before. I didn't like the predatory notion of what Ryan implied; it was as if he was threatening to rape me right there with the camera recording the whole thing. I didn't know whether he was right about help being three minutes away or not, but I did not want to find out. I stood up, hugging Hannah's file to my chest, and backed toward the door.

I wanted to run, but I couldn't leave things between us that way—I needed to work with him to get Hannah home—

so I forced my feet to stop moving. There had to be a way to shut him down without him shutting me out. It would be impossible to straighten him out and get Hannah home if he didn't cooperate with me.

Ryan stood up. His face changed, softened. There was something in it that reminded me of how Paulo looked at his guitar just before he closed the lid of its case and locked it. "I'm sorry," Ryan said. "I didn't mean to scare you away. Don't go."

Whiplash was beginning to set into my heart. First he was cold, then welcoming. He went from self-centered to enticing and then hard and aggressive before melting into a sentimental goofball. If he hadn't already been in a treatment facility I'd have guessed he was flying high on a self-prescribed cocktail of drugs. No wonder he'd lost his career and his daughter. Nancy had been right, the guy was sad and lost and looking to destroy himself.

What the hell was I doing in the middle of it all?

Ryan's eyes never left me. He needed reassurance and I could give him that much without compromising myself. "No worries." I played it cool and lowered the folder to a less defensive position. "But I have to go, have to catch my bus."

"Can't you stay ten more minutes? You're the only normal person I've talked to in weeks; this place is driving me nuts."

I understood what he meant. In-patient care had a way of shutting out the whole world until you thought maybe it was something you'd only dreamed about. Reality flipped on its head and nurses, doctors and other patients fell into the places where friends, family and co-workers used to be, sometimes even replacing them. But as much as I felt for the guy, I knew he'd put himself in the situation and he had to finish rehab if he was going to get his family back.

If I was going to get my phamily back.

"Sorry, last bus of the night," I lied, because I had no idea what the schedule actually was. "I'll come back tomorrow after work."

His eyes brightened.

"One condition," I said.

He nodded, and I felt this rush of power, like I could have asked him to do anything and he'd have done it.

"We have to talk about your plan," I said, tapping the folder. "Whatever else is going on in your head, I need you to put it aside so we can get to work getting your daughter home."

"But you're coming back?" he asked, looking like a lost child.

I backed away toward the door and banged on it with my fist. Five seconds later the lock clicked and I opened it. "See you tomorrow."

I turned and walked through the door with warring emotions in my heart: relief, sadness, hope, frustration, anger, fear and an odd sexual tension.

A new nurse met me two minutes later and led me out to the lobby. I made an appointment to see Ryan at 2:30 the next day. That would give me time to get there on the bus after work and spend a couple of hours working with him before going to the foster home to see Hannah at 6:00.

A cool breeze blew my hair back from my face as I stepped out of the lobby and walked along the circular driveway. The bus stop waited empty at the end of the block.

The schedule posted at the stop said the bus would be along in ten minutes. I knew it would take me the better part of an hour to get back downtown to Brady's apartment where I could finally relax after an incredibly long day. Damn I missed my Buick. Setting my bag down next to me, I plopped onto the wooden bench to wait, and to think. A million ideas pinballed around inside my head and I was lost to them when a low-slung, black car with huge chrome wheels purred to a halt right in front of the bus stop.

Elvis save me. A Bugatti Veyron. Cooper had dozens of photos of that car on his cell phone—or had before it drowned.

The blacked-out passenger window slipped open silently, and Laume leaned across the seat. "Need a ride?"

11

Apparently it was good to be a Faery in the human world. Very good. The Bugatti Laume rolled up to the bus stop in was sex on wheels—hot, multi-positional, take-me-to-the-emergency-room-because-I've-pulled-a-muscle sex on wheels. The lush black paint accentuated her glossy, long hair and perfect little black dress.

If a car says anything about its driver, this one screamed power, control, and excitement. The bus pass in my pocket, however, cried out dependent, poor, and helpless. Life just wasn't fair. If I had my Buick I might not have been able to take that fancy Italian ride of hers in a quarter mile drag race—it was a 16-cylinder super car, after all—but I could have smashed the hell out of that carbon fiber dream machine with my good old American chrome bumpers and still had enough car left to drive away.

"Are you going to sit there in the rain and get soaked or are you getting in?" Laume asked.

I didn't know if she caused the sky to open up and cry or if she was just good at reading the changes in the air, but it didn't matter because the rain started to fall and I had no coat. Chilly drops spattered out of the dark clouds, coming quicker and harder in a matter of seconds. I held my bag over my head—heavy binder and all.

The same voice inside me that had told me not to agree to Laume's bargain back at the lifeboat yelled at me again; *do not get into that car.* It would be stupid to give Laume that kind of control over me, and I absolutely did not want her to deliver me to Brady's apartment building. Could not let her to know where he lived. The last time she got close to the people I cared about, she stole them away to who-knew-where and locked them in a magical prison with no doors. I couldn't do that to Brady, not after he'd been so nice to me when I really needed a friend.

"Drip, drop. Tick, tock," Laume sang. "You get much soggier and I am not allowing you inside this car."

As if on cue, the pace of the rain picked up.

"I'd rather take the bus." I looked up the street, hoping to see some sign of a bus, any bus going to any place, I didn't care. There were only cars and more cars and rain falling in the beams of their headlights. Damn.

"You know you're not very pretty when you're soaking wet, little darlin'," Laume said. "Believe me, I've seen it."

"I don't care." Though part of me did not want Brady to get an eyeful of me as a drowned rat. "I'll dry off on the bus."

Laume gave me a *hmmm*, and raised one eyebrow. In the blink of an eye, without looking like she'd moved a muscle, she suddenly disappeared from the driver's seat and appeared in the passenger seat. I startled and almost dropped my bag because it happened so quickly and fluidly; one moment she had one hand on the wheel and the other elbow on the red leather console between the seats and the next moment both hands rested on the door and she was a couple of feet closer. "You can even drive. Anywhere you like. As fast as you like."

"Yeah, right," I said. "You're going to let me drive your two million dollar car."

"It's not mine."

"You stole a Bugatti?"

Her face grew stern. "Get in the car."

"Let my phamily go and I will."

"That was not a part of our bargain," Laume said. There was an odd sense of authority in her voice, like no sane person (or Higher Power, or Faery) would stand for my attempt to renegotiate our previous agreement. "You can get in the car, or we can have this conversation later, at a less fortunate place and time."

Her threat came through loud and clear: less fortunate for me I was sure—like when I was at work, or in the middle of something hot-and-heavy with Brady. I didn't know how she'd found me at the bus stop or the day before in the city—or at the airport in Dallas—but I had no doubt she could do it again any time she wanted. I might not be able to stop her, but maybe I could use the current situation to my benefit, to learn how she did it. "Okay. But let's make a new bargain."

She raised both eyebrows at me in a how-dare-you look.

"No," I said, "not a bargain for my phamily. I want you to answer a question."

Laume laughed that same condescending laugh she'd given me inside my head as I was being rescued by the fishermen on the shrimp boat. "Silly Bailey. Do I appear foolish enough to agree to answer *any* question you might ask? I was not sparked to life yesterday."

"No, not *any* question, just one specific question."

"Ask, and we shall see."

Rather than take the time to dig through all the possible quandaries I wanted answers to, I stayed on topic and asked her how she was able to keep finding me wherever I went. "It's not that big a deal, I'd just like to know," I said, playing it off as best I could.

Laume nodded her head in agreement and then she transported back over into the driver's seat. "I agree to your bargain. Get in the vehicle and I will tell you."

My hand shook as I reached for a door handle which might cost as much as my whole car. I wasn't sure if the door was going to flip upward or outward so I tugged on it lightly and stepped back. The door opened like a normal car and I sat way down into its supple leather seat. Laume slammed the shift lever into gear and launched the screaming behemoth into traffic before I could get the door closed; I almost got my toes squashed.

Laume drove like a demon. Her lack of turn signals and aggressive lane changes got her plenty of angry honks as she threaded her way through traffic along the two-lane highway. I tugged at the seatbelt six times before I could pull out enough slack to buckle myself in.

"How is it you keep finding me?" I asked again.

"Simple, object tracking," she said.

Simple object tracking. I'm sure that meant something to her, but it befuddled me. And when I thought about it for a second, it pissed me off. "Look lady, we humans may not be able to fall from the sky as a ball of light or come and go at will, but we are not objects."

"I'll be sure to tell that to the next person who says you are," she said, amused with herself. She drove in silence for a mile or so while I waited for her to explain what simple object tracking was.

If we were having the non-verbal patience-testing equivalent of a stare-down, I lost. "Are you going to answer my question?" I asked.

"I answered your question," she said. "And now I have a few of my own."

"You're not going to explain, are you?"

"I agreed to provide an answer. I did not, however, agree to clarify said answer to your satisfaction, little darlin'." There was that smug attitude again, like she was daring me to say she hadn't lived up to her end of the bargain. If I had to be objective, I would say she had kept to the letter of the agreement, but not its spirit.

Just like when she *took my phamily to safety.*

Faery Bitch.

I wished I'd never met her. Never listened to a slimy word that came out of her poisonous mouth. Never agreed to my half of the original bargain.

My internal fuming obliterated my ability to hear the first half of her next statement. I did catch, "...quite something special, yes?"

I wasn't sure what she referred to as special, but the way she caressed the steering wheel made me think she'd been talking about the car.

"I guess it's okay," I said feeling the soft grain of the red leather seat under my fingertips. "But I'd rather have my Buick."

Laume laughed like I'd made the funniest joke known to human or Faery. "Excuse me?" she asked and then snorted—and it somehow did not come across as unladylike from her. "Did you just say you'd rather copulate with your car than Ryan Williams?"

If I'd have been anywhere else, in any other company, I'd have died of embarrassment from my blunderous words, but being alone in a car with a hysterical Laume only pushed my buttons. Buttons installed over the years by vicious babysitters, drunken applicants for step-mother-to-be, and the nasty shits on my ward at the Hospital.

"If you didn't have my phamily, I'd make you eat..."

Laume's laugh cut off and she turned to stare at me, even as she drove at high-speed, weaving her way through traffic. "But I do have them. So you might want to consider your next words, very carefully."

Thinking back to how callously she had ground Maria's grandmother's ruby ring into the concrete, I clenched my teeth to keep silent. We drove on. I had no idea where we were going, but we were still on a multi-lane road in the metro area: shopping malls, restaurants, apartment complexes. I wanted to ask where she was taking us, but I was afraid if I challenged her at all I'd find myself buckled into the passenger seat of a runaway car with no driver.

"Compliance suits you," Laume said.

As badly as I wanted to tell her what she could do with my compliance, I kept my mouth shut. But in my mind I vowed to myself, *just keep thinking that, Faery Bitch, relax and assume I'm just another good little girl from Texas. One day, though, I'll have my phamily back and somehow, I don't know how just yet, I will pay you back for every violation, every humiliation.* I kept my promises, especially the ones I made to myself.

"You met Hannah today?" Laume asked the question after we'd been silent again for a while. Her even-handed tone surprised me. I was too angry to be that polite to her. I didn't trust it coming from her.

"I'm glad you're making progress." She actually looked at me and smiled. "Miss JoJo and Mister Cooper will be glad to hear it, too."

I wasn't sure if she was baiting me or being authentic, but it sure pissed me off to hear her use my phamily's names with such familiarity. I added another mark to the one-day-I'll-get-even column and kept my mouth shut.

"You understand now why you must rehabilitate Hannah Faye's father and rescue her from that horrible place."

From what Laume had said before, I knew she thought Hannah's foster parents were a danger to her, but now that I'd met Mike and Nancy I couldn't understand why. I broke my silence to defend them. "Actually, if you ask me, I think she's better off with them, where she is. Her father is a real piece of work."

"Then, you haven't thought it through."

"What's to think through? He's an addict, a narcissist, a scared little boy hiding in a grown man's body."

"And what a body."

I couldn't really argue with that. Being in the same room with him had been electrifying, until he threatened to take me against my will up against the door. A universal turn-off in my book. I wondered what Laume would think of her perfect Ryan if I shared that little story.

"He's not equipped to raise a little girl."

"A very special little girl," Laume reminded me.

Unknown to Laume, I knew what she really meant by that, and I played dumb. Compliant and dumb.

She continued her lecture, "For a moment, imagine the worst possible way you could spend the rest of your life--"

"You mean without my phamily?" I challenged.

"--what would be the epitome of hell on earth for you?" She glared at me, oncoming headlights glinting in her pale eyes.

I had no idea what motivated her question, but in a flash I knew what the answer was. For me, hell-on-earth would be a house in the suburbs: one with a white picket fence and a minivan parked in the driveway. A paunchy-waisted husband, 2.2 screaming kids, a pair of flea-bitten dogs, and working a stupid job as a cubicle zombie, answering to a boss who didn't know his ass from a hole in the ground—those things would make me spill my own blood in copious amounts just to escape.

"Being mundane. Being like everyone else would be hell on earth."

Laume slowly blinked her eyes and then nodded. "Exactly as it would be for little Hannah. She was born to be something greater. Those horrid, small-minded people she's living with will extinguish every spark of greatness she has. They will break her spirit and drain her passion and leave her empty to tumble about this world like refuse."

"I hardly--"

"Already they're forcing her into a mold of mediocrity. Small deaths each and every day. A caged angel, singing out for flight."

"And you think her father will do any better?" My voice held challenge in it. As Laume braked the car and swerved suddenly to the side of the road, I was afraid I'd pissed her off again.

She skidded the car to a halt and gave me her full attention. "He lacks. But he has the one thing little Hannah needs to reach her potential." She paused, looking for me to answer her little riddle.

"Celebrity?"

"Not quite. But close. For all his shortcomings, that man knows Greatness."

"He was great, sure. But he's a has-been."

"You must fall before you can be redeemed," Laume said, as if it were a likely scenario that Ryan Williams would pick himself up, dust himself off, and climb back to glory someday. It was a fairy tale.

Or a Faery tale.

And suddenly my place in this story became all too clear.

"You expect me to redeem him? To rebuild his reputation and make him famous again? Ryan Williams? That letch at the rehab facility?"

"As I said earlier, and you would have heard if you'd been listening, that man is quite something special."

"And if I can't?"

"That would be too bad for your friends."

"You can't be serious!"

"We have a bargain," she said.

And then she went and did it again, she frickin' vanished into thin air to end the discussion and avoid my questions. This time, instead of disappearing from a little wooden lifeboat while my back was turned, she'd done it in front of my face and left me in a two million dollar car that might or might not have been stolen. Great.

I looked around. Nothing seemed familiar in the dark and the rain. We were parked near the river, with the city to my right. I could see three of the city's grand bridges and most of downtown ahead of the car. As I tried to decide whether to risk driving the car someplace more familiar, the light-rail train trundled across the nearest bridge a couple of blocks away.

Thank Elvis for The MAX. I knew where the tracks crossed the river—the train had passed by a few times while we listened to the drum circle—and I knew how to get back to Brady's from there. Laume had tried to leave me in a lurch, and failed. I added it to the count of things she would answer for one day.

It took me a minute to figure out the car's ignition system, but I found the switch to turn the engine off and then popped my door open. After using my sleeve to rub down any surfaces

I might have touched, and checking that nothing had fallen out of my bag during the erratic ride, I climbed out of the car into the rain. It took everything in me to stuff down the temptation to turn back and take the car for a quick spin, but I found my resolve and pushed my hip against the shiny black paint to close the door. As it thudded against the body—a solid, echoing sound like the low-E string on JoJo's stand-up bass—the whole car disappeared before my eyes.

Poof. Gone. Bye-bye sexy car. Just more Faery magic. Such a pity. Though it made me realize I must have been getting used to the odd things that happened to me, because it didn't even make me jump.

As I walked toward downtown, and Brady's apartment, I wondered what it would have been like to drive the Bugatti, and I realized it would have been like making a choice between Ryan Williams and Brady. Braggart's flash or nice guy's shine. Easy choice. Brady's little Audi wagon would be my choice over the Bugatti any day. Unless of course my Buick had been around, 'cause it was still the baddest-ass hot rod on the strip.

12

The rain chilled me to shivers by the time I reached Brady's apartment building. As I stood on the doorstep trying to decipher the scribbles on the stickers and choose the buzzer for his apartment, 8C, The Second Date Nerves washed over me like a virtual tornado, turning my shivers into shakes. I hesitated ringing the buzzer—this wasn't an ordinary second date, not even an ordinary follow-up to sleeping with a guy on the first date. We'd only known each other for two days and I already felt bonded to him, felt like I was coming home. I wondered why. It wasn't like me to be so stranded and needy and that might have twigged something for him, or maybe it was just the chemistry we had together, or perhaps there was a bit of Faery magic behind it after all.

What if he didn't feel the same way about me? And yet, what if he did? What if he wanted more than I could give him?

I couldn't know what was going to happen until I pressed the door buzzer, and frankly after a day that had started at 3:30 AM and included all the crap that the world had thrown at me, I was too tired to fight with my sense of pride about continuing to accept Brady's charity. With an unsteady finger I poked the buzzer for his unit. I got halfway through a concerned thought that he might not even be home when the speaker came to life.

"Bailey?"

I didn't get a chance to answer him before I heard the remote lock release click on the front door. My heart beat a little faster at the thought he was as excited to see me as I was to see him. "Coming right up," I said.

The lobby was warm and the elevator whisked me upstairs lickety-split to find Brady standing right there when the doors slid open. I smiled. He smiled back. So nice to be welcomed. So nice to be wanted.

"You look miserable," he said as he pulled me into a hug, wet clothes and all. He took off his zip-up hoodie and draped it around my shoulders.

"It's been a long day," I said.

"Your voice came back," he said as he held my hand so we could walk down the hall together. The warmth of his touch eased my shakes from the earlier Second Date tornado.

"Yeah. Sorry about freaking you out like that. Some people get ulcers when they're stressed, my brain short circuits." There probably wasn't one single shred of scientific evidence to back up that particular hog-wash, but I had to say something. It might happen again and I didn't want him to take me to the emergency room.

Brady stopped us at the closed door of his apartment. Funny how 24 hours changed things. The last time we covered the space between the elevator and his door we couldn't keep our hands off each other. But now I was exhausted and starving and overloaded with thoughts about Hannah and Ryan and how I was going to get them back together so I could get my phamily back.

And Brady seemed distracted, too. He paused with his hand on the doorknob.

"What's up?" I asked.

He took a deep breath. "I haven't been completely honest with you."

Since people who hide things about themselves—on purpose—should not throw stones, I didn't get angry with him. But I did get very curious about what he was hiding behind that door. A wife? A girlfriend? *A boyfriend?*

"Just tell me now," I said. "In my experience the Band-Aid method works best. Just get it over with."

Brady took a deep breath like he was going to explain, but then his expression changed and he said, "Better if I show you." He opened the apartment door and led me straight to his bedroom door.

There, sprawled out on the bed in a patch of light cast by the ceiling fixture in the hallway, lay a little blond boy who was the spitting image of Brady. I've always been horrible about guessing kids' ages, but I'd put the little guy at about three or four. He was tan from a long summer playing outside. His long bangs fell across a face slack with deep sleep the way only kids can do it, not a care in the world. His right hand stuck out of his mouth like he was trying to inflate it through his thumb. A raggedy teddy bear shared the pillow with him.

"What's that?" I asked and pointed in an attempt to lighten the mood.

Brady smiled and leaned against the doorjamb. "That's my Chester."

I recalled Brady talking about Chester in our first conversations on the plane from Dallas. "I thought Chester was a sheepdog?"

He looked at me and wrinkled his nose. "That's the part where I stretched the truth."

"That's a pretty big stretch," I said. *And who would sabotage a kid's childhood by naming him Chester?*

"I'm sorry." He grimaced. "But you have to admit that with those bangs of his, he does kind of resemble a sheepdog," Brady said, leading me out to the living room.

Though I'd spent the night before in the apartment, our busy-taking-our-clothes-off-entrance had left me no time to look around, and that morning I'd been too flustered to appreciate it on the way out the door as I left for work. It wasn't the bachelor pad most single guys our age seemed to keep. Sure the couch and flat-screen TV dominated the room, but the furniture cried out look-I'm-not-that-same-crappy-hand-me-down-stuff-he-had-in-his-college-apartment, and the vintage advertising art on the walls gave the room a personal touch that you just couldn't get from neon beer signs and full-size wall clings of the Dallas Cowboy's offensive line. Cooper and Paulo could take some decorating tips from Brady.

We sat down next to each other on the sofa.

"Why would you lie about having a son?"

"Why does any guy lie to a beautiful woman?" He smiled at me and shrugged his shoulders, trying to make it okay. "I didn't want to blow my chances with you. I thought for sure that you'd be on to me the second you saw my station wagon, not the coolest set of wheels, so I lied about having a dog instead of a kid."

"Where was he last night?"

"His mom has custody. She had an unplanned trip out of town and dropped him off for an extended weekend with me."

I noticed Brady said *his mom*, not *my Ex*.

As much as I detested lying, I could understand why Brady hadn't explained things. He couldn't have known that we'd hit it off as well as we did. I had not planned to stay the night the first time, much less twice. Why complicate things with explaining an out-of-wedlock child to someone you just met? Heck, I'd avoided explaining the whole Faery bargain thing, and that was a whole lot bigger deal than the little guy sprawled out asleep on Brady's bed.

And there was the problem. Even though Brady's bed was technically big enough for the three of us, it could never really big enough for the three of us. As a child, I'd been scarred more than once by running in to wake my father up in the morning and finding some woman I didn't know sleeping naked in his bed with him. Different skin tones, different hair colors, consistently reeking from too much booze the night before. Underneath any superficial differences they were all the same woman—definitely not my mother—and they each had a way of disappearing shortly after my dad woke up.

"I'll sleep on the couch, if I can still crash here tonight," I said.

Brady seemed surprised by my statement. "I can move him out here. He'll sleep right through it."

"And then he'll wake up at some point and run in to find his Daddy, and get to meet me. No thanks." My stomach grumbled its agreement.

"Are you hungry?" Brady asked. "I could reheat you some leftovers from dinner. Mac 'n Cheese with hot dogs. You know you want some."

"Thanks." I knew the powder-based stovetop version would make me miss my father's overpriced gourmet kind, but I was so hungry it didn't matter. I kicked my feet up on the couch and laid my head back while Brady went into the kitchen to nuke the leftovers.

My eyes may have been closed, but my brain was up and running at full speed.

Two ideas kept bounding around my head from my city-wide cruise in the Bugatti with Laume: I wanted to understand what *simple object tracking* was because I was tired of the damn Faery popping up whenever and wherever she wanted; and I still had to come to terms with her expectation that I could somehow redeem Ryan Williams.

Beeps from the microwave told me dinner was ready and Brady carried in a bowl full of pasta and a glass of white wine. I accepted both and dug in.

"Want to tell me about your day?" he asked. "Things at the bakery that bad?"

I considered attempting small talk, but my brain was so spun-up I doubted I could carry on a conversation about anything petty. Brady came across like a pretty smart guy; smart and insightful enough to guess I would have run for the hills if he'd admitted the whole Chester story during our early flirtations on the airplane. Maybe he could help me understand what to do with Ryan Williams.

"What do you know about redemption?" I asked him between bites. I sure couldn't explain all of the circumstances, but Brady was a single dad who obviously had a story or two behind the birth of his son. He must have had to make amends with somebody—his mom, grandmother, or Chester's mom—for choosing to have a child without providing a two-parent family around him.

"Are we talking coupons or sinners?"

"Dads," I said.

"Look, I'm sorry I lied--"

I stopped him. "It's okay, really. This isn't about you. It's about my friend's daughter's dad. He's messed up pretty badly and I need to figure out if he can redeem himself enough to get their daughter back from foster care."

Brady thought about it for a second. "How badly did he screw up?"

"Got arrested. He's in rehab, probably in an attempt to avoid jail time. His behavior is erratic and predatory. I'm not sure he can get sober."

"Does he love her?"

I thought about that. "Not as much as he loves himself."

"Too bad he's not a celebrity," Brady said.

"What do you mean?" I asked, tempted to let on about Ryan Williams' identity but deciding to keep it to myself.

"I and the guys in my ad firm helped with the PR campaign for Tiger Woods after his life imploded. Amazing what doing the walk of shame on a couple of talk shows, admitting how badly you screwed up, and then keeping your nose clean for a few months will do to repair your reputation."

"Did it work?" I asked.

"Not so much in his home town," Brady said. "But he travels a lot and folks don't give him as much crap as they used to."

"So what was the catch? Why did it work?"

"We looked at a bunch of politicians and movie stars who screwed the pooch in very public ways and tried to figure out how come some of them still had careers and some didn't. It came down to remorse. He had to admit what he did was wrong in a way that said he didn't expect to get anything out of it. No money, no fame, no fanfare—just real remorse."

"Then I'm screwed. I don't think this guy could scrape together a cupful of real remorse on his best day."

"Until he puts his daughter ahead of himself, nobody will ever buy his redemption," Brady warned.

I knew he was right, but I wondered if I could get Ryan to patch together something that looked like remorse long enough to fool the judge in his case. When I thought back to my glance at the sample report in the back of the CASA notebook Kevin had given me—the level of detail included in its pages—I decided real remorse might be easier.

I finished my Mac 'n Cheese and my wine, which did make every bite a little better, and I thought about what Brady had said. It made sense. I wasn't sure how to do it, but if I could get Williams to understand how much he'd hurt Hannah—and I knew under that pretty face she had lots of pain stored up—maybe I could get him to apologize to her in front of a judge, straighten up his act, and convince the court he was a capable parent.

"Thanks," I said.

"At your service," he said and took my dishes to the kitchen. He came back with a refill on the wine.

"I'd better not," I said. "It'll make me too sleepy."

"If you're crashing on this couch, you're going to need it."

I accepted the wine with a smile.

"You still look like something's bugging you," Brady said.

"It's nothing."

He reached out and stroked my hair. "It'll give me a good excuse to stay up and talk. I'm not ready to go to bed without you."

I gave him the smile he was fishing for. As much as I'd love to have some help figuring out how Laume was tracking my ass down anytime she wanted, the story was far too involved to tell as tired as I was, and with a glass of wine in me. "It's complicated."

"Try me. I'm full of all sorts of useless advice and information." He pretended he had a notepad in his hand and was ready to go to work solving anything I threw at him.

"Okay, smart guy, what do you know about simple object tracking?"

"Well, that depends," he said with a mock German accent. "Are you tracking da simple objects or simply tracking da objects? And are any of da objects shaped like cigars?"

I know he was being a goofball, but something he said kindled an idea in my brain that flared too quickly for me to grab hold of. I needed him to repeat what he'd said. "What?" I asked. "What did you say?"

"What part? The cigar?" he said without the silly accent.

"No the objects."

"I just wondered if you were talking about simple objects or simple tracking."

"Simple objects," I murmured out loud. "Simple objects."

That was it. Objects. It had to be. She wasn't tracking me, she was tracking an object I carried with me. And there was one very good reason not to explain when I asked; she didn't want me to know I could undermine her ability to find me.

I grabbed the beaded bag I'd been using to carry around all of my belongings. After tugging out my uniform whites, wrinkled and dusty with flour, and a ziptop bag full of cosmetics, I pulled out the fake Texas-issued driver's license and passport that Laume had left for me in Laredo to manage the border crossing. I held them up to Brady. "Do these look simple enough to you?"

I watched his face as he touched them, wondering if he might sense their Faery origins somehow, but his demeanor didn't change. If he had any sense my ID was odd, he didn't give it away.

Taking the passport back, I flipped through its pages looking for the smallest detail that might be a tracking device. Nothing. I traded him for my license. There was a barcode on it, but no bumps in the thin plastic that would betray anything sandwiched inside.

"Looking for an RFID chip? The new enhanced licenses in Washington State have them, but these look like your regular run-of-the-mill pieces of ID if you ask me."

That was the point; they were supposed to look normal. But I knew they were anything but. I didn't know how Laume was using them to track me, but it made sense. Something about those simple objects, or maybe just one of them, allowed her to find me. Maybe because they were made of Faery magic. Maybe because she'd given them to me. I didn't know and it didn't really matter. Although I thought it was a bad idea to run around a strange city without any ID, I decided to ditch them both until I could figure out if they were both trackable or just one of them.

"You're a genius," I said and kissed Brady full on the mouth.

"Will you let me in on your secret?" he asked when I let him come up for air. He looked more closely at my passport. "Don't tell me, you're a spy, right? Are you in some kind of trouble? Are you on the run from the law?"

I shook my head with a smile. "Nothing illegal."

Gently, like it was no big deal, I took back my passport. It was superstitious of me, but I didn't want him handling either of them any more than necessary, just in case some of their trackability rubbed off on him. He looked insulted and I needed him to stop thinking about it. Laume was my problem, not his.

"I could tell you, but then I'd have to screw you stupid," I teased him. When his face got that hopeful look I felt badly for teasing him and had to temper my joke. "And your son is right in the other room."

"I can be quiet if you can," he said as he crawled over and lay on top of me. I wanted him so badly. The look on his face held an intensity I almost couldn't shrug off.

Almost.

I gave him my best kiss. "I'm sorry, I can't." I wished I could, wished I had no compunction about Chester waking up and seeing his daddy making *the beast with two backs* with a stranger. "My dad was the Original Player. I was the little kid in this situation a few too many times. I can't do that to Chester."

He pulled his hurt eyes away from mine and pried himself off me. "I'll get you a blanket."

I know he wasn't happy with me. Returning with a blanket, Brady tucked me in with more kindness than I'm sure his bruised ego wanted to show me. I kissed him goodnight and watched him walk slowly into the bedroom to sleep in the bed that he'd made.

Only when I saw the light go off underneath the door did I get up and grab my Faery-provided ID. I tucked the driver's license inside the passport and thought about what to do with them.

I didn't want to carry them until I proved whether or not they were the objects Laurne was tracking, but I didn't want to leave them inside Brady's apartment to lure her directly to him, either. That would be reckless. I could take them someplace else in the morning, but I didn't want to risk someone else finding them. I might need them.

My best plan would be to put them someplace in the common areas of Brady's floor. Safer than hidden at work or someplace public. Not directly in Brady's. I quietly got up and walked out into the hallway, keeping the door from latching shut behind me.

I considered the fire extinguisher cabinet, but the door was all glass and my ID wouldn't be completely hidden. The bits of plastic and paper might not have been as dangerous as a loaded gun, but I still didn't want them falling into naive hands.

There was a door at the end of the hall marked "Trash." I walked down and opened it to find a shallow closet-like area that provided access to a stainless steel garbage chute cover. At first it didn't seem like a good hiding spot, but then I looked up and noticed that the light fixture on the wall above the door had a large flange surrounding it. Standing on my tippy-toes, I wedged my ID between the wall and the flange until barely an inch of the passport's blue cover stuck out. It wasn't the best place, not as secure as a deposit box or bank vault, but it would do.

I slunk back to Brady's apartment, and after setting my new-to-me phone's alarm for 3 AM I crawled back beneath my blanket on the couch and closed my eyes. I sang Buddy Knox's *Rock Your Baby to Sleep* inside my head with Brady's art deco mantle clock keeping the tempo. Sleep took me before I hit the second chorus.

13

Dragging my ass off of Brady's couch on Friday morning at 3 AM was a struggle, though it was nice to wake to the sound of my own alarm and get my morning rolling independently. I hung my uniform in the bathroom to get the wrinkles out while I showered. After primping as much as bakery standards required, I made a pot of coffee, wrote Brady a note saying I'd be in touch after work, and went in and kissed his forehead goodbye while he slept. Chester had curled up against Brady's body, back tucked up to his daddy's ribs, and was kicking at the covers gently as I left.

On my way out I grabbed Brady's phone and exchanged numbers with him.

The second morning at the bakery was about the same as the first except that I got to make croissants instead of baguettes—I must have impressed Boss-man to move up so quickly—and I could listen-in on my co-workers conversations, laughing with them on the occasions I picked up enough Spanish to understand their jokes. Lunch break came when the taco truck blared its horn outside; I had tamales that were almost as tasty as the ones made by the shrimp boat's chef back in The Gulf of Mexico. Give me three days of starvation and I might have said they were right on par.

I checked my new-to-me cell phone during lunch to find a message from Kevin Butler at Human Services. Hannah's foster parents had changed the meeting place that night to a local community center because Hannah had gotten an invite to some sort of event for foster kids.

One of my co-workers lent me his smart phone so I could look up the address to the community center and check it against the bus schedule. Thankfully it was on the same bus route as the Carter's townhouse, so I'd probably have no trouble finding it. As much as all the logistical malarkey made me miss my Buick, I was grateful to Portland's extensive public transportation system because I didn't have to make the choice between carrying my Faery-made driver's license, which Laume may or may not have been able to track, or driving without it at the of risk getting pulled over in an unfamiliar city.

I finished my shift, picked up my check for two measly days pay, and clocked out for what promised to be a busy weekend. I changed into my slightly wrinkled swing dress in the bathroom but decided to stick with my flats instead of my heels as the bus stop for the southbound express was six blocks away.

The bus was fairly empty at 2:00; most commuters were still in their cubies praying for that five o'clock whistle to blow. I whipped out my phone and left a message for Brady telling him I'd probably miss dinner with him and Chester, but would love to join them for something after. Part of me wished I had someplace else to sleep so that I could keep my relationship with Brady munchkin-free, or at least munchkin-lite, until Chester's momma got back into town. The paycheck in my bag would pay for a couple of nights at a cheap motel. Maybe I'd talk to Brady about whether that would be a good idea.

Though I knew I still needed to take the time to read through the huge CASA binder Kevin had given me, my curiosity about Ryan Williams made me open his file instead. I spent the rest of the ride reviewing what the State of Oregon wanted Ryan Williams to accomplish in order to get his daughter out of hock from foster care. After drug treatment he also had to enroll in anger management classes and attend a parenting class for at-risk teenagers. I prayed to Elvis that he didn't have to complete it all before he could regain custody—I'm not sure my phamily had that kind of patience.

After a 30-minute ride, the bus let me off at the same corner stop where Laume had picked me up the night before and I walked up the circular driveway to the treatment center. The place was hopping. Cars crowded the lot. Patients, visitors and vendors streamed in and out of the building. A far cry from the peace and orderliness of the previous night.

I signed in at the front desk as a visitor for Ryan, and the receptionist explained that his doctor wanted to speak with me before I saw him. She quickly whisked me back to the office area where I sat to wait on a folding chair outside a door marked Dr. Brinn Mayweather. The closed door and active sound generator in the hallway told me she was in a session. I rested my eyes and tried not to be nosy about the parade of characters trooping up and down the hallway; none of it was any of my business.

Just when I thought I might lose my struggle to stay awake, the doctor's door popped open and a woman in her mid-fifties walked out; baggy sweatpants and Terwilliger branded sweatshirt giving her away as a patient. Behind her, Dr. Mayweather loitered in the open doorway. The doc, dressed in jeans and a green button-down blouse, reminded me of the shrinks at the Texas State hospital, as if all of them had been cloned from the same Freudian test tube full of goop and then customized with various genitalia, conservative hair styles, and facial features in an attempt to hide the truth of their sketchy origins.

Like living Mr. Potato Head-Shrinkers.

I laughed at my own paranoid commentary and thanked Elvis that I was free to walk out the front door any time I wanted. That hadn't always been the case. Usually I had been in Ryan Williams' position—a de facto prisoner waiting for parole back into a world that didn't understand me.

"Ms. Michaels?" the doctor asked, extending a hand.

"Bailey," I said. I tested her, offering a fist-bump instead of a handshake, to see what she would do about it. If she accommodated me, I'd know I wasn't about to walk into her office to sit on The Hot Seat and get grill marks from all her questions. If she insisted on a hand shake, I would know she was *that kind of shrink* and the following ten minutes was going to be intense in a familiarly nasty way.

But Mayweather turned out to be cool. She adapted to my fist bump without a hitch and invited me inside for a seat at the desk instead of at the informal sitting area that looked so therapeutic I could puke twice and die. I let her start the conversation because I had no clue what prompted our meeting or where it was headed.

"So you're Bailey?" she said with a straight face.

That didn't give me much to go from. I hated that tactic docs sometimes took, opening the door and allowing you plenty of room to step in something stinky before you knew what you'd done, so I simply agreed with her. "I'm Bailey."

"Ryan has not shut up about you since you left last night."

Her face still didn't give anything away, but uh-oh, that didn't sound good. My heart started to race. Instead of commenting, I nodded, having learned at the Hospital that when all else failed it was best just to nod my head and play along. Docs filled-in the blanks the way they chose, anyway. I wanted Mayweather to assume I was cooperating until I decided whether I actually was.

"I haven't seen him so interested in his treatment, so willing to engage, so alive, in the three weeks he's been with us," doc said, her face finally breaking into a smile.

My pulse rate dropped a little at the smile—it seemed like cooperation was still a viable option—but I continued to listen carefully because her praise felt oddly motivated and her smile came across forced for some reason I couldn't figure out.

My intuition said something wonky was afoot; not good wonky, either.

"Um, that's good to hear." Regardless of how I felt about Ryan Williams as a person, and as a parent, I really did want the guy to snap out of it, straighten up and fly right, come to the light—whatever they called it in their healing paradigm. The sooner he took responsibility for himself and for Hannah, the sooner I'd get my phamily back.

"I feel like we owe you an apology. If we'd known he had a fiancée we'd have invited you to visit after he finished his first core week."

What the hell was she talking about? "Fiancée? Excuse me? He told you we were engaged? When?"

"Ryan asked us to keep it confidential. I understand that he's trying to keep it out of the media. They haven't been very nice to him lately."

Something wonky afoot, no doubt. I didn't know what to say, so I laughed at the idea.

She ignored my discomfort, leaning across the desk to pat my hand. "I just love the fact that you were willing to move up here to be with him after all the troubles. Amazing. That man really is quite something special."

Just like that, all my Faerie magic alarms went off. *Quite something special*, that's exactly what Laume had said about Ryan, word for word. I looked closer at Doctor Mayweather's face and saw an inconsistency between the light in her eyes and the look on her face—she smiled, but her upper lip curled up in a way that took the joy out of the expression. Forced, not organic. The gap between her two facial expressions wasn't as striking as it had been on the middle-aged guy in the football jersey back at the Dallas airport—so maybe Laume wasn't fully possessing the doc—but I'd bet my signature-edition Zildjian ride cymbal that the doc wasn't feeling entirely herself.

"He's something, alright," I said. *Where was this going?*

The doc reached into her desk drawer and pulled out a set of keys on an expensive looking gold-tone key ring with the Jaguar Motors logo on it. She placed them on the desk in front of me like she expected I would recognize them. I didn't.

"Ryan said you had to leave suddenly last night to catch the bus. That was incredibly hard on him, so he had one of his cars shuttled over this morning for you to drive."

She said it all like there was nothing to giving me, the person who was supposed to be Hannah's CASA, keys to a car. Wonky.

"Oh, yes, and--" Back into the drawer the doc went, this time she came out with an envelope. She flipped it over to show me that it was sealed. "This has the codes to the main gate and alarm system."

"For his house?" I asked. Very wonky.

"He really, really needs your help, Bailey. With you near-by he can focus on the program." She shook the envelope at me impatiently. When I didn't take it, she laid it down on top of the keys. "After the amazing progress he's made in the last 12 hours, we're pulling out all the stops to keep him moving forward. I honestly can't see him completing the transition to sobriety without you. Please say you'll help him. Say you'll stay." She tapped the envelope.

Good Graceland. She believed every lie he'd told her; *hook, lie and stinker.* I had never felt so manipulated in my whole life—and I'd been raised by the king of manipulators. I wanted to storm out of her office and never look back. I wanted to forget I'd ever heard of Hannah Faye, Ryan Williams, or Portland, Oregon and run back to Austin with my proverbial tail tucked between my legs. I wanted no more to do with any of it.

But because of Laume, there was nothing left in Austin for me except my drums and my Buick. Not until I finished things here. My phamily may have been the ones locked in a Faery prison, but I was stuck in a Faery's trap, which turned out to be just as bad.

I considered the keys and envelope. I'm sure the car and house I was being offered were beautiful and amazing and a girl's dream come true, but it was all a lie. A lie built on Faery magic, at least some part of it.

I wondered if there was any way I could snap the doctor out of her Faery-affected state and get her to see how unusual all of this was. But even if I could straighten her out, I didn't know if there would be any use in trying to tell her the truth.

Would she listen to me when I explained I was not in love with Ryan Williams, not actually engaged to marry him, that it was all in his head? And that I had no relationship with the Williams family except as Hannah's CASA, and it was really just a cover I was using to get my phamily back.

I watched the doctor's face as I reached my hand out toward the keys and envelope. She wore a devilish grin which made me wonder how much of Laume's influence she was under. Was Laume watching me from inside the doc's brown eyes: willing me to take the keys, take the car and house and somehow seal my own fate in doing so?

I wanted to say no, but I couldn't. My life depended on getting my phamily back, and that depended on me getting a couple of important ideas through Ryan Williams' narcissistic skull: no more drugs, no more violence, no more self-pity—it was time to stand up and be Hannah's father.

Ryan was here for treatment, and he had to stay and complete his program to make the judge happy. I could fight against this insane version of reality he was spewing around, which would probably drag things out for weeks or months, or I could pick up the damn keys and play along until I found a way to use the situation to my advantage. Wondering if I was making a deal with a devil of another sort, I lowered my hand and rested it on the envelope. Doc Mayweather nodded at me as if to say, *it's okay little mouse, just take the nice, tasty cheese and everything will be fine.*

One day I would resist following the easy paths Laume laid out before me like a safe wooden bridge beset on all sides by snapping alligators. Someday. But not just then. Just then I felt ganged-up on, and out of options. I wanted it to be over, so I picked up the envelope and keys and slipped them into my bag.

"Wonderful," the doc said. "Now let's get you some time with Ryan. If things continue to go as well as they did last night, I'm sure he'll be home in no time."

Time with Ryan. Swell. I figured I could handle it as long as we had a chaperone. I followed her out of the office and down the hall.

My time at the Texas State Hospital had been full of moments like the one following Doctor Mayweather down the hallway, and I hoped that what I learned then still held true: sometimes life threw challenges at you that you wanted to run away from with all of your heart—like being in a room with Williams, confusing because he was so attractive and so aggressive at the same time—but unless your life was actually in danger, it was best to just suck it up and get on with it.

I almost choked on sucking it up.

Doc Mayweather led me to one of many patient dorms along one wing of the building. Apparently Terwilliger believed in the buddy system because the large room had two of everything: two bunks, two nightstands, two dressers, two windows, two area rugs. The only difference between the halves of the room was the personal effects tacked onto matching corkboards.

Ryan's message board overflowed with cards, letters, and photos of himself in uniform from his ball playing days. Hannah had contributed a banner that stretched across the top of it all; *Get Well Soon Daddy*. The board on the opposite wall was empty save for a single family photo of a middle-aged man and three teenage boys who bore a strong family resemblance. I wondered if it was more miserable for Ryan to be stuck living with a father of three, or to be in the father's shoes and stuck with a narcissist like Ryan.

We found him sitting on the edge of his bunk talking baseball with one of the orderlies.

Mayweather stopped me outside the door and said, "See how much stronger he is? Until yesterday he spent all his time locked-up inside himself. Now it's like he's back in the world."

Ryan did seem more like the man I'd seen before his fall from grace, the one I'd found sulking in the visitor's room the night before. If anything his gregariousness and energy made him more attractive, more compelling. I had no idea what it was that drew me to him even though he'd been such an ass.

Doc Mayweather knocked on the open door. Ryan looked up, first at his counselor and then to me. His face erupted into a smile without a shred of hesitation or self-control. It was as if the sun rose behind his eyes.

Being smiled at like that made me weak in the knees.

"Look who I found," Doc Mayweather said.

Ryan stood up and walked over to stand in front of me. He reached out and then hesitated, looking at the doctor.

"It's okay, she's family," she said.

I balked, but Ryan wrapped me in a hug so warm and so gentle I thought I might be ruined for all other hugs for the rest of my life. Safe. Needful. Strong. Loving. Absolutely. Ruined.

It took my breath away, not in a rib-crushing way but in how I'd never understood that a hug could communicate so much: happiness, excitement, hunger, passion, and a need to be loved so deep it felt like spider's silk pulling me in and binding me to him. He spread his hands on my back as he rubbed them slowly up and down my spine and then nestled his face against the spot where my neck meets my shoulder, breathing in my scent.

I'm not sure why, but I reached my arms around his lower back and returned the hug. He filled my arms like the best teddy bear ever handed down from big sister to little sister.

"You came back," he said quietly into my ear. His voice held a confusing intensity as if my presence again at the recovery center after a 20-hour absence was more important to him than I understood.

I looked toward his doctor to ask her if she had a clue about what Ryan meant, but she was already out of the room. I looked over to the orderly and saw him stand up and head for the door. He gave no indication that he'd heard Ryan.

"Aren't you supposed to stay?" I asked the orderly.

The dude winked at me. "I have to grab something from the other wing. It'll be at least fifteen minutes before I can get back to monitor the cameras. You two play nice."

But I didn't want him to go. Didn't want to be alone with Ryan. Couldn't he see the look of panic on my face? Sure things had started-off on the right foot this time, but I wasn't sure I trusted Ryan enough to be alone with him. Not sure I trusted myself to resist the temptation that had compelled me to hug him back.

The click of the door latch echoed through the dorm just as Ryan's hands traveled south of my belt. I quickly reached back and grabbed both hands before he could entice my body into something my heart and brain couldn't handle.

"No," I said gently and pulled away from him, keeping his hands between us.

"But, Laume--"

I dropped his hands and stepped back in surprise. Had he somehow figured out that Laume had sent me? "Did you see Laume?" I asked. "Did she visit you?"

I continued backing away until my legs bumped into his roommate's bunk and then my momentum carried me down to sit on the rock-hard mattress covered tightly in a forest green wool blanket.

"Nice try, good disguise," Ryan said, "but I know it's you in there."

"My name is Bailey. Remember," I said. I set my beaded bag down. "Who is it you think I am?"

Ryan closed the space between us in three long strides and knelt down in front of me, looking up into my eyes. His need and hunger filled the room with palpable energy that eddied like a whirlpool spa against my skin. But it wasn't anything like the night before in the Family Visiting Room when he threatened to take me up against the door so the staff couldn't stop him—I felt no danger. "You can't hide from me. I know it's you. It's been a long time, but I still know your touch, your smell." He enveloped both my hands into his.

Elvis help me, the man was deranged. He thought *I* was Laume.

"I had them bring my car for you. You'll love it; I bought it from a collector a couple summers ago because it reminded me of our trip to Monaco. You remember that classic E-Type Jaguar you loved--" Ryan reached up and ran his fingers through my hair, lifting it from my shoulder. "Remember how your hair streamed on the wind when we dropped the top and raced along the cliffside highway under the moon."

He stopped reminiscing, the focus of his eyes sharpened and he frowned at the strands of my platinum blonde hair laced between his fingers. "I like you better with dark hair."

I stopped breathing, watching as he teetered on the line between his reality and mine. Was I me, or was I Laume in disguise? I figured he was either going to grab onto that handful of hair and use it show me just how much he preferred Laume's long, dark tresses, or, I hoped, he'd lapse back into his puppy-love trance long enough for me to disentangle myself before he could toss me around like a doll.

The expression on his face wavered as the seconds slipped by. About the same moment I tensed my shoulders—because I knew, just knew, he'd come to his senses and accepted my real identity and I was in for some bad hurtin'—he drew the handful of my hair toward his nose and inhaled deeply. I don't know whether it was the smell of Brady's shampoo or *eau d'bakery*, or something else, but that whiff toppled him over the edge again. His eyes softened and he smiled. "I'm so glad you're back. Everything is going to be fine. We'll be a real family, like I always knew we would."

He lunged upward more quickly than I imagined was humanly possible, his lips finding mine and delivering a knee-quivering kiss while his hands cupped my face. Eight nanoseconds later my brain checked out completely and my body temperature jumped a few degrees. I don't recall any of the details beyond the probing of his tongue, and insistent tug on my skirt and the pressure of his body separating my knees so that he could press his body along the length of mine.

Nipped and nuzzled. Skin exposed to lips and tongue. Touched, grabbed, latched onto as if we two in that moment were all that existed. Thoughts abandoned and both panting and...

...and what the hell?

A wave of cold reality rushed up my body from my toes to the roots of my hair, prickling my skin and standing every fine body hair on end. I found that the top of my dress rested down around my waist—the zipper not unzipped but ripped from its hold on the fabric—and Ryan's left hand cupped my breast beneath my bra. His right hand struggled beneath my skirt to separate me from my panties. My hands, heeding my body's need not my brain's orders, grasped his muscular ass, skin on skin beneath his hospital-issue sweatpants. But worse than all of that was when I understood that my tongue had been seeking out all the tender places of his neck, coaxing him on as I tasted the antiseptic bite left behind by his aftershave.

Disgusted with myself, I reeled in my tongue and repositioned my hands on the front of Ryan's hips. He misunderstood my movement, and untangled his hand from my bra so that he could help me find and take better care of the bulge at the front of his pants. My body wanted me to bliss out and follow his lead, but my mind struggled to regain control.

I bit my own tongue hoping the pain would sharpen my grasp on reality. That was enough to focus all my concentration on shoving Ryan's grinding hips off of me, away from the bunk, and onto the floor. He looked up, surprised to find himself flat on his ass in the center of the room.

For the first time in my life, being good at sex was a bad, bad thing. *How could I have lost control like that?* Ryan Williams was like the best high from the most powerful drug I'd ever tried. I'd lost it with him and barely caught myself in time to want to get it back. That scared the shit out of me. He scared the shit out of me. My mysterious attraction to him scared the shit out of me.

"I am not Laume!" I yelled at him, wiping my mouth. I pulled the top of my dress up and shoved my arms into it. There was nothing I could do about the zipper, the seam between it and the fabric of my dress on the right side had been shredded. "You ruined my dress!"

Ryan's expression faded from surprised to sappy. He slithered up onto his knees and advanced on my position on the bed. "I'll buy you a new dress. A closet full of them. Just promise you'll stay this time. Stay with me."

I didn't have a closet to fill with dresses, I didn't even have a place to call my own, and it was Ryan's fault. And Laume's fault. And my own fucking fault.

I grabbed my bag from the floor next to the bunk and launched myself toward the door, grabbing a zip-up sweatshirt from a wall hook on his side of the room as I moved.

He got ahead of me, blocking the door closed with his hand. "Please, don't go." He ran the backs of his fingers along my triceps gently, begging me with the tenderness in it to please turn around and look at him. "I couldn't stand it if you left me again. It's been fourteen years of hell without you."

Fourteen years was a long time to want something the way he obviously wanted my body. Well, my body, but only because he thought Laume was hiding in it. No wonder he'd gotten addicted to cocaine and booze and thrown his life away.

I turned halfway. "I'm trying to help you," I said. "But I have to go, right now. I'm meeting Hannah."

He reached for my hand and raised it to his lips, gentle and gentlemanly. Every experience with this guy was a bad case of whiplash waiting to happen. Pull, push. Attract, repel. Don't stop, knock it the hell off. His warm smile preceded a gentle kiss on my bare back. "Come back soon. I need you."

I took my hand back and opened the door. Fresh air washed in, calling my attention to the heavy musk smell we'd filled the room with. We had chemistry, no doubt, but it was a kind of chemistry I didn't need in my life.

I walked down the hall without a backward glance, stuffing my arms into the sweatshirt to cover up my exposed skin.

14

When I got outside the treatment center and finally reeled in my panic I found the bus stop in front of the recovery center crowded with a dozen commuters waiting for their ride home. My mood could not have been worse and I had no patience for being surrounded by people who embodied so many things I hated in our culture: cookie-cutter-conservative clothing, back-crippling computer bags, the daily lemming-trek between corporate cubicle-cells and suburban family-cells. Mortgages, yard work, weekly date night so that sex with the hubby didn't evaporate entirely. Drab, repetitive, smothering. Repeat until death.

I would have preferred another trip on the stinky, noisy bus in Mexico, staring out the window at harsher lives which were at least somehow more authentic.

I wanted my life back. My phamily. My drums. My car. My rat hole of an apartment over the liquor store. My old bakery where my favorite customers came in and shot the shit with me over sticky buns and coffee while I decorated birthday cakes with skulls and tacos made of fondant. I barely had the willpower to stop myself from opening a telepathic link to Cooper so I could rant at him about it. (While I loved Maria best, he was the older brother I always wanted and he understood me best.) Cooper knew how to laugh at life in a way that put my head back on straight. I vowed to try my telepathy to contact him later, before I went to sleep, to find out if they were growing as fucking bat-shit crazy with this situation as I was.

I paced back and forth on the grass behind the clump of commuters, too cranked up from my inappropriate interaction with Ryan to stand still. Which was fine until I stepped in a hole, damn sprinklers, and almost fell. I caught myself in time but my beaded bag hit the ground with an unfamiliar metallic clank.

There's no sound in the world like the clang a ring of keys makes. Anyone who has shaken a purse or backpack trying to locate keys that have fallen into the bottom of the black abyss knows the sound. And every set of keys has its own distinct jingle. This sound was both higher and lower pitched than my keys would have been, and I suddenly remembered I had accepted keys from Doc Mayweather. Keys to one of Ryan's cars and his house.

I dug into the bag and pulled out the set—only three keys on a gold ring with a gold Jaguar pendant—which lay extremely heavy in my hand. I fought with myself not to turn around and search the treatment center's parking lot. Those keys weren't really for me, they were for Laume. I, me, Bailey, had a bus pass and no driver's license on my person, and for good reason. My ride would be along shortly; it was big and smelly and it came with a chauffeur who knew his way around the city.

I dropped the keys back in my bag and waited. And waited. I checked my phone and saw that I only had 42 minutes left to make my appointment with Hannah. But I waited, still. Waited with a growing group of commuters who made my skin crawl.

Eventually the bus rolled into view. We gathered in an orderly clump near a spot where my fellow travelers obviously expected the doors to open when the big ol' behemoth finally rolled to a stop. The doors hissed open, revealing a standing-room-only crowd—good for a concert, bad for getting across town.

To my surprise, nobody got off the bus.

And even more surprising, none of the others waiting to climb aboard batted an eye at squeezing onto an already full bus. One by one they trudged up the stairs like they were mounting the gallows to their deaths.

I. Just. Could. Not. Do. It. I couldn't force my feet to take those last three steps to the edge of the sidewalk and step across the yawning nine-inch chasm to the bus's bottom stair. The driver, a gray haired African-American woman, looked at me like I was mentally retarded. "Are you gettin' on this bus, honey? I got to go."

I looked at the crowd of cookie-cutter-commuters and shook my head.

"Suit yourself," she said and closed the door.

I dug into my bag and pulled Ryan's keys back out. Maybe it was the stupidest thing I'd done in, well, days, but I had a cocky bounce in my step as I walked up the circular driveway and scanned the parking lot for something exotic looking.

And there she was; a 1960s Jaguar E-Type convertible. Glossy green paint and gleaming chrome. Giant inverted fishbowl headlights flanking a gaping intake. An arching hood that seemed to stretch for a mile from the short windshield down to the split bumper. The soft-top was obviously new, tan canvas that went perfectly with the shape and color of the car and matched the interior perfectly. The car called to the basest parts of me. I inserted the key in the door and twisted it to unlock, getting a whoosh of that warm leather smell from a car sitting in the sun all day. It was nearly fifty years old but it looked and smelled like it had just rolled off the showroom floor.

Nice.

I slipped behind the wheel and let the supple leather cradle me. The leather-wrapped steering wheel felt like the strap on Maria's guitar—worn, soft, durable, with lots of little perforations to tickle the skin of my hand. I looked down at the keys lying heavy in my palm. I could still walk away; there would be another bus along shortly.

Another bus full of drones, zombies, commuters. I shook the ignition key loose and pinched it between thumb and finger.

I'd been through so much, hell-week of new proportions, and it would be nice to just drive myself to the community center. No bus. Just cruise and forget for a little while how messed up things were.

Besides, it wasn't my fault Ryan Williams misunderstood who I was and gave me the keys to his car.

I jammed the key in the ignition, pumped the throttle pedal to the floor twice, and begged the working bits under the hood of the gorgeous classic to be in as good a shape as the body and interior. The engine turned over on the first try, roaring to life. Careful of everything around me, I reversed out of the parking spot and literally purred my way out along the circular driveway. Guilty as hell, but loving every second of it.

At the end of the driveway I paused to drop the top and then pulled out into rush hour traffic with the sun warming my skin and diluting my guilt with mega-doses of Vitamin D. Three minutes later I passed that stupid bus as it stopped to swallow up more riders and had to curb an impulse to wave at the driver.

It was a lovely ride—sun, warm breeze, classic rock on the radio—until I realized I had no idea how to get to the community center. Needless to say the vintage Jag had not been updated with a navigator. Rather than drop back to follow the lumbering bus to the community center, I pulled into a convenience store and got directions. Thirty minutes of horrendous rush-hour traffic later, I cruised into the right address and parked the car.

The community center was about twenty years old. A high-roofed single-level affair with lush landscaping. The lot was full and a large number of kids of all ages and a few racially-unmatched parents streamed from the lot toward the building. I couldn't catch much of their conversations, but the tone was universally excited.

Feeling frumpy in the oversized sweatshirt I had to wear over my ruined dress, I joined the throng, happy to be surrounded by such positive energy. It lifted my mood, even though I had no idea what caused it. As I approached the door I saw a man and a woman in black slacks and polo shirts checking ID against lists on clipboards. They turned away a mother and her two children. I hesitated at the transition between the parking lot and the sidewalk, feeling like an attempted gate-crasher, until I saw Mike Carter standing inside the doorway. He waved me past the door guards. Apparently he was on the list.

"Glad you could make it, Bailey."

"What's going on?" I asked.

"American Idol frenzy," he said. He led me to the door of a gymnasium-style auditorium-slash-basketball-court with bleachers climbing up both long walls. The noise level grew as we walked past a mass of a hundred teenagers grouped tightly into five clusters.

"The last season's runners-up have a tour stop in town tomorrow night at the Rose Quarter. We were told one of the performers has a foster brother and so he gets some of the performers to do an event like this in every city on the tour."

"A concert?" I had to shout my question to be heard above the kids.

"Better," Mike yelled as he led me forward to the foot of the near-side bleachers. We climbed to find Nancy in deep conversation with an older couple behind her and the seats she had saved for us. "They're going to sing with the kids. The place went nuts when they announced it."

"Hannah's over the moon," Nancy shouted.

I believed her. What I wouldn't have given to perform with my idols as a teenager, but then that's the problem with 'billy tunes, most of those guys and dolls were six feet under before my father had even graduated out of diapers. But, who knew, with my telepathic talent, maybe one day I might get that chance. Maybe. One day when I'd figured out just how it all worked. For now I was satisfied just knowing I could use it to contact my phamily when I needed it.

But today was about Hannah, and nurturing one of the things she was good at, so I turned my attention outward. I scanned the five mobs on the floor and found Hannah near the center of a group under a basketball hoop at the near end. She looked like she was in her element—talking and laughing, not hiding in a dim room under a quilt. Her smile illuminated her face and in the few minutes I watched I saw the gender balance of their group of twelve kids redistribute themselves, the guys drawn into Hannah's orbit. Not a new thing, I guessed, given the way her smile turned shy.

"Fourteen going on nineteen, going on oh-my-goodness," Nancy said. I looked and found her attention focused on the same thing I'd seen with the boys gravitating toward our girl. As we kept an eye out for Hannah's virtue from afar, something interesting occurred. The singer at the center of the group, a young blonde with a heart-shaped face, appeared to have asked a question that only Hannah answered with a raised hand. The whole group focused on her and I feared she'd shrink from the attention, but she held her ground. Good for her.

Ten minutes later each of the five groups filed out of the auditorium, my guess was to get more privacy to push through that really awkward situation that was the first time running through a song with a new group. Having been *in music*, I wasn't expecting much in terms of quality-performances from the kids, but I knew their enthusiasm would make up for any lack of talent. How could it not with their idols in the building?

The noise level in the venue dropped without the kids and I could finally converse with the Carters without shouting. "They do this kind of thing all the time?" I asked.

"We've been fostering so long that we get invites to most of these events. But it's usually bowling in pajamas or a pizza party down at Izzy's," Nancy said and she smiled. "This one couldn't have come at a better time. I swear Hannah rewatches every episode of Idol three times before she'll let us delete them from the DVR. I wish her dad could've been here to see this."

I nodded, but kept my mouth shut. Though I understood the sentiment behind Nancy's wishful thinking, I didn't think Ryan Williams was ready for that stage of fatherhood. Not yet. Had he attended, he probably would have found a way to hog the spotlight for himself, or otherwise do something to embarrass his daughter. It was my job to figure out how to fix that particular problem, and soon.

"What did you think of him?" Mike asked me.

Nancy looked at me from Mike's blind-side with raised eyebrows and I got the impression she didn't want me to answer honestly. I thought back to Hannah's comment about how Mike had asked Ryan to sign a ball when they first met and realized that her foster-dad had a bit of a bro-crush on her bio-dad. I settled for saying, "He's pretty intense."

"Nice guy, though," Mike said. "I hope he'll find some answers in rehab."

"Yes." I agreed. Answers would be better than the lies he'd been spinning.

We fell into small talk about Hannah; her difficulty fitting in at school since moving up from The Bay Area, her troublesome friends, her regular migraines. Mike had said something about them the day before and I pressed him to explain.

"I know it's coincidence," Mike said, "But I swear, every time she gets one of those awful headaches we find out later—sometimes a day later, sometimes weeks later—that she'd gotten up to some kind of trouble earlier that day."

"Guilty conscience?" I asked.

"Dunno," Mike said.

"Thankfully nothing that can't be cured by aspirin and a good night's rest," Nancy said as she patted her husband's knee.

I was glad of it. There were few things as bad as waking up with a splitting headache if you hadn't done something stupid the night before to deserve it. I was about to make another comment when the house lights went down and the first course of the evening's entertainment took the stage, or court, or floor.

A group of twenty kids strolled in, ten ahead of and ten following a chubby dude who looked like he was half Latino and half African-American. I figured he was the group's ringer from TV. They do-wopped in on a steady beat that I thought could have been a 'billy song until they reached the center of the auditorium and the dude in the center lifted a microphone to his perfectly masculine mouth and belted out the first line of Lady Gaga's hit song *Poker Face*, in falsetto.

For a group of kids who'd assumedly never sung in public, much less together, their version was hilarious in a very sincere fashion. It turns out one of the foster girls had a great set of pipes and she joined in with the lead for the chorus, sharing the microphone with the Idol at center stage. She looked deep into the older guy's eyes with adoration and then turned to play to the crowd just as Gaga would have. A little diva-ish and cheesy, but way too much fun.

I smiled so broadly at them that my cheeks hurt. I knew what it took for kids to get out there, sober, and perform. As hard as it was for most kids, I imagined these kids—who were caught in the toughest times of their lives—had it even harder. The audience clapped along with the beat of the pop song as the kids in the line executed simple but righteous choreography and sang the a-capella background track for the tune. This was a simple joy that had been missing from my life lately, the joy of sharing music with music lovers—not for fame, not for money, just for the power of music.

We all leapt to our feet when the twenty of them and their Idol came together in an awkward people-pyramid at the song's finale. They laughed together, hugged, took a quick bow and then ran off stage-left to sit on the floor at the end of the court and watch the rest of the show.

Hannah's group entered next. In contrast to the excited and decidedly campy entry of the first group, they came in soberly and formed a u-shape at center court with Hannah and the blonde Idol in the middle. Both girls, the polished professional and Hannah, the adoring fan, held microphones and I suddenly felt a moment of dread for our girl—that was a lot of pressure. Though looking at her in front of a crowd like she was, face beaming, it was hard to remember she was only fourteen.

After two measures of background melody from the kids, the Idol started the song, a soulful and sultry line about a fire burning in her heart. My heart sunk. I knew the song. It had been popularized by a singer named Adele and it was a muther to sing well all the way through. I hoped in my heart of hearts that the Idol only had Hannah in the center of the group with her to sing back-up on the chorus, and only back-up. It looked like I was right as Hannah rocked in place while the Idol carried the lead and the other kids bee-bopped the backing track. But to my surprise—complete and utter surprise—as the chorus came up, the group's little blonde Idol stepped three paces to the side and directed the crowd's attention to Hannah, giving her a solo.

I dared not breathe. I gripped the edge of the wooden bleacher with my fingertips, willing the crowd to be kind to Hannah's attempt at tackling an incredibly difficult song.

And then Hannah closed her eyes and opened her mouth and sung out in perfect pitch.

While the rest of the crowd, including Mike and Nancy, went wild with cheer for Hannah's solo on the chorus, my mouth dropped open in silence. The ending word of each of those lines, *all* and *deep*, were vowel-heavy extended notes that were nearly impossible to sing at the same power level as the rest of the chorus. I know; I've seen a hundred karaoke singers bomb it. I've watched Cooper try to sing it. Usually his natural talent pulled him through any song, but at that one he sucked; fell flat like a pancake, every single time. But Hannah did it as well as—maybe even better than—the radio version.

She took my breath away.

I clapped wildly for her because I still couldn't find my voice but needed to add my appreciation to the crowd's.

At the end of the chorus she opened her eyes and I saw tears of joy, even from a distance. Something inside her had woken, burst out, and made itself known—part pain, part love, part divine spark. She smiled the most authentic smile I've ever seen. Absolutely beautiful.

The crowd's cheering and applause faded into clapping along with the beat as the chorus ended and the next verse came around. Instead of taking back the lead, the little blonde Idol pointed at Hannah and encouraged her to keep singing. Without missing a beat, Hannah stepped right into the tip-off circle and dropped her voice a half-octave to that sultry place the song needed.

As Hannah sang, the Idol added her voice to the back-up sha-la-las sung by the kids as she worked around the u-shape. She stopped for a moment with each of the kids, changing parts to sing along with them into the microphone. Her smile caught on every time and I admired her so much for taking those few seconds to focus on each and every one of them, just one at a time, to make them feel special. I didn't know her name, but I would learn it because she instantly earned a page in my book of heroes.

Hannah's powerful voice carried through the second verse and into the chorus again and I marveled at her innate talent and vocal power. My eyes, and every set of eyes in the place, watched her without wavering. We were silent except for perfectly synchronized clapping. At the repeat of the final chorus, their Idol pulled four of the other kids forward to sing into the microphone with Hannah: a lanky, long-haired Asian boy; a husky brunette dude in jeans and a flannel shirt; a mousey girl in glasses and a track suit; and a sprite of a girl with African-American bone structure and pale-toned skin. Together, those five kids, those five strangers who were joined only by circumstance—victims caught in the system—found brilliant moments of harmony and brought the house down.

The audience gave them a standing ovation—including the kids who'd already performed and the kids who had yet to have their moment in the sun. They'd all come into the auditorium, drawn by Hannah's amazing talent.

"That'll razz your berries! She's amazing," I yelled to Mike and Nancy while we clapped.

"Not bad for a small-town girl," Mike said.

Not bad? I stopped clapping and looked at both of them with tears in my eyes. Sure, they looked proud, but there was something missing in their smiles and applause—a lack of awe and enthusiasm. They clearly did not understand their foster daughter's talent.

Not bad? What the hell? *Not bad?* "She stole the spotlight from the winner of a national, televised singing competition," I argued.

"Not winner," Nancy corrected me, leaning across her husband to shout in my ear. "Third runner-up."

Good Graceland. Winner. Third runner-up. *Really?* As much as I liked Mike and Nancy, they didn't have an inkling of a suggestion of a hint of a clue at what they'd just witnessed.

I finally understood why Laume had sent me to help.

In that moment I vowed to fix the Williams family. Not just for myself and my phamily, but for Hannah. After everything she'd been through, all the pain she'd drawn up and belted out through that song, I would find a way to get her family back together and provide the support she needed to achieve her potential.

The world deserved to hear her sing.

She deserved to feel their love.

15

The last three acts of the Idol sing-along went pretty much as I expected. Good times and good music sung with a lot of enthusiasm, but not much talent. While the audience around me paid attention to the acts on stage, I watched Hannah. Her group had run to the end of the court to sit and watch the remaining groups, and as she sat, the four teenagers she'd sung the final chorus with clumped around her. They spent the rest of the show chatting and laughing, riding the high that follows a good performance.

No. The high of a great performance.

After some encouraging parting words from the Idols about how each foster family and each foster child could reach their dreams if they worked hard enough (yeah, right, my inner cynic complained about a recording contract waiting for Billy's Asylum Rats to come home from our brush with death) the audience gave one final standing ovation to the kids and the Idols and then the event broke up. I followed Mike and Nancy outside where we waited for Hannah. She walked out looking like a mother duck with a trailing-v of ducklings. Admirers. Her fans. First among them the four other foster kids she had sung the final chorus with. I hoped they would be able to stay in touch as each of them fought their way through the system.

Hannah finally saw us and waved goodbye to her new friends and followers. There was a touch of her dad in the parting. Her smile, maybe. Or the way she tossed her head. Something about it was Laume, too. The grace. Her beauty.

"Well done, kiddo," Nancy said. She looked like she wanted to reach out and hug Hannah, but held back out of respect.

I, on the other hand, knew all about the post-performance high Hannah was riding and I did reach out and hug her. "Great solo. You were on the stick like nobody's business."

Hannah hugged me back. "It was okay?"

I stepped back and grabbed both her upper arms. "That was amazing. You out diva'd the diva. That was so cool when she gave up the spotlight. Just gave it up."

Hannah giggled.

There was something warm and lovely between us as we made eye contact. I knew how hard it was to live in the shade of one attention-grubbing parent and the hole of the other one who's missing. The narcissist never says anything complimentary or real unless they somehow can make it a reflection of themselves. And though it was normal and natural to daydream about how an absent parent might react to such success if they'd been around, there was no way to know what the real person might say or do, and that was where the pain came from. For once, I just wanted Hannah to know someone had seen *her*.

And then Mike shattered our moment by punching Hannah in the shoulder. "Good job, slugger."

Hannah's eyes rolled from mine toward Mike's but got stuck on something in the distance.

"My dad's here?" Hannah's eyes lit up and a hopeful smile stretched her cheeks. "He came to hear me sing?"

"Your dad?" Nancy asked. "Where?"

"That's his car," Hannah said and pointed over my shoulder.

I turned to see her pointing at Ryan's Jag where I'd parked it in the lot. Crap.

Elvis help me; I wish she had not seen the car. I should have parked it on the street, on the next block, on another planet. I should have left it at the treatment center and taken the goddamn bus—zombie commuters and all.

"I didn't see your dad inside," Mike said, craning his neck to catch a glimpse of his bro-crush. "Nancy, did Ryan tell you he was coming?"

"No," Nancy said, joining their search.

The three of them looked like meerkats keeping an eye peeled across the African plains on the watch for hungry lions. I understood Hannah's hopeful searching and was disgusted by Nancy and Mike's star-struck gazes.

And the sad thing, it was my fault.

Sadder still, if someone had said they thought they'd seen my dad's car parked in the lot, I would have done the same damn thing—even after all this time and all that therapy. We love our parents, no matter what, and we always need their acceptance.

I knew the only kind thing to do would be to explain that I had driven the Jag.

I opened my mouth but no words came out. It wasn't anything like being D-n-D from using my telepathy, I was just being chickenshit. Best I could do was to pull the keys to the Jag out of my bag and hold them where Hannah would see them.

Eventually she did.

She turned dark red in the face. Unmistakable rage and disappointment. "You have my dad's car. How?"

The challenge in her voice was more than the usual, simple question of vehicle logistics. There was obviously something special about that car and something significant about how it affected Hannah's relationship with her dad.

I owed her an explanation.

"He found out I was stuck taking the bus and loaned it to me." Simple. Straightforward. The truth.

And it backfired in my face.

"No. Fucking. Way," Hannah yelled. "He never lets anyone drive that car." She got into my face and lowered her voice. "You were supposed to be here for me."

"I am here. For you."

Hannah stepped back, glared, and crossed her arms. "Did you sleep with him?"

"No." That was the literal truth, and I hoped Hannah couldn't read the whole truth on my face. I cautiously folded back the left side of the sweatshirt I'd borrowed in an attempt to hide the treatment center's logo. I didn't want her figuring out I needed her father's sweatshirt because he'd ripped my dress off me. We had not had sex, but it had been close. Too close. I breathed deeply trying to keep myself grounded.

"You slept with him."

"I swear I didn't."

"Then why would he give you his car."

"Loaned. Loaned me his car. It's only temporary."

Hannah bit her lip and a tear spilled out and ran down her cheek. "He won't even let me ride in it." She stared me down, blue eyes vibrant through her tears.

Damn. Damn, shit, and hell. I should have taken the bus. I should have parked on another planet. "I didn't know."

The evening wasn't supposed to end this way. This was supposed to have been Hannah's big night. A triumph. A grand moment to remember forever; the day the spark caught and ignited the first-stage of her career. Not the day she got one more piece of evidence that her daddy loved adoring strangers more than he loved her.

I couldn't stand the pressure of her gaze; I let mine fall to the ground where ants detoured around our feet as they criss-crossed the sidewalk. She was right and I was wrong, horribly wrong. I felt frozen in place, stuck in time, unable to decide what I should say or do—or even move—and the world around us got unnaturally quiet for a minute as if everyone in town was waiting for me to figure it out and fix it. The ants even stopped to listen.

I thought and thought, the question looping in my head about what I might say to fix things. All I could come up with was, "I'm sorry, I didn't know."

"Can we go now?" Hannah asked, finally breaking the silence after an uncomfortable minute. "I feel another migraine coming on."

I looked up to find Nancy's arm around Hannah's shoulder, leading her toward a gray minivan with a hundred colorful bumper stickers plastered across its back. Mike stood on the sidewalk next to me—his attention flickering back and forth between the keys in my hand and the Jag in the parking lot.

"I could offer to drive her home in it?" I asked him.

Mike shook his head, to make sure I hadn't missed the fact that I'd just given Hannah the royal shaft. "This is really not how it's supposed to go. Give her some time," he said.

I thought about it and then remembered the report I had to write for the judge, to keep up my cover as CASA. Kevin at Human Services had wanted me to spend at least four hours with Hannah before the end of the weekend and get that report to him first thing Monday morning. "I don't know if I can give her much of that. I have to do this report for the judge."

"When?"

"Monday. I need at least two more hours with her before then."

Mike nodded. "Come over for family dinner tomorrow night. We eat at six. Come early, bring dessert. Hannah likes chocolate."

"Thanks," I said. I would bake the best chocolate cupcakes she'd ever tasted.

Mike flashed a low-handed wave and climbed in the passenger side of the minivan as it pulled up to the curb with Nancy behind the wheel and Hannah buried somewhere in the back. I watched them go, feeling down, sad, deflated. Experiencing Hannah in front of a crowd—the way she lit up and filled the hearts of the audience as she sang—it was such a high. Seeing her slouch away to her foster mom's minivan couldn't have been lower.

I'd ruined her perfect day.

Scolding myself to be more careful with Hannah's feelings, I crossed the parking lot to the pristine Jag that Williams apparently held in greater esteem than his own child. I knew what that felt like, having been on the short end of that particular stick myself a time or two, and it made me sick to my stomach that I'd had any part in doing that to Hannah.

With my dad it had always been travel—all the places he visited and people he met—and I was never invited to go along. One time, when I was thirteen, I destroyed his luggage with his good kitchen knives the night before a big trip, just to get his attention. It had worked. Not that I got to go. For punishment, he emptied my piggy bank—all the babysitting money I'd been saving to get my own iPod—to help pay for replacements. The next morning he borrowed bags from a neighbor and made his flight to New York anyway.

I was so distracted by my own past that I absentmindedly unlocked the car and climbed in. It wasn't until I sat down in the driver's seat that I noticed something funny about the car's hood. At first I thought it was the reflection of the trees on the paint's surface, but then a gust caught the branches and the marks on the hood didn't sway along.

"What the?"

Launching myself out of the car, I ran around the open door to find someone had keyed the lustrous green paint.

Bitch.

It said bitch. Huge letters crudely engraved in the paint starting at the split bumper and reaching all the way back to the windshield. Both windshield wipers had been ripped off and were lying on the ground beside the front left wheel. I reached out and felt the grittiness of the bits of paint under my fingertips. The scratches were so deep I could pick at them with my nails. I'd have to work for a month at The Rose City Oven before I could cover the cost of the repairs.

Damn.

In my gut I wondered if, somehow, Hannah had done it. But there was no way she could have; she hadn't been out of my sight after she'd gotten so angry with me.

My rational mind said it had to be a mistake, some kind of misunderstanding. A stranger had confused the car with another vintage Jag or thought Ryan was driving it. Players often pissed people off. But if the message had been for Ryan Williams, wouldn't it have said *bastard*, or *asshole*, or *douche bag*? *Bitch* was definitely a female thing.

Embarrassed to be standing in front of a car with an obscenity scrawled across the hood as families from the event walked by --and noticed—I quickly got back in the car and got it out of the lot. The surface streets led me to the highway which ran parallel to The Max train tracks all the way downtown toward Brady's place.

I rode without the radio and with the top up, trying to be as inconspicuous in the fading daylight and thinning traffic as possible. I thought more and more about the scratches on the car I grew more and more confused. Throwing out coincidence and mistaken identity, I was left with only two possibilities: Hannah or Laume.

Hannah had reason to be very angry with me. And with the car, as an extension of the anger she must have for her dad. She had motive, and was certainly capable of causing the damage, but she hadn't had the opportunity.

That left Laume. And a bigger problem—two bigger problems actually.

The first was that if Laume had scratched-up the car it meant she was able to track me down even though I hadn't been carrying my driver's license or passport. And that meant my understanding of simple object tracking needed some fine tuning. Maybe I was the simple object all by myself without any additional stuff. Maybe it was the tracking that was simple, as Brady suggested, and there was no way to fool her. I didn't want to accept that because I needed to believe I could spend some part of my life—until the time I finally got my phamily back—exerting my own free-will without always looking over my shoulder for a Faery.

The other problem—the bigger one—was that my attempt at eluding Laume had obviously pissed her off enough to damage a car that Ryan Williams thought she would have a keen affection for. I couldn't imagine how angry I'd have to be to deface the paintjob on my Buick. I hoped to hell that she wouldn't take any of her anger at me out on my phamily, like the way she'd ground Maria's ring to dust.

One thing I knew for sure, this deal just got crappier and crappier all the time.

16

I cruised along the Portland waterfront in Ryan Williams' Jag as the streetlights turned on in their nightly battle against the darkness. My conscious brain had every intention of going straight to Brady's apartment, but somehow I found myself parked along the parkway across from the concrete amphitheater where Brady and I had seen the drum circle playing. A thrumming rhythm in the air said they were at it again.

Sitting and listening to the complicated beat from afar wasn't enough to satisfy my need for rhythm—I needed to feel the vibrations—so I shut the car off, locked it up, and dashed across the divided parkway to get closer to the music. The circle of drummers was smaller than it had been the night Brady and I had our first date. The main snare and bongo kept the groove that six other drummers and a tambourine riffed on. I sat at the open end of the circle next to a scraggly teenager playing twin bongos with dirt encrusted hands.

He caught me tapping my hands on my thighs and asked, "You want to play?" He held the bongos toward me.

I accepted the drums with a smile and arranged my skirt so I could tuck them between my knees without blocking the sound. The skins were old, worn, stained by decades of playing, but they were solid and extremely responsive. Rocking to the beat I played half and quarter notes as background, just happy to feel the pounding of my hands and the vibrating response of the drum bodies.

It took a couple of minutes to learn the rhythm of the group—though no one player directed the music there was a courtesy of about four measures between one player's solo and the next. Solos bounced back and forth across the circle in a clockwise pattern and when the music came around to me I played a three-measure fill I'd made up as a short spotlight when Billy's Asylum Rats played Wanda Jackson's *Whistlebait* in our second set. As I finished, and laid back into the background beat, a couple of the other players nodded their appreciation for my contribution to the greater sound, a high compliment.

The music filled me and soothed my wounded soul. I felt the inner me grounding back into *what was important* and *what I could affect*: the car was just a car, it could be repaired; Hannah would calm down by Sunday and I would explain things to her; and I would find a way to handle any of Laume's future hissy-fits when I saw her.

The truly important part was that I was still on track to get Hannah home to her father, and more importantly I had finally reconciled Laume's impression of the foster parents with Kevin's. They were both correct about Mike and Nancy, but looking at the situation with different eyes gave them diverging opinions. Kevin wanted foster parents who could provide normalcy and healing. Laume demanded her daughter be recognized and rewarded. I could see things from both perspectives and I would get the job done in a way that made them both happy. Hannah would have a chance to be as full and complete with her music as I felt with mine as I pounded the bongos; if only for the moment.

I added one more fill as the music came around to me again, and then I regretfully passed the drums back to their owner. "Thanks. I needed that."

"Anytime." He jumped back into the circle's rhythm without missing a beat.

Drummers: folks of few words.

I waved a casual good-bye to the rest of the circle, silently thanking them for the healing and grounding, and walked back to the Jag, ready to face whatever might come at Brady's. Including little Chester.

It was a good thing that Chester's bedtime was 8:30 because an hour of his company and his juvenile sense of entertainment wore me out. He asked a hundred questions in a row, thought *poo-poo* jokes were the funniest in all the land, and did not tolerate me being within two feet of *his* daddy. I know that's pretty much on par for a three year old little boy; and it's exactly why I liked them so much more after they'd grown up and learned to throw punches instead of tantrums when jealousy struck.

While Brady spent more than an hour coaxing little Chester to lie down and go to sleep in the other room, I flipped channels on the flat screen and finished off Brady's bottle of microbrew. The early news caught my attention, not because I was a news hound, but because it had been a whole week since the record company's yacht sank and I'd been completely out of touch with the world since then.

Local news in Portland was a lot like local news in Austin; it just got reported by whiter faces. Fires, bank robberies, local festivals to promote. The weather, however, was worlds apart from home—a skinny brunette touted overnight low temperatures that central Texas wouldn't see again until the holidays.

The holidays. My heart sunk when I considered my life going forward over the next couple of months. I hoped the whole phamily would be home by then to celebrate with our strange traditions and typical Austin weirdness. I saw each of their faces in my head and then realized, oddly, they weren't just in my head. The faces of my phamily were also on Brady's television.

The news showed a picture of our band, a moody black-and-white promotional shot we'd taken a year ago to use on our bar posters. I turned up the volume to hear the anchor's report.

"*...Coast Guard is now calling their scaled-back efforts in the Western Gulf a recovery operation rather than search and rescue. The yacht was last located two hundred miles south of Houston just before a brutal storm eight days ago. The boat's owners, revitalized recording label Sun Records—best known for their association with the late Elvis Presley—called the sinking* 'a tragic blow to the regional music scene and a devastating loss for the Sun family.'"

The anchor moved on to the next story and I shut the TV off. Written off already. It was nice to know someone had cared enough to look for us in that vast, unbroken expanse of water, but it would have been nice if they'd stayed at it a little longer. My first impulse was to pick up the phone and call Sun Records to report that their boat was sunk and we were still very much alive, but that would lead to all kinds of questions I was unable to answer. If I did call it's likely I'd have had to spend my whole weekend giving statements to the local cops and filling out paperwork. And none of that would help me get my phamily back.

But when I did eventually get them back, and we did contact the folks at Sun Records, I imagined we'd cause quite a stir. It might even boost our sales. *Rockabilly band returns from the dead*—story at eleven.

"You look like you're a million miles away." Brady's voice pulled me out of my daydream about Billy's Asylum Rat's comeback as he walked into the living room and sat next to me on the sofa.

"Finally alone." He leaned in and gave me a kiss. He tried to hold me there, to linger and deepen the moment, but my heart wasn't in it and I pulled back. "I promise, he's asleep, like the dead. He won't be up until the morning."

"That's not it."

"Talk to me."

Damn. I really didn't want to explain. There was no nice way to say that compared to the kiss Ryan Williams had planted on me that afternoon kissing Brady felt like kissing Paulo or Cooper. Like kissing my brother, if I'd had one. Sure, all the parts connected in all the right ways, but the heat didn't rise in me quite the same way with Brady.

Brady liked me, he was good and kind and wonderful. But Ryan Williams kissed me like he was worshipping.

Worshipping Laume.

Damn, I hated that this stupid fucking situation with Laume got in the way of what had been so good with Brady. I didn't want to explain all that, so I lied. "I'm just exhausted, that's all."

Brady patted the couch cushions. "I told you this couch had issues," he smiled, hopefully. "I have an idea. You get us a couple more beers from the fridge, I'll grab all the blankets out of the linen closet, and we can make a nest right here on the floor. Snuggle and watch dirty movies all night. Just the two of us." The way he caressed my thigh, his hand moving my skirt up to bare more skin, told me the movie might not be the only dirty thing going on in his mind.

I put a hand over his to stop him from getting any more ideas. It wasn't like me to pass-up such a well-intentioned pass, but for lots of reasons all I wanted to do was borrow one of Brady's oversized t-shirts, wrap myself up like a burrito on the couch, and check in telepathically with my phamily before I dropped off from exhaustion. I'd had less than nine hours sleep in three days, and the Chester issue was not going away for another couple of nights.

"I'm sorry, Brady. I can't," I said. "Maybe Sunday night after Chester goes back to his mom's."

He pulled away from me. "I know I should have told you about him when we first met, but you have to trust me; he's not going to wake up."

"You sure about that?" I asked and pointed over Brady's shoulder to where his son stood in the bedroom doorway, eyes half closed and hair all mussed-up.

"Daddy, I'm thirsty," Chester whined. "Juice."

"Chester, go back to bed." Brady's impatience came through in his tone though I saw him try to fight it.

"Juice, Daddy. Juice."

Brady sighed. I couldn't blame him, for all he knew he'd just gotten cock-blocked by his own son.

"Chet, get back in bed and I'll bring you some water." Brady got up and headed for the kitchen. "I'm sorry," he said to me.

I was sorry, too. I liked Brady, a lot, but I wasn't cut out for the potential-step-mommy game—I just didn't have the patience on a good day. And it had not been a good day. Disappointing one unhappy kid was enough for me.

"I'm just going to go." I got up and grabbed my bag.

Brady came back to the living room, glass of water in his hand. "Where?"

"I'll find a cheap hotel."

"It's late. Do you want to take my car?"

Leaving Ryan's Jag parked on the street downstairs and taking Brady's car for the night might get the classic car towed if I just happened to oversleep in the morning, like I really wanted to.

"Umm, no thanks."

I thought back to Brady's comment on the day we'd met; how he loaned me his car in part so I couldn't flake-out on our dinner date. He had that same look on his face as he stepped forward and touched my arm. "But the bus isn't really safe this time of night."

"Don't worry. I borrowed a car for the weekend because I have a million things I have to do tomorrow. I'll be fine. I'll come back tomorrow night after my dinner appointment," I said as I motioned to my dress and mis-matched sweatshirt. "We'll have dessert."

He looked like he wanted to ask me more but he simply said, "At least let me walk you down."

But then a forlorn Chester cried "Dad-dee-ee, I'm thirst-tee," from the other room.

"It's okay. Go; take care of your boy. I'll see you tomorrow." I kissed him on the mouth to show him I was serious about seeing him, and even Chester, the next day.

"Seven o'clock?" he asked as he backed toward his room, still facing me.

"Seven thirty, maybe eight," I said. "I'll bring cupcakes."

Brady disappeared into his son's three-year-old-kiddo-needs and I let myself out into the hallway. The elevator was to the left, but I went right down to the end of the hall and the garbage chute where I'd stashed my passport and driver's license before leaving that morning.

The building was happily quiet and my feet made a soft rustle on the low-pile carpet. I pulled the closet door open for the garbage chute—planning to step in, turn around, grab my ID from its hiding place behind the light fixture flange, and get out before anyone saw me—but my heart skipped a beat when I stepped right into Laume.

Crap. Elvis kill me now. There she was standing in the small closet that housed the garbage chute. It's a good thing she was a petite Faery or she would not have fit into the closet, much less into that amazing, gold-colored satin dress with matching three inch heels and white, elbow-length gloves.

She smiled the way a female lion might smile at the last antelope lingering too long at the watering hole. "Hello, little darlin'. Looking for these?"

She held my driver's license and passport between slender fingers and then turned and tugged down on the garbage chute's handle, opening the gaping hole that went all the way down nine floors to the basement.

17

No! Don't," I cried and lunged forward, trying to keep Laume from dropping the driver's license and passport down the apartment building's garbage chute.

"Why not?" she asked. "It appears you no longer need them."

"Of course I need them." If she tossed them down the chute, and I couldn't get into the basement to find them in the dumpster, I'd be hard pressed to get a replacement license without my birth certificate and some other form of photo ID. Neither of which I had with me at the moment.

Laume let the chute slam closed, the noise assaulting my tired nerves, and held my ID out toward me, but not quite to me, as if she were daring me to reach for them and threatening me not to take them at the same time. "If you need them, what were they doing tucked behind the lantern casing all day?"

I didn't want to answer that question, didn't want to give away my intention of testing to see how she was really keeping an eye on me—I wanted to keep some parts of my life private. But I was caught, the jig was up. If I failed to give her an answer, the conversation would probably go on until she eventually threatened my phamily and then I would have to cough it up anyway.

"It's not like you need them to track me anyway," I said. "You proved that with Ryan's car this afternoon."

Laume's smile faltered into a questioning gaze for half a second, but then she caught herself and reasserted a confident smirk. "Smart girl. Of course I don't need them to keep tabs on the movements of one mere mortal," she said with nonchalance.

But I'd seen that bobble. Something didn't add up. The hairs on my arms stood up in warning. "You're lying to me," I said.

Laume tightened her lips and then shoved my ID at me. I grabbed at it before she changed her mind and turned for the chute again. Then she shoved past me into the hallway with her back straight and her nose in the air. "The Fae never lie. We cannot."

I took the hit on my shoulder and let it turn me to follow her down the hallway. "You're shitting me."

"I would never say it with quite so much vulgarity," she said as she led the way to the elevator, "but given the track record of your species, I understand your disbelief." Laume stopped in front of the elevator and pushed the button to call the car. "Adherence to the truth is just one of the many ways in which we Fae hold ourselves to a higher standard than the wretches of humanity. A Faery never lies."

"You have to tell the truth? Always?"

"I. Never. Lie."

Well, *Ooby Dooby*. And how about that? I knew from our haggling back on the lifeboat, from Laume stealing my phamily away in the night and calling it *taking them to safety*, that she had the ability and intention to mislead me. I just assumed that all-out lies weren't far behind.

She *said* she couldn't lie, but I wasn't sure how far she could stretch the truth, what kind of amazingly fucked-up slant she could put on it, before it crossed the line into a lie. I wanted to test her, and I had the perfect way.

"I saw Hannah sing today," I said, filling my voice with pride. "I understand now why she needs to get out of her foster home and back with Ryan, but I still don't get why you care so much. What's your interest in her? Are you two related or something?"

Laume turned and studied me. The elevator dinged its arrival and the door slid open, but we stood still as statues as I waited for her answer. It took a full ten seconds of waiting, and then she must have seen something in my face, a tell of some kind, giving away the fact that I had already guessed they were mother and daughter.

"Relationships we Fae have with our offspring may not measure up to your sentimental human standards, but I am not so callous as to not care at all what happens to my progeny." Laume stalked into the elevator with her nose in the air, as if daring me to question her again.

So there it was. She hadn't used *mother*, *daughter*, *child*, or *parent*, but unless my vocabulary skills were complete crap she had just admitted to being Hannah's mother. When pressed with a direct question she proved that she could not lie. In the same breath she also admitted to abandoning Hannah to a life with a flaming narcissist of a father—a crappy life for a little girl with no one to shelter her from his bizarre behavior or to provide a role model of what was healthy.

I squeezed into the elevator between the closing doors. "So you just left her with him? She doesn't even know who you are, does she?"

Floors dinged by as the elevator descended and I waited for Laume to answer, hoping that being stuck with me in the elevator would compel her to say something, however slanted. But as the doors opened to the lobby and I just about gave up hope that she would answer me. She walked out ahead of me straightening her gloves and simply said, "There is no place in Fae for a human child. It is not at all like your world."

Funny that Laume had assumed I was griping at her for not taking her daughter to her "home" when I was just tapping into my own history and yelling at her for leaving a little girl to grow up in the world of a narcissistic father without a mother. I hadn't really thought much about where Laume went when she left in such a hurry, that she might have a whole other home. I'd read stories when I was a kid about Fae, the land of the Faeries, but somehow I'd always figured it was part of our world, hidden in tree trunks and under waterfalls, not something completely separate. And it never occurred to me Fae would be a place unfit, unsafe, or unwelcoming to human-kind.

That cold ball of fear behind my breast bone pulsed when I considered what Fae might be like, especially if there was a chance that's where Laume had taken my phamily.

Suddenly I had to know.

"Is that where you took my phamily to be *safe as moonbeams*?" I asked. "Into some land of the Faeries?"

She didn't answer as she strode across the lobby and out to the street, the heavy metal and glass door flying open ahead of her so quickly it bounced off the hard stops with a resounding *thwang*. And she hadn't even touched them.

It was hard to keep up with Laume as she strutted up the sidewalk in her heels like an experienced runway model, the pools of orange light from the street lamps giving her gold dress a life of its own. She was trying to ditch me, I knew it. But I didn't know why. Especially when she could very easily have disappeared into thin air.

"Laume, wait! I have to know if that's where my phamily is."

I chased her across the crosswalk and over to the next block where I'd parked the Jag a couple of hours earlier. At first it looked like she was going to keep on going into the night, but just as she passed the far bumper of the car she stopped, sniffing the air, and then looked at the classic car like she'd never laid eyes on it before.

She turned and stared at me. "Is this your conveyance?"

"Where am I going to come up with the money to buy a car like that?"

She smiled at me and sniffed the car again. "It smells like *him*, like Hannah's father. And you have something on you that smells the same way."

I took the sweatshirt off, exposing the back of my ruined dress, and held it out to her. She curled her lip and did not take the sweatshirt so I put it back on to keep the cold breeze off my bare skin.

"Yes, I know it belongs to him; but that's not it." Laume stalked over to me and poked one long, satin-tipped finger at my beaded bag. "It's in there."

I reached into the bag and pulled out the gold key ring.

"You must have quite a few talents for a human. A second man has given you his conveyance?"

"He thought he was giving it to you," I said. "I don't know why, but for some reason he's got you and me confused in his drug-pickled brain."

Laume laughed in a way that said there was no way in Fae, Heaven, or Hell that anyone could confuse the two of us. "He never did have the sharpest wit."

"He's still in love with you, you know. Bought this car because it reminded him of you."

Laume looked over the car, walked around it until she could read the word scrawled in the paint on the hood. "And now it's been customized for you, I see."

Her arrogance made me angry, but I knew had to stuff it down so she wouldn't decide to retaliate against my phamily. Yes, I knew I had to, but couldn't quite bring myself to do it. I think a little of it got out. "You know that was a pretty fucking lame thing to do." I pointed at the car.

Laume had leaned over the hood so she could trace the letters with her gloved finger. She stopped to look at me and stood up straight, her perfect posture making me feel like a slobby teenager in my torn dress. "What exactly are you referring to?"

Uh-oh. I knew that tone. She'd used it on the lifeboat, making me want to scrape and bow, and then again right before she ground Maria's ring to dust. I really needed to learn how to get my mouth under control.

"Be mad at me all you want," I said, "but please don't take it out on my phamily. And don't take it out on a defenseless car. Do you know what it's going to cost me to get that fixed?"

"I'm sure I have no idea what you're referring to." Laume wiped her gloved hands together like she had just squished a wasp or a scorpion into their shiny fabric.

What? Was she playing me, or could it be possible she hadn't been the one to scratch the word *bitch* into the hood? I thought back to her earlier insistence that she could not lie and wondered if she was just giving me a slant of the truth.

"So you didn't scratch-up the car to get back at me for leaving my license and passport behind?"

Laume laughed, turned on her heel, and strode off up the street. "No, little darlin'. I would not do such a petty, childish thing. When I have a bone to pick with you, you will know it," she shouted over her shoulder.

I watched her walk up the block, heels clicking on the asphalt street, until she reached the next corner, turned it, and then disappeared behind a building. Ten seconds later the fading sound of her clicking heels disappeared as well.

I stood on the dark sidewalk next to the Jag feeling lost. Part of it was trying to figure out how the damn car had actually been damaged. If Laume had not keyed it, then it was back to a stranger and a coincidence, which I doubted, or Hannah, which I doubted even more. But Laume's denial, and the way she had confronted me about leaving my license and passport hiding in the closet all day, had pretty much confirmed that she needed some kind of an object to track me down as I moved through my day. Now I just had to decide whether to ditch (or maybe even destroy) my ID and drive around in someone else's car illegally without them, or hold onto them and risk her finding me any damn time she wanted to.

Thankfully, given that I'd just gotten my daily recommended dose of Faery, that was a decision I could hold off for the moment. It had been an incredibly long day; too many extremes had fried my little brain. I would decide what to do in the morning, after talking telepathically to my phamily and then getting some desperately needed sleep.

Bouncing the keys to the Jag in my hand I thought about my next problem: would it be better to go to a cheap hotel for the night (like I told Brady I was going to do) or did I dare take Ryan Williams up on his offer to use his house? He wouldn't be there and I still had the codes to the gate and the alarm system in my bag.

The good girl in me hollered to go find a cheap hotel. The bad one tried to convince me that it would be okay to go to Ryan's for just one night. Who would care?

Hannah would care, the good girl voice warned. It would devastate her if she found out—knowing that she couldn't go home, but I had free run of the place.

I weighed the possibility of Hannah somehow figuring it out against the reality that a cheap hotel would eat up more than half of my money. I didn't like either outcome, but after the way I'd left things with Brady, I sure couldn't go crawling back upstairs and beg to use his couch for the night. Unlike Brady's station wagon the Jag was too small to sleep in. I was too proud to find a shelter and I had no desire to camp out on a park bench, it was too cold and the air smelled like rain.

What would Cooper do? I asked myself.

"*Do about what?*" Cooper's voice jumped into my head with such clarity that I had to look around and make sure he wasn't standing next to me on the sidewalk. But he wasn't there, he was inside my head. I must have inadvertently opened up a telepathic channel to him.

Cooper? Elvis help me, I'm so glad to hear your voice.

Knowing that my hearing and voice would be gone 'til I got some sleep and the sun rose in the morning, I climbed into the car and locked myself in.

"*Well if this ain't the biggest tickle ever,*" Cooper said inside my head. "*We weren't sure if Maria was really talking to you or if there was some kind of drug in the wine. Score one for the piano-girl. I'll have to apologize."*

Still blows my mind, I thought to him. *Sorry it's been a couple of days since I called last. I've been busy here.* I explained about my new job at The Rose City Oven and about how using my telepathy with Maria had made me D-n-D until sunrise.

"*Couple of days?*" Cooper asked. "*Maria said she talked to you just before we all went to sleep. Have we been sleeping for days?*"

I had no idea how to answer him. *None of this makes any sense. Though I think I did figure out how the Faery Bitch is tracking me.*

"*Tracking you?*"

She shows up anyplace she wants and makes me do whatever she says.

"*I'll bet that goes over like a fart in church.*"

Cooper knew me so well. Knew I had history with being told what to do. Rotten history.

At least I figured out how to shake her. She gave me a driver's license and passport so I could get back into the country after the yacht went down. If I don't have them on me she has no idea where I am.

"*I don't get it.*"

She called it simple object tracking. Like as long as I'm carrying something of hers—because I know that wasn't my original license and I've never had a passport—she can track my ass down. She just shows up.

Cooper gave me a thoughtful harrumph in my head. "*Nice trick. Wish we could have used that when she stole Maria's ring.*"

How is she? I know that ring meant a lot to her.

"*Meant a lot? It* means *a lot, right?*"

I'm sorry. Don't tell Maria. Laume trashed it; totally destroyed it. Like turned it into a million bits of used-to-be-a-ring dust sparkling in the cracks of the asphalt now.

"*Shit. I'm not going to be the one to tell her.*"

She's taking it that badly?

"*She's been drunk or asleep ever since, and sleeping hasn't kept her from raving. I think she's going to try one of her grandmother's curses the next time that Faery Bitch shows up to drop off food and wine.*"

Tell her good luck, I said. *Make it a real good one.*

"But we're okay. Maria explained what you've got to do for that kid. You worry about that, and we'll take care of finding some way out of here."

I'm not so sure that's safe.

"Come again?"

I think you guys might not be where you think you are.

"This isn't Hotel Hell in beautiful downtown Burbank?"

Seriously, Coop. I think you guys might be in Fae. Like actually in the land of the Faeries, not in our plane of existence. I'm not sure getting out *is going to be possible. Could even be dangerous. Maybe it's better if you just hang tight until I get things settled with the kid.*

"Come on, Bay. Quit the shit."

The way she teleported you guys out of the lifeboat. She could have taken you anywhere.

"But another plane of existence, another reality. No way. It's weird here—I mean weirder than Austin—but not that weird."

Okay, but just be careful. I will get you out of there as soon as I can.

"How's that whole thing going?"

The girl is amazing, sweet as can be and voice like an angel. I figured out she's the daughter of our least-favorite Faery Bitch. The dad, well he's about the biggest prick you'll ever meet, except maybe my dad. But I promise, I'm going to make it work.

"*Good luck,*" Cooper said.

I'll touch back after I'm done with everything tomorrow, see how you're doing.

"But you have to promise to call Paulo next time."

He okay? I'd forgotten Maria's implication that Paulo still wasn't recovered from the time in the lifeboat and I worried that he'd taken a turn for the worse.

"Sure. But he's never going to believe this unless you reach him directly. He's been giving poor Maria so much crap."

Okay, but tell him I'm coming so he doesn't think he's hearing those voices again, I thought to Cooper. *And you take care. I love you guys.*

I was about to sign off but Cooper thought, "*Wait a minute.*"

What?

"You started this whole thing asking what I'd do. What I'd do about what?"

Just trying to figure out my living situation for the next couple of days.

"And the choices are?"

Spend half my cash on a cheap hotel, grovel my way back in to spend the night on the couch at my new friend's place, or crash out in the mansion of a former professional baseball player.

"New friend. Male or female?"

Apparently Cooper had heard something in my voice.

Male, with a three year old ankle biter.

"Take the mansion."

It has potential strings, nasty ones.

"Take the hotel."

I knew he'd say that. It would be the smart choice.

Thanks, I thought. *Goodnight, Coop.*

I pulled away from my connection with Cooper and felt cool tears on my cheeks that matched the drops of rain just starting to fall on the Jag's windshield. Talking with Cooper that way was the most intimate experience I'd ever had with him. It was somehow different that linking to Maria, who already knew all my dirty secrets and loved me just the same. Cooper was phamily, but he was my second conscience, and so there were things I'd always kept from him, keeping him at a safe distance. Connecting telepathically had crushed that distance like a beer can against a drunken frat boy's forehead and it felt like inviting him inside of me. Pulling away felt like saying good-bye, forever.

He was right. It was time to find a cheap hotel. I started the car, oddly feeling the vibrations of the engine through the seat even though I couldn't hear them, and headed over the river to look for a hotel. Along Sandy Boulevard I found a series of flea-bag-wannabes and quickly recognized the whole strip as a red-light district by the number of nearly naked girls and tricked-out low-riders trolling slowly back and forth. Being D-n-D, I felt too vulnerable to sleep in a place where hookers, drug dealers and gang bangers did their business. If all hell broke loose I'd never even hear the alarms and sirens in time to run, so I decided to look for a little higher-rent cheap hotel.

My gut said I'd probably find something near the airport—I wouldn't hear the planes until sunrise—so I followed signs further east along the interstate, and then turned north. As I exited the highway and turned onto the main drag I was shocked to see dozens of people, mostly in their teens and twenties, roaming the area in packs. And most of them wore oddball costumes. Some I recognized from old movies and TV shows. Some I did not.

The answer became clear as I passed hotel after hotel with their No Vacancy signs lit up. The ones with reader boards out front all posted welcome signs for a regional Science Fiction and Fantasy convention. I cruised for five minutes, searching carefully while trying not to run over any aliens, and the only place that appeared to have a vacancy was The W. I knew that would cost every penny I had, and more, just for one night.

I turned the Jag around in the vacant parking lot of a giant IKEA store and stopped to think. The old dial-style clock in the dash said it was after midnight. I was exhausted. Instead of listening to my conscience, or the advice of Cooper-my-second-conscience, I dug into my bag to find the envelope Dr. Mayweather had given me. Inside I found the address for and directions to Ryan Williams' house and two six-digit security codes, one labeled gate and one labeled main-house. I had to stop twice on the way there to check my map because the place was tucked way up in the hills among curving roads and trees so tall their tops disappeared into the moonless sky, but when I got there it was all worth it.

Completely worth it.

18

Ryan Williams' house could have stood shoulder to shoulder with any mansion in Texas and come out with nothing more than a black eye. The solid white gate at the roadside swung open silently after I punched the six-digit code into the touch screen. The driveway itself looked like its cobblestones had been lifted from the streets of Boston or New Haven and rebuilt for just him, stone for stone. The Jag's tires tapped out an asynchronous rhythm as I drove up the rise, past a good-sized gatehouse, and up to a two-story monstrosity surrounded by towering evergreens and ample lawns.

Exterior lights blinked on as I drove up to the house. Rather than try to figure out how to open one of the five carriage-style doors to stash the Jag in the garage, I parked it in the circular driveway in front of the main doors. A fountain at the center of the drive gurgled.

Though most of me knew I should re-start the engine and drive away as fast as I could, part of me couldn't go without at least taking a tour of the house. If the inside was half as beautiful as the outside, with its rough hewn stone—real rock, not a facade—and white wood accents, I couldn't miss it.

I plucked the keys from the ignition and grabbed the house alarm code and my bag from the passenger seat. Cobbles gave way to textured concrete at the front porch which gave way to smooth, inlaid stone at the threshold. Since two of the three keys were obviously for the car, I inserted the last one into the door and felt the tumblers roll as I twisted it. At the same moment the door eked open, lights inside came to life.

Nothing quite like a good welcome home, even if it wasn't my house.

The interior was magazine perfect. Though I knew Ryan had been in rehab care for three weeks, someone had been in to clean and placed a fresh flower arrangement on the antique table in the entry. Mail was sorted into three piles and left for the master of the house among photos of him and Hannah in sterling silver frames. Separately each of them was gorgeous, together they were unstoppable; the camera adored them. Hannah favored her dad, no question, but her eyes were all Laume—deep, piercing, almost inhuman in their beauty.

I clicked the door shut and then quickly located the alarm panel on the foyer wall. Six digits disarmed the system and then I immediately rearmed it. Leaning against the wall I took in the rest of the soaring entry, beautiful arching staircases and open living areas. Amazing. Breathtaking in the details and in the whole—no expense spared—granite, stainless, highly polished maple, nickel fixtures, leaded glass. As I moved through the house it became clear to me that it was Ryan's house—magazine covers, trophies, pennants, balls, uniform jerseys, gloves—a monument to his good looks and career in major league baseball. Poking through his master bedroom, bath, and closet I got a clear sense of his tastes in clothes (designer, tailored, high-fashion), electronics (bigger, newer, expensive) and sex (adventurous, naughty, tasty). Snooping was never my thing, but after two awkward meetings with the guy, I had to understand how he could be so creepy, so fascinating, and so unforgettable all at the same time.

The answer was not in his oversized bed, or his walk-in closet, or his four-headed shower. Each was amazing, but frankly impersonal; nothing a well-paid decorator couldn't throw together with six months and a couple hundred grand to shop.

I wondered where in the house Hannah actually lived and ventured down the hallway, back across the main living areas and into the opposite wing of the house. As I expected, that side of the house had a small gym, library, home theater and office on the ground floor. A spiral staircase at the far end led up to four different bedroom suites on the second floor off a hallway filled with more *Ryan-obilia* photos, jerseys and signed paraphernalia. At the furthest end of the hallway—as far as you could get from the main living areas and Ryan's master suite and still be living in the same damn house—I found the only room that had any personalization, and it said very clearly, *go the fuck away.*

Hannah's room.

The room was dark until I flicked on the light switch. I could tell that the decorations had started out fit for a princess, but Hannah had marked-up the walls, torn apart the closet, covered the furniture with stickers, and destroyed the carpets. A rumpled comforter on the unmade bed matched the heavy, black-out drapes, but beyond that the room made no attempt to conform to any sense of style. Hell, my bedroom was better coordinated.

How long had it been since Ryan had last seen the inside of his daughter's room? How could he know it was this way and not understand how unhappy she was? I'd lingered in the doorway for two minutes and could hear the cry for help from every scribble, stain, and sticker. The room personified her anger at being ignored by the only parent she'd ever known, the man she loved and who she desperately wanted to love her back. He'd given her everything but his love, time and attention; and I intended to make sure he figured out how to fill in those holes. They deserved to be filled in.

I turned off the light and slowly closed the completely generic door to Hannah's room, immediately glad that her room at Nancy and Mike's had been clean, cozy and inviting. With their help, I knew we could make it happen here, in this place that was supposed to be her home.

I yawned and stretched, realizing how tired I was. As I wandered the hallway back to the main living area I passed a sleek, new-fangled grandfather clock that said it was after one in the morning. I was exhausted, having been up since three. I had worked a full shift, and then dodged a bullet with Ryan only to walk right into one with Hannah. After I disappointed Brady, I'd managed to get into it with Laume even though I hadn't meant to. My telepathic conversation with Cooper had been the second brightest part of my day, because watching Hannah sing had been the best part.

And, of course, I'd ruined it. And now I was in her house, exhausted and pretty much expecting to stay for the weekend. I hated myself.

Problem was, it would be stupid, if not down-right suicidal, for me to get back into the Jag and go looking again for a cheap hotel. I put my chances of successfully finding my way back toward the city and locating a room at less than ten percent. As dumb an idea as staying overnight was, I knew it would be the smart thing to do. Cooper might even agree with me. If I still felt guilty in the morning when my hearing and voice came back I could try for a hotel again.

I wandered back toward Ryan's room in search of a ratty old t-shirt I might use for pajamas. In the back of the closet I found a stack of built-in drawers and rifled through them until I found what I knew had to be there—a stash of faded, old logo-ed t-shirts. Feeling nostalgic, I found one from the Texas Rangers and took it with me to the kitchen where I swiped a bottle of water from the fridge and a box of granola bars from the pantry.

Gnawing on a granola bar on my way up to the guest rooms, I picked the one next to Hannah's, the one decorated in teals and browns. I helped myself to a shower in the attached bathroom—odd to feel the water but not hear it pattering on my skin or dribbling down the drain—before donning Ryan's t-shirt and climbing into a bed so plush I almost checked to see if it was made of marshmallow fluff. After considering whether or not to set an alarm on my cell phone, I decided that I deserved a chance to catch up on some sleep and turned the ringer off before dropping it onto my beaded bag.

Clicking off the lights, I lay in my cocoon of D-n-D silence and drifted off to a very deep sleep.

19

I didn't wake up Saturday morning until ten o'clock—nine solid hours of sleep felt so good, as did waking up with my hearing and voice—but I had to hit the ground running, so much to take care of before seeing Hannah at her foster home for dinner. Not only did I have to bake cupcakes (and not just any cupcakes but my award-winning chocolate malted cupcakes with chocolate Swiss meringue frosting) as a huge apology to Hannah for messing up so big with her dad's car, but I desperately needed to go clothes shopping. Wearing a ripped dress was getting old; my ego couldn't take it any longer.

After ducking into Hannah's room-from-planet-pissed-off to borrow a pair of sweats and a t-shirt that was baggy-but-closer-to-actually-fitting-me, I showered, chowed down on the last granola bar from the box, chugged a glass of water and then wandered downstairs into the kitchen to see what baking staples I might find.

I understood that Ryan had been in rehab for a few weeks, but damn, there just wasn't any food in the house—cupboards bare except for a bag of dried spaghetti noodles and a jar of red sauce, fridge full of nothing. Not even flour and salt and sugar. Who lives like that? What if Hannah suddenly got the urge one night to throw together a batch of chocolate chip cookie dough and sit on the couch to watch a whole season of Jersey Shore? Damn. No wonder the state took her away.

I added the grocery store to my list of errands.

My purse and the keys to the Jag were still on the entry table where I'd left them. As I approached the Jag the word *bitch* screamed at me from its hood. The fact that it was there bothered me. The fact that it was true bothered me even more.

Laume had played coy when I challenged her about causing the damage, but I believed that she hadn't done it. After watching her grind Maria's ruby ring into dust, I had to say it felt too childish for her level of revenge. It felt like the kind of thing angry-teenager-Hannah would do, especially after seeing what she'd done to her bedroom, but she hadn't had an opportunity to get close enough to the car to maul its paint like that at the Community Center.

I couldn't bring myself to drive the Jag in the daylight. And not taking the Jag out for my errands caused problems.

I knew from doing a little research on the PC in Ryan's office that the places I wanted to go—Goodwill and the best supermarket in town for chocolate, Whole Foods—weren't within walking distance. I considered calling a cab, but my funds were limited and I really needed a new outfit more than I needed to overpay for a trip into town. I spun around searching for an answer and saw the five closed garage doors.

Surely there was an answer hiding in there. A guy like Ryan didn't have a garage like that and not fill it up with status symbols. Beautiful, fun-to-drive status symbols.

I peeked through the window of the closest door and saw a speed boat, a pair of motorcycles, another sports car that I couldn't identify in the gloom, and a you-don't-know-it's-me-inside-because-they-all-look-alike-with-tinted-windows black Cadillac SUV. Jackpot.

I found the keys to the SUV dangling from the ignition. Must be nice to have a garage—my poor Buick was currently locked-up tight in the alley behind my building, collecting dust and fingerprints and who knew what else as the desert sun faded its interior - I hoped.

A remote for the garage was clipped to the Caddy's driver's side visor so I used it to let myself out, and took off, watching the door slide closed in the rearview as I tippity-tapped my way down the cobblestone driveway in hulking anonymity. If I wasn't careful I was going to get used to living like this.

I was glad to find the SUV had a nav system. Not as nice as Brady's Audi, but it did the trick. I started at the Goodwill, taking more than an hour to find a form-fitting pair of skinny jeans and a black, button-down Oxford that could have been tailored just for me. I added a silver-studded belt, a pair of barely worn wedge heels—with black accents to match my new top—and a package of plain, black bikini panties (new, of course) and got out the door for under $16.

It pained me to go into the grocery store in Hannah's borrowed sweatpants and tee when I had a perfectly-good, perfectly-flattering outfit hanging in the SUV. But my day was running short, and I had to get back to Ryan's place and start baking his little girl the best apology she'd ever gotten, so I slummed it into the high-end grocer. Mostly no one cared what I looked like—except for me as I cruised through the produce section and caught my reflection in the mirror behind the lettuce. I really needed to get my shit together.

Because I had to buy all of the staples and a cardboard carrier to get the finished product across town, my trip to the store for cupcake fixings cost more than my new outfit, go figure. My wallet was getting skinny, just $145 and an uncashed paycheck, but I got everything I needed, including a decorating bag to give my frosting that professional touch. With two and a half hours to bake and clean up, I hightailed it out to the parking garage and then followed the navigator's instructions to take the SUV back home where I parked it in the driveway.

Ryan's expansive kitchen was a baker's wet dream. Not only did it have acres of solid granite countertops, he had every tool, toy and temptation—though he had no food. Sadly my chocolate cupcake recipe only called for a double-boiler, a stand mixer, some muffin tins, a couple of bowls and various measuring utensils so I didn't have reason to play with the butane torch or the titanium springform pans or the wood-fired pizza oven.

I cranked the stereo to keep me company as I worked. It wasn't Rockabilly, of course, but Ryan's satellite system had a 50s channel and that was good enough for me; they played Elvis.

My cakes baked perfectly in an oven nicer than the one in my boutique bakery back in Austin and I set them to cool on chromed wire racks while the egg-whites got-busy with the sugar and the butter in the mixer for frosting. The scent of chocolate filled the house and soothed my soul. More melted chocolate went into the mixer where the frosting whipped at high speed into cloud-like fluff—apology perfection, I hoped. I finished swirling it onto the tops of those little cakey bites of heaven just in time to go upstairs and change into my new outfit and head out the door to go to Beaverton.

Because I could not risk Hannah seeing me in another one of her father's cars, I picked the Caddy again and only drove it as far as the nearest MAX station and then hopped on the train for the rest of the 20-minute ride to Mike and Nancy's house. I walked from that familiar transit station a few blocks along the sunny sidewalk to the Carter's townhouse.

As I walked I tried-out my apology in my head. *I'm so sorry, Hannah. If I'd known what that car meant to you I'd never have accepted the keys. It was wrong, selfish of me.* My gut knotted-up as I imagined Hannah's lingering anger and I kicked myself for being so desperate that I was still being selfish. I promised myself she wouldn't find out I crashed at her house for the weekend. Ever.

I reached Mike and Nancy's door at ten after four and was welcomed by the rich smell of simmering tomato sauce and the sound of singing. Hannah's singing. It made my heart soar with hope because it seemed impossible that an angry teenager could possibly make such beautiful music.

And Hannah wasn't singing alone. I heard three or four other voices harmonizing with her, and not the voices of adults or little children. It sounded like teenagers, and that puzzled me. As far as I knew, Hannah was the only teen living in the townhouse.

I knocked on the door and waited, but no one answered. My arm was getting sore from holding the cupcakes so when I saw there was no longer a sign on the door about Hannah and her migraines I rang the bell. A little boy about five years old answered. He had the same green eyes as Nancy. One of her biological kids, then.

He stared up at me with those eyes open wide. "What's the password?" he challenged.

I knelt down. "Chocolate cupcakes for dessert, if you let me in," I said and lifted the lid on my cardboard carrier so he could see I was telling the truth.

"Mommy!" the little boy yelled in my face and then turned to run upstairs, leaving the door standing wide open. "Mommy, the lady with the chocolate cake-cups is here."

I let myself in, closed the door, and left my shoes in the entryway before climbing the stairs into the Carter's living room. The space was crazier than I remembered it from my first visit. Both TVs were on. The big one displayed a rated-E-for-Everyone video game with cartoony characters and even more cartoony music; the smaller one played the football game, with the sound turned down. Mike crouched on the floor with his two young boys and a little Asian girl, who must be their other foster kid, waving his arms to make the characters on the big TV shape bubbles.

"Hi, Bailey," Mike said, not looking away from the screen. "Sorry, can't talk; have to sculpt some clouds into circus animals before they evaporate."

The kids looked at me, though. I waved at them because I had no idea what their names were.

"Bailey, you any good with a grinder?" Nancy's voice yelled at me from around the corner in the kitchen. "If you are, I could use some help. My prep cook deserted me for her new career as a rock star."

I followed the smell of tomatoes, basil, and garlic into the kitchen to find Nancy elbow deep in raw meat. She was feeding cut-up pork into a hand-cranked sausage grinder clamped to the counter and trying to manage the casing to catch the ground meat coming out while she nudged at the crank with and elbow to keep the process moving.

"I'll stuff 'em, you catch 'em?" she asked.

I set the cupcakes down and rescued the sausage that was about to escape the counter and dive onto the floor. "Sure."

"Thanks," Nancy smiled. "I get these crazy ideas sometimes." She nodded at the meat grinder, hands slick with fat from her project. "It always looks easier on TV."

I washed my hands so I could really help. "Takes a little practice." I took over where Nancy was holding the casing at the output spout and nodded for her to keep feeding and grinding as I corralled the results into the casing, stopping to twist it into five-inch sections every 30 seconds or so.

"You do that like a professional."

"My father didn't believe in paying a butcher," I said, but let my comment trail off, not really wanting to think about father-daughter kitchen-time. In my house that usually resulted in a shouting match and dinner that smelled amazing but nobody was in the mood to eat.

"Where's Hannah?" I asked, changing the subject.

"They're holed-up in her room, rehearsing." She shoved another handful of pork chunks into the grinder and kept cranking. The cartoon music from the other room changed its tune.

"They?"

"Those four kids she sang with at the end of the song last night." Nancy stopped and smiled in a way that said her National-bank-of-karma-account-balance was getting a positive hit on the scale of my credit card balances. "After they hit it off so well yesterday, I told Hannah to call the group home where they live and invite them all over to spend the day with us—

one of the advantages of being a state-approved foster home. The five of them have been holed-up trying out songs since ten o'clock this morning."

"The skinny Asian guy with the amazing head of hair is Noah. His buddy is Jacob, don't-call-me-Jake—kid's been in the system a long time, earned himself an attitude. The girl with the glasses is Danni and the tiny one with the braces on her teeth is ML, short for Emmaline. Great name, right?"

I nodded. We were both quiet as we tried to listen to their singing through the walls. I couldn't make out any of the lyrics, but the vibe I got gave me happy tickles up my spine.

"Sounds good," I said. "Really good."

"They have a private concert planned after dinner. Cupcakes and song on the balcony, the neighbors will be so jealous." Nancy joked. "It's the happiest I've seen her since she got here. Maybe she can dodge getting a headache today."

Nancy shoveled the last bits of cubed meat into the grinder, cranking it through the blades, and I twisted off the last sausage, a little one that reminded me of the tuning pegs on JoJo's stand-up bass.

"You think it's a good time for me to go in and apologize?" I asked as Nancy and I stood side-by-side at the sink washing the bits of meat from our hands.

"You can try," Nancy said as she flicked the water from her hands and grabbed a towel. "She's been bottling it up, not talking to Mike and me."

That did not sound good. I remembered being an angry teenager; I lived most of my life that way.

Crap.

I frowned as I tried to figure out how to make my apology better.

"I have to try." I dried my hands. "Wish me luck."

She did and started hustling sausages from the counter onto a cast iron griddle as I headed toward Hannah's room. I waited outside in the hall, listening, until I heard their harmony stumble and they broke into laughter. I knocked.

"Come in," Hannah's voice said from behind the closed door.

I opened it, but didn't breach the threshold. That felt too pushy for the role of the apologizer.

Hannah sat at the foot of her bed, ML next to her on the right and Noah on her left, looking at something on a laptop computer. The other two kids, Jacob and Danni, sat on the floor, completing a tight circle, girl-boy-girl-boy-girl. I got sense of déjà vu and my mind flashed back to my phamily trying to get comfortable as they slept in our dinky-ass lifeboat the night Laume fell out of the sky. My fingers went up to my lips to prevent a gasp from coming out.

The kids looked up at me simultaneously. Hannah had a smile on her face at first, the computer's pale light making her teeth shine ghostly blue, but she frowned as soon as she recognized me. "Not interested." She looked away, but not back at the computer, away toward the corner of the room.

The others had also started off smiling at me, but one-by-one their faces hardened in response to the tone in Hannah's voice. None of *them* looked away. Tough kids, protective of Hannah already. They were going to be a tough crowd.

"Hannah, please, I came here to apologize. I'm still your CASA."

"That's your CASA?" Jacob asked from his spot on the floor and then he whistled. "My CASA is a fifty year-old hag with a bad perm and twelve cats." He turned to look at Hannah. "Want to trade?"

Hannah glanced at me for a fraction of a second. "You can have her. She's useless. Worse than useless." Like I was just a baseball card for some has-been, ball player...like her dad.

"Be reasonable, Hannah," I said. "I couldn't have known about the car." I stepped into the room. "If you give me another chance I'll make it right. I promise."

That was the wrong thing to say, I knew it in an instant when all five of them grunted at me in disgust at the same time. Three of them even rolled their eyes. A really tough crowd. But they were right.

I needed to start thinking before I opened my damn mouth. Promises meant less than nothing to kids who'd spent their whole childhoods listening as false-regret, empty-sentiment, and bold-faced-lies dripped from the mouths of people who were supposed to look out for them. I'd given Hannah absolutely no reason to believe anything I said. I was being a hypocrite, and all of them had called me on it.

I turned around so they couldn't see my face and balled my hands up until my nails bit into my palms. I wanted to leave, wished I could walk out, close the door, and then knock again, starting fresh. I could do better. I knew where these kids were vulnerable, why they didn't trust anyone, how they saw everyone over the age of eighteen as an enemy. I should be able to talk to them, but my mouth kept screwing it up. "Elvis help me. This is so fucked up. How am I going to fix this?"

"What?"

I turned back around. Hannah's eyebrows were raised and her forehead wrinkled. "What did you say?"

I saw a teeny-tiny crack in her angry-teenager mask. It was small, and already starting to seal back up as I watched her forehead smooth back into apathy, so I jumped on it.

"I don't blame you for doubting me," I said. "I fucked up, big time. If I were you I'd say the same thing."

I wished I'd had a camera to capture the look on those five young faces. It was like they'd never heard an adult admit to being wrong before.

Taking advantage of their surprise, I sat down on the floor with them. Not forcing myself into their circle, keeping back a bit, but doing my best to be on their level. "Yeah, you heard me. I was wrong. Big deal."

"Where's my dad's car?" Hannah challenged me, nose turned toward the window.

"It's not out there, I took it back." My guilty conscience treated me to goosebumps for not explaining that his SUV was as the train station and I'd slept and cooked at her house. I shook it off.

She finally looked at me.

"I know you don't care, and you shouldn't have to care, but this has been the worst ten days of my life," I said. "When somebody offered me a shortcut I took it. Can you give me a break? Please?"

"What's wrong?" asked Danni, the girl who sat on the floor next to me.

I was touched that she would ask, but I had to think for a second about how to describe my situation without sounding daffier than a lady with a cat problem. I also didn't want to give them enough information that they could use their savvy technology skills and dig up the fact that the world thought I was still lost at sea. "Let's just say I'm a long way from my home and my phamily, I have a job I hate and a guy I'm starting to fall for even though I don't want to. And I made a deal that I'm not sure I'm going to be able swing."

"What's your family like?" Danni asked.

I wasn't surprised that she was curious about my phamily.

"We're not your traditional family; none of us is actually related. They're more like the best friends I've ever had. We met in the Texas Loony Bin for teenagers when I was about your age." I went on to describe Maria and JoJo and Cooper and Paulo.

"What'd you do?" Hannah interrupted me. "How come you got stuck in the hospital?"

"I was really angry when I was a kid. I never knew my mom," I nodded toward Hannah so she'd get the commonality. "Like I said before, my father's a big-shot chef and he was never-ever around. Most of the time the closest thing I had to adult supervision was our housekeeper, and she had four kids of her own to worry about."

"Did you get in trouble?" Noah asked.

I wanted to be honest with Hannah and her new buds about the trouble I'd gotten into, not to prove I was cool, but to try to earn Hannah's trust. But it didn't seem smart to confess drinking, drugs, and malicious mischief to a bunch of impressionable kids. "Let's just say I have an arrest record, and leave it at that."

"But they don't put you in the hospital for getting arrested, do they?" ML asked.

I took a deep breath. "No. That happened because I tried to commit suicide."

I hadn't talked with anyone about my attempt in a long time and I never thought I'd be talking about it with a bunch of foster kids I'd just met. Their eyes were all on me and I knew these were the dark places their lives had visited from time to time. I didn't want to glorify what I'd done, but I didn't want to hide it either. I looked toward Hannah and saw that she was leaning forward, listening intently, and I hoped that if I shared with her she'd understand me a little better and accept my apology.

"I was angry, alone, scared—all the time. I hurt," my hands instinctively came up to press against my chest, "all the time. I didn't really have any friends, just people who hung around to mooch off me and my father. School was impossible for me, my grades always sucked; I was always in trouble—fights, boys, skipping class. I think I spent all of seventh- and eighth-grade being completely confused about everything. And nobody was ever around to listen to me, to help."

I stopped talking and realized how hard and fast my heart was beating. The cold ball of loneliness grew frostier as I remembered how empty my life had been before the hospital.

The kids' mouths hung open as they stared at me, except for Jacob's. He looked like he was going to grind his own teeth flat. "How'd you do it? Pills? Cut your wrists?" he asked.

Nancy said he'd been in the system a long time and I could see that there wasn't much room in his heart for other people's troubles...too crowded already. He'd probably heard stories like mine from every kid that ever moved through his group home. I shuddered to think of how crappy it must be, feeling like you've been warehoused. Racked, stacked, and packed until you aged out of the system and no one had a legal obligation to care what happened to you anymore.

More for Jacob than the others I decided not to go into the details. "Doesn't matter what I did. Not really. What matters was finally getting someone to pay attention to me. I got some help and got myself straightened out."

"Must be nice," Hannah said.

Her poor-me routine was starting to get old. Or maybe all that tripping down the halls of my memory made me see her as if she were a JoJo or a Maria. Whatever it was, I suddenly remembered what it felt like to be an angry teenager, and I remembered how my counselors at the hospital finally got through to me.

They stopped pitying me.

They stopped buying into my bullshit sob-story.

They told me I could be a victim for the rest of my life or I could grow-up and help myself. It took six weeks for that message to start to sink in, but it finally did and I grew stronger for it.

I looked right at Hannah and waited until she looked back at me to speak. "Okay, I get it. Your life sucks."

I looked at all of them. "All your lives suck. But ten minutes ago, you were all laughing and you'd forgotten all about the suckage. You made something amazing. Something wonderful. Isn't that better than getting all wrapped up around the axle about things you can't control?

"In a way you're lucky, you five are already learning something that most people don't learn until they're 24 or 25 years-old, the only way to be happy is to make your life what you need and want. Not that you can do that right now—because you aren't allowed to make those choices yet—but by the time the world is ready to let you, you'll hit the ground running and be miles ahead when everyone else finally gets a clue."

I looked back to Hannah. "You can be angry at me, you can fight against me, you can make my life a living hell. If that makes you feel better, fine. But I won't put up with you acting like a five year-old, not any more.

"I apologized, twice. Accept it so we can move on. I'm here to get you back home. The only way I can do that is by convincing a judge your family is getting straightened out.

Your dad is doing his part—he hates it, but he's getting clean for you. Mike and Nancy are doing their best for you. I screwed up, and I'm sorry. I know better now, and I will make better choices. You can't ask more than that."

Hannah thought about what I said for a minute, head bent over her lap, hair falling into her face. For the first time I wished we'd done this just the two of us because I wanted her to feel free to say whatever was on her mind, but having allies in the room for her had also been good.

I could see the moment when Hannah finally let go of being pissed-off at me, her shoulders dropped a little and she reached up to pull her long hair back from her face as she looked up at me. "Dad hates rehab?" she asked.

"But he's making progress. His counselor said he's finally participating in group sessions and taking things seriously."

"And that's what you're going to tell the judge?"

"Yup. And I'm going to tell him that you shouldn't have to take piano lessons or go to soccer. I'm also going to ask him to make sure you guys have practice time together at least twice a week."

"Really?" ML asked at the same time Noah asked, "Why?"

"There's no money for stuff like that," Jacob said as if it were something he'd been told a hundred times, or maybe a thousand.

"You doubt me?" I asked Jacob and then I smiled at Hannah, thinking about Nancy's comment that Hannah had had such a good day. "I'll just say it's medically necessary. Call it migraine prevention."

I expected Hannah would like that, maybe even smile at me. But she didn't. Her face went flat, her eyes tried to meet mine but couldn't, and the corners of her mouth couldn't decide whether to turn upwards or down. My instincts screamed in my head that she looked guilty.

But why? Guilty of what?

20

I never did figure out why Hannah got that incredibly guilty look on her face when I mentioned my plan to ask for mandatory visits with her new friends by calling them "medically necessary." But I was glad that she tried to live up to her decision to accept my apology. She stopped scowling, mostly, only rolled her eyes at me twice, and her tone of voice evolved almost all the way to pleasant. Pretty amazing, for a teenager who'd been shit on all her life.

Nancy and I finished prepping dinner and then eleven of us sat around a pair of patio tables on the balcony and enjoyed one of those family dinners that every kid ought to have on a regular basis. Or maybe I just regretted they weren't a part of my formative years. Grounding. Connecting. Humbling. Mike told tall tales about camping trips among the towering trees of the Coast Range, exaggerating every detail, I was sure. Nancy corrected him, and then exaggerated more. The young-uns gasped at the scary parts and laughed riotously at the funny parts—egging Mike on, daring Nancy to go bigger or go do the dishes.

The teenagers had better manners than I expected—instead of bundling into a small group and chattering amongst themselves they integrated with Mike and Nancy's family. ML helped their youngest boy, Tony, learn to twirl spaghetti on a fork and Jacob got into a slurping contest with Tony's older brother, Mikey Jr., until they both had faces covered by tomato sauce whip tracks. My job was to watch and listen, and I did. This was a good place for Hannah, as good as any, until Ryan got his shit together.

Best of all, Hannah showed no signs of a getting a headache.

During the dessert course, the kids sang us a gorgeous song called *She Will Be Loved* about a girl with a broken smile, and it just about broke my heart. ML laid down the beat, Danni and Noah be-bopped behind Hannah while Jacob harmonized with her to build emphasis. I was so impressed with how easily Hannah moved into the perfect pitch—yesterday's sultry had become today's haunting soulfulness—and loved how her joy for singing shone on her face.

We clapped and hooted when they finished the song, and then got overrun by the sound of applause from others listening on neighboring balconies and standing below on the grassy square between the buildings. Danni blushed and ducked into the corner. Jacob played the fool: grand bows and throwing peace signs toward the crowd, such as it was. Noah gave Hannah a high-five, very old school, and ML couldn't help but hug each of them. For a minute I forgot how much I missed my phamily and the cold loneliness in my chest slipped away leaving a welcome sense of peace.

Once again I considered how much better Hannah's life was here in her foster home than living in a giant house where nobody gave a shit what she did with her time, or her room. Sure, the Clarks didn't have the interest, connections, or vision to nurture Hannah's amazing singing talent, but would it be so bad for her to grow up like this and attempt to be just a well-rounded kid rather than a superstar?

A sprawling mansion with a 5-car garage is nice, but doesn't a well-taken-care-of townhouse in the suburbs keep the rain off and the cold out just as well?

If Laume had not been holding my phamily hostage I might have made an argument in my report for keeping Hannah with the Clark family until she hit her eighteenth birthday. But my phamily was hostage, we had a deal—as much as I hated it—and I had to get Hannah home to get them back.

Ryan was making strides in rehab, and I would do my best to make sure that when he proved himself sober he would provide more than just a platform from which Hannah's talent could rocket into stardom. He would also provide those dull things in life like warmth and protection and a weekly dinner with friends and family.

At seven o'clock I said my goodbyes, grabbed three cupcakes from the leftovers, and left Mike and Nancy's as Nancy herded Hannah's buddies into the minivan for the ride back to their group home. I noticed, but wasn't surprised, to see Hannah's smile slip away when her friends left like clouds hiding the sun. The five of them had clicked, even in such a short time, and I was grateful for their place in her life while everything else was so up-in-the-air.

As I made my way on foot and by train back to Ryan's SUV at the train station I thought about what I'd write in my report for the judge. Ryan's progress in rehab, check. Hannah's stable situation—except, of course, I had to note the headaches—and her growing bond with new, not-troublemaker friends, check. To make Laume happy I'd also include a strong suggestion that Hannah and Ryan have mandatory visitation a couple of times a week. Getting them in the same room, maybe even with a counselor, would be a great first step to getting them back into the same house. And the sooner that happened, the better, because the cold ball of loneliness in my chest had come back with a vengeance.

I was glad my next stop was at Brady's apartment. I couldn't imagine being alone right then; those familiar inner hurts had bubbled too close to the surface from talking to the kids.

The closest parking spot I could find to Brady's was two blocks away. I ignored the meter, grabbed the cupcakes, and hustled to Brady's building. He buzzed me up right away, and the difference between the reception he gave me (a sensual full body hug and a quick, but deep, kiss) was the exact opposite of Chester's reaction—crossed arms, lowered brow, pouty bottom lip—until I showed him the cupcakes.

The little guy was interested in the treats like a teenager with a new smart-phone. He ended up wearing about a quarter of the frosting while the rest of it went down his gullet in sixty seconds flat. Brady had set us up at the kitchen table for this, and Chester's beady brown eyes zeroed in along the length of shining glass to the untouched cupcake in front of me as Brady oohed-and-ahhed his way through the frosting.

"Did you want some of mine?" I asked Chester as I peeled the wrapper off my cupcake and split it into two halves with my fingers, trying to keep the frosting from sliding off onto the table.

"Daddy, can I?" he asked with big eyes.

Brady acted truly surprised at his son's manners. "I don't know," he said. "You've had a whole one already and Bailey hasn't had any. That doesn't seem fair."

I smiled and leaned toward Chester as though I was sharing a secret. "Don't tell your dad, but already I had two of them."

"See Daddy, she had *two* already." Chester's eyes flicked back and forth between the cupcake and his dad until Brady finally gave in. I gave the little guy the choice of halves, he took the big one, and we ate them at the same time, at a more leisurely pace.

"Did you make these?" he asked me with his mouth full.

I swallowed. "Sure did."

"Can you teach my mommy how to make them? They're good."

I didn't know whether to laugh, snort, or dodge.

Brady saved me. "Chester, your mom makes great cupcakes. She doesn't need anyone to teach her how to bake."

I liked that he stuck up for Chester's mystery mom, even though they weren't together. It said as much about him as it did about her.

"But these are better," he whined.

"That's because Bailey is a pastry chef. She went to school and does this for her job. Your mom is a really great hair dresser, right?"

"You can go to school for making cupcakes?" Chester asked. It was as if he had never considered that school could be something fun. "Will they teach me in kindergarten?"

"Later, probably," I said.

"Will you teach me?" he asked.

"Okay," I said. "But on two conditions."

Brady watched our back-and-forth with an amused smile.

"What's a con-mis-shun?" Chester stumbled over the big word.

"Condition," Brady said. "It's like a rule, or a trade-off."

Chester nodded at me enthusiastically. I suddenly thought of Laume and the way she bullied me into our bargain and wondered if she thought she was smarter than me as much as I thought I was smarter than Chester.

"Condition one: you must never tell anyone my recipe, it's a secret."

Chester crossed his heart, even though it was over his left shoulder. I figured that would still count.

"Second, we have got to get you a cool nick-name," I said. "Chef Chester would never do."

"Mommy calls me Boo-boo."

"Chef Boo-boo." Brady snickered. "Nope, wouldn't eat anything he cooked."

"Nah. It's got to be something really cool." I pretended to think. "Got it. How about Chef Sheepdog?"

Brady laughed at my joke, but Chester wrinkled his nose.

"Chef Half-pint?"

Wrinkled nose with vigorous head shake.

"Chef Mini-me?"

That got me a full-bore groan.

"How about Chef-ster?"

"Chef-ster!" he yelled and then wiggled out of his chair and ran around the apartment hollering it. "I am Chef-ster! I make cupcakes!"

"Okay, okay," Brady yelled after a few minutes and corralled his sugar-fueled son. "But not tonight. Tonight you're Good-Boy Chester who goes to bed. It's getting late. Go get ready to brush your teeth and I'll read you a story before bed."

"No," the little guy shouted and wriggled loose from his dad. I expected him to run from the room so his dad would chase him down, but as he landed on his feet he stopped and looked at me. "I want Bailey to read me a story."

Goodness Graceland. A couple of cupcakes and a new nickname and suddenly the kid was my biggest fan. He ran over to me and threw his upper body into my lap. I pulled my hands out of the way, not sure what I was supposed to do with them. When he looked up—brown eyes peering through those shaggy bangs—I saw an uncanny resemblance to a sheepdog. Though I couldn't actually say I liked the little guy, it was getting awfully hard to ignore how cute he was.

I was afraid to look up at Brady's face, worried he would be unhappy that I'd bribed his kid into liking me. But when I did finally meet Brady's gaze, I saw a happy man. He raised his hands in surrender. "Fine by me. Just watch out for the one with the monkey on the cover...he'll make you read that one twice."

Chester reached up and grabbed my hand, nearly pulling me out of my chair in his frenzy to get ready for bed. I let Daddy manage the tooth brushing, changing into PJs, and washing of the face—not ready to get that cozy with the little guy just yet.

After two stories, a short glass of water, and more whining than I thought could come out of three kids his age, Chester's eyes finally started to go droopy and Brady and I left him wriggling around in a sea of blankets to sing himself to sleep.

Brady clicked the bedroom door closed behind me as I led the way toward the living room. He surprised me by grabbing my arm and spinning me around. The way he lunged forward to kiss me brought out an instinct to pull away that confused the hell out him. I knew immediately that it was because of Ryan Williams' move the day before, and how that had turned out.

"Did I do something wrong?"

I took a deep breath. "Sorry. Just a little shell shocked."

"Did someone hurt you?"

Now that was a question with a complicated answer.

I could explain about Hannah's dad, but I didn't know how Brady would take to knowing about my involvement with their family, or that I'd been kissing someone else while the two of us were in the feeling-each-other-out stage of our relationship. I did not want Brady to know that I had been making comparisons, even though I'd been on the receiving end, not the seeking-out end of those kisses. In my experience the male ego didn't handle that kind of thing well, and it would take too long to explain the reality, because I didn't fully understand how it had happened myself.

I could use Brady's open-ended question as an opening to explain more about my past and my father. I guess my reminiscing with Hannah and her friends that afternoon had made me nostalgic, and the loneliness that swept in afterwards had given that nostalgia a dark edge. But I'd had such a good day, a positive day, that I didn't want to let any of that out.

I decided to keep it to myself. "No. Nothing like that. I'm sorry, you just surprised me."

"Is this better?" Brady asked as he slowly moved in for a kiss. It started lips on lips and added a body part at a time, starting with his stubby chin, until he had me gently but solidly up against the wall. The warmth of him against the whole length of my body soothed me. Tasting my chocolate cake and frosting on his tongue gave me a foolish rush of pride. He really liked my cupcakes, almost as much as his hands enjoyed my ass.

Once I heard a line in a movie; something about a long, deep, wet kiss that lasted for three days. In reality, that would probably not be as romantic as it sounded—like covering a lover in honey and licking it off from head to toe, that would be too much, too sticky—but that was how my kiss with Brady unfolded like a little taste of heaven.

My breath came harder as my heart pounded faster. I could tell where the kiss was eventually headed: nekkid, sweaty bodies slapping together on the living room floor as we chased each other to orgasm. I wanted it as badly as Brady did, really I did. But I couldn't do it. Even though Chester and I had come to some kind of fragile agreement for sharing his precious daddy, I still didn't feel right having sex with him in the apartment.

Achingly, I broke off the kiss.

Brady's head fell toward his chest. He was so hot and bothered he was panting, too.

"Sorry."

"Damnit, Bailey," he said quietly as he turned away from me and stomped off toward the kitchen where I heard the fridge door open and a short hiss followed by the clinking of a bottle top in the sink.

I followed him and saw him already half finished with a bottle of beer. I leaned against the wall and waited. He stopped chugging and leaned against the counter, beer bottle clinking against the laminate. He opened his mouth a couple of times before anything actually came out.

"I just don't get you."

I held my hands out to my sides as if to say, *this is me, what you see is what you get.*

"We hit it off so well on the plane. And the way you kiss me." He paused to take another drink. "When you're not around, I can't stop thinking about you. When you're here I can't stop thinking about you naked."

I wanted to take that as a compliment, but it obviously caused him pain. I'd had guys get attached this way before. Something I thought was meaningless physical attraction gave some guys the impressions I wanted them to be possessive and start talking about the future—not good. But with Brady it was different. It hadn't just been sex. And I wanted to talk about the future, someday, but not just then, not like this. I didn't know how to tell him.

"I want this," I said.

"I want it, too. But you're so closed off, so damn private. Just when I think you're going to open up to me, you get that look in your beautiful eyes."

Look? What look? I had no idea what the hell he was talking about. "I do not."

"Yeah, that's what I thought." Brady drained the rest of his beer and set the bottle next to the sink.

The apartment got very quiet and the sense that I was not welcome oozed toward me out of the kitchen.

"I think I should go."

Brady nodded and remained leaning against the counter.

I walked over to the table and grabbed my beaded bag and then offered a smile across the counter before walking to the door.

I'd just gotten the door open when he spoke from behind me. "Bailey, wait." He walked across the room and stood four feet away, weight shifting from foot to foot, hands uneasy by his side.

"Don't go. I want you to stay."

I wondered what it had cost him to say that.

"But, Chester..."

"I get it." He raised his hands and then clasped them behind his back. "I'll keep my hands to myself. Just stay, please."

The look on his face just about ripped my heart out of my chest. He wanted me. And it wasn't like the way Ryan Williams wanted me. Brady wanted all of me, not just my body. Given how I'd grown up, it was the kind of thing I dreamed of, the answer to a million wishes.

Brady stepped closer and reached out to me with both hands. "I think I'm falling in love with you."

Elvis help me.

It felt real.

And it scared the shit out of me.

If Chester wasn't falling asleep in the big bed in the other room I would have caved in, buckled under, given myself over to my need for Brady to love me and make love to me. After all the crap that had happened in the last week I knew I could lose myself in the joy of sharing sex with him, just climb into bed and forget the world until we were satisfied, or until we ate through every last crumb of food in the house and he was at risk of losing his job because he kept calling in sick.

But hiding from the world would not make it go away.

I was still thousands of miles from home.

My phamily would still be held hostage by a Faery.

Hannah would still be in foster care.

Ryan Williams would still have to complete rehab.

I still had a report to write for the judge.

And Brady's cute little boy was not going anywhere. Even after he went back to his mom's house, he was still going to be Brady's son.

I needed some time to think, to work it all out.

There were so many things to say that the words got all caught up in my throat. Brady's face looked so expectant, and he deserved an answer. He'd gone out on a limb to tell me how he felt about me, that he might be in love with me, and even though I wasn't sure I loved him, yet, I liked him enough that I needed to give him an answer of some kind.

I launched myself at him and threw my arms around him, burying my face in his neck. I held on tight while my brain wrestled with what to say.

Give in?

Get out?

Hide?

Take the plunge?

Run?

Stay?

I inhaled Brady's masculine scent as I held him—warm, musky, minty—and somewhere between the second and third breath I figured out that I was so frightened by his confession of love because I was falling for him, too.

I pushed myself up onto my tip-toes and whispered in his ear, "I've never said this before..."

I swallowed. And swallowed again to get the fear out of my throat.

"...I think I might love you, too."

Brady's arms wrapped around my waist and he lifted me off my feet and rocked me in his arms. It was a good thing, too, because I felt too shaky to stand on my own.

"I thought you were going to run," he said into my hair.

He finally set me down and I looked into his eyes, the depth of our connection was deeper than anything I'd ever had before, it was like a taut rubber band that ran all the way down to my belly button.

"I almost did," I admitted.

"So you'll stay?"

I released my arms from around his neck and grasped his hands. "That would not be smart. I really should go."

"Fuck smart. Stay." His smile fell away.

"I know." I chased Brady's sightline as he tried to look away from me. "But it's not just me and you here. You have responsibilities. I have responsibilities. I don't want this to blow up in our faces because we acted like a couple of horny teenagers."

He tried to turn away from me but I held onto his hands until he stopped avoiding me and could think about what I said for a moment, to know I was right. When he stopped straining against me, and my ideas, I released his hands.

"I am not running away from you." I picked up my bag from the floor where I'd dropped it. "I'm asking you to wait. Just until tomorrow. Chester won't be here, and I'll have gotten some things taken care of so I can really be here. Think of it as foreplay." I smiled at him.

"Really long foreplay. Unbearably long." He scowled, but a smile hid under it.

Neither of us said *I love you* before we kissed goodnight, or after, but I was thinking it and the warmth of sharing that kept me smiling all the way back to Ryan Williams' guest room. My only real regret was that I hadn't thought to ask to borrow one of Brady's t-shirts so I wound-up sleeping in Ryan's Texas Rangers tee again.

I fell asleep fantasizing about Brady.

21

I woke to feel the warmth of the late morning sun on the side of my face. But it wasn't the light of day, or the purring sound of lawnmowers nearby that pulled me out of slumber, it was a passionate kiss from a man with a stubbly chin and minty-fresh breath. At first I thought I was kissing Brady, but then I remembered I hadn't slept over at his apartment even though we'd shared I-love-you's because of Chester (and besides, Brady didn't have a lawn to mow, he lived in a downtown high-rise). I snapped my eyes open to find Ryan Williams' tanned face and closed eyelids too close to pull into focus, kissing me for all he was worth.

Groggy and still half asleep my brain reminded me I was in the guest room of his house and then scrambled to figure how the hell he was there, too, and why I was letting him kiss me. He was supposed to be in rehab not playing creepy, scary, wake-me-up-out-of-a-dead-sleep with a passionate kiss.

I twisted my face away and he opened his eyes and stared deep into mine as he dropped the weight of his body onto me in a full-body tackle. Leaning on his left elbow to free his right hand, he smoothed the hair away from my face and laid it across the pillow with a chilling sense of possessiveness. "I knew you'd be here, but I thought I'd find you in *my* bed."

"What the hell are you doing?" I asked him. "How did you get out of rehab?"

"I take it back," he said, completely ignoring my questions and concentrating on my hair. "Keep the blonde. It's perfect. You're perfect."

He continued to study me with eyes that darted around too quickly. I could tell he was Jonesing, an addict chasing a high. And I was in the wrong place at the worst possible time.

The asshole tried to kiss me again and I bit his lip.

"That's my dirty girl," he whispered in my ear as he pressed down on my whole body again. "You always knew how to make it hurt so good. I've missed you. I couldn't stop thinking about you. I need to be inside you again."

Again? We'd never been together that way. He was still under some delusion that I was Laume. I'd been sleeping with my arms over the covers so I wriggled them loose and wedged my hands under his shoulders to push him off of me. "Get off."

He worked hard to stay on top of me, and his strength gave him an undeniable advantage. My force of will and increasing fear were all I had to stop him. And they weren't enough against an athlete as big as Ryan.

I slapped him across the cheek to get his attention.

He pulled back, starting to figure out that I wasn't playing with him. "Baby, don't be that way. We're almost there."

"I am not who you think I am."

"I know who you are inside." He pushed himself up to his knees, straddling me across the hips and burying me in the soft bed. "How can you not know who you are? Did something awful happen to you? Is that why you had to leave me, why you went away?"

He was absolutely convinced I was Laume. I struggled to get out from under him, but his weight trapped me against the mattress.

Ryan reached out and touched my face with eerily tender fingertips. "You came back to me. That's all I care about. Just trust me. Let me remind you of how good we were together. This time you'll want to stay."

My continued struggling didn't buy me anything beyond tangled blankets and a face full of my own hair. Ryan corralled my thrashing arms, bending them against my body and pinning them at the wrist to the bed. His face hovered over mine. I stopped struggling to save myself some bruises.

He stared deep into my eyes. "I have to make you remember."

In all my life, in all my one-night-stands, back-room-trysts, love affairs and friendships, I had never been so afraid of a man. Not since my father, when I was a teenager and had pushed him a step too far. The look in Ryan's eyes was like that look in my father's eyes, that all-consuming need to control me, to impress his will over mine, to make me into that thing he needed to feel good about himself and right with the world.

Ryan Williams was going to rape me. Whatever twisted logic he used to back it up, the end result was going to be his dick in my body, thrusting until he broke me and then claimed me with the gush of his semen.

Fear drove shivers through my body. Flooding cold started from that ball in my chest and engulfed me. I'd known women who'd been raped and I never thought I'd get caught in that situation, this situation. So damn helpless.

I thrashed with renewed strength born from panic, but it wasn't enough. Ryan lowered his full body weight onto me again. His muscular chest crushed my breasts, pinching them brutally, and prevented me from drawing enough breath to scream.

He took advantage of my open mouth to kiss me roughly and invade me with his tongue, no longer gentle the way it had been when he woke me. Instead it probed deep into my mouth until it pinned my tongue against my teeth.

On instinct, I pulled my tongue back and bit down forcing Ryan to pull away to avoid real injury.

I yelled, "No. Stop."

He let go of one wrist long enough to slap me across the face. "Stop fighting me."

The slap got the effect he wanted. I couldn't deny that I was physically outmatched and the more I fought, the worse it would be for me. Avoiding pain is a powerful motivator. Besides, I could tell by Ryan's stiffening bulge pressing into my pelvis that my fighting back was only turning him on. He was getting off on my fear and pain. I was trapped in his gigantic house, too far from the nearest neighbors to hope they'd hear my pathetic screams, unable to get to the window and signal for help from the people outside in the yard running the lawn mowers I'd heard.

Elvis help me. This was as shitty a situation as I'd ever been in.

My thoughts zoomed off to Brady. I needed to reach my phone and call him to come and save my ass. It wasn't a fair thing, ditching a guy after he just said *I love you* and then asking him to save me from being raped the next morning, but I knew he was that kind of guy. He might be too late to stop Ryan, but I knew he'd come if I called.

As Ryan's mouth came down on mine again for another crushing kiss, I used his shifting weight to push us both toward the edge of the bed, nearer where my bag lay on the floor.

"We're not done yet," Ryan said as he pulled me back to the center of the bed and pressed his cheek to mine, pinning my head to the pillow. Hot pain flared across my face, drawing a tear.

He brought my right hand closer to the left side of my body so that he could pin both of my hands to my chest with one of his while he pushed his pants down with the other. His dick sprung out of his underwear, stiff and angry red. Ready for action. The blankets and my underwear were all that stood between us, until he quickly and awkwardly pushed the blankets toward the foot of the bed with his feet. My underwear gave him no challenge and I quickly found myself naked from the chest down with his hot body pressed to mine.

He pushed his knees into my thighs, fighting to get in position between them.

"Stop! Ryan, don't do this." I begged, hoping I could break through his obsessive need to take my body because he thought I needed to be reminded I was actually Laume.

He pressed his knee into the muscle of my right thigh until I cried out and had to give in and move it before he broke the bone.

"I have dreamed about this so many times."

"I'm not Laume. I'm Bailey. Bailey Faye Michaels. Not Laume," I said through tears.

He smothered my complaints, mouth to mine, as he pressed his dick against me, looking for the way in.

I couldn't let him do it. But there was no one to call for help. I couldn't get to my phone. Sure, I could reach out to my phamily telepathically, but they couldn't help me from where they were and I would not put any of them through the nightmare of being raped with me. Nobody could help me. And as Ryan got the head of his penis into me I knew I was going to lose the fight. He was going to rip my body and trample my soul.

Stronger. I wanted to be stronger and tougher and meaner and badder. I wanted to hurt Ryan the way he was hurting me. I needed him to know how badly I wanted that. It was so unfair that he could do this to me and I couldn't do a thing to stop him. If I could somehow turn the tables on him I would. I would pull in my knees, wedge my feet between us, find the superhuman strength to push him off of me, off of the bed, and onto the floor—half naked and afraid of me. And I wouldn't stop there—because he wouldn't stop when he was hurting me, even when I was crying, even when I begged him.

I would drop into a low stance and kick him with every ounce of energy I could dig up. My foot would find the softness of his gut and shove his bellybutton right against his spine, regardless of what might be in the way. As he fell onto his side I would push his thighs apart and kick him between the legs again and again until I felt his testicles flatten between my bare foot and his body. The more he cried out, the more I would kick, and harder, until he couldn't say a word. Until he was broken the way he wanted to break me.

Suddenly Ryan pushed off of me and he leapt away as if a giant puppeteer had grabbed imaginary strings from behind and yanked him to the other side of the bed. One heartbeat he was on top of me, trying to get inside of me, and the next he just wasn't. I could hardly believe it. I clenched my legs together and scooted back against the headboard until we stared at each other, eyes even, across the disheveled bed. His arms braced against the mattress between his knees and his chest heaved as hard as mine did—his eyes showed fear. He was afraid, of me. We looked like a couple of wildcats who'd bitten off more than either could chew, but were squaring off to go another round, because we had to.

I saw Ryan's lips and jaw moving, but the son-of-a-bitch rapist wasn't actually able to form words. Like a spoiled fucking child, that big, powerful man had been willing to take from me what I wouldn't give him, until something stopped him and now he babbled like a baby.

Something stopped him. But what?

I didn't know if it was his conscience finally getting him to behave, the smell of my fear as I struggled, or some odd Faery Magic clinging to him after his relationship with Laume and preventing him from having sex with anyone else; and I didn't care. All that mattered was the three feet of space that was suddenly between us and the stark look of fear on his face.

Something had changed.

Hysterical laughter bubbled up from my chest, but instead of bursting out and mocking him for our sudden change of circumstances, my laughter made no sound. I did, however, get the quickly-becoming-familiar tickle of imaginary junebugs in my throat that said something odd was up.

Then it hit me. Ryan wasn't too scared to talk, I was deaf and dumb, again. He was talking, I just couldn't hear him.

Damn.

Ryan's mouth moved again, and I watched his lips closely, trying to understand what he said. I think it was something like *How in the hell did you do that?*

I had no idea what he was talking about, I hadn't *done* anything. I'd wished awfully hard about some stuff I'd like to have done to him, but I recalled being the one pinned to the bed, damned helpless, until he went flying off of me.

It was my turn to take advantage of his fear, of him being paralyzed. I slid off the side of the bed into a crouch, snatching my panties and my bag from the floor, which was a start, but I needed more clothing. Unfortunately I had hung my new outfit up in the closet before I went to bed, and Ryan was between me and that door. As I backed toward the door to the hallway I saw my ripped swing dress and borrowed sweatshirt stuffed into the trash can next to the door. I snagged them, and my second-hand flats that were sitting next to the bin, and kept moving.

Only when I had crossed the threshold into the hallway did I turn my back on the room, the bed, and Ryan. I ran. Took the staircase at full-speed, half-stumbling down more than a dozen steps and then across the foyer to the front door. I yanked it open, actually feeling the siren for the house alarm start to blare, and didn't stop running until I hit the tall hedge at the far side of the lawn. Barefoot, bare-assed, and unable to hear a damn thing, I balled myself up amid the leafy greens and tried to catch my breath.

What the hell had happened?

As grateful as I was to be sitting half-naked in the bushes rather than being raped in a luxurious bed made of marshmallow fluff, I had no clue what had happened to get Ryan off of me. The look on his face sure matched how I would have expected him to respond if I'd been able to do all those things I wanted to do. If I could have fought back. Even the way he held both arms to protect his crotch seemed like...like he'd be kicked in the balls. Repeatedly.

That thought came together with my current state of D-n-D to make me wonder if I had somehow given Ryan a taste of the images in my head. Had he understood what I wanted to do to him? Had I unknowingly exercised my telepathy, using it to defend myself?

I knew my current inability to hear or talk wasn't from the Friday night's telepathic conversation with Cooper. This current round of silent-me *had* to have happened because I'd used my telepathy when Ryan was trying to rape me. Every cell of my body had wanted him to experience my little fighting-back fantasy and it was possible that had been enough to create a mental connection between us and telepathically insert those thoughts and images into his head. After all, I'd contacted Cooper the night before without really intending to. The situation with Ryan hadn't been all that different.

Elvis help me. Maybe I had *done* something. But was it really telepathy?

Maybe it was, but just running one-way.

It made sense that it could be the case considering how quickly things happened. The whole exchange exploded lightning-quick, much too fast for Ryan to send me any response before the connection between us had been broken by his surprising leap away. All of my other telepathic exchanges had been longer, had included time for back and forth with the person whose mind I touched.

Though every experience with my telepathy had been a part of the trial-and-error method of learning, and I sometimes I didn't learn my lessons quickly enough, I knew one thing about telepathy for certain: I didn't ever want to have a back and forth with Ryan Williams. Never. Ever. Not after that.

I wanted out of his goddamn t-shirt, off his property, and out of his fucking life. Immediately.

22

Hiding in the tall hedges at the edge of the lawn surrounding Ryan Williams' enormous house I earned a few scrapes and pinpoint bruises as I took off and discarded his Texas Rangers t-shirt and wriggled into my panties, and reluctantly struggled into my torn dress. I did not want to put that sweatshirt, his sweatshirt, back on but the cool air on my back was a more humiliating reminder of what happened between us, so I sucked it up and plunged my arms into the sleeves. I waited to put my flats on until I ducked out the far side of the hedge and wiped the dark earth from my feet on the softest, greenest grass I'd ever felt.

The men who kept that lawn so beautiful, a white-haired old Latino guy and a younger man who looked to be his adult son, were weeding a flower bed ten feet from where I emerged from the bushes. I startled them as much as they startled me if their reactions were any clue. Being D-n-D from telepathically defending myself against Ryan, I did my best to pretend everything was fine, that I was supposed to be there, and both men nodded their heads in deference to me until the younger one got a very concerned look on his face.

I didn't blame the guy. I'm sure I came off a bit like seeing the Grim Reaper riding on a Moped—scares your ass off at first glance, but then you laugh when you look closely enough to see the itty-bitty motorcycle hiding beneath his flapping robes. I wiped at the mascara streaks I knew must be drying under my eyes after my encounter with their employer.

The son said something to me that I couldn't hear or understand, so I just waved him off and slipped into my shoes as quickly as I could. Both he and his father dropped their tools and took a step toward me, but I was in no mood to play charades with strangers about what had just happened. I turned my back on them and hustled down the driveway to the street.

It was a beautiful, sunny morning and I wished it had been pouring rain to match my mood. I'm sure the birds were singing and the leaves on the trees were rustling in the breeze that tugged the hood of the sweatshirt I was counting on hiding my tangled hair under. Unable to hear the cars as they approached me from behind, I decided to walk against traffic along the two lane rural road beyond Ryan's big white gate; keeping my head down, taking any turn that lead downhill or toward the rising sun, knowing the city lay that direction.

I desperately wanted a shower to wash the smell of Ryan Williams off of me, to clean away the creepy lingering feeling of his hands pinning me to the mattress, his lips kissing me, his hard-on pushing into me.

I'm not sure that Ryan had ruined sex for me, but he sure changed my definition of what it could be. Until that morning, sex had always been about pleasure, experimentation, exploration, novelty, and the undeniable curiosity about how to slip Tab-A into Slot-B in any configuration I could dream up. Now my feelings about sex also had to include helplessness, fear, pain, and agony. I hated him for that, hated him for ruining something that had been so pure for me. The sadistic part of me considered walking back up to the house in the hopes of seeing him still cowering on the bed so I would know for certain that I had seen what I thought I had—that he'd paid some price for what he'd taken from me.

Most of me wanted to curl up in a ball at the side of the road and cry, even though I wouldn't hear the sound of my own sobs.

Underneath it all I wanted to talk to someone; I wanted someone to tell me the even though I'd been in his house I hadn't asked to be raped. That I was the victim and that eventually, someday, somehow, maybe...possibly...everything would be alright. But I couldn't. This price for my power was getting to be awfully high, even if I could use telepathy to defend myself.

The soles of my feet complained about the thinness of the soles of my shoes, and I missed hearing the slap they made against the pavement as I trudged along the pine-cone littered roadside. It was as if the lack of sound stole away some of the satisfaction I should feel as my feet carried me further from harm. The muscles in the front of my thighs ached from step after step of following gravity's pull down the steep hills toward the city. I finally came to a street I recognized, Burnside Road, and turned downhill one more time knowing that the safety of the city lay a mile or two ahead of me.

Elvis help me, I wanted my phamily. Every other time I'd felt as low, as sad, as helpless, they'd been there for me. Maria would hug me and hold tight until I no longer felt like the world was going to chew me up and spit me out. Paulo and Cooper would either plot to kick the snot out of whomever had hurt me...or if it was something I'd done to myself, they'd run to the store for Jack and Cokes. After sitting silently and listening to my blithering, JoJo would kiss me on the top of the head and say something particularly witty that took an hour before it would sink into my brain and make some kind of sense—usually after a couple of rounds. Only then would I feel hope that there was a way through the pain, the darkness, the fear. They'd help me dig through the crap to find my anger and my will to survive. Only then would Maria tenuously release me and stay close, like a momma deer steadying her fawn as it takes its first tenuous steps, until I was strong enough to be out in the world again on my own.

I missed my phamily. I needed to touch base with them, but not until I was someplace farther away from Ryan Williams. But how far was far enough to be safe? Could I ever be far enough?

I kept walking in silence and the events with Ryan replayed in my head. I didn't want to think about it, but I couldn't seem to stop remembering the worst parts.

Shameful tears clouded my eyes and I had trouble keeping my feet tracking in a straight line. Oncoming traffic on Burnside was heavier than it had been on any of the side streets leading from Ryan Williams' house. I'm sure if I wasn't D-n-D I'd have heard a few annoyed honks at the hung-over blonde girl who was obviously making her way home on a Sunday morning after too much partying the night before.

A couple of police cruisers coming up the hill complicated things by forcing a driver to pull his delivery van over onto the berm in front of me as the cops raced up the hill with their lights flashing. The guy waved at me as he pulled the hulking truck back onto the road, but I didn't return his gesture. I wasn't feeling all that friendly.

And I kept walking.

About a mile further down the road, the woods to my left opened up and I noticed a small park nestled into the hillside. It wasn't much, just a stone monument to some historical figure surrounded by a half acre of manicured garden barely different from the surrounding wild space. My tired feet carried me to a concrete bench out of easy sight of the road where patches of sunshine broke through the tall trees and lay warm on my exposed legs. For the first time since waking up beneath Ryan Williams that morning I took a deep breath. It seemed the perfect, calm, safe place to reach out to my phamily and get some help.

Resting my hands on my grateful-to-not-be-walking-downhill-anymore thighs, I closed my eyes and took another deep breath. Thinking about Maria, I felt the connection with her open immediately.

Maria? I nudged her thoughts, hoping she wasn't drunk again—or still.

"*Not now Kitty-kat,*" she thought back to me. "*Busy. Can't chat.*"

In the twelve years we'd been phamily Maria had never, ever said anything like that to me. Her voice in my head was clipped, the telepathic equivalent of swatting at a mosquito buzzing at her ear.

I need help, I begged.

"*That makes five of us.*"

Oh, crap. That did not sound good. The hair on the back of my neck stood up until it pulled the rest of my spine straight up with it. I sat on the bench as stiffly as a Barbie Doll. Maria treating me like that meant something was wrong. Really, really wrong.

You're scaring me.

"*Talk to JoJo.*"

I hoped that meant she and JoJo were together in whatever situation had Maria all tied up. Maybe even all four of them were still together, if I was lucky. If they were together, then they'd be okay. I hoped they'd be okay.

Letting my connection with Maria close, I imagined JoJo in my head; her bright green eyes, perky little ski-slope nose, jet-black hair cut in a sleek, front-heavy bob. I imagined her smile and her sass and the way she cut across a room, drawing all attention to her just by the way she strutted on her stacked-like-a-brick-house legs. We teased her about being shorter than her stand-up bass, but she had sexier curves and always took front stage right at our shows—drawing in the shy guys who might otherwise linger at the bar. I kept imagining details about her until I felt a mental connection open up between us. It was different than it had been with Maria or Cooper—there was soft background music, something melodic and dark.

Jo-bear, it's me, Bayster. Can you talk? I used our special nicknames so we could avoid wasting time swapping authentication questions. *Maria just blew me off. What the hell is going on with you guys?*

"Bailey, thank God. Everything's gone to shit."

Yep, that was JoJo—profanity and God's name in the same sentence. I think she was the only one of us who actually believed he existed.

Talk to me.

"I'm so humiliated. They're making us stand here, buck naked, while that Faery Bitch tries to dig herself out of a hole the size of the Grand Canyon."

Naked? My protective instincts for my family kicked into gear, even though there wasn't a damn thing I could do to help them. *Who the fuck is* they? *Where are you?*

"We're in the Faery Court."

Faery Court? It took a few seconds for the concept to sink into my over-stimulated brain. Since my conversation with Laume about why she had abandoned Hannah with her daddy I'd feared that Laume had taken my phamily away from the world I knew, and now I had some confirmation from JoJo that she had. Damn.

You guys are really in Faery?

"And standing here naked while they all stare at us. It's horrible."

Why are you naked?

"*Cooper's plan to get us out of Hotel Hell worked, but it turns out we climbed out of the frying pan only to fall right in the fire. It didn't take them very long to figure out how we'd done it and The Queen took all of our possessions away from us. Stripped us right down to our skin so we couldn't do it again.*"

Cooper's plan? The Queen? What was she talking about? *What the hell did you guys do?*

"*He figured it out from what you told him about Laume using object tracking to show up any time she wanted and fuck with your life. He and Paulo planted one of my earrings on Laume's dress when she came in with a platter of food and wine. When she disappeared again, I followed her, carrying Paulo's glasses. I just thought really hard about my earring, what it looked like, felt like, the weight of it in my ear...and I magically transported out. It was like flying through a freezing cold blast of air—took my breath away. The glasses let Paulo follow me with Cooper's lucky guitar pick in his pocket and then Maria was able to follow Cooper because he had her toe ring. It was real slick—pop, pop, pop, pop—and I was so excited to get the hell out of there, until we realized where we were. I think maybe we should've stayed put."*

Now you're in some kind of courtroom?

"Not that kind of court, dweeb, the kind with thrones and crowns and lots and lots of pissed-off Faerie attendants. We showed up and the guards surrounded us before we could run. The Queen, they keep calling her Mab, is the most pissed off of all. She's so gorgeous, Bay, and so scary. I can't stand it when she looks at me.

"I don't think we're supposed to be here. Laume's in deep shit. And I don't like the way they talk about humans, like we're dumb as cows and about ten percent as valuable."

As JoJo talked I tried to imagine where they were, what kind of trouble they were in. My mind kept dredging up elfish village scenes from the Lord of the Rings, but I knew by the fear in JoJo's voice that those lofty halls with their towering arches standing proudly over plunging waterfalls weren't anything close to what my phamily was dealing with. Elvis help me; I wished they hadn't tried to escape Laume's Faery prison on their own.

"Bailey, I'm so scared."

How much worse things had just gotten? The only time I'd ever heard that much trembling in JoJo's voice was back at the hospital. JoJo was a cutter, had been a cutter. Her path to a cure was only possible after the counselors made her stand in her fear, face the fact that life was a horridly messy ordeal over which none of us actually had any say. I really don't know how she managed it, choosing to accept the lack of control that the rest of us sheepishly and unquestionably accepted from birth—or denied deeply, like me—so we felt safe enough to step out of the door each day. All I know was she finally coughed up her razor and her hat pin and her pen knife and kept all her blood inside her skin where it belonged.

Skin that was on display to all the Faery Royalty, thanks to Laume.

What's Laume doing about it? She promised me you'd be safe.

"It doesn't look like she's calling the shots anymore, Bay. From the little I understand, that promise she made you might be the only thing keeping us safe from Queen Mab right now."

Fuck.

"You said it."

What can I do?

"Besides wishing us a whole lot of luck? I don't think there's anything anyone can do. The way everyone bows and scrapes to the Queen, I get the feeling it's her way or the highway. The more pissed-off she gets, the colder it gets in here. My nipples are growing icicles."

I had to laugh.

"You think that's funny, I've got something you're going to think is fucking hilarious."

What's hilarious?

JoJo paused.

I waited, heart pounding like a double-footed 8/4 rhythm on my bass drum, knowing from the sarcasm in her tone that I wasn't going to like it.

"You sitting down?"

Why do I need to be sitting down?

"Because I just met to your mom, Bailey. She says to tell you hi."

My what!

I almost yanked my consciousness away from JoJo, back to the little park in the trees along the road in Portland, where it was quiet and peaceful and although I'd just about gotten raped, my life actually made some kind of sense. I wanted to scamper back there to stay in that world where the sun was warm on my skin and my mother was just a collection of nasty phrases my father spewed when he drunkenly complained about his life. My life would never win any top-ten prize for best life story, but I was comfortable in it. Until a week ago it was what I had made for myself, and even now I was dealing. I was not prepared to have it rocked by JoJo's Mama-revelations from Faery.

I wondered if it was possible that JoJo wasn't clear about what she'd said. Not because she was intentionally lying to me—she sounded awfully convinced that she'd met a woman claiming to be my mother—but because I hoped whoever had said it to her was lying.

I did not want to believe it. Did not. Did. Not.

No.

But I couldn't just leave her and hide in my head in the sand, I had to stick with JoJo, hear whatever she needed to say. And if I were being honest, part of me—the sad, little three year-old girl who hides deep inside and whines about things that aren't fair—had to know the truth. Had JoJo really met my mother?

Are you telling me you actually met my mother—in Faery?

"Her name is Sunny."

"You know how everyone always says you don't look a damn thing like your dad? Well now we know why. You look exactly like her, Bay. Exactly. Except Sunny is taller and fairer-skinned than you, and doesn't have your taste for tattoos."

Damn it. I wished she hadn't said that about how we looked alike. Except for that I could have stayed in denial, chocked it up to a bad joke, a cruel game, a Faery thing.

JoJo's thoughts cut through my thoughts.

"No, ma'am. I did not have any clue that my best friend's mother is a Faery. No ma'am, I'm pretty sure she didn't know that either."

Either JoJo had abruptly changed the topic while I dawdled in denial, or she was letting me in on her conversation with someone else.

JoJo, who the hell are you talking to?

"I apologize," JoJo said and then paused for a few seconds, there was real fear and submission in her voice and I hoped there were no sharp-edged instruments or shatterable objects nearby. *"I meant, no, Your* Highness. *Of course, Your Highness."*

JoJo, talk to me.

"Bailey, I can't do two things at once. Go bother Paulo."

Just like that, JoJo was gone from my mind. And my awareness was fully back in the park.

Wind-blown strands of my hair tickled my cheek and the chill of the concrete bench had worked its way through my dress into the backs of my legs. My breathing was fast and shallow, something I had not noticed while piped-in so closely to JoJo's mind. I squeezed my fingers together to stop them from shaking and tried to quiet all the thoughts racing around in my head before I reached out to Paulo.

One breath, better.

Two breaths, better still.

I breathed in again, real deep like I was just about to jump off the bridge into the river at Zilker Park, but hesitated before linking up to Paulo. Going zero-for-two like that—getting shut down during telepathic conversations with both Maria and JoJo when I called for help—was like walking smack-dab into a brutal right-left combination punch at the end of a twelve-round prize fight where I was getting the snot kicked out of me by a guy twice my size. I felt the sting of their rejection burning behind my eyes, drawing tears, until I realized neither would have done what they did except that they were both dealing with Mab, the Queen of Faeries.

The name Queen Mab meant less than nothing to me. When I tried to tie an image to what JoJo had said, I could only recall news clips I'd seen of the Queen of England on television—and she didn't exactly come across as frightening in her fussy, pastel-colored hats as she waved stiffly from the balcony of Buckingham Palace. But if what JoJo said was true and Queen Mab had the authority and power to call Laume on the carpet in front of other Faeries—Faery Royalty, no less? I had the feeling this Queen wasn't some wrinkly-old, benevolent figurehead like the Brit's Queen. Caution, in the form of a million imaginary bugs crawling up the back of my neck, warned me Mab was more like a force of nature.

As upsetting as all that was, the thought that ricocheted around my brain like the winning contestants in a swing dance competition—that last pair of hep cats showing everyone how they owned the floor—was the fact that JoJo said she'd met my mother. I would've brushed it off as some kind of Faery magic except that JoJo said I looked just like her and then something about it to The Queen. And she hadn't said it in the you-remind-me-of-someone way a stranger says it at closing time after five double-tequilas. She had said it like someone who really knew me and saw me most every day.

In all my travels with Billy's Asylum Rats, playing Rockabilly in seedy little bars in every piss-ant town across the southern United States, I'd never met anyone who looked much like me. Never.

And now I knew why.

Elvis help me, I finally got it, my mother was a Faery.

23

Sometimes, there are scary or Earth-shattering details in life that make you re-assess everything you've ever understood about the world in a new light. Like when a friend comes out of the closet and suddenly all the odd bits and pieces you knew about their life came together in a picture that finally made sense. Or after you have sex for the first time, and you cross an invisible boundary into the adult world where no guy ever looks quite the same again because all those jokes (wink-wink) and stories and pictures are suddenly less gross and a whole lot more titillating.

Nearly drowning in the Gulf of Mexico should have done that to me. Finding out that my phamily and I had been rescued by a Faery, an actual Faery should have done it. Discovering I had a talent for telepathy should have done it. But no, none of those things made me re-evaluate my life. It took learning that my mother was a Faery named Sunny to really rock my world.

Realization after realization slammed into me and I'm sure my body shook from each one as if being riddled with automatic gun fire.

So many things started to make sense.

I knew why she left me as an infant. Why she never came back. Why I could never find her. Why my father never talked about her when he was sober.

I understood why my father hated her. If Ryan's response to Laume was any indication of what happened to human men who fooled around with Faeries, then my father was likely to have been hit at least as hard by his relationship with my mother. He hadn't turned to drugs and self-destructive behavior, the way Ryan had, but he'd obviously thrown himself into his career so completely to avoid something. Her. His Faery lover. The one who left.

I finally understood why things had gotten worse between my father and me as I got older. Not that things had ever been *good*—when I was a little girl he had been incredibly demanding and distant, which my therapists thought was normal for an unplanned baby who presented a consistent reminder of the woman my father hated so much. But when I hit puberty, it was like he couldn't even stand to be in the same room with me. I always thought it was because he hated me. Now, looking back—how he could never sit still when we were in the same room, the way he looked at me and then looked away so quickly when I caught his eye, the fact that the only time he complimented me was to tell me how beautiful I was—I wondered if it wasn't something else. I wondered if he was somehow attracted to me, a part of me, the way Ryan Williams was attracted to me, because he thought I was Laume.

Because I was half-Faery.

That thought rocked me so hard I had to brace my hands against the bench to keep from falling over. It made perfect sense; Ryan thought I was Laume because I was half-Faery.

Maybe that's why I had the gift of telepathy, and why I'd never known about it until my interactions with Laume, the first Faery I'd ever met.

Half-Faery. What a weird thought to think about myself. Half human, and half Faery.

Just like Hannah.

Between one heartbeat and the next, that thought combined with my new understanding of Ryan Williams' little Faery-addiction problem took me someplace horrible that made me suddenly and violently sick to my stomach. My skin flamed with hot prickles, my mouth flooded with saliva faster than I could swallow it down, and all the muscles in my belly clenched at once. I leaned forward and vomited onto the patchy grass, but there was only yellow stomach acid coming up. I kept heaving even after my stomach was empty of that.

Eventually my body gave up on trying to expel the offending idea from my head as if it was just something rancid I'd eaten.

No, this idea wasn't going away quite so easily.

I wiped my face on the hem of my skirt and leaned back to breathe through my mouth. It took a few minutes for the muscles in my torso to loosen up and feel mostly normal. The smell of vomit filled my nose so I got up and moved to another bench with the sun on my back. The breeze swirled under my skirt and chilled the sweat on my skin, coaxing goosebumps up and down my legs.

Fitting, since I had similar goosebumps on my soul.

I finally understood why Laume had picked me to make a bargain with; I was half-Faery, like her daughter—my special talent.

The thing that had made me throw-up was considering a new deeper, darker dimension to the outcome of our bargain.

Until that moment my understanding had been that I'd agreed to get a little girl home to her daddy in exchange for saving my phamily. A win-win situation, if all went well. But after having met Ryan Williams, and understanding in a very personal way how fucked-up he'd become from his relationship with Laume, I was horrified to finally realize that the only way I was going to get my phamily back was to deliver half-Faery-Hannah into the control of a man who was obviously and hopelessly addicted to Faeries.

And when he couldn't get a Faery, a half-Faery would do.

He'd tried to rape me because my Faery side reminded me of Laume. He was sick, delusional, self-destructive, and he didn't care who he hurt as long as he got his fix.

What were the chances he would do something horrible to Hannah once she was home?

I thought about sweet, empathetic, angel-voiced Hannah, and the way she'd trashed her fit-for-a-princess bedroom. Could something have happened already? The possibility of sending her back into that house forced me to put my head between my knees to keep from hurling again.

Elvis help me.

If I was going to get my phamily back I might have to send Hannah into the hell I'd just escaped.

That was assuming my deal with Laume hadn't just imploded because my phamily tried to escape her plush little prison cell by tapping into Faery Magic. JoJo had said their Queen was beyond unhappy with Laume, angry enough to suck all the warmth from the room where they were being held naked.

I had to talk to them again.

JoJo had said to contact Paulo, so I pictured him in my head—tall, sandy-haired and balding, with wire-rimmed glasses. He was our guitar virtuoso, not that 'billy music required any advanced musical talent, and had the most amazingly long fingers. He was the core of us; the reason we first came together as a band for the talent show at the hospital and the heart and soul of our music ever since. We could not have survived losing him in the lifeboat.

The link didn't seem to want to come, until I imagined him not standing naked in humiliation in some nondescript Faery Court, but sitting on a stool at center stage with the spotlight flashing off his vintage Gibson as he bent his head to play his way through a solo, feeling the strings beneath his fingers rather than looking at them. When I saw him lift his chin and smile in my mind, I felt the connection snap into place.

Paulo's head was a very loud place to be. Not just music, like I'd heard in JoJo's thoughts, but at least a half a dozen muted voices speaking all at once. Wondering if this was a part of his schizophrenia, I listened, but couldn't really make out more than an underlying tone of fear and concern. The doctors had always said Paulo was lucky, his disease was mild and well-controlled with the medication we (as a phamily) made sure he took, but it didn't feel mild to me. It felt scary.

Paulo, can you hear me?

I didn't sense any change in the muffled conversations.

I intensified my thoughts to raise my voice above the din. *Paulo, man, I got to talk to you.*

"*Not funny guys*," Paulo's voice rang clearly above the conversations that quieted in the background like a bunch of puppies that'd been sprayed by a hose. "*We've talked about this; no imitating the phamily. It's not fair.*"

At first I thought he was talking to Maria and Cooper and JoJo, but there was sternness in his voice that I'd never heard him use with us. For all his intimidating size and expertise at the guitar, Paulo was never a dominating presence like that in our group, on or off the stage.

Paulo, hon, it's me, Bailey. It's me, just like Maria and Cooper said it would be. I'm not a voice inside your head.

Paulo laughed at me. "*Prove it*," he said like someone might when the guys from Publisher's Clearing House showed up on the doorstep with a giant check for a million bucks. Like he wanted it to be true, but he'd been fooled too many times before and couldn't get his hopes up on my say-so alone.

I thought about that for a second. I knew the simple Q&A I'd performed with Maria about my car wouldn't be enough to convince him I was not only real, but separate from his own brain. Neither would tossing around our pet nicknames for each other. I had to tell him something true that his mind wouldn't already know and therefore couldn't tell him by itself. My only hope was that he was with the others and I could betray one of their secrets to him, something he could verify with them to know it was me.

Unfortunately we didn't have too many secrets in our tightly-knit little group; and the ones we did keep—at least the ones I knew about—were pretty big, or otherwise humiliating. It made me feel weak and disloyal to even consider breaking a confidence with one of the others just to prove myself with Paulo.

I didn't really have to talk to *him* to find out what was going on in Faery—I could go back to Maria or JoJo or Cooper—but it felt reassuring to have contact with him the way I'd already had with the others. And I had to admit, I was curious about how his brain worked, he'd been living with this disease for so long.

I decided to stay with him and choose a secret.

Maria was always the most forgiving, so I thought about all the moments only she and I had shared. I had to throw out the one about the abortion and the one from our trip to Las Vegas, but then I remembered that horrible prank we'd played on him for his last birthday. He'd never known which of us had sent that stripper to his job at the warehouse.

Okay, I thought to Paulo. *Ask them who called Serena Swallows for your birthday and almost got you fired.*

"Hang on," he said, like a call-center employee putting a customer on hold.

After about ten seconds Paulo came back into my thoughts, *"Okay, I got it."*

It was me and Cooper. I'm sorry.

"Holy shit, Bailey, it is you!" Paulo thought at me. *"What the hell took you so long?"*

What do you mean?

"It's been two days since you talked to JoJo."

Two days? No way. Sure, I'd lost track of time as I re-evaluated my whole life after learning I was half-Faery, but maybe an hour at most. No way it had been two days. Except that I was in my reality, and they were in Faery. Cooper had already hinted that time wasn't quite the same thing there as it was on my sunny bench in the park.

Sorry, dude. It wasn't that long on this side, I swear. Please tell me you're haven't been standing around Faery Court naked all this time.

"Nope. We got an upgrade...to Queen Mab's dungeon."

Dungeon? Like underground with bars on the door?

"And damp, and dark, and cold—with the biggest fucking rats I've ever seen running along the walls."

Oh, no.

"Oh, yes. Don't you wish you were here with us?"

Actually, I hate to say it, but I kind of wish we were all still on the lifeboat. I wanted desperately to travel back in time, tell Laume to stick her deal where the sun don't shine, choosing to let fate have its way with us.

"Sing it, sister. I know exactly what you mean."

Of course he couldn't know. As bad as things were for my phamily they had no idea that the only way I had to get them back—if I still could—would be by selling Hannah out to her Faery-crazed father.

Can you guys do the object tracking thing again and try to get out of there?

"It looks like we blew our wad on the first try with that one. The Queen kept our stuff when her guards brought us down here."

You're still naked? Two days naked in a dungeon. Good Graceland, what a horrible thought.

"*Nope, we got us some new, fancy Faery duds. Long tunics with lots of embroidery and jewels. Very classy shit. You'd look good in it, Bay."*

Maybe you could exchange outfits and try it again? It worked with the license and passport Laume gave me.

"Nope, we tried. The damn things won't come off. Faery Magic."

So you're stuck. Crap.

"And we're not going anywhere until Queen Mab decides whether or not your deal with that Faery Bitch violated their laws."

Huh?

"You want the good news or the bad news."

I couldn't take any more bad news, so I asked for the good.

"If it turns out Laume didn't break their laws she gets us back."

Well, fuck, it wasn't really such good news after all. But I hoped that meant the deal was still on and I could get them home if I held up my end of things...as horrible as that might turn out to be for Hannah.

And the bad? I asked.

"If she did break their law, she gets some magical slap on the wrist and our lives are forfeit to Queen Mab."

The idea of that chased every thought out of my head except the repetition of one word: no. No. No. No...

No.

No!

NO!

"We need your help, Bay."

Anything.

"The Queen wants you questioned. She said she's going to reserve her judgment until she hears your side of the story. I don't think she likes Laume very much."

That seemed pretty reasonable. We all thought she was quite the bitch; no reason Queen Mab should feel any differently.

How can I help?

"She wants to send her emissary, The Winter Knight, to ask you some questions."

Send him my way.

"Queen Mab says you have to summon him."

I have a new cell phone. Can I just call?

"*Easier than that,*" Paulo thought at me. "*All you have to do is say his name three times and he'll come to you. But she told us to warn you never to summon another Faery that way, ever. Her exact words were that you're under her protection for the purposes of this inquiry, and that's it. After that, you're fair game just like any other human idiot stupid enough to summon a Faery across The Veil.*"

Summoning a Faery across The Veil, sure, sounds like a kick in the pants—I would have laughed at Paulo except for the fear I remembered feeling in JoJo's thoughts about Queen Mab. When a force of nature offers me a warning, I'm smart enough to heed it.

What's his name?

"Sir Ansley Devon Stannard. You have to say it just like that, Sir Ansley Devon Stannard. Exactly. Three times, and he'll come to you."

Sir Ansley sounded like a pompous asshole; like one of those dudes who struts into a 'billy bar wearing a black biker jacket and brand-new jeans with turned up cuffs and thinks we'll be impressed because he's the third or fourth person in his family with the same goddamn name. *Hello, I'm Sir Ansley Devon Stannard the Eighth.*

Okay, Paulo, I got it. I'll call him right now. I was about to say goodbye when I realized that all the other voices inside Paulo's head had suddenly gone silent. Far from being soothing, it gave me the willies.

"*Bay, be careful,*" Paulo warned. "*I met this guy. He's not like anyone you've ever dealt with before. Smart. Brutal. Icy. Calculating. Really fucking dangerous. Do not underestimate him.*"

That was the most sober thing I'd heard Paulo say in all the time I'd known him. The tone of his thoughts tapped into that cold ball of loneliness that had been living in my chest all week and shoved it down in to my vacant stomach. I could feel the chill of it pass through my abs and through my skin and through my dress and through the sleeves of my sweatshirt into the flesh of my forearms until my bones ached from it.

I promised Paulo no funny stuff, and pulled away before I lost my nerve.

Aware, again, of the dappled sun on my back, I shook my head to clear a swarm of distracting thoughts out of my brain so I'd be clear-headed when I called The Winter Knight. But one persistent little bugger of an idea held on: *Bailey, you're fucked, you can't call him.*

I was still deaf and dumb from using my telepathy.

Communicating with telepathy had been so easy with Paulo and JoJo that I forgot I couldn't hear or talk in my reality. How was I going to summon Mab's emissary without a voice? And if I could somehow figure out how to call The Winter Knight, how would I hear or answer his questions when he arrived? Being D-n-D in the presence of a dude who scared Paulo so badly was not a good idea.

I was screwed. My phamily was sitting in a Faery dungeon, in a place where time didn't exactly mean the same thing as I knew it to be, and I couldn't do a thing to help them until I got some sleep and the sun rose Monday morning: about 19 hours away. If relative time stayed the same—an hour here taking two days there—that could mean over a month in the dungeon. What if The Queen didn't have that much patience?

And I thought almost being raped would be the worst thing that could happen to me all day. Damn.

24

I figured I had two choices: I could sit on the bench for the rest of my life or I could stand up. It was the only choice I had to make in that moment: stay and sit or stand the fuck up.

I stood up.

The next choice was almost as easy: hang around all day or take the first step of the rest of my life.

I turned and walked toward the road.

At the edge of the asphalt I paused while traffic whizzed silently up and down Burnside Road. If I turned right I'd be headed up the hill, back toward Ryan's place. Turning left would eventually get me back down to the city. Since standing, staring vacantly by the side of the road would probably, eventually, make someone notice me—and I really didn't need any more unwanted attention—I knew I had to choose. Right or left?

It had been years, twelve in fact, since I'd been so overwhelmed by the shittiness in my life that the simple act of deciding what to do next took all my willpower. Last time hadn't ended so well, except that when it was over I had Maria and JoJo and Cooper and Paulo in my life. Last time the maid had found me on the floor in the bathroom, unconscious and bleeding from a deep, self-inflicted stab to the chest.

My right hand unconsciously reached up and touched the three-inch scar hidden carefully beneath the flaming heart tattooed over my breast bone. The rough ridge felt hot to the touch as if those flames were more than just red and orange pigment forced into my skin.

And, of course, they were.

I'd gotten the ink done on my eighteenth birthday because my goddamn father wouldn't sign the consent form to get it done any sooner. He'd happily pay for a plastic surgeon to fix the scar for me, but that was his fix, his shame. I wasn't ashamed of it, I wanted to remember. It's who I had been, where I'd come from, an honest response to the pain.

The artist who'd done the tattoo asked why I'd picked a flaming heart. I'd told him it would serve as a reminder not to let the fire die.

The thin skin over my sternum must have ten times the nerve endings of any other place on my body; the pain of the needle had been intense; scraping, burning, deliberate and unrelenting as plain skin became an outline and then a work of art. As the ink permanently changed my skin, I let that pain permanently change my thoughts. I would no longer doubt myself, ignore my own needs, or give my love to someone who didn't want it or need it. I accepted that I was only ever going to be good at three things—pastry, drums and sex—and devoted myself to being really, really good at them.

That tattoo had been a rite of passage and its reminder had never been as important to me as it was right then. I did not want the fire to die. Not mine. Not my phamily's. Not Hannah's. I wasn't sure it was possible to get all those things, given the craptastic situation I found myself in, but standing there on the side of the road wasn't getting me anywhere I needed to be.

Right or left? Choose one and worry about the rest later.

I turned left toward the city, placing one foot after another, imagining a drum cadence in my head to hold back the silence and keep myself moving. I followed Burnside all the way down to the riverfront park at the center of downtown where I was surprised to find a large street-fair and farmer's market in full swing. The place crawled with tourists, even in September.

Although I couldn't hear a damn thing, I could smell a million different things: garlic, roasting beef, lavender, candle wax, sawdust, wet wool, wet dog, body odor, antiseptic cleaner mixed with urine. I melded into the crowd and wondered at stall after stall of hand-made crafts and fresh-from-the-field produce. I had planned to find my way back to the Buffalo Exchange to buy another second-hand dress but abandoned that plan when I came across a lady selling organic hemp clothing and hand-made sweaters imported from South America. I picked out a khaki sundress with red embroidery and an airily-knit, three-quarter sleeved Alpaca sweater. Together they were a hundred and thirty bucks, all but ten dollars of the cash I had left from my bank account. I couldn't really afford to do it, but the silky texture of the sweater was exactly what I needed to soothe my sorrowful heart.

My money spoke for me as I paid the lady running the booth and then took advantage of a changing area curtained-off at the back of her stall. She smiled, threw a couple of hand-gestures that were either gang signs or sign language, and closed the tie-dyed curtain behind me. I changed quickly; glad to be out of my ruined dress and sweatshirt I'd taken from Ryan. I bundled them under my arm and slipped out of the changing room while the woman was busy with another customer to avoid my inability to communicate in real sign language.

That was a handy skill I was going to have to pick up, and soon, if I continued to use my telepathy.

The nearest trash can sat thirty-feet away, outside a small area filled with tables where people of all sizes and colors sat eating food from paper plates and Styrofoam to-go containers. I dumped my clothes into the bin and then realized I had no plan for what came next.

It had been an hour, at least, since Paulo had told me I was supposed to summon The Winter Knight. But an hour to me could have been a minute or a day or a week in Faery time, I didn't really know. Any amount of time was too long for my phamily to be stuck in a Faery Queen's dungeon.

I wondered if I could get away with asking a stranger to help me summon Sir Ansley. If I wrote his name, and a short explanation—like I was on some kind of oddball, initiation-type-scavenger-hunt for my deaf college—on a piece of paper, maybe I could work around my current disability. But Paulo's warning about Mab's protection being limited and his caution about pronouncing the Knight's name exactly made me worry that plan could endanger some innocent bystander. My conscience had enough to make amends for without that.

A tap on my shoulder startled me, spun me around, and brought me face-to-face with the last person I wanted to see right then, Laume. Her beautifully glossed lips flapped at me, and I felt somewhat satisfied that I had an excuse for ignoring what she said—I could tell I was getting a lecture. But there was something different going on. Unlike my previous interactions with her, she gave off a different vibe—a sense of desperation. I didn't know if that was just me knowing she'd gotten in deep shit with her Queen for taking my phamily to Faery, or if she really was the hot mess she looked to be. Either way, it didn't matter; there wasn't anything I could do to help her until after sunrise.

Laume's rant wound down and I could easily read her lips as the spoke her last sentence: "Are you listening to me?"

I shrugged my shoulders and shook my head, covering my ears in the hope she'd figure out that I couldn't hear her. At first she gave me that look I'd gotten earlier for asking a dumb question, that puppy/dim-witted child glare, and then I saw her realize I wasn't bluffing and she worked it out.

I dropped my hands.

She reached into an amazing red leather purse (I'm sure JoJo would have known which designer's bag it was) and pulled out an iPad which she shoved in my face. When I looked at the screen it said, "Why have you not yet summoned The Winter Queen's emissary?"

I touched my throat and shook my head as if to say, *No voice, either.*

Laume shoulders moved in what I assumed was a sigh and then she pointed back and forth between our heads. She wanted me to use my telepathy. I hesitated. I'd already used my gift that day to defend myself against Ryan Williams, touch base with Maria, and then chat with both JoJo and Paulo. It was the first time I'd used it so often between sunrises and I was honestly a little afraid that I might remain D-n-D longer this time, maybe even the rest of the week, as the price for overusing it. I certainly didn't want to give up a whole extra day just so Laume could yell at me inside my own head. Again.

Her gestures got more and more aggressive, so much so that the people around us were starting to take notice. Most looked once and moved on, but I could tell two young guys down the aisle were talking about us, I was sure of it. Maybe they were expecting a cat fight, but I didn't want them to come to my rescue and get a dose of Laume for their trouble.

She was in a Bad Mood. Nobody deserved that.

I decided to risk another day of D-n-D to keep the Faery Bitch from exploding in a crowd of innocent civilians. Closing my eyes for a second I imagined Laume the first time I'd seen her, hanging onto the back of the lifeboat under the stars. I felt the connection pop into place, and apparently she did too because she immediately started flooding my mind with more thoughts than I could separate.

About three seconds of that was plenty for me. I imagined an ear-splitting siren's wail and opened my eyes to stare her down. She got the message and her assault on my mind stopped.

Better.

I couldn't call him, I told Laume in answer to her iPad question. I explained in detail the price I paid for my telepathy, leaving out the fact that I wasn't sure about all of the specifics, and told her that the best I could do would be to summon him in the morning.

"Not good enough."

Of course it wasn't good enough. I didn't need her to tell me that.

"You understand that your people are in the custody of The Faery Queen of Winter."

They told me.

"You seem blissfully unconcerned. Did they not tell you they are being kept in The Queen's dungeons?"

The Queen's dungeon, or your glorified prison cell, what difference does it make? They're prisoners all the same.

Laume's face transformed from tight-lipped anger to eye-flickering indecision. "*Either you are very stupid, or they didn't really tell you,*" she thought at me. And then, rather than explaining things to me in words, that gauzy blindfold feeling came over me again—like it had in the lifeboat, when she showed me the fast-forward video of Paulo's fate—and she filled all five of my senses with the horror of Queen Mab's dungeon.

I felt things so clearly that for a second I worried that she had actually transported me there.

Paulo had mentioned the rats, and they were huge and terrible like he said, but he hadn't mentioned the spiders and the biting flies and a dozen other nasty bugs I'd never seen before and might not even exist in our reality. Nor did he bother to share that every one of the little creepy-crawlers had a taste for human flesh and considered bare skin an open invitation to feast away. No way could anyone sleep in there, the bugs would take you a bite at a time if you ever stopped flicking them off your skin.

The moldy grout between the stones that made up the dungeon walls sweated foul-smelling water and the damp moist air carried a chill deep into me each time I breathed it in. My skin felt clammy where it was exposed and sticky and grimy where it wasn't. I knew in my soul I would never be clean again, not if I took a year-long shower.

Worse than all of that were the noises. Erratic. Haunting. Blood-chilling. Sometimes it was screams of pain, other times it was gasps of ecstasy—often paired too closely not to be related. The rock walls thrummed with vibrations, low and deep and mechanical. Footsteps marched along the hallway outside the heavy timber door—some fairly human, some skittering, and the rest were heavy in a beastly way. My curiosity got me looking toward the door, and my fear kept me from looking away.

The cell was larger than the lifeboat we'd been trapped in for three days on the Gulf, but not large enough for four scared, angry, frustrated members of my phamily to hang out in and maintain their sanity. They'd been locked up together for the better part of a week and I'm sure they were pacing like caged tigers most of the time. Three steps, turn, three steps, turn, shove someone out of the way, three steps, turn.

Laume's details of the dungeon painted a different picture than what Paulo had led me to believe about their circumstances under The Queen's care. Somehow I knew in my heart that Laume had gotten her details in a very personal way—not from a brief tour of the facility, but from an extended stay at the Queen's pleasure. If that hell was what my phamily faced, then Laume was right. I was stupid. I was so very stupid.

Details of the dungeon faded back into lightness, and my awareness drifted back to the sunny street-fair. My skin still crawled from the feeling of dampness.

What do I do? I asked Laume telepathically. *How do I help them?*

"You help them by convincing The Queen's emissary that our bargain is fair and just and that you entered into it of your own free will."

I tried to laugh in her face and felt the flutter of junebugs in my throat. Fair and just? My own free will? The whole thing had been about her manipulating me from the get-go. She'd used every strong-arm tactic in the book to get me to agree to help Hannah—or actually to condemn her—to life with her father, as I finally understood. Technically I'd had a choice, I could have said no to the bargain, but Laume had all but guaranteed Paulo's imminent death and the destruction of my phamily if I had not agreed.

I suddenly wondered if she'd set the whole thing up. Had she somehow sent the wave that capsized our record company's yacht? Was she somehow behind my efforts to convince my phamily to take the boat out and clear our collective heads before we went into the studio? Had she and her Faery Magic puppeteered the recording deal that tied us to Sun Records? Had she manipulated the owners into resurrecting the label, Elvis's first label, so Billy's Asylum Rats couldn't possibly pass-up the offer?

My mind reeled at the possibilities. I couldn't decide how far Laume would have gone to make all of this happen, but her insistence that I back up her side of the story said there was something more important going on that I didn't understand.

Though none of that mattered. Not anymore. All that mattered was getting my phamily out of The Queen's dungeon so that I could get them home. I could lie to a Faery Knight; convince him that Laume and I were just doing a little business—Faery-style.

But I couldn't convince him if I couldn't summon him. I still had not figured out the solution to that little dilemma. Maybe the Faery Bitch could fix it for me.

How do I contact him if I can't talk? I asked her.

Laume smiled and tucked her iPad back into her bag and pulled out a small, crystalline statue of a mounted knight, like an ornate chess piece. She presented it to me, my own little Winter Knight. When my fingers touched the ornate shape, my first thought was that it was made of ice, but the heat from my hand didn't melt even its sharpest edges.

"Carry his token to a private venue. He will seek you out. You should be able to converse with him the way you're conversing with me."

Okie-dokey, artichokey. I thought toward Laume. *One big, fat lie, coming right up.*

I closed my hand around the little horse and rider and tried to leave, but Laume stopped me. She put both hands on my shoulders so I was forced to look her in the face.

"Communicating telepathically will make it very difficult for you to hide your true feelings. Whatever your petty little heart believes about the circumstances of our agreement, you must be convincing—very convincing—if you hope to free your friends from the dungeon. Stick to the facts."

I wanted to say, Fact is: you're a bitch. Or, Fact is: you bullied me into it. And mostly I wanted to say, Fact is, you must hate your daughter as much as you hate me to do this to her, why couldn't you just leave well enough alone. But I didn't. I shrugged her hands off my shoulders and carried the little knight figure toward the river. I walked along the waterfront until I found a public restroom—a park-style unisex: a wide-open one-holer with thick concrete walls and a functioning dead-bolt lock on the door.

Seemed as private a place as I was going to find in the middle of a street fair.

I locked myself in, sat on the closed toilet, and set the little crystal likeness on the edge of the sink. I stared. I waited. I slumped. I studied the details of the carving, committing each one to memory. I doubted, until The Winter Knight arrived.

25

The Winter Knight wasn't quite what I expected.

He popped into the bathroom on a gust of silent, cold wind—but that could have been me being D-n-D—and settled into a slight crouch as he immediately started assessing everything in his new surroundings.

Paulo had called him *brutal, icy, and dangerous* so I had been expecting a dead-eyed, Norse demi-god—muscular and tall enough to cast a shadow on the moon—wearing full plate armor and hefting a battle axe heavier than my Buick. Instead, Sir Ansley was compactly built, just under six feet tall, with curly dark hair and silver-toned eyes. More assassin than thug.

He was graying at the temples, and his face was careworn with wrinkles, which led me to guess he was older than Laume—whatever that meant for Faeries. He wore polished wingtips, charcoal gray slacks and a matching vest over a tone-on-tone dress shirt with the sleeves rolled up to the elbows—no tie in evidence. The only weapons I could tell he carried were a pair of odd, non-metallic knives criss-crossed snugly against his back in an ornate, leather sheath. I wondered what else he might have concealed.

He was breathtakingly handsome. Also he was sad. Not in a my-puppy-just-got-run-over way, but I got a sense that he was tired—sick and tired—and there was someplace else he would rather have been.

As soon as he saw the little crystal knight, he took two strides toward the sink and snatched it up in his knobby-jointed hand. From that new position, in front of the sink, he put his back to the wall and finished scanning the restroom—concrete block walls, unpainted concrete floor, pitted-chrome water tap on the sink, empty soap dispenser, and the bare scar on the wall where a hot-air hand dryer used to hang. His gaze lingered on the stainless-steel handicapped rails around the toilet for a moment before fixing on the heavy door. His eyes narrowed and he unsheathed both knives, holding them at the ready, tips just above eye-level and pointed at the door. The blades—maybe made from some kind of ceramic—threw back the fluorescent light from the lone ceiling fixture. Standing there, wound-up and ready to spring at the door, Sir Ansley looked like the devil's own jack in the box.

Although there was plenty of floor space in the bathroom for both of us, his presence made me pull my feet up and hug my knees against my body. I did not want him to decide I was his enemy, or accidentally put myself between him and the door. I waited at least two minutes for him to calm down and lower his blades, which he finally did, but he did not put them away.

He finally barked something at me, but I couldn't catch a word of it by reading his lips. I hoped Laume had prepared him for my D-n-D situation and he was offering to make a telepathic link with me, because I'd gotten enough detail about him that I was ready to try it.

I stared at him—my eyes locked with his eyes, even though it made my heart race in fear to do it—and kept repeating two thoughts over and over: *I'm not your enemy*, and *Please don't hurt me.* At my third repetition I saw him shake his head as if to discourage a pesky mosquito (or one of the other horrific insects from Queen Mab's dungeon) from landing on his car and snacking on him. When that didn't seem to relieve what was bothering him, he cocked his head sideways and listened. After three more repetitions he looked to have gotten my message and started nodding in time with the cadence of my thoughts. I winced as the tips of his weapons came up again, but then relaxed as his blades rotated over his shoulders and hissed into their sheath; the right one first, and then the left one.

The curt bow he offered me surprised me almost as much as the timbre of his voice as his thoughts entered my mind. "*Sir Ansley Devon Stannard, Winter Knight to Her Majesty Queen Mab of the Winter Court.*"

His Irish accent was incredibly melodic. (I almost wanted to hear him introduce himself again so the tingles dancing up my spine wouldn't fade to nothing.) He dominated the room as he straightened, eyes first then shoulders then his whole back, and waited for me to introduce myself.

Bailey Michaels, I said. *From Austin, Texas.*

"*Bailey Faye Michaels?*" he asked.

What was it with Faeries and full names? Thankfully, that was an easy question.

Yes.

The rest of them would not be so.

"*My Queen bids me to convey her gratitude, and requests your assistance in establishing the veracity of claims purported by Lady Laume in regards to the binding agreement between you. But first, may I ask an important question?*"

Sure.

"*Why have you been incarcerated? Lady Laume did not prepare me to assist in an escape. I would have arrived more properly equipped.*"

Incarcerated? I looked around the restroom again, seeing it through his eyes—the eyes of someone who *wasn't from around these parts*, as we said in Austin—and recognized that in many ways the utilitarian bathroom did come off like a prison cell with its block walls, crappy lighting, and shortage of windows.

I stifled a laugh. Making light of such an easy misunderstanding would start things off on the wrong foot with Sir Ansley.

It's a public bathroom, I explained. *The door locks from the inside, Sir.*

Ansley eyed the door. *"The handle and lock knob are steel, are they not?"*

I looked more closely and decided he was correct, like most bathroom fixtures in public facilities they were made from rugged and easy-to-clean stainless steel. I nodded my agreement, which seemed to increase his tension rather than relieve it, making me worry those odd knives were going to come out for an encore performance.

"I would like to propose a bargain," he said telepathically.

I don't know.

I wanted to convey to him how bargaining with Faeries had been a 0-1-1 proposition for me—Laume won the first round, and it was mostly a draw when we agreed to a bargain so I would get into the Bugatti. But to explain that to him would give away that I'd felt cheated in our original bargain, which was the opposite of what I needed to convince Sir Ansley of if the Queen was going to rule in Laume's favor and return my phamily to her.

"What would you ask of me in a bargain?" he offered.

Man, if that didn't come across as the Genie offering Aladdin three wishes. My first reaction was to wish for my phamily back, but circumstances as they were meant that would probably be as effective as pushing on a rope. Sure there were other things I wanted: fame, money, an Elvis concert for me and ten of my closest friends...but none of those things were in the same category as getting my phamily out of The Queen's dungeon.

What I really needed was information. Ever since I agreed to Laume's bargain, I felt like I'd been flying blind. Laume may not have been able to lie but she was awfully stingy with the details. Maybe if I knew a little more about the situation going on in Faery I could get ahead of her a little better, get this whole thing settled sooner.

Answers, I said. *I could really use some answers.*

Ansley smirked at me. *"That's a very vague request."*

I remembered a similar response I'd gotten from Laume when I asked if I could ask her a question. She'd said, "Do I appear foolish enough to agree to answer *any* question you might ask? I was not sparked to life yesterday." I got it that I needed to be more specific with what I wanted in a bargain with The Winter Knight.

How about a question for a question? For every question you ask of me, I get to ask one in return.

He considered my deal and then nodded. *"In return, you will unbolt the door and we will move this conversation to a more agreeable venue."*

I doubted that's all he wanted and wondered what else was going on. *What kind of knight doesn't know how to open a simple dead-bolt?* I asked him.

"I comprehend the technology. It's the materials I object to." He held his bare hands out to me, palms facing up. *"If I'd known I was to manipulate iron on this little quest, I would have packed my goblin gloves."*

Iron?

"*The steel*," he said as he nodded toward the door. "*It's essentially a fancy form of iron. Most unpleasant to come into contact with.*"

You're allergic?

"Extremely."

The tone in Sir Ansley's voice said that his aversion to iron was worse than an allergy, and his willingness to blindly trade questions told me how much worse. I got the impression that the lock knob, door handle and door might be able to do some serious harm to him if he touched them with his bare skin. I finally understood his unease. Most likely, if I didn't open that door, the only way he could leave the bathroom was the same way he'd come in—Faery Magic. Given that Queen Mab had sent him to question me, he was stuck in here with me until I gave him the answers he was looking for.

No wonder he was willing to deal. Damn! For the first time, I had a Faery right where I wanted him. It felt good to have the upper hand for a change. But then I looked at Sir Ansley, just a guy trying to do his job who got stuck in a bad situation, and suddenly it didn't feel good anymore.

I'm sorry. I didn't know. I stretched the cramps out my legs from sitting all balled up on the toilet and hopped off to get to the door. I opened the lock, twisted the handle, and pulled the door open inward, holding it for him. *Honestly, if I'd known the steel was such a problem for you, I would have opened the door immediately.*

"But then you wouldn't have the chance to ask your questions." He nodded his head and stepped out into the sunlight and the noise of the street fair.

We presented an odd pairing as we walked silently along the riverside, side-by-side: me in my hemp dress and loosely-knit alpaca sweater and he in his precisely tailored slacks and vest with a pair of knives strapped to his back. We got a lot of looks from folks walking by.

"*We appear to have everyone's attention*," he said, telepathically, as we continued. "*Is my attire not appropriate?*"

Not too many people strap-up to walk around town in the daylight. I pointed to the hilts of the knives that protruded above his shoulders.

"I should remove them before the authorities detain us."

Nah, leave 'em, I said. *Besides, there's a Geek Fest in town. If anyone asks, just tell them you're here for the convention.*

He gave me a raised eyebrow.

Trust me. It would take too long to explain.

He nodded.

We walked a block more in telepathic silence until we reached a huge circular planter full of lingering summer flowers beneath a spreading oak. High clouds gave the sky over the hills to the west the look of December in Austin. I hated the way the tension had grown in my belly as we walked—its heat clashing with the cold loneliness that filled my chest. This wasn't just any old interview; my phamily's lives hung on whether or not I answered The Winter Knight's questions to Queen Mab's satisfaction. He made me wait while he brushed the dirt off the cement and then we sat, side-by-side, backs toward the tree, me in the sun and Sir Ansley in the shade.

"You know why I'm here?" he asked.

Does that count as a question?

He nodded. *"As does that,"* he said.

Damn, despite all of his courtesies, The Queen's emissary was no push-over. This was going to be tricky. Just as Laume warned me.

"Let us begin."

I nodded, better to get it over with before the hot and cold forces in my body got together and caused some kind of internal tornado that ripped me limb from limb.

"Will you please describe the circumstances in which Lady Laume approached you and proposed the bargain which resulted in your friends' presence in Faery?"

I was tempted to be cagey and just answer "yes" to that question so he'd have to ask me another one to get the actual information he needed—and then I'd be up by two questions instead of just one—but something told me Sir Ansley had a lot more experience at this than I did, and I'd regret being a bitch about it. Probably sooner rather than later.

Agreeing to be agreeable wasn't the same thing as laying it all on the line, though. I still had to be careful about what I said so that The Queen wouldn't decide against Laume. I thought back to what Laume had said about "stick to the facts" and decided that was the best course to follow. All fact, but not all the facts. No attitude, no exaggeration, no sob stories. Nothing that would make Laume look bad—even though I wished I could tell someone the truth about her, someone as powerful as The Queen or her handsome-yet-sad Winter Knight.

I was in a lifeboat, adrift in the Gulf of Mexico, with my phamily. We'd been lost at sea for three days without food or water.

He nodded and held up one finger. At first I thought he was trying to shush me, but then I realized that his face held no sternness and he was just keeping count of the questions he would have to answer for me in return.

"Were you, or your family, in immediate danger when she proposed the bargain?"

I clamped down on all the unhelpful comments that ran through my thoughts in response to that question. My memory tried to revive the horrific images Laume had shown me about Paulo dying in the lifeboat, but I squashed those so I could tell Sir Ansley only the facts. This whole inquisition thing would have been so much easier for me if we could have done it traditionally, not mind-to-mind.

No, when she offered me the bargain none of us was in any immediate danger.

He held up a second finger.

"Were you aware of your responsibilities, what your side of the bargain would entail, prior to agreeing to the bargain?"

I thought back to the lifeboat—remembered Laume pushing it through the water so fast it actually left a wake and how wonderful that was after three days of floundering around with no direction—and tried to piece together what had happened before I said yes, and what had happened after. I remembered a great deal of arm twisting to get my agreement and not a lot of information about what I was agreeing to, but as I thought longer there were two things I could say in Laume's defense.

She made sure to remind me that I had a choice in the matter, and she assured me that I would not have to kill anyone. Then I agreed. It wasn't the whole story, but it was the truth.

The Winter Knight held up a third finger.

"Did Lady Laume explain your role before or after she executed her responsibilities?"

Before, I told him, not having to think that one through. *After I agreed, but before she took my phamily to safety.*

I almost choked on that last phrase. It took every bit of concentration I could muster to keep my comments to myself.

Some of my feelings might have leaked through in my tone of thought because Sir Ansley raised an eyebrow at me. I felt like he was trying to coax me into making clarifying comments, and I wanted to, but I knew it would be the wrong thing to do. I had to stick to the facts that would keep Laume in the best light.

After waiting three breaths for me to elaborate, and I didn't, he raised a fourth finger.

"One more question, and I'll be done." He paused and I wondered why. I feared it meant he was laying a trap for me. *"What do you think was Lady Laume's intention when she carried your family to Faery?"*

Intention?

"Intention is everything. The Queen must understand Lady Laume's intention in transporting your family across The Veil. That choice carries with it unintended consequences which ripple across both our realities. Queen Mab must quiet those ripples in her realm, but she cannot do so until she is clear about the intentions of all those involved."

I wanted to take some time to think about that question—an hour, a week, my whole frickin' lifetime—because I'd assumed I'd understood Laume's intentions without ever really looking at them: she was trying to strong-arm me. The way Sir Ansley conveyed the idea startled me—it was as if intention backed the Faeries' currency of bargaining like our money used to be backed by gold and silver.

Intention is everything.

I didn't know what I believed in my heart about Laume's intentions, but I knew what she'd said—what she wanted me to believe—and I knew she couldn't lie, so in a way that was the truth. What that added up to, I had no idea. But I could parrot her words to The Winter Knight if that would save my phamily.

She said her intention was to keep them safe, I told him. *She said they were safe as moonbeams.*

I don't know if it was my hesitation, or the way I phrased my answer, but he tilted his head as if he might understand my answer differently from that perspective.

"I see. Those are all the questions I have for you."

You didn't give me a fifth finger.

He smiled, slyly. *"You already asked a question of me."*

I did not. I replayed our conversation until I realized he was right. I had asked him about intention.

Very good, sir, I told him telepathically the way a champion chess player admits defeat to his opponent—that is if the champion has any class. I almost asked Sir Ansley if I might have a few minutes to consider what questions to ask, but then I realized he would construe that as a question in itself and then I'd only be able to ask three more.

I will think a moment and then ask my first question.

"Very good, Miss." His face showed genuine appreciation that I'd protected my remaining questions. He waited patiently, watching the crowds as the clouds overtook the afternoon sunshine. The children made him smile.

There were a million things I wanted to know, but my first question was very easy to decide on. *Is my phamily safe and well?*

"*Yes,*" he said, and he lowered a finger.

Knowing that Faeries could not lie, his answer gave me some relief, but not much. I gave him a raised eyebrow of my own, begging details from him beyond that simple one word answer.

He obliged me. *"The Queen has provided secure accommodations for them, including food, water, and bedding. Only myself, my brother, and my son have access to their chamber. They are angry, and frustrated, but they are safe and well."*

Thank you, I told him and I wanted him to know I meant it.

My second question was harder to pick. So much had happened since the concept of Faery became part of my reality. In a week my life had flipped completely upside-down. New city, new guy, new job, new ability. Hannah's face kept popping into my mind. Poor little Hannah, the one caught in the middle of all this bullshit. And she didn't even know she was half-Faery. Like me.

Half-Faery.

Suddenly my next question came clearly into my head. *What can you tell me about my mother, Sunny?*

"I have known Princess L'Estatia all of her life. She is a relative to Queen Mab, and therefore a member of The Winter Court, with many responsibilities to her people. She is a great deal like you: beautiful, bold, brave, and brilliant. Unlike you, however, she is cold, calculating, and condescending."

My mouth hung open by the time Sir Ansley got to the end of his description. He hadn't really said much, but he'd given me ten times as much information as I had before I asked. There was so much I still didn't understand.

Does she even talk about me? The question slipped out before I could stop it.

"Bailey, you have to understand how Faeries see humans."

I tried to mentally butt in, to share JoJo's assessment that we were less than cattle to them, but he placed a hand on mine, sending electric tingles up my arm.

"I have studied your culture, and the closest analogy to Faery-Human relations is the way racial discrimination divided your people during the time of slave-keeping. A master sometimes relied on the efforts of his slaves for his own success, sometimes he even interacted with them—and might occasionally have been impressed by one who displayed a particular talent—but the line between person *and* thing *held true, even with the master's own progeny."*

Sir Ansley eyes were apologetic as he said this, but it didn't make me feel any less pissed-off to hear it. To hear my mother had abandoned me because I was *less than.* I wondered if Sir Ansley felt that same way as we sat together, that he was a *person* and I was a *thing.*

I'd be damned if I was going to blow my last question on that. But I was too angry to keep the next thought that popped into my head from coming out as a question to Sir Ansley.

"So if Faeries feel so fucking superior towards humans, why do humans get so hung-up on Faeries?"

The Winter Knight pressed his index fingers together and raised them to his lips in thought. His icy silver eyes stopped focusing on anything around us and it looked like he disappeared into his own mind trying to find the answer.

I expected he was trying to find a way to tell me the truth in really big words I probably wouldn't understand, so that he wouldn't have to give away any secrets. I was starting to see that in Faery circles secrets were power. The longer he took to think, the more complex I expected his answer would become, and it got to the point as I waited that I figured there was no way I was going to be able to understand the complexity of what he said at all.

And then he gave me my answer.

He took me in his arms, and he kissed me.

...and I lost touch with reality.

...and I didn't care if I ever came back.

...and I knew.

I knew why humans got so hung up on Faeries.

I knew, and I wished I had never asked.

26

I wanted to lose myself forever in that kiss with Sir Ansley. My body lit up. Every nerve tingled with pleasure; and though I would not have thought it possible, he brought me to orgasm by the touch of his lips alone. And not an ordinary orgasm, it was like the best sex I ever had, mixed with the best chocolate mousse I'd ever eaten, and the coldest drink of water I'd ever chugged on a hot day, set on the most beautiful white sandy beach in the world.

It was too good to be true.

Well, no. My body told me it was absolutely true, just sit back and enjoy the ride. But my eyes wanted confirmation that I was not just experiencing a particularly vivid hallucination based on Faery Magic, so I opened them. It struck me funny that I'd never kissed anyone with my eyes open before.

Sir Ansley's eyes were open as well. I met his gaze. But instead of getting lost in the depths of his bright silver irises, seeing him looking back at me rattled something loose in my brain. There was something wrong. We shouldn't be doing this.

The kiss wasn't too good to be true, but Sir Ansley—he and his kiss—were too good to be good for me.

I tried to pull away from the kiss, but my body, still engulfed by wave after wave of orgasmic pleasure, did not want it to stop. Never. Ever. Part of me would do anything to keep those intimate sensations flowing.

Unfortunately, I couldn't yell at him to stop either. It wasn't because I was D-n-D; it was more about the fact that the tip of my tongue refused to stop the flickering dance it had started with the tip of his tongue. Our touching was deft and light and his mouth tasted sweetly of fresh herbs.

I hated the sensation of losing control like that; it reminded me of kissing Ryan Williams in his room at rehab. This nonsense had to stop. Had to. And soon, or it would have horrible consequences, I knew that with every part of my soul.

Since my body disobeyed me, I was forced to resort to my telepathy.

No! I shouted at Ansley in my thoughts. *No, I don't want this. You have to stop.*

But I did want it. I wanted it to go on forever. I didn't care about food or drink or sleep. I just wanted to keep riding the waves of lust that pulsed through my whole body.

Bittersweet relief filled me as Sir Ansley pulled back his flickering tongue and his lips left mine. (I think I may even have leaned toward him at the last moment to keep the heat of our connection for one microsecond longer.) It was a good thing he stopped the first time I asked; because I knew there was no way I had enough control to ask again.

A hollow feeling flooded in as the tingles of pleasure drained out of me. My arms suddenly felt heavy, my legs might as well have been made of wood for all the good they did me when I attempted to stand up. A dull headache started behind my eyes, making me squint.

"*You have incredible self-control,*" Sir Ansley's voice said inside my mind as he sat back and smiled at me.

I wiped my mouth on the back of my hand. *Why the hell did you do that?*

"*Tut-tut.*" He waved his one remaining erect finger at me before he tucked it into his fist. "*I have answered your five questions.*"

That wasn't an answer; that was a sexual assault.

"*But now you understand the human-Faery dynamic a little differently than you used to.*" His smile turned dark. "*I'd call that a very effective answer.*"

I couldn't argue with that. I wanted to, but couldn't.

If a picture was worth a thousand words, I'd say The Winter Knight's kiss was worth the Library of Congress. It made me understand in my gut what Ryan Williams was chasing when he kept coming after me. Ryan thought it was Laume he wanted, but it was the erotic and incomparable sexual release of being with a Faery he was chasing—the way a simple touch from one of them exploded into full-body bliss for one of us. His actions over the previous few days made perfect sense to me. Not that I was willing to excuse him for trying to rape me, but I finally got why he did it. He was chasing a high he'd been after for fourteen years. And what a high.

And I even understood my father a little better, too. If he thought my mother had implied a lifetime of sexual pleasure that intense—and Sir Ansley had only given me a taste of a kiss, not the Full Monty—and then dropped a little blonde screaming bundle of responsibility on him instead, I could see that making him angry. And sad. And extremely disappointed.

"*It's even harder for full-bred humans,*" Sir Ansley said, as if he were reading my thoughts. "*I've never met a human who could resist me.*"

I almost told him how close it had been for this half-human, but decided I'd try the Faery approach and keep the details to myself.

His eyes held mine for a moment more and then he jumped to his feet like someone had jabbed him someplace sensitive with a cattle prod.

"*It is time for me to take my leave.*" He touched his head like he was tipping a hat.

You're just going to pop-on-home?

"*Well*," he thought as he looked around at the folks walking along the riverfront, "*I think I will find a less conspicuous location. But, yes, something like that.*"

When you see my phamily, please give them my love.

He nodded. "*Someone will be in touch.*"

I'm afraid to ask what that means.

"*It is wise to listen to fear. But in this case, have hope that you will get what you desire.*"

I hoped that meant I had convinced him of the lie that I'd entered a fair and just bargain with Laume of my own free will. I hoped he'd report to Queen Mab quickly, and that she would release my phamily just as quickly. I didn't like how that shifted the pressure onto me to get Hannah back home with Ryan-the-Rapist, but at least it would get Queen Mab and the rest of the Faeries out of the picture. Maybe. If I was lucky.

With that, Sir Ansley blew me a kiss and walked back in the direction of the public restroom where we'd started this insane little interview. I watched his back, stiff and straight, as he descended a set of stairs toward a floating restaurant on the river, and then The Winter Knight simply vanished.

I readied my mind to restrain my body from chasing after him, but it turned out not to be necessary. Apparently my little dalliance with Queen Mab's emissary had not been enough to ruin me for the male of my own species.

That encouraging thought lead me to thinking about Brady—which made me feel guilty—because I ought to have been thinking about my phamily. Maria and JoJo and Paulo and Cooper were still stuck in The Queen's dungeon. At the very least I should give them an update on what happened before I ran off trying to fill the hole that Sir Ansley had hollowed out inside me with his kiss.

I did my best to clear my mind of the slight headache leftover from my lengthy telepathic conversation with Sir Ansley and reached out to Maria's mind. The connection clicked in to place as easily as breathing.

Hey Doll, y'all hanging in there?

"Hey you. We're okay, Kitty-kat."

I'm sorry about the bugs and the damp and the screaming down the hall, I thought toward her. *I'm doing the best I can to get you guys out of there as soon as possible.*

"Bugs? Screaming? What the hell are you talking about, Bay?"

The Queen's dungeon. Laume showed me how bad it is. I know you must not be sleeping.

"I'm confused."

And that confused me. It wasn't like Maria to sugar-coat anything, especially when there was something worth complaining about. Those bugs were worth complaining about, even if Paulo had not mentioned them because he was being a guy.

Laume showed me the dungeon. I tried to send Maria a mental copy of the impression Laume had implanted in my brain.

"*Bailey, where are you?*" Maria asked, concern in her voice telling me that something got through. *"We've got to get you out of there. Immediately."*

No, that's not where I am. I'm still in Portland, trying to get you guys out of that hell hole.

"Then who's in the stinky-ass dungeon?"

You guys.

"Wait. That's where Laume said we were."

Hold on, now I'm really confused. Paulo said you were in a dungeon full of big ol' rats. And then Laume came to find out why I hadn't summoned Sir Ansley yet and she showed me where you were being held by Queen Mab so I'd be sure to get my answers straight.

"Oh my god. That fucking bitch."

I suddenly realized I'd been played.

I don't know how, but she lied to me when she showed me that horrid dungeon. She said she couldn't, but she did because she let me assume that's where my phamily was being held. I felt my face get warm. *So you guys are okay?*

"Laume's little hotel room from hell was more comfortable, but, yeah, we're doing okay. It's nowhere near as bad as she let you think."

I got an image in my head, a Maria's-eye-view of a large, concrete room with a wooden table, chairs, and four low cots.

I could feel goosepimples on Maria's exposed skin but nothing like the sensation of the bone-invading chill Laume had fed me. Cooper and Paulo and JoJo were sitting at the table playing a game of some kind with stones that looked like jewels the size of walnuts. The firelight from the hearth at the end of the room made them look like they were alive with their own fire.

Okay, I said. Glad they weren't suffering the agonizing screams and fetid stench.

"*You don't sound any better.*"

Bad day.

"*How bad?*"

I paused to decide how much to tell them. Earlier I had no hesitation to call them for help after escaping my almost-rape at Ryan Williams' house. But now, knowing what they'd been through with Laume and The Queen, I couldn't load them up with any more worry. But I had to say something. Maria knew me too well. If I didn't explain, she would worry more.

You remember that time at the Hospital when they split the five of us up into different wards and Paulo quit taking his meds and JoJo got stuck rooming with that girl who was bulimic and nobody knew?

"*Sure.*"

Not quite that bad, I lied.

"*So what are you going to do about it?*" Maria asked me.

I hated it when she did that. More than once she'd said that accountability saved her life, it was her own personal bullet-proof vest. Unfortunately, she thought the rest of us needed to get accountable with her, all the time.

It wasn't always easy loving someone who made you be the best version of yourself. But I did, and so I admitted that I had no fucking clue what to do next.

"*You need to take care of yourself.*"

Since the fishermen on shrimper fished me out of The Gulf, my intuition for self-preservation hadn't been running at full steam. *Not sure I'm the best person for that job, right now.*

"*Until we get out of here, you're the only person for the job. Where can you go? Who can you hole-up with until you're stronger?*"

I immediately thought of Brady and his confession of love for me. But I couldn't unload this pile of shit into his life. He had a son to take care of.

Nobody, I told her.

"*That's bullshit. Cooper said you made a friend. Go there.*"

I was about to complain about Brady having an ankle biter who got in the way, but then I realized that it was Sunday and Chester's mom was going to pick him up. I *could* call Brady without interfering with his daddy-duties.

Okay. I give up. I'll call him.

"*You promise?*"

Pinky swear.

"*I love you, Bay. We all love you.*"

I love you, too. I'll be in touch soon. Take care of each other.

I reluctantly signed off with Maria and dragged my full awareness back to the park in Portland. The sun was angling toward the east, its light sparkling off the river, indicating evening would soon be on me.

My little borrowed cell phone had fallen to the bottom of my beaded bag, so it took a bit to find it under the big CASA binder and my work uniform. I pulled it out and flipped it open hoping to find it had texting capability.

It did.

That was great. And it sucked. If I had not been able to send Brady a text, I probably would have procrastinated about contacting him until my voice and hearing came back in the morning and just found someplace to crash at for the night. Instead I had to figure out what to say to him.

I hated to ask Brady to drop everything in his life to help me with my problems. He didn't ask for that, even when he said he loved me. Sure, we'd had great sex, but how far does that get a girl, especially when she leaves a guy hanging with a raging case of blue-balls because she's got hang-ups about his kid. How far would this possibility of love really take us?

I did not want to go to Brady in this condition. It made my arms itch, my scalp sweat, and my brain wanted to shut down.

If I'd been in Austin I could have texted a dozen different people to shelter me for the night and some of them would even have been capable of giving me some good advice.

I hated Laume so much for orchestrating this whole situation I could taste the acid of it in my mouth. But acid and hate and fear and anger weren't going to help my phamily, or me.

Maria was right, and I had to suck it up and follow her advice. But asking for help meant Brady was free to say no, free to say he realized that he didn't really love me after all. I wondered what I'd do if (or maybe when) he said so. I didn't know which was worse: not actually having control over the situation, or the possibility that I might find out that without his help I was incapable of dealing with it at all, or the fact that I was absolutely going to have to explain all of this shit to him now.

I took a deep breath and started keying a note.

[Brady, if Chester's mom came to pick him up can I come over? I really need your help.]

My thumb hovered over the Send button. I considered blanking out the whole thing. I fought with myself for a minute and then finally triggered the message.

It only took Brady's reply fifteen seconds to come back.

I couldn't get the smile off my face. Some of it was relief. Some of it was the joy that he hadn't fallen out of love with me overnight. There was a hint of embarrassed shame as in it as well: I hated to be so needy, vulnerable, dependent. And, oddly enough, part of me was really happy because the cool nickname I'd given Brady's little boy had caught on.

[Chef-ster's mom is on her way over to get him right now. What's up?]

Talk about an explanation that wasn't appropriate for delivery via text.

[Thanks a bazillion. Too complicated, I'll explain when I get there.]

Brady's immediate reply was just one word.

[Hurry.]

And I did.

The walk from my meeting with Sir Ansley to Brady's apartment took twenty minutes. I spent most of that time oblivious to the people and buildings and cars around me and concentrated on how I could link up with Brady telepathically without freaking him out. I stopped a block away and typed a message into my texting application to show him: [Voice is gone again. Have something cool to show you. Do you trust me?]

I planned to show him the note when he opened the door to his apartment and hope that he'd come along for the ride.

27

Turns out I didn't have to wait to get up to Brady's apartment to see him, he was sitting on a bench in his lobby—hands pressed together between his knees—watching people come and go. He jumped up as soon as he saw me and met me at the door.

I didn't get a chance to show him my phone before he swept me into his arms. His skin smelled like BBQ smoke and the warmth of sunshine. I held him back, feeling the movement of his jaw against my face and the vibrations of talking in the muscles of his back. In all the times I'd been D-n-D, this was the worst to bear. I needed to hear what he was saying.

When I didn't answer him he pulled back to look at me. My opportunity to show him my phone. He read the message quickly and nodded his head without hesitation, though his eyebrows were arched in concern.

If only he knew what he was in for. I was about to blow his mind.

My fingers laced with his and I pulled him toward the elevator. He pushed the button for his floor and as soon as the doors closed I pounced on him, hungry to feel his lips on mine. Part of that came from the emptiness left behind after

Sir Ansley's demonstration kiss, but most of it came from the joy I felt at simply looking at Brady's face. His strong jaw, thin lips, strong eyebrows. My need for him reassured me. I knew in that moment that I hadn't just said I might love him because he said it first. It was true.

Now I had to hope that dumping my story and my new ability on him wouldn't scare him away.

He broke from our kiss first, and I saw that the doors had opened on his floor. He led me to his apartment and once inside I lead him straight to the fridge for a couple of beers and then dragged him over to the sofa.

We sat facing each other and I admired his patience because I could see a million questions racing across his face. With one last deep breath and a hopeful prayer to Elvis that I wasn't about to make the biggest mistake of my life I grabbed both of Brady's hands and stared him straight in the eyes.

Brady, can you hear me?

I squeezed his hands in time with each word in the hopes that he'd pick up the pattern and not dismiss my voice in his head. I had to repeat myself three more times, but then his eyes got really huge and he pulled his hands away.

Expecting some resistance, I reached out and took his hands again. *Please, I know this is strange, but it's the only way I can talk to you right now, and I really need your help.*

Brady tried to pull away but this time I held onto him.

Just think something back to me. It's telepathy. It won't hurt you. I won't hurt you.

"Am I crazy?"

I'm not a doctor, but given all the crazy people I've met, I'd have to say no. I smiled at him so he'd take the joke the way I meant it.

He shifted uncomfortably on the couch and I felt bad for making him feel that way in his own apartment.

"How is this even possible?"

It's all part of the story, and I'm finally ready to tell you, if you're ready to hear it.

"You're telepathic."

And that's not the most fucked-up part, I'm sorry to say. Last night you gave me the impression you wanted to know me, really know me. I'm scared, but I want to tell you. All of it.

Brady hesitated and I was glad that he didn't just say yes. Our relationship had a strange start, and this might turn out to be an even stranger end if he couldn't accept what I was about to lay on him. I hoped that his ability to handle my telepathy pretty easily indicated he would be able to wrap his head around the rest.

He scooted nearer to me on the couch until our knees touched and then he leaned forward and offered me a kiss. I accepted and used it to convey all the passion I felt for him. It was sweet, and needful, and reassuring.

"That won't change?" he asked with a tiny smile when we finished.

The cold ball in my chest warned me to mitigate my answer, I didn't really know what would change and to say otherwise would not be the truth. But I knew what my heart wanted the truth to be, so I went with that.

No, that will never, ever change.

"Hang on." He cracked open his beer. After he downed the whole bottle in three breathless gulps and then opened mine and held it in his hands like a drowning man holds onto a life preserver he said, *"Okay, tell me."*

I started at the beginning and described our band, our amazing fortune at landing a recording contract, and the wave that rolled the record company's yacht out from under us. He handled all that well so I gave him a few details about the days and nights in the lifeboat, watching for lights on the horizon.

And this is where it gets weird, I thought to him, and then launched into the description of Laume's arrival and her offer to save us if I'd help Hannah.

"So that's why you were on the plane to Portland. It wasn't a friend's kid, it was hers."

It turns out that Hannah is hers, but that's getting a little bit ahead. I smiled and he nodded for me to continue. The story of getting to the airport made him smile in places, except the part about the middle-aged guy in the airport.

"So she's a Faery, and she possessed some poor guy to keep you in line? What a bitch."

That's what my phamily calls her, Faery Bitch.

"What happened to them? Where are they?"

They're hostage. I described their hotel room from hell, then glossed over the details of getting settled in Portland because he knew them already—he'd been so helpful—and I got to the part about Hannah and Ryan Williams and how I got hooked up with them through Children's Services.

"So she can just fake paperwork like that?"

You remember my license and passport?

He nodded.

All Laume. The guy at the border never even blinked when I used it.

"That's why you were looking at them so closely."

She'd been tracking me down and I wanted to know how. I figured out that she was tracking those documents, but something strange happened that I still don't really understand.

I filled in more of the story, meeting Hannah and then her father at the treatment center. I paused for a moment, covering it with a drink from Brady's beer, as I decided how much of my interactions with predatory-Ryan to share. I wanted to tell Brady about Ryan trying to rape me, I needed someone to know, and I knew he'd be more likely to believe me if he knew there had been other incidents leading up to that morning. But I was afraid that the details would make Brady too angry to listen to my whole story.

This whole damn exercise was about trust, though. So I decided to give him the whole ugly story and hope that he'd keep his cool. I described the first meeting with Ryan in the visiting room at the treatment center and Brady's hackles went up, I saw it in the way he flexed his biceps beneath his tattoos. If he'd been drinking beer out of a can the couch would have been drenched from the unconscious tension in his hands.

I reached out to calm him with my touch. *It gets worse. I can spare you the details, but I'd rather you knew the whole story.*

"I'm going to kill the bastard."

If he felt that way already he was not going to deal well with the rest of the crap that had gone down.

You can't. I need to straighten his ass out and get his daughter home if I'm going to get my phamily back. Promise me that you will let me handle this. Please.

"I don't know."

I'm trusting you with this, I reminded him. *This situation sucks like nobody's business, but it's what I've got to deal with and it would be a whole hell of a lot easier if you were with me, not making it harder.*

"Tell me the rest."

I described my interactions with the psychiatrist at the treatment center and then my second meeting with Ryan, sparing no details except maybe how turned on I'd gotten and how lost my brain got.

"You were wearing that dress on Friday when I saw you. How the hell didn't I notice?"

We had Chester that night. You were a little pre-occupied.

Brady shook his head in disbelief, and maybe even disgust. *"I was so wrapped up in my own shit that I didn't even notice you'd been attacked."*

I didn't want you to know. And dealing with the Williamses hasn't been all bad.

I told him more. The part about Hannah singing at the American Idol event was easy to describe to Brady. Partly because I knew no part of it would hurt him, or make him angry, and mostly because it had been such an amazing experience.

"If I didn't know better, I'd say you already loved that little girl."

That was an interesting observation. I wasn't sure if he got it from the look on my face or the intimacy of telepathic conversation, but I took from the smile on his face that he thought it was a good thing.

We have some odd things in common, I told him. *But I'll never be able to get to that part of the story unless you stop interrupting me.*

He gave me a time-out sign so he could run to the kitchen for two more beers and then he came back to listen to the rest of my story.

It was hard to tell him about Hannah's reaction to seeing me with her father's car, but Brady didn't interrupt—like he promised he wouldn't—so I got through it and made him laugh with my story of trying to find a hotel room in a city full of hookers and Sci-Fi conventioneers.

"So where have you been staying these past two nights?"

My answer, *Ryan Williams' house*, didn't make him happy.

"After he attacked you?"

I'm not proud of it, okay. I figured he was all locked up at rehab and it was better than blowing all my cash on an overpriced room at The W.

"You could have come back here."

I wish I had.

Elvis help me. If I'd only come back and stayed the weekend with Brady—Chester or not—my life would have been so much easier. My phamily would still be in the dungeon of a scary Faery queen, but I wouldn't be feeling as humiliated as I was. Thinking about Ryan's attack brought all the feelings back as if it were all happening again and I started to cry.

"Baby, what's wrong?" He moved in to hug me, not that he was trying to stop my tears, just that he sensed the change in me.

Can I borrow a t-shirt, I asked him, *looking into his eyes. I really, really need to take a shower.*

Brady didn't want to let me go, I felt it in the strength of his arms around me. Instead he swept me up and carried me into the bathroom where he set me on the counter and cranked on the shower.

"Be right back," he said as he dashed away and returned with a t-shirt and pair of sweats that smelled fresh from the dryer as the water in the shower started to steam up the mirror.

I stripped out of my sweater and dress and handed them to him. *Can you hang these up for me?*

"You want me to go?"

No. Please stay.

He helped steady me while I stripped out of my undies and then helped me into the shower.

The hot water felt like a clean slate sliding over my body, not quite new skin or a new me, but a chance to clean myself of the crappy memories that clung to me like cobwebs.

I took advantage of the way the shower curtain gave me some privacy. Even though my mind was linked in conversation with Brady's it was better that he couldn't see me for the part of the story I still had to tell. Skipping over Saturday—parts he already knew and the other parts were not really significant to the story—I told him about the way Ryan Williams had woken me up that morning.

I didn't spare him the details, and as I recounted the pinning and the crushing and the invasion of his penis penetrating me I watched the water slide down the drain and imagined my pain going away with it. Down. Out. Good riddance. It was not easy to tell my story, but by the time I was done I felt better. Not good, but better.

Turning off the shower, I pulled the curtain back to find Brady waiting with a fluffy towel. He wrapped me in it and held me gently.

Tighter, I begged him with my telepathy and my arms. *Tighter and please don't ever let go.*

We held each other in the steamy bathroom for a minute, my wet hair soaking his t-shirt until I felt strong enough to let go. Our telepathic link was quiet so I pulled back and looked into his eyes to see what he was feeling.

"You have to go to the police."

I can't. If he gets arrested and goes to jail he can't get his daughter back. I can't do that to my phamily. But, that might not matter anymore, anyway.

"I don't understand."

While I dried off and got dressed I explained to him all that I'd learned from JoJo and Paulo and Sir Ansley about Queen Mab and her court. Especially the part where JoJo said she'd met my mother and Sir Ansley confirmed it.

Brady had plopped down on the counter to listen to me so I sat on the closed toilet seat. *So, that's where the telepathy comes from. Turns out I'm half-Faery.*

He didn't budge. He didn't smile. He didn't add anything to our conversation.

You want to run, don't you?

"It's a lot to take in." Brady shook his head and blew out a breath. *"I thought I had a lot of baggage."*

It is, and you do, but I have more. How about you sit and think about it for a while and I'll make us some dinner. I'm starving.

"I can't ask you to do that after all you've been through today."

Baking focuses me, really. I could use some time in the kitchen that isn't repetitive mixing and kneading. I led him out to the couch and sat him down with the rest of his luke-warm beer. *Sit. Don't think too much. Just don't freak out on me.*

I left him there, shell-shocked, and rummaged through the kitchen for ingredients. His cupboards and fridge were stocked well enough for me to pull off a quiche Florentine. I was surprised to find myself humming *Blue Suede Shoes* in my head as I worked. Not happily, but not completely destroyed like I'd felt for most of the day. I blamed it on Brady—blamed it on his strong arms, big heart and steady nature.

Yes, it was very possible that I loved him.

While the quiche baked I tiptoed back into the living room to see if Brady was still there (he was) and if he was ready to talk some more. He patted the sofa next to him and I took the clue.

"What are you going to do about the girl?" he asked me telepathically. *"Knowing what you know, you can't send her home to him. If you're right about his obsession with Faeries, sooner or later he's going to go after her. It doesn't matter that she's his daughter."*

I knew Brady was a smart cookie, but he figured the crux of the problem a whole lot faster than I thought he would. I was really impressed and I showed him with a kiss.

I have to write a report outlining my recommendations for Hannah's future and turn it in to a judge tomorrow. If she doesn't go home Laume will never let my phamily go.

"Assuming she's going to get them back."

I have to believe I convinced Sir Ansley. Queen Mab will release them. I can't even think about what might happen to them if she doesn't let them go.

We talked until I sniffed the buttery, eggey and spinachy smells that said the quiche was done cooking, but neither of us had come up with any answers. We ate in silence, like an old married couple and I felt oddly soothed by how comfortable it made me. After dinner Brady brought me his laptop and I sat at the table stumbling over my report while he washed the dishes.

An hour later I had a two-page report that looked like the example in the back of my CASA binder with all the right names and dates and doofy little logos. I included observations of how well Hannah was doing at her foster home with her new friends and a fierce recommendation that they all spend at least three afternoons a week together. I noted how Ryan Williams was finally getting on the stick at the rehab center, but I could not bring myself to include the reason for his sudden change in interest or that he'd skipped out on Sunday morning for a little field-trip home.

The worst part was how easy it had been to recommend that Hannah and Ryan start visitations as soon as possible and that she be returned home as soon as he completed rehab. It felt slimy and cheap and betraying and I never thought I'd be the kind of person who would put my own interests ahead of the protection of a little girl. Part of my brain chocked it up to the fact that no one had ever protected me when I was little and I'd made it, sort of.

Brady noticed my stretching in my seat at the table and came over to rub my shoulders. *"So, what did you write?"*

It's awful, I whined. *If I do what I need to do for my phamily it's just selling her out. I keep trying to tell myself that he might not ever go after her like he did with me. My dad never came after me that way.*

"But your dad sounds like he's a better person than Ryan Williams."

I glared at Brady. After everything I'd shared with him, I couldn't believe he would side with my father.

"I'm not saying he was a good man, but he was good enough. I'm a single-father by choice and I know how hard it is. I can't imagine Chester suddenly dumped on me full time."

Brady's words felt like the kind of thing one of my counselors might have said. I could wallow, or I could open my eyes, see what was going on and accept the situation, the reality.

If I applied that to the Williams family, I suddenly got very scared for Hannah. Sir Ansley's kiss had been a real eye-opener. If that's the kind of experience Ryan had been missing and looking for since Laume ditched him, I had to admit there was a real possibility that he would go after Hannah as soon as he had any inkling she was half-Faery.

I looked down at my report and felt horribly ashamed.

What do you do when one of your ad campaigns just isn't working?

"I start from scratch," he explained and grabbed the mouse to print out a copy of my report and then brought a clean page up on the program.

Suddenly it made all sorts of sense. If the last week had taught me anything it was that nothing was predictable and I couldn't give up. My report wasn't actually due until I walked into Kevin Butcher's office the next day. In Faery time that could be a week—a million things could happen between now and then. I would write two reports, the one saying Hannah should go home, and write the truth in the other: that I didn't think Hannah should be allowed anywhere near her father. Armed with both of them I'd be able to make a decision before I had to actually turn it in.

Okay, I'll write two versions and decide later.

Brady kissed me on the top of the head. *"I'll be watching TV. Come get me when you're ready for bed. I can call in sick for you in the morning and then drive you over to Human Services."*

I turned to look at him. *Call in sick? I can't, I'll get fired.*

"Baby, you've had a hell of a week. You have to take a day to take care of yourself. Who cares if you get fired from that lousy bakery?"

I swear you've been talking to Maria behind my back, I teased. *She would have said exactly the same thing.*

"That's because we both love you." He kissed me on the head again and left me to wrestle with my truth draft.

It felt good to put the truth in words, but only because I had the "save the phamily" draft written and sitting in the printer already. The second report only took fifteen minutes to write—fewer schmooozy details, more gritty truth—and I was incredibly tired and ready for bed when I'd gotten it all out and Brady printed it for me.

I was so grateful that Chester had gone home to his mom's and I could stay the night without my conscience nagging at me.

Snuggled into Brady's arms looking at the patches of orange light on the ceiling I wasn't quite at peace, but I could see it from there. He surprised me when I spooned against him and felt his erection, and I surprised myself when I took him up on it. Though I was tempted to use a telepathic link to talk dirty to him as I rode his sweaty body, I decided the physical connection was intense enough. We were good together, better than good, better than the first time, and afterwards I collapsed onto him and rolled off to lie at his side, head to toes, tucking my cold toes under the pillow next to his.

Brady's touch was light as he traced the line of star tattoos running up the backside of my right leg. I took that as a request for a little afterglow chit-chat on a telepathic level.

Tickles, damnit, I told him.

"What are these?" he asked as his fingers worked their way up toward my butt.

I guess you could call them my scorecard.

Brady pulled his hand away and I felt the mattress shift as he sat up. *"One for every what?"* His tone in my head was colder than I expected after what we'd just done for each other.

And then it suddenly hit me that he thought my tats were like notches on the bedpost.

No, not lovers. I would never, ever be stupid enough to tattoo a star for each man I'd been with. That was my private business, and would probably scare most guys away. *Gigs, I have a star for every packed house Billy's Asylum Rats ever played.*

"Oh," I heard him think and he settled back on the bed. *"If you did have a scorecard for lovers, how many stars would it have?"*

Damn, he had to ask. Maybe one day I'd tell him, but in that moment I was too exhausted to start a conversation like that.

I twisted to lie on my side and propped my head on my hand so I could see his face.

If you really want to know, I'll tell you. But if you ask me, the more important questions are how many more stars will I add, and how high up my list would your star be?

"*I'll settle for that.*"

I turned around on the bed so I could prop my chin on his chest. I made him wait until his breathing got faster and I knew I had him beyond curious.

I think I might be done adding stars, I thought to him as I examined his handsome face. *You're the top of my list.*

Brady smiled. I loved it when he did that. Especially since I earned it by telling him the truth. He pulled me up into a sleepy and content kiss, in the middle of which he turned off the light. We lay in the darkness and I wondered what might happen next.

Only after Brady's chest rose and fell in a steady pattern indicating sleep did it occur to me that while I made love to him I hadn't once thought of Ryan's perfect body, Sir Ansley's enthralling kiss, or anyone I'd ever been intimate with. Proof that I was truly, madly, deeply in love with him.

At nine the next morning Brady delivered me, wearing my hemp dress and alpaca sweater again, to the state offices on 2nd street downtown. We parked in a garage across the street and he said he'd make some work-related calls while he waited for me. My badge got me in the building, past the metal detectors, and I made my way up to Kevin's office.

I took the stairs, hoping that extending the stress of my impending deadline would help me finally decide which version of my report to turn in for the judge. My gut said to give them only the truth, but every time I thought I'd decided that way the cold ball of loneliness in my chest would act up. By the time I hit the third floor I was more confused than ever.

The halls to Kevin's offices were a beehive of activity. I found my way to his door and knocked on the frame, interrupting some work on the computer.

"Bailey, I was just trying to reach you."

Good Graceland. I'd shut the ringer off on the cell phone he gave me so I could sleep in on Saturday morning, and I'd never turned it back on

"Sorry. I've got my report," I said, tapping the folder with both versions.

"I'm not sure how much good it will do now," Kevin said.

"Why not?"

"You haven't heard the news."

The little hairs on the back of my neck stood up, suddenly afraid for Hannah. It wasn't that I thought my admission of attempted suicide to her and the kids was likely to give her any ideas, but Hannah was obviously one unhappy kiddo and anything could happen if anything pushed her too close to the edge. "What news? Is Hannah okay?"

"She's down the hall with a counselor. Her father's dead."

"What? How?" I almost said that I'd just seen him, but I clamped my mouth shut because of all the questions that would raise.

"Yesterday morning. The police were called out to his house. We don't have all the details but we know he came outside and pointed a pair of pistols at them. The police bureau is calling it *suicide by cop.*"

My legs went weak and I collapsed against the wall and found myself sitting on the floor before Kevin could come around the desk to catch me. I suddenly remembered the two police cars rushing up Burnside, forcing that big truck onto the side of the road where I was trying to walk. They must have been headed for Ryan Williams' house.

Ryan Williams was dead.

Elvis help me.
I was never going to get my phamily back.

28

I slumped into the passenger seat of Brady's Audi, slammed the door and buried my face in my hands. Leaving Kevin's office, the third floor, and the building had hardly registered in my thoughts. I barely remembered crossing the street and climbing the garage stairs to the second floor. There was no explanation for how I found Brady's car again, except blind luck. I'm sure my face was ghost white because my skin felt cold and clammy.

"Went that well, huh?" Brady asked, a tinge of humor in his voice.

I hated to obliterate his good mood with my devastating news, so the band-aid approach seemed best. I sat back in the seat, propping my head at an uncomfortable angle as I stared at the garage's giant steel support beams through the moon roof. "Ryan Williams is dead, and I just got kicked-off the case."

Brady was awfully quiet for an awfully long time. When I looked over I saw him staring straight ahead, thinking. His face alternated between a smirk of satisfaction and the creased brow of disbelief while his hands wrung the steering wheel in a death grip. He finally looked at me and said, "I can't say I'm sorry he's dead after what he did to you. What happened?"

"The gardeners who saw me leaving his house called the cops because they heard me screaming and crying after their boss came home early from rehab. When the officers arrived, maybe twenty minutes after I left, they found a truck in the driveway; they'd been looking for it since it was reported leaving the scene of an accident at daybreak. Hit and run."

I took a deep breath to try and distance myself from the next thing I had to say, but it didn't really help.

"He busted out of rehab and killed someone to get to me. That bastard killed someone to get to me."

The tears I'd been bottling up since Kevin's office finally broke loose and my whole body convulsed with sobs as I doubled over. Brady reached across the console and wrapped me in his arms the best he could, his head heavy on my shoulder. I appreciated that his strokes and kisses were meant to make me feel better, but I was too far gone down the road to hell to think that was possible.

I kept talking into my lap. Not that Brady would understand half of what I said, but I had to get it out so it didn't eat me alive. "After they ran the plates and the registration didn't match the address, a dozen cops surrounded the house so he couldn't escape. They said he came out the front door in a pair of boxer shorts, screaming nonsense and waving a pair of chrome-plated semi-automatic pistols. He took a shot at one of the cop cars and they took him down. Seventeen shots. He took seventeen bullets before he gave it up."

"Bailey, it's not your fault."

"But I'm still fucked," I said through my tears. I sat up. "He's gone and so is any chance of getting my phamily back from Laume, whether Queen Mab decides to give them up or not. And poor Hannah."

"What's going to happen to her? Why are you off the case?"

"She's still a ward of the state until they figure out if her father made any arrangements for her in his will. But I can't help her anymore. The shock of hearing what happened struck me stupid and I opened my mouth at the wrong time. I confessed to Kevin that I was the woman at the house, that Ryan had loaned me his car and his house to help me.

"Kevin got pissed. So pissed. Apparently I broke a bunch of rules. I wasn't supposed to accept gifts. I didn't know someone would see it as a gift. I never read that far in the binder. The damn thing was thicker than the lenses in Buddy Holly's glasses. I just didn't have the time..."

I lost it again and Brady held me and waited out the storm.

Stupid, stupid, stupid. I knew I should never have accepted the keys and alarm codes from Ryan's Faery-befuddled psychiatrist. I'd known it was wrong at the time, but I was being selfish and didn't understand how serious a problem it would be until Kevin explained that the defense's lawyer would have a field day because of my lack of impartiality.

Impartiality. Heh. That was fucking ironic. I'd never been impartial in Hannah's case. I'd connived my way into Kevin's office on a set-up of Faery lies with an outside agenda driving every choice I made. The only time I'd been impartial was the half hour I spent writing a second report telling the judge the truth; a report that I couldn't even convince myself to turn in.

I wasn't saying I deserved all that had happened to me, but I sure didn't have a lot of room to cry foul at being kicked off the case.

"Kevin said the Children's Services department would take it in the teeth from the court if the 'bribes' I'd taken from Ryan Williams ever came to light," I told Brady and buried my face in his shoulder.

Bribes. Sure. That's not even where the real trouble had been. I wondered how the judge would feel if he found out that Hannah's delinquent father had sexually assaulted me and then tried to rape me. Who'd get in trouble for that?

Eventually I cried myself out, but not before I'd soaked the shoulder of Brady's good work shirt in mascara-stained tears. He looked like he'd lost a fight with a mime.

"I'm going to call the office, take the day off," he said softly. "I'll get you home and we'll figure this out. We'll think of something."

I was so grateful for Brady. Grateful that I'd told him everything and he'd stayed. Grateful for his optimism. Grateful that his brain was still working because mine could only cycle one thought over and over: *The moment Laume finds out Ryan is dead, my phamily is in trouble.*

Brady made his call while I stared vacantly out the window at the rain-spattered cars rolling through the garage on the hunt for the perfect parking space. It felt wrong that anyone within a ten mile radius of me should be allowed to go on with their day as usual when my world was falling down around my ears.

The whir of the car's starter and the purr of the engine pulled me out of my pity-party just enough for me to ask Brady if we could stop by the liquor store. He agreed without questioning, even though the clock on his dashboard said it was barely ten in the morning.

I intended to spend my last ten dollars on a cheap bottle of tequila and drink myself into oblivion.

Telepathy and tequila, not such a good match; like drunk dialing at three in the morning—which I could no longer do because I was without a cell phone, again—but stupider. Especially if the other end of the link were dear friends you were about to disappoint horrendously or a Faery Bitch who wouldn't be happy to hear a word coming out of your brain.

Brady had chipped-in at the liquor store so we got a good bottle of tequila instead of the eight dollar swill from the bottom shelf—we'd get just as drunk but the hangover promised to be less obnoxious with the good stuff. I was so pissed-off, stressed-out and self-obsessed that I didn't even pay attention to whether or not he kept up with me as we sat at his dining table and drained most of the bottle, one shot at a time.

By noon our conversation stopped making any kind of sense, but we'd come up with a plan of attack. First, I decided that I had to connect with my phamily right away. Their lives were hanging in the balance of what happened next more than mine and I had to let them know that the situation had gone to shit...but I was still trying to fix it. Second, and this was Brady's idea, I had to be the one to tell Laume that Ryan Williams was dead. She had to hear it from me.

After killing of the last partial-shot in the bottle I picked Maria for the first conversation. She yelled at me for being drunk to the point of slurring—that much I expected: pot meet kettle—but she took the rest of the news without making any comments. She said she'd talk to the others, but she didn't think there was much they were going to be able to do from their cell in Queen Mab's dungeon. After babbling *I'm sorry* for the millionth time, I ran out of things to add and told her I'd be in touch as soon as I figured something out.

When my whole brain was back in the apartment with Brady I answered his hopeful smile with a slow shake of my head. He stroked my hair and cupped my chin in his hand. As I tilted my head to the side to rest it on his warm skin, my stomach lurched in a very demanding way. Straightening up and taking a deep breath didn't settle things down so I slapped both hands across my mouth and ran for the bathroom.

Tequila on the way back up burns almost as much as it does on the way down, especially when you drink more than half the bottle in one sitting. Stupid. Unbalanced and unable to stand, I knelt on the floor in front of the toilet and vomited again and again. And again. When I was done, all that remained inside of me were the aching muscles that held down that cold ball of loneliness in my chest. No amount of brushing or gargling made that better.

I reached out to Brady telepathically—hell, I was already going to be D-n-D until sunrise, so using my telepathy to talk to the man of my dreams in the next room was quite convenient. I told him I was okay, but what he said in return gave me goosebumps on every square inch of my skin.

"Bailey, get out here. There's someone, something, in my living room and I think it's that Faery you told me about."

My feet slipped on the wet tiles as I launched myself toward the door but I managed to keep from bashing my brains out on the edge of the counter. It took three tries to get the door open and I sprinted down the hall to find Brady and Laume standing on opposite sides of the coffee table, each pulling on a handle of my beaded bag like a couple of naughty terriers. I crashed into the couch to stop myself and that distracted Brady just long enough for Laume to gain the upper hand. She clutched my bag in both hands, but held it away from her as if she didn't want it to snag her floor-length, sky-blue sequined gown.

Talk about being overdressed for the occasion.

Her arrival solved one problem—I didn't have to try to locate her telepathically—and the way she dug through my bag, came out with my passport and license, and tucked them down the front of her dress confirmed once and for all that's how she tracked me. But I could not stand having her in Brady's place, his sanctuary, standing just three feet away from him.

Maybe the tequila made me brave, maybe I felt like there wasn't much left to lose, or maybe I was just fed-up with Laume. No matter why I did it, I charged at her, pushing Brady out of the way as I shoved past him, and grabbed fistfuls of her long, silky hair. It was pretty clear that I surprised her, and that was probably the only reason I controlled her long enough to drag her through the dining room toward the sliding glass door that sat partially open to the balcony.

It took every ounce of strength I had, but I managed to force Laume to her knees and wedge her head through the ten inch opening between the door and the frame. Still holding her hair with one hand, I slid the floor-to-ceiling glass door closed until there was barely a quarter-inch between Laume's bare neck and the brushed steel frame that held the glass to the door and the door to the wall.

I was acting on a hunch, a desperate and pathetic guess based on intuition and a whole lot of desperation in the moment. Sir Ansley's confession of a *severe allergy* to iron and steel had stayed in my mind, and in the heat of the moment I hoped it was not just a Winter Knight thing, but a Faery thing, to react badly to iron. The hunch was backed by my memories of Laume in her elbow-length gloves as she handled the stainless steel handle of the garbage chute hatch and the fact that she chose to drive me through town in a two-million dollar supercar that was made mostly of composite materials. I'd never seen her actually touch metal except for Maria's ring, which was made of silver. The way Laume held perfectly still, as if her head were perched in a guillotine, not just the frame of an ordinary sliding door, verified my hunch was dead on.

I let her hair go, but held tight to the door and the wall—knuckles white and hands shaking—as I tried to catch my breath and figure out what the hell I was going to do next.

She had ruined my life. Eight days ago I had been sopping wet, miserable, hungry, thirsty, and afraid of dying in a lifeboat with my phamily when she found me—and yes, I had plead to the sky for help—but as I stood there with her life in my hands I wished Laume had never fallen out of the sky as a shooting star and devastated my life. Sure, that might be the same thing as wishing myself dead, and I know that any version of Billy's Asylum Rats perishing at sea would have sucked rotten eggs, but at least we would have been together.

I would have died with my phamily, not alone and incapable of doing anything but offering empty apologies for the consequences of my crappy decisions.

Somehow that would have been better.

Nearly staring holes in the back of Laume's head, I forced a telepathic connection. *Did you do this, you bitch? Did you set this whole thing up from the start? Did you send the wave that sank the yacht? Were you there, just watching and waiting for me to get desperate so you could force me into this hell?*

Every question drove my anger to a higher level as I telepathically yelled and yelled and did not stop to listen. I didn't even want to know if she was trying to answer me. I swear if Brady had not stepped up behind me to pull me away from the door I would have found out how disgusting the decapitation of a Faery could get. I fought him to keep a hold of the door but he carefully wrapped his hands around my torso with his fingers spread wide and applied pressure until I gave in, sagging in his arms.

He reeled me in against his body, moved away from Laume and then placed me in one of his dining chairs where he knelt on the floor between my legs and tucked the wild tangles of my hair behind my ears.

I couldn't hear him, but I could read his lips. "Settle down, Bay. Breathe. Just breathe."

I forced breath in and out around my clenched teeth and snarled lips. He meant well, I knew it, and I should have been grateful for his interference, but all I could do was turn and watch that Faery Bitch palm the glass panel to push the door open, pick herself up off the floor, and then smooth the front of her dress as if I had not just almost killed her.

"*He is quite an intelligent human,*" she said to me telepathically, her face as unrevealing of emotion as a marble statue. "*Perhaps I underestimated him from a distance.*"

Perhaps he just saved your fucking life.

"*Perhaps he just saved yours.*"

We glared at each other across the dining table, neither willing to look away as if this moment would somehow settle all of the matters between us. I felt Brady's hand running down my arm from my shoulder to my elbow, stroking me the way a cowboy might calm a horse by stroking its neck. His touch grounded me, diffusing some of my adrenaline and calling my attention to the fact that I was still severely intoxicated.

My jaw relaxed, my breathing came easier and slower, but I dared not take my eyes off of Laume.

"*I sense something has changed. You stink of desperation, mint-tainted-vomit and fermented* pulque." She pulled one of the chairs away from the table and perched on its edge, showing me that she wasn't afraid of me, arrogant Faery Bitch. "*That wouldn't have anything do to with why I cannot locate either Hannah or her father?*"

I was surprised to learn that Laume kept tabs on her jilted human lover and their "less than" offspring. She'd never once expressed any real emotion for either one of them beyond calling Ryan "something special" which in light of Sir Ansley's comments on the universal Faery disdain for humanity might mean just about anything.

Her inability to find Ryan didn't surprise me. He was done with this life, no longer vainly searching for that high, maybe even feeling some peace after his years of torment. But I had no idea why Hannah had gone AWOL, and it scared me.

Let's make a deal, I offered. *I'll give you Ryan Williams' current whereabouts if you tell me everything you know about Hannah Faye: where she was last time you checked on her, who she was with, what they were doing.*

Laume nodded her head in agreement, but I had learned a thing or three and knew that wasn't good enough.

You must say I agree.

She smiled like a crocodile and hesitantly said, "*I agree.*"

You first, I insisted.

"*Very well. This morning I observed Hannah Faye travelling with members of your justice brigade in one of their conveyances with the flashing lights and false-made siren's song. The conveyance entered a garage beneath ground and I have not sensed her presences since.*"

Well, hell. That didn't tell me anything that I didn't already know except that Hannah had been taken to Human Services in a police vehicle.

"*Your turn.*"

I crossed my arms and tried to decide if there was any way I could play the situation out that I knew for sure wouldn't get my phamily killed. For the first time I was grateful that Queen Mab had taken them away from her, and that only Sir Ansley and his trusted family members could gain access to their dungeon cell.

The crap part was that sooner or later Laume would figure out what happened to Ryan, so I might as well get it over with.

You can't find Ryan Williams for a very simple reason, I said.

She stared at me, looking bored, not looking like someone who was prepared to hear about the death of someone she once knew, and once cared about enough to mother a child with.

So I sucker-punched her with it...

...He's dead...

...and cringed, waiting for her to explode.

29

I wished Laume had been standing when I gave her the news about Ryan Williams' death, because if she had I might have seen some kind of physical response: a teeter, a sway, a hand propped against the wall seeking balance.

Laume gave me no immediate reaction. After a minute I wondered if she would give me any reaction at all.

Well? I asked her telepathically. *Don't you have anything to say?*

"*It's a pity, I suppose.*" Laume brushed invisible dirt off the skirt of her dress where I'd forced her to her knees. "*He was admirable when naked.*"

It's a pity? It's a pity! Brady had to hold me down in my chair. Elvis, Carl and Roy, was that all she had to say?

Laume had turned my entire life upside down to get my assistance in returning Hannah home to Ryan—took my phamily, wouldn't let me go home, put me at the mercy of a rapist, and then subjected me and my phamily to the whims of a Faery Queen—and now her only regret was that she'd miss seeing Ryan's naked body. Good Graceland.

I stopped fighting Brady and went limp in my chair from disbelief.

What's going to happen to my phamily now?

"Well, Little Darlin', that's up to Queen Mab, isn't it?"

But we had a deal.

"And you've delayed so long in delivering your part of the bargain that it is no longer possible to do so. That means I am no longer obliged to deliver my portion."

But they're my phamily. I could feel my drunken tears running down my face, dripping on my hands and cooling in the path of the breath I huffed.

"They are no longer my problem. Their safety is not my concern anymore."

Elvis help me, I hated her. I fantasized for just a moment about what it would have been like to slam the sliding glass door closed on her neck. It wasn't blood I pictured gushing out of the stump of her neck as her body writhed on the floor, knocking over the chairs, but silver-blue liquid about the same thickness of over-used engine oil. I imagined her head rolling across the balcony, leaving patches of the same pale-blue goo and trailing her gorgeous black hair, until it bounced against the railing and stopped. Pale blue eyes aimed skyward but not seeing the beauty of the last days of Summer before Autumn coated the Portland sky in high clouds.

"*That's not a pleasant image*," she said telepathically. "*I didn't think you had it in you. Perhaps your paramour did save my life.*"

It shocked me for a moment that my imaginings had passed through our telepathic link, but then I got over it and was glad she knew exactly how I felt.

"*My turn*," she said.

That fake gauzy veil slipped over my eyes again and Laume transported my senses back into her horror-show dungeon. Biting bugs. Ginormous rats. Hair-raising screams stealing through the bars on the door to assault my ears. My phamily lying on the floor in much the same way they'd laid in the lifeboat, except without me. The lack of sun from their time in the dungeon had faded their sunburns to sickly pale. Paulo's hair had all but fallen out. Maria had bruises which were coincidentally the same size and pattern as the scuffs on Cooper's fisted hands.

No! I shouted at her mind. *This is not the truth. You are trying to manipulate me. Trying to hurt me.*

The moment I rebelled, the images faded and I found myself still sitting in the chair but braced against the table. Brady stood halfway between Laume and me, motionless as a mannequin.

At first I thought he was preparing to act as a barrier between the two of us, standing still but wound up tight and ready to spring whichever direction Laume chose to move. But then I realized no part of him was moving, not his lips or his fingers or his knees.

I quickly established a telepathic link with him. *Brady?*

I heard a muffled sound, like a word spoken through a gag. I was glad it wasn't the sound of a muffled scream, but my pulse kicked up a notch and my palms broke out in a sweat just the same.

Shoving off the table and the chair, I leapt to Brady's side in an instant, to find him warm and pulsing with a heartbeat, but otherwise doing his best impression of a vegetable. No expression on his face. No sound beyond the passage of breath through his nostrils.

Brady wasn't panicking, but I felt anger building in the pit of my belly.

I broke the connection with him and went back to my connection with Laume.

Even though my brain said it was the stupidest thing I could do I danced around Brady and lunged after her again. Without Brady to hold me back I didn't imagine anything would stop me, but Laume pointed one long, silver-tipped finger in his direction at the same time she narrowed her eyes and said, "Tut, tut, little darlin'."

The threat froze my muscles in place three feet away from her. I wasn't restrained physically, but some part of my pickled brain understood she wouldn't retaliate against me, she'd make Brady pay. She saw my true vulnerability. I backed off the way I would give room to a rattle-shaking snake.

Release him. Fucking let him go. You have no right.

"He broke his agreement with me."

What agreement?

"When you had me pinned to the floor I warned him I would kill you both. He said he'd get you to let me go and neither of you would harm me if I promised not to do that."

He would never hurt you. He's still five feet away from you.

"Never underestimate your influence on humans, Little Darlin'. Your mother always does." She stood up and stepped closer to look Brady deep in the eye. *"This one will kill for you. It was in his eyes, I saw his intention as clear as day."*

She smiled as if I should feel honored that Brady would make such a sacrifice.

A stupid, meaningless, amazing, heartbreaking sacrifice.

And she'd gotten him for it. It was like he was in a coma, standing up, and I was scared to the depths of my frozen-heart that he might never come out of it.

Everything I was trying to avoid had happened. My phamily was lost. Not dead, not yet anyway, but lost as surely as we'd been lost at sea in that damned lifeboat. I'd led Laume straight to Brady and his generous nature had gotten him turned into a statue.

I never meant for any of it to happen that night I lifted my head to the stars and asked for help. It was never my intention to fuck up anyone else's life.

Intention.

The word rattled around my brain like it was supposed to mean something.

Intention.

I remembered Sir Ansley's voice in my head, his Irish accent throwing a 'y' sound into it between the 't's that didn't belong there: in-tayn-tion.

Sir Ansley.

Intention.

I suddenly remembered his answer to my accidental question—the fifth one, the one I thought I'd blown because I shot off my telepathic-mouth rather than listening to him and exercising patience.

Intention?

'Intention is everything,' Sir Ansley had said.

Good Graceland. I might not be fucked after all. There might still be a way to get my phamily back.

I sat back down, hoping that opening a larger gap between Laume and me would make her more likely to listen to the wild-ass idea forming in my brain.

What if our bargain is not finished yet?

"*How could it be otherwise?*" she asked, but she mirrored my movement and sat down opposite me.

I was glad for the breathing room—it gave me a chance to think—but even happier for the distance it created between her and Brady.

When you asked me to get Hannah home to her father, what was your real intention?

"*To get her home to her father.*"

But it was more, I thought toward her. *You wanted her to be someplace where her talents, her half-Faery nature, would be supported, helped to grow.*

"*Perhaps.*" There was something behind Laume's eyes that said she was not telling me the whole truth. She might not be able to lie, but I didn't trust her to be forthcoming.

You said her foster parents put her soul in jeopardy. I understand. I get it. They're lovely people, but they don't see Hannah the way a parent would see her, even a Faery parent. Mike and Nancy are just trying to keep her alive and get her evened out a bit. Trying to give her a normal life.

"*She deserves better than a normal life.*"

I had no idea why Laume felt that way, especially when her reaction to Ryan's death was 'It's a pity,' and I wondered what reason she still wasn't sharing. I didn't have time to figure out what it was, but I knew it was there and I needed to leverage it. I felt like I was like playing Reverse Poker: I didn't have to know what the card was to play it from my hand; I just had to believe it would work before I laid it down.

What if I could convince the Carters to do a better job with Hannah? I felt guilty for implying that they were doing a bad job, they weren't. But I needed to revive my chance to get my phamily back.

"They'll never love her as their own."

But they already love her. Nonetheless, I'll convince them to adopt her, legally, it'll be just the same as it is with their own kids. She'll be theirs, forever.

"But they have no resources."

True, but Hannah has resources, I said, stretching what I suspected about Ryan's estate into an argument for my plan. *Her father must have millions from his days in professional baseball. I'm sure he has debts as well, but I know there's enough left for Hannah, even if it's just life insurance.*

With their love, their stability, Hannah's resources and my vision I'm sure we can give Hannah what you expected from Ryan, only better. Better for Hannah.

I sat back in my chair and kept an eye on Brady while Laume pondered my interpretation of our bargain.

"*And this is more difficult than returning Hannah to her father?*" Laume asked me, and she seemed happy about it.

I ignored her snide smile and said, *Yes, much more difficult.* That was an understatement. Not only was I no longer a CASA, so I no longer had any legal standing to comment on the case, but there were so many more variables in play now that Hannah was heir to a small fortune and there were more lawyers involved.

"*And you think you can make this happen?*"

I nodded. I wasn't sure how much convincing it was going to take to get Mike and Nancy to adopt Hannah and get her out of the merry-go-round that is the foster system, but I had four very important reasons to make it work—five if you counted Hannah. And, for the first time, I really believed that I was working to get Hannah into the best place for her. I was no longer divided internally between what I needed to do for my phamily and how I should protect a teenager the way she needed to be protected—the way I wished someone had protected me.

"If you fail, what do I get?"

That sounded a hell of a lot like she was asking for double-or-nothing to me. If I hadn't already talked to Sir Ansley about the way intention worked in the world of Faeries I might have been tempted to fall for her ploy. It was good not to feel stupid, well not as stupid, in my dealings with Laume like I had been that first night.

No way. Same deal: no new consequences for either side as the intentions are the same as the original bargain. I said it with as much conviction as I could muster, and being a telepathic statement, I felt that intention go across to my adversary.

Laume pondered and I waited, feeling like I had a chance to save my phamily for the first time since I'd heard Ryan was dead.

"*Fair enough,*" Laume finally said. "*If you can secure these adoptive rights for Hannah, demonstrate that she has at least two-million United States Dollars available for her care, and if her new parents freely profess their love for her, I will agree you have fulfilled the original bargain.*"

She sounded like a fucking lawyer, spelling it all out like that, but I could make that happen. *Good,* I thought toward her.

"But none of that will matter if Queen Mab does not return your friends to my care. I cannot overpower the will of The Winter Queen, not even during the months of Summer."

I understand. It sucked, but I felt like my phamily and I had better odds with Queen Mab than with Laume. At least The Queen had sent Sir Ansley to get my side of the matter.

"*Then get to work,*" Laume said, and then she disappeared, leaving behind a sulfurous smell that made me gag.

If the overwhelming stink of rotten eggs made me want to vomit again, I knew Brady would also be breathing it in with a similar reaction and regurgitation in his condition might be fatal. I skirted his statue-like presence and slid the glass door to the balcony all the way open. I saw his fingers twitch as the fresh air washing into the room reached him.

It made me feel good that I was there in time to catch him, and strong enough to keep him from slamming into the floor like a six-foot tall log.

Our telepathic connection clicked into place. *I'm here. I've got you.*

I laid his head in my lap and ran my fingers through his hair as Laume's Faery Magic slowly slipped away. His neck muscles loosened allowing his shoulder to touch the floor and then his spine sagged and then his arms and legs released. Eventually his fingers wiggled, his toes flexed and his face lost its sense of plastic-ness.

Slowly he smiled at me. "*That was intense,*" he said into my mind.

You heard it?

"No, but I saw everything. You had her going over something."

Just the folly of a last ditch effort, I told him, and explained how I played the intention card and bought some more time. All the while I wondered if I'd actually be able to pull it off.

30

The crappy part about having a game plan is when the game goes on and you've run out of plan. Brady and I improvised the rest of Monday after Laume left in her gush of sulfur. I was D-n-D and struggling to get sober after having soaked myself in too much tequila. Brady's brush with Laume's Faery magic freeze-ray had somehow short-circuited his well-earned buzz, so as he regained control over his body the poor guy went straight past delightfully dizzy right into his hang-over.

I was sure Laume had done that on purpose.

We snuggled on the couch and watched a bunch of syndicated episodes of *How I Met Your Mother* on TV with the captions on. I napped a little—jolting awake at least six times from terrifying dreams: darkness, cold, bugs, rats, dead phamily, a faceless Faery Queen with a stunning jeweled crown and an uncanny ability to put a room into deep-freeze with a single word. Each cycle took less and less time to figure out where I was, curled-up in Brady's arms on his couch, but the disorientation never quite went away. He had a box of veggie-burgers in the freezer, so I dolled them up for late-late supper and we watched the evening news.

Ryan Williams' death was a hot story for the locals. His career, his fall from grace, and his notorious drug-bust all led to wild speculation about what had driven him to fire on police, drawing their fatal fire in return. Wild and wholly-incorrect speculation, I knew, because who in the hell would have guessed Ryan had badly needed some Faery-tail and couldn't find it on the corner near the local Seven-Eleven. Toxicology results were pending, but given all the possible hiding places in his huge home—and his history of addiction—I was sure the reports would not come back clean. Thankfully they left Ryan's parenting troubles out of the story and Hannah's name was not mentioned.

I wondered how Hannah was coping. I hoped she was back at the Carter's home. Kevin had taken her file back before I learned whether or not she had any relatives nearby. My guess was that any family she had must be very distant—physically or emotionally, or both—if the state had chosen to place her in a non-relative foster home after being removed. More than ever I was grateful for Mike and Nancy Carter. Their wall of transformed faces proved they were the best port in a storm for Hannah and I knew they'd rise to the occasion for her. And for me.

They had to.

As the news touched on funeral plans for Ryan Williams—there was going to be a private service for the family the next afternoon, and a public memorial at the local minor-league baseball stadium on Friday night—it struck me that I would have to make my next move at the funeral.

Officially off the case was not the same thing as *not allowed to speak with Hannah or the Carters*, I hoped. It was incredibly tacky to crash a funeral, I knew that, but dressing properly and acting like I belonged might get me close. Close was good enough. I could make close work.

First thing the next morning Brady took me shopping for an appropriate black dress, stockings, and heels. He insisted on paying and further insisted we visit an actual department store with actual choices and actual class. It hurt my pride to accept his generosity when I'd given him such a case of blue balls over the weekend and then dumped my horror story in his lap, but I was dead broke (and without my normal phamily options) so I did what Maria would have wanted me to: I smiled and thanked him like I actually had some manners.

With my new long-sleeved, mid-calf length dress and stockings covering my tattoos and Brady's dark suit and tie hiding his, we made quite the respectable couple. The phamily would puke twice and die if they saw me.

Brady had made a couple of educated guesses from the information he heard in the newscast and then called-in a favor from a friend who worked for the Portland Police Bureau to track Williams' funeral service to the Sunset Hills cemetery. Oddly, it was the same graveyard in the West Hills I'd passed beneath a few times on The MAX train. For all eternity, people would ride a train beneath Ryan Williams' body. Creepy.

There was no security checking cars at the entrance, so Brady drove in like he owned the place. We headed toward a pair of black limousines at the north-end of the property and found the Carter's minivan parked a hundred feet from a hole in the ground where what was left of Ryan Williams would soon be buried. Thinking of him, of what led us to this moment under gray skies, I shivered and my knees clenched together of their own accord. Most of me wanted to turn around and find another way to get to Hannah, to not be anywhere near Ryan. Apparently 52 hours was not long enough to gain perspective and heal from being raped.

While I did believe it was unwise to speak ill of the dead, especially where their relatives could hear you, my thoughts were my own and they were blacker than Laume's version of The Queen's dungeon. The petty part of me still wished there was some way I could hurt him because I hated that a dead man could still frighten me as he waited to be lowered into his grave. Asshole had gotten off easy.

Brady parked behind the minivan and escorted me to the graveside gathering. The doctor from the rehab facility stood at the foot of the gravesite with four others who looked like colleagues; she looked much more sober and grounded than the last time we'd spoken.

The group at the far side of the hole was all men and my instinct said they were former teammates by their haircuts and the way their tight bodies tried to bust through the seams of their off-the-rack suits. Though the polished-mahogany casket rested less than six feet from the closest of them, not a one of them looked at it directly. Their muted comments brought half-hearted smiles and shrugged shoulders all around, but I could not have cared less about what they said.

Across from the athletes, between us and the grave, sat a smaller group, including Hannah. She wore a black sweater and black slacks with a pair of patent-leather Mary Janes. Her face showed no signs of make-up, just the tracks of too many tears; she looked stark and lovely in a very sad way. To my surprise her four new singing friends from the group foster home sat with her in what looked like the-best-outfits-they-could-piece-together-for-the-situation, insulating her from five adults who took turns trying to talk at her. I classified these well-dressed folks as distant relatives or attorneys, but I couldn't tell exactly which because nothing brings both kinds out of the woodwork faster than hearing a rich man has been read his Last Rites. Mike and Nancy Carter stood together, but slightly separate from everyone else, behind the bank of chairs where Hannah sniffled. The sadness on Nancy's face was only exceeded by her husband's. I knew he had a man-crush on Ryan.

I approached Nancy and she greeted me with a sad smile and a great-big Momma-Bear hug. "Hannah will be so glad you're here. We talked about you on the way over. She was hoping you would come."

I was surprised to get a warm welcome from anyone at the service—making me wonder if Kevin had shared my role in Ryan's last morning with the police at all—and even more so to find out Hannah actually wanted me there. The relief instantly drained the stress from my shoulders. Brady felt it through our clasped hands and smiled at me.

The minister, a ninety year-old version of Ward Cleaver in a black suit and shirt, welcomed everyone to the ceremony. Brady and I stood hand-in-hand, next to Mike and Nancy, to listen. Being a man of the cloth, his remarks were of the generic "Yea, though I walk through the valley of death" type and I felt badly for Hannah that it was so impersonal. She deserved better, because funerals were for the living, not the dead. This one was definitely for Hannah.

Almost at the same moment I started shifting my weight to relieve sore-spots from my new shoes, the minister announced that Hannah had prepared a song in tribute to her father.

Of course she had. It was the perfect thing; it's what I would have hired someone to do in my place if we'd been standing beside my father's grave.

She stood and walked with somber grace to the head of her father's grave, but she avoided actually looking at it. The flower-draped lid was fastened shut: Ryan's had not been the kind of death that welcomed the up-close-and-personal goodbye of an open casket. My morbid imagination got the better of me, wondering how badly his body had been torn-up by the seventeen gunshots, as Hannah brushed stray hairs from her face and breathed deeply in preparation for her song.

She sang the first line clear as a bell up until the last word, *heaven*, when her voice quivered and she wiped at her eyes with a handful of crumpled tissues.

"*Would it be the same*?" Hannah's voice hiccupped and I watched her heaving chest fight between sobbing and breathing as she tried to do the song justice.

Her voice shrank more and more with each word and I realized I had filled-in the end of the line in my head rather than hearing her vocalize it.

I knew the song, Tears in Heaven, a heart-wrenching ballad written and recorded by classic rock legend Eric Clapton after the death of his young son. Such a sweet and sad goodbye. So full of guilt and regret. Perfect.

The amazingly strong start told me Hannah had been practicing her perfect song, but it didn't look like she was going to be able to finish it. She bowed her head until she looked at the toes of her shiny black shoes and I saw her struggle to lift it back up again. I felt more than saw Nancy take two steps forward, but she stopped when a clear voice rang out.

"I must be strong."

It was Hannah's friend, Jacob, the young man who'd spent most of his life bouncing around the foster care system. He stood and approached Hannah, whose head had jerked up at the sound of someone else singing and then dropped again to avoid having to look at the casket and the hole.

Suddenly ML, Danni and Noah launched out of their chairs and as the four of them surrounded Hannah, they finished the second melancholy verse of the song in perfect harmony. I recognized the way each of them reached out to touch Hannah, even though she wasn't reaching back. It was steadying, supportive, grounding, and it made me bawl for the loss of my own phamily.

And for Hannah.

But not for Ryan.

Their touches slipped naturally into mutually-held hands as the five of them stood in a tight bunch at the head of the casket: an impromptu choir of angels in borrowed black outfits edging out the minister with a much more personal message about the deceased. In the middle of the third verse Hannah's wavering voice joined back in, growing stronger as she raised her chin and stared defiantly at the coffin and the hole.

At the beginning of the bridge, Hannah's voice jumped in volume and the others faded into a gentle background hum underneath. I'm sure it was unconscious how they all rocked back and forth to the slow rhythm of the song. Hannah carried the next verse of the song all by herself, delivering pain and sorrow and anger with every note, until the chorus, when all five of their voices joined together again.

In the recorded version of the last four lines of the song, it's obvious that Clapton struggles to accept that his lost, beloved-boy is in a better place and that there will be a time when fate will rejoin their paths. But in the meantime it's best that he, Clapton, remains in this life, no matter how painful, and his little boy rests in the loving grace of Heaven.

But that's not how Hannah sang it. It was a subtle change of the lyrics, and with the other four voices delivering the song as-written I'm not sure anyone else caught it. The original admits that the singer doesn't belong in Heaven. But Hannah sang, "*'Cause I know* you *don't belong,* there *in Heaven.*"

I would have chocked it up to a mistake, a misstep because of her grief and obvious lack of sleep, but she sang it that way both times, and her eyes squinted in time with the change.

Apparently I wasn't the only one who was still pissed at Ryan. She was angry, incredibly angry. I felt it, I knew it, and I understood it because the cold ball of loneliness in my chest responded to it, throbbing in time.

Getting the Carters to adopt Hannah became even more important because I knew that only a few, very special people in this world were capable of healing injuries which triggered such intense emotions. And it was obvious to me that Nancy Carter was one of them. Now I just had to get everyone to agree, any way I could, for my sake and for Hannah's.

Still hand-in-hand, the four teenagers escorted Hannah back to her seat where they ignored everyone and everything else. After a final comment from the minister about the importance of lifting our chins and carrying on, the service ended without any other personal messages. I was glad the minister had not asked if anyone else wanted to speak because I had a few things on my mind that were much better left unsaid.

In silence, we watched them lower the casket into the ground and I felt my chest relax, just a little, knowing that the broken, unfulfilled, arrogant, monster-of-a-man wasn't going to get out of it. He was dead. Buried. Gone.

Surprisingly, no one drizzled in a handful of dirt into the grave as they left. No one deposited a single-stemmed flower or nodded their head in a private prayer. Williams' teammates shuffled off toward five year-old luxury cars in groups of two and three. The folks from the rehab center made their way back to a small shuttle bus with the facility name painted on its side. The well-dressed crowd around Hannah tried in vain again to talk with her, but her friends, bless their hearts, formed a walking barricade around her and delivered her to the Carter's minivan.

Nancy and Mike invited Brady and me back to their townhouse for a late lunch. I asked for a moment alone before we left. As the employees of the funeral home stacked chairs and took up the artificial grass that had been laid down to hide the bare earth around the grave, I stepped close and whispered so no one else would hear me. "I think you got what you deserved, you son-of-a-bitch."

I had to fight the urge to spit into the hole.

Brady followed the Carters home toward Beaverton with a short stop to drop off ML, Jacob, Danni and Noah.

"What is this place?" Brady asked me.

"Warehouse. Time-out. Cold-storage."

"Beg pardon?"

I studied the large gray house with white trim that sat on a huge, fenced-in corner lot, surrounded by dozens of sun-faded, half-broken toys.

"Group foster home. Hell on earth if you're a teenager and Mom and Dad don't want you around anymore."

"You lived in one?"

I turned away from the house and smiled at Brady so he would understand I'd healed from my ordeal. "Not long. Six months."

"But you made it."

I grunted, not really feeling like *A Success Story* given my current circumstances.

"They will, too," he said of the four teens dressed in various faded tones of black who stood on the curb and waved goodbye to the Carter's minivan as it headed down the street.

"I hope so," I said as Brady pulled the Audi away from the curb and I waved goodbye to the kids. I felt badly for them. I felt like hell for me. A compelling need tingled in my palms, pulsing in time with the cold ball of loneliness throbbing in my chest, until I had to borrow Brady's cell phone and make a call.

Dialing from memory, I heard the ten familiar tones of his number and waited through five rings for the voicemail to pick up.

"Trevor Michaels." It was all the greeting he ever needed.

"Hi, Dad, it's me, Bailey," I said, trying to prevent the torrent of emotions inside me from oozing out through my voice. "Sorry it's been so long since I've called. I just wanted you to know I'm okay. I can't explain right now, but please don't call anyone or do anything until you hear from me. This is a good friend's number in Portland, Oregon. You can reach me here in an emergency."

I hesitated, the pulsing and throbbing and tingling I felt betrayed that my part of the conversation was not yet complete.

"I love you."

I pressed the end button and my hands settled and my chest went back to just-plain-old-chilly. Brady brushed my hair away from my face but showed the smarts not to ask the questions I couldn't answer with tears trickling down my cheeks and my lips clamped between my teeth.

When we reached the Mike and Nancy's townhouse complex it took a few minutes to find an open parking spot for the Audi, and for me to compose myself. The Carters and Hannah had already gone inside and she had headed into her room to change. Brady hit it off with Mike and Nancy right away so I felt okay leaving him with them in the loud and wonderful living room looking at its wall of *Real Success Stories* and went down the hall to talk to Hannah.

I knocked on her door, still decked out like an American Idol's dressing room, and Hannah invited me in. She'd already dumped the fancy funeral duds for a gray hoodie over a bright pink t-shirt, bare toes peeking out from beneath the flares of her yoga pants. She plopped onto the bed, and after asking permission I sat next to her.

It wasn't hard to know what she was feeling. It was in her puffy eyes, red nose and stringy hair. It was also in her slumped shoulders, crossed arms and downcast gaze. I knew she didn't need my pity, but it was impossible for me not to feel sorry for her. She'd lost her dad, the only parent she knew. At fourteen kids don't often know a fucked-up parent from a good one, and so it doesn't really matter; it didn't matter to Hannah. All that mattered was Ryan was gone and she had not gotten a chance to say goodbye to him.

I got that.

"Did you like my song?" Hannah asked while making intermittent eye contact.

"I liked the way you sang it, with your friends. Though I'm pretty sure that wasn't the way the end of it was supposed to go."

Hannah's head dropped in shame. She mumbled something I heard as, "You caught that."

Her shame looked awfully familiar. I wore it on my way home from the Sheriff's station a time or three, sitting in the third seat of my father's behemoth Expedition with his assistant or his accountant or his attorney behind the wheel and him in the passenger seat explaining my behavior to some stranger I didn't even know. On those occasions I hated him with furious anger, and I felt guilty for not being a better daughter.

"You have every right to be pissed at him. I'm pissed at him for dying like that and he's not even my dad."

"My counselor says I'm supposed to remember only the good things." She picked at the hem of her pants, avoiding eye contact.

"Then your counselor is a complete douche-bag."

She looked up at me and gave me a half-hearted smile. "I wish you were my counselor."

"You know I can't be your CASA anymore, right?"

She nodded. "Kevin said you were off my case. I didn't think I'd see you again."

I was surprised Hannah didn't ask why I'd been removed, but given all she'd been through in the past couple of days I could understand that the inter-workings of The System weren't as important as what the hell was going to happen to her next.

And that was a huge question. I knew what I wanted to have happen, needed to have happen, but my part in this whole cluster had changed drastically.

"I still care what happens to you. So CASA or not, I'm still here to help, if you'll have me...on one condition."

Hannah raised her eyebrows in question.

"There's something you need to know. The reason I got on your case in the first place. You're very special, Hannah Faye Williams."

She ducked her head in that typical I-am-not kind of way teenagers always respond to being called special, whether they think they are or not.

"You and I are special in a very unique way."

That got her attention, and I'd been counting on it because I figured she would be much less likely than Brady to buy into my incredible Faery explanation.

I decided to skip over the part about being lost at sea and Laume's rescue. There was no way to tell that part without explaining my bargain with Laume and my phamily being held hostage. I would not put that issue into Hannah's head; I could not let her feel one inkling of responsibility for my phamily's situation. I just started by telling her that her mother had asked me to come to Portland to help her.

"What?" Hannah asked as she pushed herself back on the bed and pressed her back against the headboard. Though I'd obviously scared her, it was a much tamer reaction than I had felt when hearing the news about my mom's identity from JoJo.

I wondered why, and what, Hannah was holding back, so I decided not to say anything until she had a chance to respond.

Seconds stretched into a couple of minutes while I saw her struggle with the idea. "You're kidding. Right? Are you, like, a friend of hers?" Her tone was accusatory, angry.

I shook my head. "I had never met her before, but she knows my mother," I said, feeling odd at uttering that sentence for the first time in my life. "They're kind-of related."

"So, we're related?" Hannah asked.

"Kind of." I took a deep breath and thought for a second about how to explain. I'd been tossing phrases around in my head since Brady did his research and I had decided to crash the funeral. The explanation that floated to the surface in the moment bubbled out of my mouth. "Both our moms are Faeries."

Hannah narrowed her eyes. "Is that a country?"

A laugh snuck out of my mouth before I could stop it. I hadn't expected Hannah's question and it tickled me for its honest naiveté and denial. Three flippant answers jumped to my mind, things I was afraid would sound racist if I said them out loud, likely to confuse Hannah more than she already was. I decided to keep it simple. "Honey, I'm trying to say they're not humans."

I didn't know a lot about Faeries, so I considered all the things that Laume and Sir Ansley had in common. "They're magical beings that are taller and cooler and more beautiful than you can imagine. Hannah, you and I are half-human, and half that...half-Faery."

"Half-human?" Hannah's brow could not have been any more crinkled if it had been made of frozen French fries. "How is that possible?"

I watched her think and then her eyes took on a sparkle and her face contorted from sadness into a painful version of comedic relief. She started to laugh at me. "You're kidding. It's a joke to make the poor girl with the dead father quit crying. Supposed to make me stop feeling sorry for myself."

She laughed five seconds longer, but her smile turned back into a frown when I didn't join in. Instead I sat still and let the awkward possibility sink in to her brain. She covered her mouth with both hands and her eyes went wide. "You're not kidding."

I gave her a half-smile and shrugged my shoulders, my way of trying to show her my own confusion and regret, and then shook my head.

"What's my mom's name?" she asked with doubt in her voice.

I didn't blame her for challenging my story, I felt the same way with JoJo, and I already trusted her with my life. "Her name is Laume." I didn't know what Ryan had told Hannah about her mom, but I saw some recognition for the name in her eyes.

"A stupid name doesn't prove she's a Faery. She could still just be from someplace foreign, like Paris or Hoboken."

I didn't have the heart to correct Hannah that you didn't need a passport to get to Hoboken.

"She found me and asked me to help you get home to your dad so you could grow up to reach your potential. You are special, Hannah Faye."

"How do I know you're half-Faery? How do I know you're not just making this whole thing up to fuck with my head?"

I was hoping I could get her to believe me without using my telepathy, but my gut said we'd be at it all night and she was still never going to believe any mundane explanation I told her.

I was going to have to show her.

Reaching out toward Hannah's mind, I made a connection and then I shoved my thoughts at her so she couldn't possibly ignore me. *Does this feel like I'm making things up?* And then I showed her an image of Laume, focusing on her face and the beautiful pale blue eyes they shared. *That's your mom.*

I could tell Hannah had immediately gotten the message because her mouth dropped open. When she started to rub at her eyes with both hands I let the image go. I needed Hannah to understand, I didn't need to torture her to make that happen.

"What was that?" Hannah mouthed.

Telepathy, I thought toward her and then explained that if she wanted to talk more it would have to be mind-to-mind because I was going to be D-n-D until the sun rose the next morning.

"How come?" Hannah asked out loud, ignoring my instructions. Typical teenager.

Best I can understand it's a price I have to pay for using my cool Faery super-power, I explained.

Hannah pulled her knees up to her chest and wrapped her arms around them. She chewed on her bottom lip and then asked me something that I couldn't read from her lips. I shook my head and tapped my temple.

"*Would my singing be considered a Faery super-power?*" she asked telepathically, her words tenuous.

I don't think so. I think your vocal talent is more like me playing the drums or making pastry... Or having amazing sex, I didn't add. *None of that makes me deaf-and-dumb.*

"Oh." And that guilty look I'd seen the other day took over her face.

Hannah, is there something you need to tell me?

She shook her head, but I didn't buy it.

Tell me.

She shook her head again.

Normally I would let it go there. It wasn't in me to push. Pushing was reserved for mothers and fathers. But Hannah's mother didn't give a shit and her father was done. As great as Mike and Nancy were at being foster parents, I couldn't depend on them to dig it out of her, and I sensed, because of her repeated guilty expression, it was important. If I didn't push her, no one would.

Tell me, or I'll break into your head and dig it out for myself.

I was bluffing—I didn't know if I could actually do that—but Hannah didn't know that. She turned her face as if breaking eye contact could prevent me from digging around in her skull.

Hannah Faye Williams, I admonished her, *don't force this.*

Apparently using her full-name did the trick because a flood of words in her voice rolled over my brain so fast I couldn't catch any of it. Suddenly she was crying and rocking back-and-forth on the bed.

I reached out with one hand to steady her. *Slow down. I can't understand.*

Hannah's sobs were so brutal that her breath hitched in her throat like hiccups in the middle of a 'roid rage. I moved over and hugged her, surprised that she let me. We rocked together until her body-quakes slowed to irregular trembles.

I pulled back and looked her in the eye. *Try again.*

"Bailey, I think I have a Faery power, too."

Wow. It made perfect sense, but still I had not expected it. Her confession came at me from left-field because I had no way to expect my situation would have more parallels in hers. I stroked her hair, gathering it back behind her shoulder.

Do you want to show me?

Hannah's whole body tensed and shook her head violently. Her eyes were wide. "*That's how I get my headaches.*"

The migraines. Nancy's comment from a couple of days ago ran through my mind...*Thankfully nothing that can't be cured by aspirin and a good night's rest.* Good Graceland.

Thinking of the way Hannah had been suffering the first time we met—balled up under her quilt in a cold, dark room—was like a punch to the gut when I realized that was the price she paid to utilize her Faery-given talent. Talk about bad luck. Suddenly being D-n-D until sunrise didn't seem so bad.

I want to help you, I thought at her, *but you have to tell me all of it. How do you trigger the headaches?*

"*I can stop time. Not for long, maybe a minute, tops. But I always get a migraine after. Don't make me...*"

I held up both hands. *Okay, I believe you. You don't have to show me.*

"You've already seen me do it."

It was my turn to have a forehead full of wrinkles.

"*At the Community Center. My dad's Jag.*" She looked sheepish, chin down, shoulders up, bobbing in and out of eye-contact again. "*Bitch.*"

Hearing that word was like getting hit up the side of the head with a sledgehammer.

It was *you.*

I thought back through that few minutes standing on the sidewalk outside the Community Center: from the moment Hannah spotted her dad's car in the parking lot to when I saw the grooves scratched in the green paint of its hood. *When? I don't remember.*

But then I did, sledgehammer part two. I remembered how everything got quiet for most of a minute. At the time I was so deep in my own shame at being caught with the car that I hadn't even noticed the world going completely still around me, time itself stopping, except I remembered thinking that everything was waiting for me to say something. Even the ants seemed to be waiting as they paused on the sidewalk.

It finally made sense.

I knew you were pissed, but damn girl. I smiled to show her that I wasn't really angry.

"*I hate that car.*" She pulled away from my arms. "*I hated you, too.*"

I deserved it.

That thought hung in the air while Hannah grabbed a tissue and blew her poor, red nose.

"*What happens next?*" she asked me in my head.

First thing, no more stopping time.

Why not?

Migraines aren't just ordinary headaches, Hannah. I tried to remember what I knew for fact and what might have been urban legends gleaned from the internetz. *You could be doing damage to your brain. Only do that in an emergency. Okay?*

She finally nodded and I hoped she was playing it straight with me, not just telling me what I wanted to hear.

I have a plan. Your dad dying doesn't really fix anything as far as your mom is concerned. If that wasn't the biggest understatement

I'd ever made. *I told her that I'd make sure you had a loving, permanent home where you would get all the support you needed.*

"But she doesn't want me?"

Sadly, Hannah seemed hurt by being unwanted, once again, by a parent who had never shown any interest in her life. Amazing how the label "mother" carried such power that even applying it (and all that it implied) to a stranger could crush Hannah's tender heart in a single squeeze.

She's a Faery, Hannah. Trust me; you're the one who doesn't want her. From my experience, the only good Faery mother is an absent Faery mother.

"Your mom sucks, too?"

Don't know, never met her.

"Never? But you're old."

I ignored her ignorant comment and stayed on topic.

Nope, and don't you be sad for me. I created a phamily of my own. And we're doing just fine. Or I planned for us to be just fine as soon as Hannah's adoption papers got signed.

"If she doesn't want me, what do I do? Where will I go?" Hannah blew her nose again at the same time she was talking to me in my head. It was weird, unnatural, and it gave me the chills.

I really think the best plan is to get Mike and Nancy to adopt you. Given that's what I'd promised Laume, I hoped Hannah would see the sense.

"*I guess I could handle that. Mike's kind of lame, but Nancy is amazing. And she never gets mad when I get my headaches.*" That guilty look came back, but I decided to let it go. Given Mike's earlier comment about Hannah usually getting headaches after she'd done something to get into trouble, I had a clearer understanding of what might be going on while she was freezing time. I'd be jealous of her gift if not for the horrid headaches.

I want to talk to them, see if I can convince them that you becoming one of their own will be best for everyone. I admitted to myself that it was *best* for me and my phamily—if Queen Mab would just get out of the picture—but I still thought it was a good thing for everyone else.

"Papa-Mike says Dad's lawyers need to talk to me tomorrow. I have an appointment at 10:30."

I assumed that meant there was some kind of declaration in Ryan Williams' will for what he wanted to happen to Hannah in the event of his death. And hopefully also something about a very large inheritance as well.

I'll work on Nancy and Mike tonight. By tomorrow we will have a plan to give the lawyers when you meet with them.

"What if the lawyers won't go along with it? Aren't they supposed to be scary and mean?"

I used to be afraid of lawyers, then I met my first Faery, I joked. *It'll be okay, I promise. I can be very persuasive.*

As soon as the promise crossed from my mind into Hannah's I saw her tense up.

I know, you've heard it all before. But this time, I really do promise.

Hannah looked into my eyes and I was glad they did not waver. *"Okay."*

I reached over and squeezed her hand and then hopped off the bed. *Hang out here for a bit. I'm going to get Brady's help to talk with Mike and Nancy.*

Before I closed the door I saw Hannah pull out her iPod, stuff bright pink earbuds into her ears, and hug her pillow tightly to her chest. She looked like a lost, little girl, not the confident young woman who had sung her heart out in front of a crowd four nights before.

Before everything went to hell.

As much as I hated that Hannah would have to live her life without her father, I was so glad she didn't have to live it with him. He died before he could become the monster who tore her life apart. She was understandably angry with him, but their relationship hadn't disintegrated to the point where she wanted to spit in his grave the way I had.

For the first time in a week the proverbial light at the end of the tunnel I felt bearing down on me wasn't the speeding headlight of an oncoming locomotive as it attempted to squash my future into the corpse of a failed dream on the tracks.

Instead it had the heat and fire of the spotlights that shined on Billy's Asylum Rats when we rocked on stage.

With that image warming my heart I went into to find the Carters and kick the rest of my plan into action.

31

You want us to adopt Hannah?"

We sat around the Carter's patio table on the balcony and Nancy was the one asking the question. She looked directly at me, while Mike stared at Brady. Both of their mouths hung open wide enough to catch one of the bats that flew out from under the Congress Avenue Bridge on summer nights in Austin.

Brady had been the voice for my plan because I was D-n-D from convincing Hannah that Faeries were real—and that we both had their blood in our veins. He'd given the Carters my cover story about how stress induced neurological hiccups in my hearing and voice, kind of like temporary Multiple Sclerosis, and he needed to help translate for me. They both looked dubious, but they did a fair job of playing along to see where we were going. If Brady hadn't been with me, hadn't attended Ryan Williams' funeral with me and come back to the Carter's for lunch, I would've had to hold off until the morning to beg Mike and Nancy to adopt Hannah.

"Bailey, I thought you understood, we're not that kind of foster home," Nancy explained. "We only take in kids that the state social workers expect to go home in less than a year."

Brady relayed all that to me telepathically while flailing his fingers in mock sign language and I fed him my answer the same way.

"She says Hannah really needs you, needs your help if she's going to make it without her dad. If you don't adopt her, she'll get stuck with some cold-hearted, money-grubbing leech of a guardian who will ignore her and rob her blind. Or worse, if her father hasn't made plans for her care she'll get tossed into a group home and age-out of the system. Do you think she's going to graduate high school that way? Go to college? She might even follow her father's footsteps into drug use."

I didn't really feel that way but I wanted Brady to make the argument. The Carters had to know the statistics for teenagers who didn't get enough supervision—inside or outside of the system. I'd walked that knife edge most of my teens and without my phamily I was sure I would have strayed even further from what I knew in my heart was the right thing to do in any tough situation.

They didn't bite at that lure, so Brady fed them my next idea. "She'll be a wonderful big-sister for your kids and to all of the foster kids who are lucky enough to stay in your amazing home."

Mike looked around at the townhouse and said, "Without the money the state gives us to take care of two foster kids every month we'd have to move to a smaller apartment. It's a catch-22: if we adopted Hannah there'd be no room for her."

I'd prepared Brady for that argument already.

"As his only child it's reasonable to expect Hannah will inherit from her dad; it'll probably go into a trust fund that would pay you two to manage her money until she turns 18 or 21. That should more than make up the difference."

Nancy's face grew more thoughtful at the same time Mike's face lit up like a kid on Christmas morning. His comment was easy to lip read. "You mean we could move into Ryan's mansion?"

Ughh. Of course that's where Mike's man-crush would take this discussion. I shook my head, but before I could convey my explanation to Brady, Nancy said something. "Mike, you know she can't ever live in that house again."

Two points for Nancy. No, three points.

"Besides, it's likely there's still a mortgage on the house," Brady added for me. "They'll probably have to sell it to cover his debts."

The resigned looks on both Mike and Nancy's faces told me that my hey-why-don't-you-adopt-a-half-human-teenage-girl-in-trouble idea wasn't going over as well as I had hoped it would. In my fantasies Nancy said *yes, of course*, before I'd gotten the whole question out of my mouth. I hadn't considered that the Carters didn't want to adopt *any* foster kids, much less that they wouldn't jump at the chance to give Hannah Faye a permanent home.

This isn't working, I thought to Brady.

"*Should we try the diamond-in-the-rough argument?*" he asked me, mind-to-mind. "*It's obvious she's going to be somebody one day. Doesn't everyone love to back a winner?*"

I understood what he meant. There were plenty of movies about compassionate people who saw the potential in a down-on-his-luck kid who was in a tough spot and did the hardest thing by giving him a home chock-full of unconditional love so that he could grow into the man he needed to become. In the end, always, the adoptive parents got paid back a hundred-fold in love, adoration, fame and money.

Sometimes Sandra Bullock played the mom in the movie. Bullock could do Nancy, easy.

Nancy who started looking at us funny as we sat quietly, so I pretended to sign to Brady some more to cover up our telepathic conversation.

I don't think it'll work. They just don't see it, they can't for some reason. I remembered back to Nancy's reaction to Hannah's performance at the American Idol frenzy, how she had said Hannah was good for a small-town girl and corrected me that Hannah had only upstaged a third runner-up, not the Idol winner.

But Brady was right; I had to make them see it. My phamily was counting on me to make the adoption happen to satisfy Laume.

Okay. Tell them we think she's going to be a huge success someday. Say she's going to make Lady Gaga look like a one-hit-wonder.

Brady explained what I'd said and I was shocked when Nancy rolled her eyes at me.

"Bailey, everyone wants to think these kids have a happy ending coming to them. The sadder the story, the worse they've been treated by their birth parents, the bigger the fairy tale ending grows. It just doesn't happen that way. It doesn't."

Brady translated for me.

I grunted involuntarily, getting a junebug flutter in my throat but failing to share my disgust with Nancy's short-sightedness. *If Nancy only knew she was in the middle of a Faery tale, not a fairy tale.*

"*Then tell them*," Brady thought toward me. "*Explain what's really going on. Give them some proof that Hannah's not just another statistic waiting to happen because she's inherently different, down to her genetics. It worked with me.*"

I smiled at him thinking about the beers he'd chugged as I explained myself. *I don't know.*

Before I could decide whether or not to cross that line, Mike and Nancy stood up. I felt the scrape of their chairs against the rough concrete floor of the balcony, and Brady explained that they were going inside to have a private conversation. I wanted to tell them to wait, that I wasn't done with my sales pitch, but they moved with purpose, like they didn't want to hear any more from me.

Brady and I sat and waited. A cool breeze drifted across the patio, one more sign of autumn bearing down on us. I shivered, but not because I was cold on the outside. The cold I felt drove its ache from inside my chest.

We had tried everything rational: appealing to Mike and Nancy's sense of obligation, their need to do the right thing, their love of family. We offered them money; we even offered them fame.

What was it going to take to get them to say yes?

I reached over and clasped Brady's hand. His warmth anchored me, kept me from pacing around the small balcony like a caged tiger. The longer we waited the more I considered that Brady's suggestion was the only way I was going to make them see. Hannah was special, very special. When I finally managed to convince Mike and Nancy of that, they would have to adopt her. Have to. In a heartbeat. That's what good people did in a situation like this.

But if I didn't have to blow my secret to make it happen, which was also Hannah's secret, I didn't want to. Once those words were out, there was no getting them back. Sure, Brady had eventually accepted my cockamamie story, but we'd known each other—in the Biblical sense—and he'd had more reasons to believe me.

Mike and Nancy came back, and they didn't have to say a word for me to know they'd decided against adopting Hannah. They both sat rigidly as if their consciences wouldn't let them relax in the padded patio chairs.

"We can keep Hannah here for another three months while she processes the loss of her father and give the Executor of Ryan's will time to find a fitting guardian. But, I'm sorry, Bailey, we just aren't the right fit for Hannah."

Brady translated the details for me; my blood boiled and my ears got hot. How could that be their decision? How could these reasonable people, these amazing foster parents with big hearts, compassionate minds, and comforting arms not make Hannah one of their own?

I'm going to have to go for it, I told Brady.

He nodded.

Do me a favor? I asked him. *After you warn them that something weird is about to happen, sing a song to me in my head for the next couple of minutes.*

"Sure, but why?"

You're mind is calm and quiet when we aren't talking and I need to know that you're still with me. I'm going to try to make this one a conference call.

All of the previous times I'd used my telepathy it had been one-on-one; even that first time with Laume and Maria, even though I'd conversed with them both I had only chatted with one of them at a time. This time, though, I really wanted to see if I could keep Brady's voice in the conversation as well as linking to both Mike and Nancy at the same time. If anything would convince them how serious I was about how special their foster daughter was; that would be the way to do it.

"Before you make up your minds for certain, Bailey has one more thing she needs to say," Brady said to them and they both stared at me like winged monkeys were about to fly out of my mouth. It wasn't the most astounding introduction I've ever gotten, but it was as good a preparation as we could give them for my telepathy.

I nodded to Brady to start his song.

"*Well it's one for the money...*" Brady sang in the back of my mind and was shocked at how much he sounded like Carl Perkens belting out the original version of the song.

You're singing Blue Suede Shoes. My heart loved that he'd picked *the* original Rockabilly anthem to let me know our connection was still open.

"*That's because you're my Blue Suede Darlin',*" Brady thought towards me.

I don't get it.

"*As in 'you can do anything, but lay off of my blue suede shoes...' I guess that's how I feel about you. I hate to think of anyone, or anything, hurting you.*"

My eyes filled with tears because that was the most romantic thing anyone had ever said to me. I'm not sure that anyone outside my phamily had ever felt that way about me, ever. Sure, I'd been wooed and chased, wined and dined, but this was the first time...

Damn, I thought to Brady as I wiped my eyes. *Can we talk about this later?*

As his answer, Brady simply restarted the song.

The delay had gotten Nancy's attention and she was trying to talk to me, but I couldn't make out what she said. I held up a finger in the universal sign for hold-on-a-second-will-ya and closed my eyes so I could settle my brain and focus.

With Brady's song taking about up about three percent of my attention I concentrated on a remembering how Mike's face had looked when I first met him at the door to their townhouse. It was not a simple thing to force the click of connection with him, but after three deep breaths I sensed a slight tug from his direction and mentally tuned in to a splash of a melodic kiddie-tunes, much like the ones from the video game he played with the kids. I knew I was in. I opened my eyes to see if he knew something was up, and saw I had his undivided attention.

Good. And Brady's song was still there. *Ooby Dooby*, my first telepathic conference call.

Connecting with Nancy was harder. I imagined her in the kitchen wrestling with the sausage grinder. I imagined her sitting on the patio, reading the book with the dragon on its cover. I imagined her behind the wheel of her minivan. Nothing worked, nothing clicked, until I imagined her standing and cheering on the bleachers at the Community Center, face beaming with pride as Hannah wowed the crowd with her awesome talent. The connection finally went through.

Are we all here? I asked.

Brady nodded and stopped singing to me. Mike put both hands on top of his head and his eyes narrowed. His comical, internal tune quieted to plinking background muzak. Nancy seemed tuned into Mike's odd behavior, but not to me, until I repeated her name a few times.

"*What the fuck?*" Nancy asked both out loud and in her head. She gripped her chair with both hands as if the earth were quaking and her face went slack, losing all color.

Uh-oh! I was floored that she cussed, impressed but floored, and not at all happy about the way she paled. There once was a guy who got knifed in the back at one of our shows in a San Antonio Honky Tonk, he looked about that bad as the paramedics carted him out.

"*Nance, what's happening*?" Mike asked. I hoped that indicated he had heard her thoughts in his own head because this conversation would prove to go a whole lot easier if I didn't have to repeat everything three times.

"*It's okay*," Brady said, inserting his mental foot, wearing a size-13, steel-toed boot, into the conversation. "*Just concentrate on your breathing. The buzzing and the nausea go away pretty quickly.*"

They both looked at him like he was a lunatic.

I hadn't known that talking to me telepathically gave Brady, or anyone, any physical discomfort. Nobody had mentioned it before. But if what he said was true, and it was temporary, I figured I had more important matters to discuss.

Mike, Nancy, I'm sorry to come at you like this, but I'm out of options. This is the only way to convince you to adopt Hannah.

"*What the hell are you*?" Nancy asked, pushing back in her chair with the whites of her eyes showing. "*What is this? How is this possible?*"

Damn, I had figured her to be the more open-minded sort. *Let me explain.*

My reaching across the table to steady her with a touch of my hand didn't help. She launched out of her chair. Mike followed. They both slid their chairs aside to so they could put their backs against the sliding glass door.

Their anxiety scared me. I didn't know how long they'd stay tuned-in, how long I could get them to listen before they shut me out completely. I hurried my thoughts. *Hannah is like me, and she's so special. She has some extraordinary gifts—things that are great, and things that aren't so great. With Ryan gone she needs you two...*

"*You mean Hanna is like this too?*" Nancy interrupted.

No, I said, but then realized from her point of view that wasn't really true. *I mean yes, she's a half-Faery, like me, but not exactly the same. She's not telepathic, though she has a power of her own. She can manipulate time.*

Mike shook his head in disbelief. As what I said sunk in, he grabbed Nancy's arm and pulled her up against his chest, backing them both into the corner as far as they could get from the opening of the sliding glass door. He pointed at the door handle like you might gesture when showing a stray dog the hole under the fence to leave your yard. *"Get out."*

He held Nancy tighter and she remained quiet. I noticed her dead-white hands were shaking at her sides. My window of opportunity was slamming shut with my fingers still sitting on the windowsill.

Mike, please, if you will just listen to me for a minute, I begged.

"*I don't want to hear it,*" he growled in my head. "*I want you out of my house and away from my family. Get out! Get out, and take that...that thing...with you. Go! Now!*"

Good Graceland, talk about unintended consequences. My stomach flip-flopped.

It made sense that he wanted to kick me and Brady out of his place, but not Hannah. Not Hannah. No, Hannah needed to stay. She had to stay and become part of their forever family. She had to stay so I could get my phamily back. I had been so damned desperate to get Mike and Nancy to adopt Hannah that it had not ever occurred to me that my revelations would get her kicked out of their home, their lives, their future.

I thought they loved Hannah. Really loved her.

I stood up hoping to not feel so powerless. *Mike, please. Just...*

"*Out!*" Mike did not make a move toward us, I think he was too frightened of me, but I did see him fiddling in the pocket of his slacks where I assumed he kept his cell phone.

A ton of cops arriving on the scene and aiming their guns at what they thought was a hostage situation would blow this problem out of control, especially two days after Portland police officers had shot and killed Hannah's dad. I couldn't do that to her.

I pulled away from Mike and Nancy's minds so I could talk just to Brady. *I don't know what went wrong. What the hell do I do now?*

"*Sorry, I've got nothing,*" Brady thought to me.

Of course he didn't. How could he? There wasn't a textbook on this kind of thing, *The ABCs of Total Mind Invasion and Brainwashing.*

I saw Brady say something to Mike out loud, but Mike barked one sentence and then clamped his mouth shut as he tightened his hold on Nancy.

"*He said he's calling the Social Worker.*"

Nancy said something in a very tight-lipped manner that I didn't catch, but Mike's response was easy to read, "No, Bailey will have to take her."

Take her? Take Hannah? Where? What's he talking about?

"He wants us to take her to the Group Home," Brady told me.

That knocked the wind out of me like a punch to the gut and I sat abruptly into the chair.

How had it all gone so wrong? I'd left Hannah in her room fifteen minutes before; convinced that was where she'd sleep every night until Nancy joyfully-and-sadly packed her into the minivan to move her into her college dorm room. Now Mike wanted us gone, Hannah gone, and he wanted me to be the one to take her to the group home.

I couldn't do that to her.

I'd promised her that everything was going to work out.

I'd promised her that I would convince Mike and Nancy to adopt her.

I'd promised.

But neither Mike nor Nancy looked to be in an adopting mood. As the seconds ticked-by his face got redder and redder and hers got paler and paler. They were obviously disturbed by what I'd shared with them, afraid for themselves and for their kids.

Didn't they understand that we weren't going to hurt them? That Hannah would never hurt them?

Brady, tell them they're making a mistake, I begged.

He reached over and tugged at my arm to get me back on my feet. *"I think it's too late for that, Bay."*

But, my phamily.

"I know. But we better go," he thought at me with the same tone of voice I'd heard him use with Chef-ster when trying to get the little terror to lie down and go to sleep. *"It's time to get Hannah and leave."*

Can we take her back to your place? I asked as I inched toward the door into the townhouse.

Brady shook his head and stayed on my heels. *"They're going to report this as an emergency relocation to the Social Worker. If we don't take her straight to the Group Home we're asking to get slapped with kidnapping charges. Maybe we can work something out...later."*

He had to push me over the threshold into the house and point me toward the hallway. Every part of me wanted to run away, but...

...Hannah stood in the doorway to her room, waiting for us with tears streaming down her face and a half-full, black plastic garbage bag dangling heavily from her left hand—Samsonite for the foster-care set. It was safe to assume she'd heard Mike yelling and packed up her shit.

Hannah dropped the bag and lunged in my direction, and for a second I thought she was going to run past me and down the hall, but then she veered toward me and wrapped her arms around my waist, burying her face in my shoulder.

I hugged her back, rocking back and forth a little bit, crying as hard as she was and thinking again and again how sorry I was for appearing out of nowhere and fucking-up her life so badly...

...exactly what her mother had done to me...

...Faery Bitch.

It was ironic and poetic, but it was also fucking horrible.

32

Hannah and I shared the backseat of the Audi in silence while Brady retraced our route from the Carter's townhouse to the Group Home. Neither Mike nor Nancy had come into the apartment to say good-bye to their foster daughter after so heartlessly booting her out.

Chicken-shit sons-of-bitches. I wished I'd learned one of Maria's grandmother's curses to drop on their heads as we walked down the stairs and out the door.

But it was possible I wasn't the best person to throw those kinds of stones. I showed almost as much bravery during the ten-minute drive, keeping my mouth shut and my telepathy to myself. Nothing that came into my mind was worth saying, none of it would help the situation, and not one syllable was PG-rated. But I did hold tightly to Hannah's hand and I think that made a difference to her. It helped me.

Danni, Jacob, ML and Noah were waiting on the front stairs of the huge gray and white house until they recognized Brady's car, and then they ran to meet us in the driveway. Brady pulled in behind a mammoth white van and Hannah launched out of the car before I felt the engine shut down.

Being D-n-D made it impossible to hear what Hannah and her friends said to each other between hugs, but I could guess the tone of it by the grave expressions on their faces and the scowls they gave Brady and me.

Brady opened my door for me and then he grabbed Hannah's trash bag full of belongings from the back of the car. We followed the kids through the front door where a college-aged woman waited to check-in Hannah at a beat-to-hell front desk.

My skin crawled with how full of kids the house was: talk about Antsville. I saw at least ten ankle-biters—from Chester's size on up—in the living room playing video games and another six doing homework at the biggest, scarred-up dining room table I'd ever seen. I'm sure it was a very loud situation. Every single one of those hopeful, young faces turned toward us when we walked in the door, until they figured out we were just dropping-off, not picking-up. Damn. How could anyone be expected to bring a kid here, especially a teenager, and just turn their back and walk away? It was fucking inhuman.

The house attendant gave Hannah a manila envelope with her name written on it and Jacob claimed her things from Brady, a hard glare passing between them, even though Brady had ten years and thirty pounds on Jacob. The four teens escorted Hannah upstairs.

Funny, I'd always pictured the staircase to hell leading downward, not upward.

Hannah paused on the landing to look back at me, so I mouthed the phrase "I'll be back tomorrow morning," and blew her a little kiss to send her on her way. She needed her friends right then more than she needed to worry about my feelings.

I waited in my silent state while Brady handled the necessary arrangements with the attendant. Although I no longer had legal standing to be involved in Hannah's life, or legal obligation, I planned to be the one to take her to the appointment with her father's attorneys the next morning—and I wasn't taking any shit about it. There was absolutely no way I would trust anyone else to handle the important details of Hannah's future after being the one who screwed up her life up so badly.

In the end, Brady had to drag me back out to the car. I cried all the way to his apartment, soaking the sleeves of my beautiful new black dress in snot and tears.

It was impossible for me to decide whether I felt worse for Hannah or for myself.

After having begged and pleaded and sold a line of bullshit to Laume about how everything was going to be alright because I was going to get Hannah Faye adopted, I'd executed a belly-flop on a cosmic scale. And unlike the way I'd been anxious to be the first one to inform Laume about Ryan Williams' death—hoping the door to our bargain had not yet slammed shut—I was scared to death about what was going to happen when Laume found out that I had fucked-up, again. Worse this time.

Brady tried in vain to comfort me, but I couldn't talk with him and I resisted every invitation he gave to start a telepathic conversation. I just didn't want to share headspace with anyone, not even the first guy I was ever truly in love with.

I didn't even have the balls to reach out to my phamily and warn them about the stinking pile of shit we were all about to step into. My last ditch effort to get them home—assuming The Queen eventually decided to release them—stank worse than the urine soaked alley behind my favorite bar on New Year's morning.

It was all too much. I honestly felt like the world was caving in on me. Tequila didn't hold any promise to make it go away, so after we got back to Brady's place I changed into some borrowed sweats and sequestered myself in his kitchen. I stared into a pot of boiling sugar while he watched old movies on TV. By midnight, when he came in to kiss me goodnight, perfect salted caramels cooled on every flat surface of his kitchen.

But even that could not make me feel better. I threw all the dishes into a sink full of suds and turned the light off on the whole mess.

With the dark apartment to myself, I pulled a bottle of Pinot Grigio out of the fridge, poured myself a glass and sat at the dining table, staring blankly out the windows at the sleeping city.

Initially it was the faces of my phamily that filled my mind. We'd had such a chaotic beginning. Bonded so tightly in the hospital as each of us fought our inner demons and struggled to find something-close-to-sanity. Relied on each other to stay on the right path once we got out because none of us fit into our old lives anymore.

We fought.

We loved.

We rocked.

We lived.

JoJo had completely surrendered her proverbial razor, stopped cutting herself, and came to grips with the chaos of the outside world—so long as her apartment remained ready for a Martha Stewart photo-shoot and we gave her enough time to re-tune the strings of her stand-up bass between songs.

Paulo had made a grudging peace with the voices in his head, relegating each one to a know-nothing role or an insignificant purpose, and trusted us to help him remember to take his meds every day.

Cooper quit being so damned angry all the time, told his meth-crazed mother to find another piggy-bank to loot, and found out that living a life of inner peace on the verge of achievable dreams was the best possible revenge.

Maria...well Maria was still a little fuckin' nuts and she held tight to some of her grandmother's outlandish beliefs, but she learned how to hide it, except from the phamily, because we really didn't care. She was our Maria, and we loved her.

And me, I'd managed to keep the fire alive. At least until recent events overwhelmed me. But I would, I really would, figure out how to keep the fire burning.

I had such gratitude for my phamily.

But what did Hannah Faye have?

A Faery Bitch mother who didn't care.

A father in the ground who couldn't.

Freaked-out foster parents who had given up.

A bunch of heartless lawyers with a dead man's last wishes to heed.

And me.

Her hug as we stood in the hallway of the Carter's townhouse had been intensely needful. Her hand in mine as we drove to the Group Home had been as cold as ice, the familiar cold of the ball of loneliness throbbing in my chest. Her look back at me from the landing as ML and Danni and Jacob and Noah escorted her upstairs had been agonizing in its naked fear. She'd been kicked pretty hard and fallen pretty far from her father's mansion in the West Hills to that overcrowded Group Home.

I was grateful she already had friends there, that she wasn't spending the night alone in a strange place two days after her father had been shot and killed. Instead of tucked into her assigned, well-used bunk crying herself to sleep, I imagined Hannah and ML and Danni sitting cross-legged, crowded onto the same twin bed as they bitched about grown-ups in general and parents in particular while they made their own plans for the future—just like Maria and JoJo and I used to at the hospital. I wondered if she would share her Faery secret with them the way Maria and JoJo and I had eventually confided in each other about how fucked-up each of us really was.

I wondered if Hannah and the girls—or maybe even the five of them given how beautifully they sang together at Ryan's funeral—could help each other keep their fires alive. They really were a powerful bunch and if they stayed together I could imagine them going far.

So far.

Ooby Dooby.

In that moment, the beginning of an idea gobsmacked me in the middle of my forehead. An idea so appealing that the sub-zero ball of loneliness in my chest responded. That cold throb behind my breastbone, the one I'd been feeling since the moment I found myself alone in the lifeboat, transformed instantly into a hot beat.

A heartbeat.

My heartbeat.

Turns out I didn't need the wine. When Brady came out shortly after sunrise to kiss me on the top of my head and say good-morning, the still-full glass and mostly-full bottle of Pinot sat on the table next to me, warm, forgotten, ruined.

Standing and stretching, I pulled Brady into a full-body hug and gave him a closed-mouth-no-morning-breath-for-you kiss with as much passion as I could muster after my sleepless night. "Thank you," I said when we finished.

"For what?" he said in my ear, the feel of his breath giving me goosebumps in some very private places.

I released the hug and pulled him over toward the couch. "For giving me some room to think." I sat down and gave him a big smile.

He sat next to me. "Please tell me that smile means you figured something out."

I took a deep breath because what I had to say next was not like me at all. It was antithetical to everything I saw myself as: a late-night drummer, an early-morning baker, an anytime—everytime—patron of the sexual arts. If someone had told me a year before that I would make such a hasty, crazy, life-changing decision—and do it on my own without any input from my phamily—well, I would have given them the phone number for my favorite head-shrinker at the Texas State Hospital.

But that was before I met my first Faery. Lots had changed since then.

"I'm going to volunteer to be Hannah Faye's guardian."

"You're what?"

"If she'll have me, I'm going to be her guardian."

"That's crazy."

Considering how much grief I'd given him when I found out that his dog Chester was actually his little boy Chester, I didn't blame Brady for feeling that way.

Not to mention that he was right. It was a crazy idea. Pretty much fucking insane. "And that's not the craziest part."

I could tell by the bewildered look on his face that Brady didn't have a guess at what I was up to. So I told him instead of playing 20-questions.

"Congratulate me. I'm about to become the mother of five."

"Five?"

"I'm going to have my very own Partridge Family. Hannah, Jacob, ML, Danni and Noah."

"The kids from the Group Home?"

I nodded. "Hannah's phamily. I'm going to be their guardian until they're old enough to take care of themselves, to take care of each other."

It made complete sense. To me.

Hannah's dad was dead. Her hope for a life with the Carters as their adopted daughter was gone. But those kids had been there for her when she needed them the most. It was obvious to me, when I finally looked at the situation the right way, they needed each other. They were already a phamily. Once Hannah's resources came into play that would take care of most of the problems, they just needed a place to live outside The System so they could stay together until they got old enough that the state would leave them alone.

"Why you?" Brady asked. "Why take them all? It isn't your responsibility to save every foster kid in Oregon."

"It's the only way to save my phamily. If I can secure Hannah's phamily, make sure they're able to stay together without any outside interference, then maybe I get Maria and JoJo and Cooper and Paulo back from Laume."

Brady got really quiet for a minute. "Do you have any idea what you're going to have to give up to make that happen?" he asked.

"It's all I've been thinking about."

To make it work with Hannah and the kids, I'd pretty much have to give up everything. My apartment in Austin. The life I'd built for myself down there. Any hope of getting back to my little boutique bakery and all my loveable, wacky customers. My role as drummer in Billy's Asylum Rats and my dream of recording with them in the studio that Elvis Presley made famous. My taste for tequila. My less-than-responsible-adult pursuit of carnal pleasure. My freedom, for a little while.

But, if it worked, I'd get my phamily out of Faery, away from Laume, and back to Austin. Back to their lives.

"Do you know what the worst part is going to be?" I asked Brady with a sigh.

"Since they're already teenagers, probably not the diapers. They do come potty trained, right?"

I sneered at him. "The worst part is the goddamn minivan I'm going to have to get to drive them all around. Elvis help me. Me. In a minivan."

He laughed. A snort turned into a chuckle turned into a full-on belly roller. I tried not to join him, but the more I thought about myself behind the wheel of a mommy-wagon, the harder it got to stay morose. I gave up, gave in, and laughed with him.

It felt good to laugh. I'd been crying so much over the past week; and although those tears had been necessary and helpful in their own way, they had been feeding my loneliness and stealing the heat from my fire. But laughter—hearty, joyful, heart-warming laughter—that's what my life used to be about. I needed to find my way back there again, and laughing with Brady made a good start.

As we settled down, Brady had a serious question for me.

"What if Laume doesn't play along?"

"You mean what if she isn't satisfied that I met all the conditions of our bargain?"

Brady nodded.

I shrugged. "It meets the intention. But I learned my lesson. I'm going to wait until everyone agrees and the paperwork is underway before I tell her about it."

"You know her better than I do," Brady said. "But it seems to me that she's been looking for an excuse to screw you in this deal. Any excuse. All she'd have to do is say no."

He was right. There was no way to know whether or not I could convince Laume that my guardianship and building a phamily for Hannah would guarantee her success in life. But I had run out of options, and I really did believe this would work best for Hannah. It was a better solution than sending her back to Ryan had ever been. Better even than betting on the Carters and hoping they'd support her budding career.

And it worked for me. It had worked for me, I had my phamily to thank for all my successes. My heart was at complete peace with my decision.

Assuming I could convince Laume.

"She won't say no."

"But what if she does? Are you still going to go through with it? Will you still be their guardian?"

The certainty I felt about my answer, and how quickly it popped out of my mouth, surprised me. "Of course I will," I said with a smile. "It's gonna be Fat City."

"What does that mean for you and me?" Brady asked.

I could tell by the look on his face that some part of him was extremely disappointed about my choice. Maybe it was because I made it without consulting him. Though honestly, it wasn't the kind of choice I could let him get into the middle of. I had to do this for me, for my phamily, for Hannah, and for her phamily. I hoped he would be willing to come along on whatever winding path lay ahead of us, but I wouldn't blame him from shying away from the whole thing—telepathic half-Faery mother of 5 teenagers, not the kind of thing that gets lots of winks on the dating sites.

"It means I'm absolutely staying in Portland," I said with a hopeful smile. "The rest, well, I guess the rest is up to you."

When he was slow to respond I reached out and touched his face.

"It's a lot to think about," I said. "We should take some time and talk later."

He nodded.

I wished he'd given me a more positive response.

33

After dropping Brady at his office I borrowed his Audi for the day and, against my better judgment given how our conversation about the future had ended, fifty bucks. My first stop was returning to The Buffalo Exchange. I needed a new outfit, since the funeral-gear-day-two dress I wore was not the message I wanted to send and the hemp was too casual. I also wanted to surprise Hannah with a new outfit as well—get started on the right foot with this guardianship-thing, assuming she said yes, and give her a little ego boost for the meeting with her dad's attorneys.

I found a vintage dress in blue with a beautiful lace collar that I could wear off the shoulder on days I wasn't trying to impress an attorney. Adding a chunky black leather belt with a big sterling buckle from the men's section and a pair of four inch pumps gave the outfit the boost it needed to fit the current decade and look less 1950s.

Shopping for Hannah was harder. I figured she was right there on the size 0 line, or maybe a well-tailored size 1, and the second-hand shop didn't carry much that was both vintage and that small. I gave up as the clock on the wall pushed closer to nine-thirty—I still had to get to the Group Home to pick up Hannah and then to the attorney's by 10:30—so I settled for some red skinny jeans and a gray t-shirt to go under a cropped cardigan printed with a Union Jack. The outfit would have looked great with a set of heels, but not knowing Hannah's shoe size meant guessing wrong would be painful or comical or humiliating, or all three. Instead I picked up a pair of barely worn Chuck Taylors in a coordinating blue from the boy's department and gray socks that would just peek out the top.

Not bad for my first attempt at picking out my kid's clothes. Maybe. I cashed it all out and then fretted about the choices all the way across town. The outfit was my style, hipster with a side of punk, but given my track record with Hannah it was possible everything was wrong and she'd have been happier in a pink cashmere sweater and jeans.

The house attendant admitted me to the Group Home and escorted me up to Hannah's temporary bedroom. It was a small space, too small for two sets of bunk beds, three mismatched dressers, and the three girls she had to share with, but the southern wall was almost all windows that let in the warm sunlight to cheer things up. Hannah lay on the bed with her iPod cranked, singing quietly along with the tune. Adele. Rolling in the Deep.

Nice.

She was obviously not a happy camper, but I had expected a whole lot worse. I was pretty sure we had ML and Danni to thank for her not lying in pieces on the floor or hiding in the closet.

I set both bags on the nearest bunk.

"What's that?" Hannah asked as she got up.

I was so glad she was curious, not withdrawn and angry at me.

"Consider them you-can't-bully-me-around outfits," I said as I pulled clothing and shoes out of the bag. "I've found that it's best to wear something fun and outrageous when meeting with lawyers. Gives you a sense of invulnerability, like a suit of armor, but cooler."

Jeans, t-shirt, sweater, shoes, socks. I laid them out on the bunk and then looked to see her smiling. Turns out I pegged her taste in clothes pretty well.

"You got this for me?"

"Unless you have something else you'd like to wear?"

"But why?"

"It's all part of my brilliant plan. The first step, actually. If you think it's a good idea, we'll go for it."

She cocked her head to the side and I couldn't help thinking of an Afghan puppy with long, floppy ears.

Since I was still wearing my funeral dress, and Brady had spent a ton of money on it, I sat on the edge of the bunk instead of sitting on the floor. Hannah sat across from me, careful not to sit on her new outfit.

I took a deep breath and my eyes dropped to the floor. "Hannah, I'd like to be your guardian. Yours and Danni's and ML's and Jacob's and Noah's. All of you. If you agree, I'm going to ask the attorneys to figure out how to make it happen, legally. The only way it's going to work is if your dad left you enough to cover the bills, because I'm probably out of a job after not going to work for the last few days. I think it will work. All of us pulling together. We'll help each other."

I slowly raised my eyes to see Hannah's face streaked in tears.

"I think we can make it work," I said. "Us half-Faery kids have to stick together, right?"

Hannah's chin started to tremble and she crossed her arms over her chest.

I wasn't sure how to interpret that. "Would you please say something?" I asked.

She roughly wiped her tears away, face mushing out of shape beneath her fingers. "Why would you do that? Why all of us?"

Damn. The *why* questions. I knew she was going to ask them. Given all she'd been through I'd have been more surprised if she hadn't.

I had already decided to come clean. If I wanted her and four other emotionally damaged teenagers to trust me, to choose to behave like adults, I had to start by treating them like adults.

"It's all of you because I think you need each other." I took a few minutes to tell Hannah all about my phamily, starting with how I spelled it differently than the dictionary. I described JoJo's ski-slope nose and how it crinkled when she laughed at my stupid jokes. Cooper's temper and loyalty and how they both came from the same passion. Maria's fierce Italian pride and her love for her grandmother. Paulo's ability to play as many notes on the guitar as he had voices in his head. Our music. Our insanity. Our love.

"After the way your friends stepped up at the funeral, I knew that they already loved you like phamily. Like my phamily loves me. Like it or not, those four forgotten-about, left-behind kids are the difference between you just-getting-by in life and having the life you deserve. Together you're going to be unstoppable."

"But why would you do that?"

"My phamily," I said. I told myself I wasn't going to cry. I hated crying. Not only was it going to ruin my make-up before a very important meeting, but it was a ridiculous thing to do. Crying didn't help. Except when it did. "I'm doing this to help my phamily."

Obviously Hannah was confused.

"Do you remember how I said your mom asked me to come and help you?"

Hannah nodded, still confused.

"She didn't really ask. She bullied me into making a deal and then she took my phamily hostage. They're in a dungeon in Faery."

Hannah's mouth dropped open.

"The only way I might get them back is to make sure you get the support you need to grow up the right way. That was supposed to be with your dad. But then he went off the deep end and got killed."

I sniffled, trying to stop crying.

"And then I convinced her to let the Carters adopt you. Except I fucked that up, too. Now the only way to make sure you have a chance to grow up and become the most amazing, half-Faery, singing diva the world has ever heard is to do it myself.

"Well, not all by myself." I stopped to wipe my face, being careful of my mascara. "I need your help, and Jacob's and ML's and Danni's and Noah's—'cause, face it, Kitty-kat, you are going to be one hell of a handful when you figure out how beautiful and talented you really are."

I smiled through my tears and was so grateful when she smiled back.

"So, what do you think," I asked her.

"I think you're crazy." She laughed.

"Me too." But I couldn't laugh with her, my heart was too raw.

I pushed myself back on the bed until my feet hung off the edge and I could rest against the wall, content to wait as Hannah thought about my plan.

Telling her the truth felt good. It sucked to lay all that on her while the rest of her life was up in the air, but if we were going to be in it together, we had to be in it together.

"Will we go back to my house?" she finally asked.

"Do you want to?"

She shook her head. I was glad she didn't want to live there. I wasn't sure I could go back.

"Then we'll find someplace else," I said as I looked around the room, crowded, worn, utilitarian, impersonal. "Someplace better than this."

"Can we all pick it out together?"

"Since it's going to have to be your money, maybe I should be asking you that."

Hannah started nodding her head; small movements became larger and bolder as she convinced herself that it could really happen. We could make it work. "If we agree, how soon do you get your phamily back?"

I sure liked the fact that she used the word *we*. It felt right. But I didn't really have an answer for her. I wished I did.

"I don't know." I explained how Laume had not yet agreed to this new proposal of mine. I left out the part about Queen Mab. It was too much to explain.

"What happens to us if she says no? Do we have to come back here?"

"No, absolutely not." I slid off the bed and went to sit next to her. "I'm doing this whether she gives me back my phamily or not."

"Really?"

I nodded.

"You must really love them if you're willing to take on all five of us," she said.

"Darn tootin'," I said. "And this is going to sound really corny, but I love you too, kiddo."

And then there was no more to say, so we got dressed. My dress fit pretty well and Hannah looked smashing. I stuffed my black dress back into the Buffalo Exchange bag while Hannah corralled all of her possessions and then I helped her stuff them in the other bag. It was overly optimistic of us to do that way, pretending she absolutely wasn't coming back, but I was feeling optimistic for the first time in days.

We had to park Brady's Audi ten blocks from the lawyer's building in downtown Portland because I had no money for parking. The long walk got us there a few minutes late, but Ryan's attorney's staff made no fuss. After all, she was just a teenager and her dad had just died.

An assistant showed us to a conference room where two young lawyers waited and a third older one, one of the partners, eventually joined us. After the big Kahuna boss, Mr. Matthison, explained the arrangements Ryan had made for Hannah in his will, and about all of the distant cousins who'd been calling his office to ask about *Darling Little Hannah-pooh*, she surprised the hell out of me by telling him *exactly the way it was actually going to go.*

I knew that growing up with money made some kids feel entitled, but I had never seen that side of Hannah before. It was freakishly cool. She sounded confident, knowledgeable, responsible—14 going on 40. Though her dad's lawyer was old enough to be her grandfather she laid it out for him like a blackmailer with thumb drive full of compromising pictures and the local news station on speed dial. I was going to be her guardian and manage her trust fund: no questions asked, no background check, no kidding around. She also detailed how she wanted to have her friends placed under guardianship with her, and even if it took an emergency injunction she wanted them all out of the Group Home immediately. That afternoon. No more sleepless nights for any of them wondering if they were ever going to find a home of their own.

Then she asked for a check for living expenses. And someone from Matthison's staff to handle the legal end of our real estate needs. And lunch, because she was hungry, please. And a car service to take everyone to a nice hotel when we were finished.

Elvis help me, she got them to agree.

While Matthison and his staff made calls and tapped away at their laptops I leaned over to ask Hannah, "Where did you learn to do that?"

"My dad's agent. Uncle Milty. Best damned negotiator in major league ball."

"I guess so," I said. "You think they'll make it happen?"

"They'll probably find some hiccup, something that's going to get in the way, but I'll offer them an eight percent bump in their fee and they'll figure out how to make it happen."

"Way to go, Uncle Milty Jr.," I said and fist-bumped her.

Things dragged into the late afternoon. Hannah's guess about the hiccup proved true, and Uncle Milty would've been proud of how she handled it. I called Brady and he arranged to come pick up his key and his car after work—I gave him a quick kiss when I met him in the lobby, explained things were going well and promised to call. By six-thirty, just as the signed paperwork was being couriered back from Family Court, a social worker arrived bearing four wide-eyed gifts: Jacob, ML, Noah and Danni with their matching Hefty-bag luggage.

With five final signatures on five interim-not-likely-to-ever-be-contested custody documents it was official: I was their guardian. We shared hugs all around. Even though it was a big surprise and had gone down faster than some Rockabilly festivals I've played at, the moment felt as good as it would have if it had taken years to come true. They were a phamily, and for the first time in a long time—maybe in their whole lives—they knew they were going to be okay.

The car service sent a limo, the first one I'd ever ridden in so it felt as magical as a carriage grown out of a pumpkin, and the six of us cruised to The Marriot where one of Matthison's team had booked us two adjoining suites.

For the kids it was the happy ending they'd never dared to wish for. No it didn't come with the perfect mom and dad and two dogs and a swimming pool in the back yard, but compared to another few years in that overcrowded Group Home their futures looked like one big party.

As they got more and more excited peeking through cabinets, poking buttons, and studying the room service menu I felt more and more anxious. The work was done, and the hard part remained.

Laume.

There was no more putting it off. It was time to see if this foolhardy gamble of mine was going to pay off. I winked at Hannah so she would know I needed some privacy in the other room and grabbed the new gigantic binder from Matthison that had become the driving force of my life: proof for Laume that Hannah's future was as secure as it had ever been, could ever be.

And this time I read the binder—from cover-to-cover—as I punched the holes in each page and assembled it.

Locking the door behind me so I would have the sitting room of the adjoining suite to myself, I pulled a chair over to the window that overlooked the city. The kids' rowdy noise from the next room made me want to contact my phamily first, before I talked to Laume, but I didn't want to get their hopes up until I had convinced her to say yes.

I took a deep breath and tried to get my muscles to relax. So much had happened in the thirteen days since the yacht went down. Surreal, as a concept, didn't even cover it. My ideas about what was possible and what was not had been thoroughly shaken and reset. My new understanding about my birth family alone was enough to rock the foundations of my life; finding out more about my mother had been almost enough to send me back to the hospital. If my phamily's lives had not been at stake I would have given up, curled up in a ball on that bench in the dappled sunlight and waited to die. But now I had Brady, probably. And I had a new ability. And I was the mother of five.

It was time to reap the rewards of all that insanity and get my phamily back.

I sat back and closed my eyes. I imagined Laume. My first thought went to my fantasy of her decapitated head rolling across Brady's balcony, but I shook it off. That would never get me the kind of telepathic connection I needed. Getting serious I thought of her in that copy of my red and white swing dress as she twirled in the middle of the Portland street.

That didn't do it.

I tried thinking of her bobbing in the water at the back of the lifeboat, moonlight shining on her hair.

Nope.

Picturing her in the Bugatti didn't work. Neither did bringing to mind the sky blue sequined gown. Not even thinking of the way she held my passport and license and threatened to drop them down the garbage chute did the trick.

In a last ditch effort I thought back to the middle-aged dude in the Cowboy's football jersey who confronted me at the Dallas-Ft. Worth airport.

Nada. Zilch. Not a damn thing.

She would not answer me; there was no click to say she was even there. Maybe she was ducking me, like my telepathy had a built-in *Ignore* button I wasn't aware of. Whatever it was, it was horribly inconvenient.

But telepathy wasn't the only way I knew to reach out and touch a Faery, I remembered another way.

Paulo had told me when we talked. It's how I was supposed to summon Sir Ansley, by speaking his name three times, but I couldn't at the time because I was D-n-D. Since the aversion to iron turned out to be a Faery-wide problem, I hoped that method for summoning one of them worked across the board too.

"Laume," I growled, trying to sound exactly like she had when she'd introduced herself the first time.

"Laume." I repeated.

"Laume." One more time to make three.

And I waited.

And waited. And waited.

And the Faery Bitch did not show up. That meant I couldn't talk to her. Couldn't explain. Couldn't fix it. Couldn't get my phamily back.

"Laume!" I screamed at the top of my lungs. "Laume, you bitch. How dare you pull this shit now? Talk to me."

I heard a knock at the adjoining door, and a small voice call my name, and a rattle of the door handle. I ignored it. The kids did not need to see me until I calmed down.

Taking a deep breath to even my voice and settle the roiling in my belly that had replaced the cold throb in my chest I raised my voice so they could hear me through the door, "I'm okay. You guys order some dinner and watch a pay-per-view, okay. Something PG-13. No horror movies."

The jiggling door handle stopped. Thank you, Elvis, because I sure as hell was not ready to calm down until I got some goddamn answers.

If I couldn't summon Laume, there was one Faery I knew I could summon.

Queen Mab's Winter Knight.

34

Sir Ansley Devon Stannard." Going once.

"Sir Ansley Devon Stannard." Going twice.

"Sir Ansley Devon Stannard." Third time's the charm.

And that time, my powers of summoning worked.

Good Graceland, did they work.

Instantly, silently, Sir Ansley just appeared in the sitting room. His slim body was clad in head-to-toe leathers, stiff stuff that would probably have saved his ass in a high-speed motorcycle accident. His hair dripped sweat, a two-inch gash on his forehead bled like it had just happened, and the smell of wood smoke washed off him to overpower the room.

And, just like the last time I saw him, he held both of his wicked-scary knives. They dripped blood as he completed a lunge forward, away from me, and then turned and looked at his surroundings with an astonished look on his face.

In the time it took for my heart to beat a single lub-dub he had me pinned to the wall with the sharp edge of his right blade pressed to my throat. The cold line of pain I could try to ignore, but the confusion, that had my heart going.

"Sir Ansley, it's just me, Bailey Michaels."

"I know damn well who you are," he said in his thick Irish brogue. "And it won't keep me from parting your head from your shoulders."

He pressed harder with the blade against my skin, so hard that swallowing was out of the question. I didn't feel a trickle of blood, yet, but if he budged the knife a millimeter one way or the other I was sure it would happen.

"I need your help," I begged. I wanted my voice to be calm, rational, but instead it wavered and gave away my fear.

"You need a lesson in fucking manners, is what you need." He eased the pressure of the knife but didn't pull it away. "Or at least a heaping dose of self-preservation."

I had no clue what he was talking about. The wild look in his eyes was beginning to scare me. If all he wanted to do was teach me a lesson, I was pretty sure I'd gotten the message. But he did not let up.

"If I were to carve my knife into your delicate, white throat right now what would you do? You are alone," he said as he stopped to listen. "Well, at least you're alone in this room. The keepers of those voices cannot possibly reach you in time."

Especially since the door between the rooms was locked. But Sir Ansley was right even discounting that point.

"You are unarmed." He looked disapprovingly around the room and I held my breath as the pressure of the knife on my throat wavered. "You did not even take the precaution to construct a circle of protection. What are you, an idiot?"

"A circle of what?"

Sir Ansley drew his face so close to mine that his breath warmed my skin. "Stupid girl. Summoning a Faery Knight while defenseless and unarmed. I should kill you now, just to save you from a more torturous fate the next time."

I pressed myself into the wall as hard as I could, but there was nowhere for me to go. I hadn't been that scared since Ryan Williams' guest room, when he had my t-shirt hiked into my armpits and he was trying to rape me.

Suddenly I realized I was not as defenseless as Sir Ansley thought I was.

I had telepathy. Telepathy for powerful defense.

The hard part was that I didn't want to hurt Sir Ansley, or seriously freak him out. I still needed his help. But I had to get his knife off my throat because he looked awfully serious about teaching me a lesson.

I closed my eyes and pictured a wicked blade of my own; Cooper's highly-illegal switchblade came to mind. I saw its rugged plastic grip, the *Born to Rock* inscription on one side and the belt clip on the other, and most especially its four inch blade with the gnarly serrations at the base. I imagined how it would feel in my hand and then pictured exactly how I would have to hold my arm—the angle, the twist, the grip—to place that blade hard against the inside of Sir Ansley's thigh, aimed at his most precious body parts.

I held onto that image and breathed shallowly as I thought about the blade sliding up along his hard leather pants until I found the gap in the material that allowed him to move freely. When the tip of the blade stopped in my mind I opened my eyes and looked into Sir Ansley's.

He leaned his lower body into me and I rotated my mental grip so that the pointy part of my imaginary blade was unmistakably up against his dangly parts.

Your move, I told him telepathically.

"*You can't actually hurt me with that*," he said.

I can't draw blood, but I can give you an unfading memory of having your balls sliced off. One at a time.

"*That would be most unpleasant.*" He pulled his knife away and then stepped back two paces. "*Why have you summoned me?*"

I've been trying to reach Laume. I finally completed my half of the bargain and it's time for her to give my phamily back. But I can't get her to answer me telepathically, and she wouldn't come when I summoned her.

"*That's exactly what I was talking about*," he thought toward me as he pointed both blades in my direction. "*You're lucky to have failed. Summoning her might have been one of the stupidest things you've ever done. Stupider than kissing me.*"

He noticed the blood on his weapons, and his gaze wandered the room until it settled on the burgundy and gold drapes framing the city view. My jaw dropped as he used them to wipe his blades clean and then slipped the weapons back into their sheaths.

I almost chewed him out for doing that to drapes I was going to have to pay to replace, but then I noticed the red blood morph into some kind of clear slime. It evaporated as I watched.

Way cool.

What was that, I asked.

"*Oxidizing Faery blood. Bad for the blades. But it cannot persist on this side of The Veil without Connection and Intention.*"

Whatever that meant. It wasn't really important, not as important as getting my phamily back.

So how come I could summon you, but not her?

He cocked his head. "*And just how did you execute this so-called summons?*"

I gave him a repetition of my attempt to say Laume's name as she had said it to me the first time we met.

Sir Ansley's body spasmed in what I interpreted as a snort. "*You don't even have her full name, and the part you do have you butchered to bits. It's a lucky thing you didn't accidentally summon something worse: an Elemental, or a Giant.*"

What's her full name? I asked.

"*Tsk, tsk. Did your father raise you without any manners at all? To know a Faery's whole name is to have some small bit of power over that individual. Any time. Any place. No matter the cost.*"

Oh. It had not occurred to me that summoning a Faery was considered a rude, power-play. How was I to know it wasn't the same thing as making a person-to-Faery phone call? But then I re-considered Sir Ansley's current state—sweat cooling, cut clotting—and I suddenly wondered what he had been doing when I summoned him. What I might have yanked him away from.

I'm sorry. I didn't mean to call you away from something important.

Sir Ansley nodded, but he kept the details of whatever he'd been doing to himself. "*I'm here. Let's just get this trouble of yours sorted so I can get back to it.*"

I need you to help me contact Laume?

"*I'm afraid that's not something I'm in a position to do.*"

Fuck. I need to get my phamily out.

"*I suppose Queen Mab might have something to say about that.*"

Has she decided about the bargain yet?

"*Queen Mab deliberates.*"

And?

"*And Laume faces her judgment just as you do.*"

But, I explained to you that our bargain was just and fair and that I entered into it willingly.

"*Never lie to a Faery, Bailey. We're much too practiced at the art of deception. I've had your lifetime and much longer.*"

I didn't lie.

He nodded his head in concession. "*But you didn't tell me the truth, and Queen Mab saw through your attempt to manipulate her judgment.*"

Oh shit. Elvis help me. Oh crap.

She's going to decide against Laume, isn't she?

Sir Ansley took two steps forward and laid his hand on the upper part of my arm. "*Let's go see, shall we?*"

Before I could disagree, or explain that I had five kids in the next room who needed me, my world suddenly blurred with the kind of acceleration I would expect from a rocket launch, making me close my eyes so I wouldn't vomit. The next sensations I felt were my feet pressing against soft ground and the air surrounding me growing so cold it had teeth.

I opened my eyes, expecting to be standing in a blizzard on the edge of a glacier or inside a giant rubber-floored, walk-in freezer full of hanging beef, but I found myself someplace much more familiar: Graceland.

Or almost Graceland.

At first I would have sworn I was standing in the middle of Elvis's living room. White carpets. White chairs and a sofa. Mirrored walls with gilded accents and a sunburst clock over the fireplace. The ambient light felt like daylight, but I couldn't tell because all the windows were covered by shears. Stained glass panels adorned with peacocks divided the seating area from the room where his glossy, black grand piano still waited to be played. How Maria had begged to lay her hands on those ivory keys when we'd toured the house on a trip through Memphis.

But it did not take long to realize I wasn't actually in Graceland.

Even though he was The King of Rock 'n Roll, Elvis never had a throne. Or attendants. Or a living room that magically elongated into a grand hall with room for dozens of the most beautiful people I'd ever seen in my life to stand and talk in clusters of four and five. I always considered Maria and JoJo to be lookers, and little Hannah Faye was going to grow up to be breathtaking, but not one of them could hold a candle to the ugliest of the beautiful people in that room. And each of them wore the slickest 'billy outfits I'd ever seen; like what Billy's Asylum Rats wore on stage, but in cooler colors and classier fabrics and with way more amazing accent touches than we could ever afford.

Faeries. It had to be Faeries. And that made the room Faery Court. I shuddered to think of Maria and JoJo and Cooper and Paulo standing naked in front of this curious, powerful, stone-faced crowd.

In the middle of all of it perched Queen Mab, I assumed, on her throne, wearing a brushed silk, white-on-white swing dress and white patent-leather saddle shoes with three inch chunky heels. Her glowing Auburn hair waved back from her too-perfect-to-believe face and down over her snowy shoulders in the perfect 1940s hairdo. But it was her eyes that really got my attention. I only glimpsed them for a moment, but the depth and sparkle of their quicksilver color seemed the source of all the cold I felt biting into me. Terrible, hypnotic, nightmarish eyes.

Beside me, and obviously a whole lot less disoriented from the trip, Sir Ansley immediately knelt and bowed his head to

The Queen, dragging my arm down with him so I had no choice but to kneel next to him.

"Lower your eyes," he growled quietly.

I did, studying every fiber in the carpet next to my right shoe, as I realized he'd spoken to me out loud, not in my head. Apparently D-n-D didn't hold its grip across The Veil.

"Rise, my dear Winter Knight."

Sir Ansley stood, leaning one leather-clad knee against my shoulder so that I could not stand up. But I could raise my head, and I did. I couldn't help it.

"What surprise have you brought for us today, Sir Knight?"

The words sounded like they ought to have come from Queen Mab, but her perfect lips never parted. Instead the voice came from a female Faery, tall and dark and regal, who stood motionless next to Mab's throne except when she spoke for The Queen.

"If it pleases you, my Queen, may I present Miss Bailey Faye Michaels: daughter of L'Estatia, friend to me, and chosen-sister of your human prisoners."

The Queen nodded, just the barest motion. "And this half-human has business with the court?" the Voice asked.

"No, Your Highness, she has business with your subject, Laume."

"I see," the Queen said, this time giving voice to the words herself. I wished she had not. It was an evil sound: intense, grating and invading. It rattled every part of my body and triggered my flight instincts. Sir Ansley had to place his hand on my back to keep me from bolting. It reminded me of Laume laughing at me in my own head.

"Let the daughter of L'Estatia rise and speak for herself," The Queen ordered through her Voice.

Sir Ansley knelt down again, as if he needed to help me to my feet, and he whispered as he pulled me up next to him, "Your best behavior. Humble. Submissive. No eye contact. No attitude. Tell your story plain, tell it true, and then shut your fucking mouth. No matter what she says, show no surprise.

Keep your wits about you and you might get to see your family again. With their heads still attached."

My stomach flipped over and raced for my toes as I struggled to my feet. It was a warning I would not ignore.

"Thank you, Your Majesty," Sir Ansley said as straightened his back and then elbowed me in the ribs.

"Thank you, Your Majesty," I said, following his lead, and focused my eyes on the white fur pillow propping-up her shiny shoes to keep from looking at her terrible eyes.

"Well, child, we don't have all day. Speak."

"Your Highness, I've come to get my phamily back. I've done everything Laume wanted, and more, and I deserve to have them back, home, with me."

The Queen leaned over to consult with her Voice and then sat up straight and nodded. "You refer to the contentious bargain over the fate of the half-human child Hannah Faye Williams?"

"Yes, Your Highness."

"So Hannah Faye has been returned to her father's residence and is reunited with him in loving family bond?"

I dropped my head and sweat prickled coolly all over my back. I had not considered having to explain the big ol' monkey wrench that got thrown into the bargain to Queen Mab. "No, Your Highness, the girl's father, died. But Laume and I..."

The Queen slapped her hand against the golden arm of her throne, sending an echoing *smack* across the room and cutting me off. "His passing from the mortal world forces the bargain into limbo. You cannot have fulfilled your obligations."

"But..." I tried to say.

"Do not *but* me, little girl," The Queen said, for herself again, and the force of her displeasure landed on my bowed neck and shoulders, driving me to my knees. "I am The Winter Queen of Faery. I could snuff out your life with a whisper, so you will show the proper respect."

Good Graceland. I hated authority figures who thought that their ability to unmake me was enough to kowtow me into behaving. My father had been the first—and he nearly broke me, almost made me take my own life to escape him. And then doctors at the hospital had tried to coerce me into things I knew were not right for me. I'd learned, or I thought I'd learned, until my life ran smack-dab into Laume. She'd bullied me, tricked me, forced me to make agonizing decisions to help out a strange kid to save my phamily, a kid I'd actually come to love enough to take care of for the rest of her adolescence. But I was done with the bowing and scraping shit. It was time to stand up for myself.

I had no idea whether Queen Mab would admire me for my audacity, or if she'd just decide to turn me into a giant Bailey-shaped ice cube. I was so desperate to get what I had earned that I threw caution to the wind.

I straightened my back until my shoulders were directly above my feet and pushed against the echoes of The Queen's words in my head with every ounce of strength in my legs until I was standing at my full height and looking directly into Queen Mab's nightmarish quicksilver eyes. It was hard to hold her undivided attention, I wanted to squirm and run, but I had nothing left to lose. So I went for it. I put my shoulders back, raised my chin, and told it true.

"Your Highness, regardless of Ryan Williams passing from the mortal world, I have fulfilled my end of the bargain in line with Laume's intentions for her daughter. Hannah Faye has a phamily where she is loved and protected and we will see her achieve her highest aspirations." Damn if I didn't sound like a well-educated college-type. Or a Faery.

"Intentions," The Queen's puppet voice said. "What does a half-human know of a Faery's intentions?"

"I know intentions are everything for one of you. I know Laume intended for me to create a loving, stable, permanent home for Hannah that would enable her to become one of the most popular performers in our world. Adoration. Fame. Fortune. Glory. She'll have it all. I promise."

The Queen started to laugh, but there was no humor in it, there was only chill and nerve endings grated raw. "Laume," she called. "Where is Laume? Front and center, little sprite. Interrogation time."

The crowd of Faeries who had gathered to the left side of The Queen's throne jostled and parted to make room for Laume to appear before Queen Mab. She stood as far away from me as she could while still technically being in front of the throne. Standing in Faery Court, among her own kind, Laume came off as merely pretty, partly for her dark coloring among such fair company, but also for her unadorned sweater and poodle-skirt combination in Pepto Bismol pink. It didn't do anything for her eyes, or for her complexion.

"Yes, Your Highness," Laume said meekly, not using the familiar boastful, power-hungry, arrogant tones that she'd always used with me.

"Explain to this half-human child your intentions."

"Might I inquire, does this indicate you have concluded deliberations regarding the veracity of our bargain, Your Highness?"

"I have not, nor will I until you explain your intentions."

"I intended for Hannah Faye to have an appropriate home among mortal humans."

"And?" The Queen's Voice asked, raising her own eyebrow in time with The Queen's. Every ear and eye in the hall focused on the tension between Laume and Mab.

"The rest is inconsequential."

"Tut, tut," again the words came from Queen Mab and I could see the syllables hit Laume like sacks of invisible flour to the chest. "The whole truth."

Laume put one foot back to keep her balance and crossed her arms over her chest. "In truth, I intended for the feat to be more difficult and punishing than Bailey Faye could endure. I set her up to fall flat on her face, as her fellow humans would say."

What? The Faery Bitch had been setting me up to fail? I thought back to our conversation after Ryan Williams' death. Laume had asked me point blank whether getting the Carters to adopt Hannah and change their tune about her potential would be more difficult than getting Hannah home to her dad. Both resolutions had turned out to be equally impossible in the end, but she'd agreed to let me keep trying because she thought I couldn't do it and she wanted to watch me fail.

"Why?" I asked. "Why would you do that to me?" If I hadn't been so bewildered I might have rushed her, wrestled her to the ground and tried to beat her to a bloody pulp, but my confusion rooted my feet in place. Or maybe it was Sir Ansley's death grip on my wrist.

"Perhaps someone with a more poignant point of view could provide the answers you seek," Queen Mab's Voice said. "Lady L'Estatia, come forward little darlin', I have a task for you."

L'Estatia. It took me a second to place the name and then I remembered that's what Sir Ansley called my mother.

My mother was in the room.

I whipped my head around, searching the crowd of Faery faces for one that looked like me. There. The crowd behind me thinned and the most beautiful woman I had ever seen approached us. Pale. Unbelievably tall. Platinum blonde. Slim and curvy at the same time, in a perfectly tailored tank dress—sage green silk. My eyes were the same shape as hers—lashes, brows, and lids—but my color had obviously come from my father as hers were silver like Sir Ansley's and Queen Mab's.

Sir Ansley dipped his head and I tracked, open-mouthed, as my mother passed by, eighteen inches away, and knelt at the base of the throne. "Your Highness."

"Rise."

My mother rose to stand on her bare feet as if lifted on the graceful wings of angels.

"It seems I now have sufficient information to resolve this most diverting dilemma. While I deliberate, you will escort your...daughter...to the dungeons..."

My heart stopped dead in my chest and all feeling left my body. I finally got a chance to meet my mother and she'd been ordered to take me to the Faery Queen's dungeon?

"...to visit with her chosen-family. On your way, explain to her the intricacies she has missed regarding Laume's intentions."

Leaping painfully back into action, my heart coursed welcome warmth through my whole body. My phamily. They were close. The Queen said I could see them.

I took a huge breath and let it out as a sigh.

The Queen shifted her gaze to me. "I will summon you when you are needed."

"Thank you, Your Highness," I said, meaning every syllable. The Queen's phrasing was flush with typical Faery vaguenesses, including not specifying a timeline, but I didn't give a shit. As long as I could spend it with my phamily, she could take thirty years to make up her mind.

My mother turned toward me, making my skin crawl with the way it was like looking in a trick-mirror that erased tattoos, and motioned for me to follow her. Faeries opened a wide pathway ahead of us toward a set of thirty-foot tall double mirrored doors at the far end of the hall.

I followed my mother's rigid back as she glided across the stone floor. It was weird. Absolutely fucking weird.

35

Maybe it was a characteristic of being in Faery; our surroundings changed drastically after we stepped through those palatial mirrored doors. Where the throne room had been alive and airy and full of light the hallway, though just as grand, was dark and dank and smelled of age. Every surface of the walls and ceiling had been carved, painted, or papered. Nothing held an edge, not corners of the moldings, not the colors in the landscape scenes, not the arms of the gas-powered, gilded light fixtures. Even the joints in the stone floor were worn and rounded. And though I was still cool, the cold did not bite like it had in the presence of Queen Mab.

My mother strode down the hallway ahead of me with purpose. The intersections did not give her pause, though they all looked the same to me, she turned and turned again as she led me toward the Queen's dungeon. I studied her back, the way she moved with very little wasted energy, the way her hair—which could have been my hair—surfed the air she moved through. Being my first interaction with her, it just wasn't enough.

It took me a second, but I realized I was mad. Really pissed. At her. For everything. Every step I took promised to bring me closer to my phamily, but those steps also took me closer to seeing red. I stopped walking.

She stopped two steps later and turned to face me. Even in the dimmer glow of the gas lights I couldn't deny the resemblance between us was more than close.

"Yes?" she asked.

"Aren't you going to say anything?" I asked. "You're a mother meeting her 26-year old daughter for the first time. Don't you want to know about me?"

She stepped forward, causing me to take a step back. "Do you want to tell me something about yourself?"

I did. I wanted to tell her everything about myself. As I considered where to start she interrupted my thoughts.

"Perhaps you'd like to share your joy at being the youngest applicant admitted to Culinary Institute of America's Master Baking program because your lemon meringue pie beat out 49 professional chefs at the Texas State Fair. Or maybe you'd like to brag about the 67 drop-dead-gorgeous men who you've shared your body with, intimately, since your were sixteen years old; all of whom still pine for you in one way or another. And yes, I know all about how you fell out of a tree and broke your arm when you were six, and that the maid had to put calamine lotion on your chicken pox when you were three, and that your father did a horrendous job of rocking you to sleep when you were an infant."

She stepped back with her right foot and crossed her arms.

"Or maybe you'd like to explain why you aren't in the damn studio this week recording your first professional performances. Oh, that's right, you got yourself in some trouble and now your bandmates are stuck in the Queen's dungeon."

I staggered sideways until the wall could hold me up. My mouth hung open and I could taste the mildew in the air.

How the hell had she known all of that? Sure, some of it could have come from discussions with my phamily, but not all of it. I'd forgotten all about having the chicken pox and crying and scratching until Miss Lucille dabbed my raw skin with something pink, and then I felt better. I was three?

She stepped closer and touched my arm with her delicate fingers. "I am very proud of you Bailey Faye. Maybe too proud. This is probably partially my fault."

"What the crap?" I asked her as my legs went slack and I slid to the floor.

She crouched down to look me in the eye. "You and your friends are here because I bragged about you, about how well you managed your father, how you refused to let a little hardship stifle your dreams, how you took life by the throat and made it do your bidding."

"How does that have anything to do with Laume or Hannah?"

"Laume has what you could call a severe competitive streak. Her tiny ego could not abide that you, my daughter, flourished where her own daughter tripped and fell flat on her beautiful little face."

I listened to her, but the words didn't make a whole lot of sense. Laume was competitive with my mom over how successful or unsuccessful their half-mortal children were? My struggle to survive and some lucky breaks were somehow better than Hannah's struggle and unlucky breaks, and that made my mom better than hers somehow?

Suddenly I felt like a prize poodle being paraded in a dog show. Or a rare strain of cattle. Or a slave who figured out how to irrigate the cotton field to save the crop from drought.

She had been watching. My whole life, my mother had been absent but watching with her Faery friends like my life was some goddamn reality TV show. As if it wasn't horrible enough that she could have seen all my pain and fear and anguish and loneliness and not done a damn thing to help me, she actually got some kind of status boost from her people because I managed to keep it together enough to chase after my dreams.

On the other hand, Hannah had not been as fortunate. And her mother suffered humiliation because of it. And she made me suffer because of that.

Maybe I was tougher than Hannah. Maybe I was born under a better star-symbol. Maybe Texas was just easier than Oregon for a teenager. Maybe my dad was just a little bit less of an asshole than hers.

The reasons didn't matter. Hannah was an amazing young woman with unbelievable talent. All she really needed was a chance.

"That's what Laume meant by my *special talent.*" I pushed against the wall until I could stand again. "Because of you she knew that I survived my fucked-up childhood and she thought I could do the same for her daughter."

My mom stood as well. "If you look at it from Laume's perspective it was a winning proposition either way."

"How do you figure that?"

"Either you were successful and her little girl would grow up to be one of the most popular, best-loved performers in your culture—giving her endless tales to bore us all with. Or you would fail and she'd never let me hear the end of it. She would finally see me disgraced."

A bleat of laughter forced its way out of my throat. Not that a thing about what she said was funny. It wasn't. But it was so the opposite of funny that I couldn't help but laugh.

"Unbelievable. You people are fucking unbelievable." I started walking in the direction we'd been headed, even though I had no clue where I was going. "You give birth to us, you leave us with these men who don't want us, then you pretend to care about us, but you'll throw us to the lions just so you can settle a childish dispute with your lifelong frenemy about who's fucking cooler than who."

"Whom. Who is cooler than whom."

I stopped and turned to find she was right behind me. I raised my hands because I wanted to throttle her, but my instincts told me that would go badly. "Whatever. How could you do that? We're human beings for Elvis's sake."

"Yes," my mother said, her tone as cold as ice. "You are. Aren't you?"

As we stared at each other I quickly realized there was no way for me to win. What I saw as the pinnacle of importance—being a human being with a heart and a soul and free will—would never mean anything to a Faery, not even my own mother. We were less than. I was less than and always would be.

I placed both hands over the fiery heart tattoo on my chest and calmed my breathing. I knew what was important. My phamily. My joy for baking. My skills with the drums. The pleasure of sharing my body, especially with Brady. My responsibility to Hannah, regardless of how it had come to be my responsibility.

And I was important. Not because my father was a celebrity chef or because my mother was a Faery. I was important because I survived, I vowed to keep the fire burning, and I deserved to live my life and be proud of myself.

I balled my hands into fists and dropped my arms back to my sides. "Just take me to my phamily."

The door to my phamily's dungeon cell was at least fifteen feet tall and made of solid timbers with all-wooden hinges, latches, and handles. It sighed gently, like a tree blowing in the wind, as a young Faery who looked a hell of a lot like Sir Ansley opened it to let me in.

He raised one unnaturally long finger to his unnaturally kissable lips and told me they were all sleeping.

My mother had left me at the dungeon entrance and though I couldn't help but watch her walk away, I didn't care if I never saw her again. My phamily, on the other hand, I couldn't wait to see. To hug. To just know whether they were okay or not.

I stepped through the door into a warm room; bare stone floor, stacked rock walls, ceiling made of heavy timbers and a fire crackling in a giant fireplace at the far end of the room. On the opposite wall there was a crude sink, a countertop full of ceramic plates and cups and wooden utensils, and a bent-willow shelf stacked with breads, wax-sealed jars of fruit, and a small Styrofoam cooler.

I tiptoed quietly over toward two benches set up with a table right next to a row of cots. The top of the table held books and that game board with all the gems I'd seen in Maria's mind.

Lowering myself gently onto the bench, so it wouldn't squeak, I motioned to Sir Ansley's son that I'd like to rest a while. He nodded and closed the door with the same gentle sigh.

My phamily lay sleeping on their cots, side-by-side, in front of the fire. They had fluffy pillows beneath their heads and intricate quilts draped over them. As always JoJo set the tempo with her snoring. Cooper and Paulo riffed along. And as I heard them all go silent, Maria ripped out a snort and then rolled over in her sleep.

We'd come so far from that little lifeboat in the Gulf of Mexico. Come so far to wind up in almost exactly the same place. Regardless, it was good to see them with my own eyes.

Maria snorted again, and when her attempt to get comfortable pushed her pillow off the end of her cot she came half awake to look for it. Her face turned to me—no make-up, hair flattened to her skull—and she saw me. It took a second for her to realize I wasn't supposed to be there.

"Kitty-kat?" she said drowsily.

"Hey Dolly." I smiled at her with tears in my eyes.

"Bailey!" she yelled and leapt off of her cot. In her hurry to get to me she bumped Cooper's cot and nearly rolled him out of it. Half a second later she flung her arms around me and I stood so that I could hug her back without dislocating my neck.

Maria's hug was quickly joined by another and I looked up to see Paulo's smiling face just two inches from mine. I reached over and kissed him and then turned to see Cooper and JoJo barreling toward us.

It wasn't a jump-up-and-down like a fool kind of group hug. It was an I-can't-believe-your-alive kind of hug. Just as intense, but less giddy-school-girl. But that kind of intensity could not hold us forever and we settled onto the benches around the table to catch up. We shared tears and smiles. We held hands. We asked questions and uttered curses, mostly at Laume. I was glad to know that they'd actually been treated well, for prisoners. They all knew Sir Ansley and he had given them my message.

I didn't explain about my mother. It was too raw for me; I didn't know what to say.

"So what happens next?" Cooper asked when Maria got up to get everyone a glass of wine. "Are we free? Are you staying with us?"

I shrugged my shoulders. "The Queen is making her decision about Laume. I really don't know how it's going to work out."

I explained how Sir Ansley and Queen Mab had seen through my attempts to hide the truth of my bargain with Laume from them.

"My only real hope is that how it happened won't matter so much now that I've delivered my side."

"Wait, I thought you said Ryan Williams was dead and the foster family chickened out," JoJo asked.

Oops. I'd forgotten to tell them the biggest news. "Well, Auntie JoJo, I figured out another way."

"Auntie JoJo?" Maria asked.

"Yes, Auntie Maria," I said and smiled at them. "You're all now officially aunts and uncles. You have two nephews: Jacob and Noah. And three nieces: Hannah, ML and Danni. I signed guardianship papers a few hours ago."

Their faces looked comically similar: mouths open, eyes wide, and they all cocked them at about the same angle.

"You're going to love them," I said, but their faces didn't change. "Come on, this is an Ooby Dooby moment, right?"

I saw Paulo's face soften first, and then Maria's, but before we could really talk about it, I heard the creak of the door opening behind me.

Sir Ansley's son stepped into the room. "Miss Bailey Faye, it's time."

My heart thudded a mile a minute as it tried to escape my chest. It was time to go. Time to get it all over with, for better or for worse. Queen Mab had made her decision.

My phamily walked me to the door, but their guard would let them go no farther. I kissed each one of them, squeezed them tight, and tried to remember how each of them felt in my arms.

Just in case it was the last time I'd ever see them.

36

Queen Mab's court looked far different when Sir Ansley and his son led me back to it. Gone were the white carpets and furniture of Graceland. No stained glass. No mirrors. Elvis's piano was absent.

Faery Magic was really amazing.

It was still fucking freezing, though.

The Queen's throne now dominated a cavernous stone room that looked more like a French cathedral than anything else I could name. The Queen herself appeared almost as different in a dark jade, body-hugging dress that shimmered with the slightest movement. Her eyes—those terrible, scary, beautiful quicksilver eyes—looked out from a face that had been made over to show how powerful and frightening she was.

I leaned over to Sir Ansley as we walked. "I think I liked the Rockabilly version better."

"Hush!"

Sir Ansley's son left us at the door and The Winter Knight walked me up the center aisle of the room as if I were the bride, he was my father, and all the Faeries who watched were guests at my wedding. Except I wanted to run down the aisle instead of walk up it.

Laume lounged in a high-backed chair at the base of Queen Mab's throne pedestal, her jet black hair piled on top of her hair in an updo as elegant as her ivory, scoop necked dress. As Sir Ansley sat me in a twin to Laume's chair, sitting to the other side of Mab's throne, I felt awfully underdressed in the vintage garb I'd purchased at the Buffalo Exchange that morning. No one else's clothes had buttons. Perhaps they were held in place by Faery magic.

Sir Ansley took up a position halfway between me and Laume and bowed to his Queen.

Queen Mab's Voice spoke, filling the room. "The fierce and noble Mab, Winter Queen of Faery, has decided."

The voices behind me cackled like a barnyard full of chickens and then quieted as the Queen surveyed the crowd, her jeweled crown catching the light.

I felt like maybe I should stand, but Laume remained in her seat, and Sir Ansley didn't motion for me to rise, so I fidgeted as I waited.

"Laume, daughter of Orion and Calliope. I have decided that you willingly executed an agreement with a mortal under duress. Your methods relied on intimidation and concealment rather than honest bargaining due to your subversive intentions. While I uphold your right to provide aide to your half-mortal offspring, even through negotiations with other mortals, your behavior undermined the security of my castle and my kingdom.

"Furthermore, as you commit these atrocities during the waxing of my power, while my sister, the Summer Queen, still holds sway, your actions endangered the whole of the realm of Faery."

That sounded an awful lot like Laume had fucked-up, but you sure couldn't tell from looking at her. Her casual posture never changed. But me, my fidgeting turned into an anxious lean forward with my fingers intertwined and pressed against my lips as I wondered how Queen Mab would handle my phamily.

"As your punishment, and since you seem to enjoy playing gaoler, I decree that you shall serve three moons as assistant to the assistant to the assistant Gaoler.

"You certainly won't need to dress so lavishly for the dungeons." The Queen gestured and Laume's beautiful dress transformed into a dun muslin shift belted at the waist with a length of rope. Her beautiful shoes, gone. Her jewelry vanished. Her hair magically transformed from an elegant knot at the crown of her head to frumpy, fly-away bun at the nape of her neck. It was like watching Cinderella in fast-rewind.

"But Your Majesty," Laume started to say, but then Queen Mab tilted her head, raised one eyebrow, and looked down her nose at Laume as if to say *I dare you, just one more word and you'll be in a cell rather than tending them.*

"Sir Ansley," the Queen's Voice said. "Please escort her to the office of the Goaler and have her put to work immediately scrubbing the floors."

Laume lunged out of her chair in a huff, shrugging off Sir Ansley's grip, and she hurried out of the court chamber—bare feet slapping on the stone floor—so that he could not escort her by force.

"That is all," the Queen's Voice said as Queen Mab summoned a chalice of wine out of thin air and began to sip at it.

"Wait," I cried out. "What about my phamily?"

"Yes, little half-human," the Queen said in her own voice, sending chills up my spine. "We have further business."

The Queen's Voice took a deep breath and she shouted to be heard, "The court's business is concluded. Clear the room."

Grumbling, and obviously as curious about what came next as I was, the Faeries sitting in the chairs behind me stood and slowly exited the room through the doors at the back. The Queen and her Voice waited in regal silence as the room emptied. I wanted to turn and watch them go, wondering if my mother was among them, but that would mean giving the Queen my back and there was no way I was going to do that. She might stick something pointy in it.

At last the room went silent, punctuated by the heavy doors closing, a sound that reverberated in my chest like the beat of one of my bass drums...only more ominous.

The Queen studied me. "I have reports of your creative solution to the situation Laume cornered you into. Are they accurate?" her Voice asked.

"Yes, Your Highness," I said. "I am legally responsible for Hannah Faye, to make sure she behaves, until she turns 18. But it's not just that. I understand her. I can help her make better choices and see that she doesn't waste her talent."

"And this ragamuffin group of human children. You think they will provide the stability she requires?"

"If you had seen them at Hannah's father's funeral, you wouldn't even have to ask," I said, and then added, "Your Highness."

The Queen got up from her throne and slipped down the stairs to stand in front of my chair. My heart pounded and fear filled my throat. "Show me," Queen Mab said in her own voice and reached out her delicate hand.

As if compelled, I raised my hand and gently wrapped my fingers around hers. Her skin was colder than ice and softer than fleece. I swallowed my fear so that I could take a deep breath, close my eyes, and bring to mind the way Hannah and the kids had looked and sounded as they stood at the head of Ryan Williams' open grave. I might have exaggerated their youthful good looks and the way they huddled close to Hannah, but I recalled their singing as closely as I could for the Queen.

When I reached the end of playing back that memory for Queen Mab I opened my eyes and looked into her face. "Do you see?"

Queen Mab extracted her hand from mine and flicked it nonchalantly at the chair Laume had sat in to face her judgment. The chair slid across the floor and came to rest beneath the Queen's rump just as she sat down.

"This is how you feel about your chosen-family?"

"My phamily." And I did not 'Your Highness' her. "Yes. I love them more than I love my own life."

"You are aware that they trespassed in my domain. They practiced Faery magicks that they had no business using. They entered my throne room without permission, interrupting royal business and embarrassing me."

I nodded.

"Those are not trifles."

"In their defense, Your Highness, they'd been unfairly taken prisoner and it's not the human way to sit around and wait to be rescued. They did what they thought they had to do."

The Queen gave me a small nod of concession, but I could tell she was not convinced.

But I had to find a way to convince her.

The few things I knew about Faeries were they were beautiful, magical, proud, crafty...and they loved a bargain. Underneath all of that was their need for clear intention. If I could get the Queen to understand it was all an accident, maybe she would find it in her frozen heart to offer us some leniency.

"It was not their intention to embarrass you, Your Majesty. They had no idea where Object Tracking would lead them, only that it would take them out of their cell. That was their only intention."

"And you swear to this?" the Queen's Voice asked. "On your mortal soul?"

"Yes, Your Majesty. I do."

Queen Mab sat back in her chair, bringing the tip of one perfect fingernail to her bottom lip.

"You are resourceful and intelligent, young Bailey Faye." The Queen used her own voice and this time, instead of rattling my innards, it felt like being stroked.

"Thank you, Your Majesty."

The Queen stood and the chair magically slid back to where it had come from. "Rise and kneel," the Queen's Voice said.

I complied, but when I started to bow my head I heard the boom of the rear doors and I looked back. A man who looked like an older brother to Sir Ansley stood just inside the doors with my phamily. They looked as confused and scared as I felt. The Queen motioned them forward until they stood just behind my chair.

"Bailey Faye, for your service to my crown in the furtherance of the safety and security of Hannah Faye, daughter of Laume, I bestow my thanks and will allow you to choose one of your comrades to return with you to your world."

"What?" I stood up. The Queen was at least ten inches taller than me, but I held my ground and stared up at her. "My bargain with Laume was for all of them."

"I have nullified that bargain, which you would understand if you had been paying attention. Now you have a choice to make. Which one will accompany you home?"

I had been paying attention. But she had not exactly been easy to follow. I turned to look at my phamily. Maria and Cooper looked furious. JoJo looked like she was about to burst into tears. Paulo had a slightly amused grin on his face, probably because this wasn't the weirdest thing going on in his version of reality.

How in the hell was I supposed to choose one of them?

I turned back, "What will happen to the others?"

"That depends on you, little darlin'," the Queen's Voice said. "Queen Mab believes you could be helpful to her interests in the mortal world. She offers you a bargain. In exchange for agreeing to remain in retainer for future service at Queen Mab's discretion, your three remaining companions will be kept securely here in the kingdom. As you complete specified tasks for Her Majesty you will gain the freedom of each of them in turn."

Elvis help me, not another Faery bargain. And Queen Mab wasn't really giving me any more wiggle room than Laume had back in the lifeboat. Somehow, I thought, bringing the irony of that to Her Highness's attention would probably not help the situation.

"Will they have to stay in their cell?"

The Queen nodded. "It's what's best and safest for them. But they will have Laume to see to their every need," her Voice said and they both smiled like crocodiles.

Good Graceland. That was all I needed to make my decision.

My phamily hated Laume, but it was obvious to me that Maria hated her more than the others did. If Laume had to be in Maria's face every day it's likely that one of them would kill the other, and my vote was on my feisty Italian friend.

But it wasn't the kind of decision I could make by myself.

"May I have a minute to talk this over with them?" I asked the Queen.

She nodded.

I walked towards my phamily but didn't stop where they stood at the back of the chair; instead I motioned for them to follow me a short distance away. As I walked, my back to the Queen and her attendant, I plucked three buttons off the front of my dress, and hoped that no one would notice.

We huddled tightly and spoke in whispers, not really sure how keen the Queen's ears were.

"I'm sorry you guys," I said. "I thought I had this all figured out."

"You should take Paulo with you," Cooper said. "He needs his meds."

"I'm okay," Paulo disagreed. "I can handle it."

I reached out and squeezed Paulo's hand, smiling at him and secretly passing him one of the buttons. He looked at me funny until he saw that I'd given him a button and I pointed to the matching one at my collar.

"JoJo, are you okay?" I asked as I reached out to her, trying to use my concern to cover my second covert button delivery. She'd seen what I'd done with Paulo and kept her face still.

"I'm fine. You should take Maria with you."

"What?" Maria asked. "I can't go and leave you all here with that Faery hosebeast."

"Hosebeast?" I laughed. Definitely a step down from Faery Bitch.

"I read it in one of Sir Ansley's books," Maria said with a snide smile. "Apparently it's one of the nastiest insults a Faery can smackdown on another Faery. I can't wait to unload it on her."

"And that's exactly why I'm getting you out of here." I reached out to Cooper, palming my last button. "Coop, you okay with that."

He took the button and disappeared it between two meaty fingers. "Yeah, I can handle it."

"I'll use my telepathy to stay in touch," I promised. "You guys just stay buttoned-down, okay."

They agreed, and after a round of really intense hugs we walked back over to Queen Mab who sat atop her throne drinking wine like nothing Earth-shattering had just happened.

"You've decided."

Maria and I stood together, hand-in-hand, with Cooper, Paulo and JoJo standing right behind us. "Yes, Your Highness."

"Away with you then," Queen Mab said, and with a flick of her hand I felt that familiar, nauseating, bitter-cold acceleration sensation yank at my belly button.

I closed my eyes, tightened my grip on Maria's hand, and gasped. The first half breath brought down lung-freezing air, but the second half felt warm and tasted like freshly cleaned laundry.

I opened my eyes and found myself standing in the sitting room of the Mariott hotel with Maria. The adjoining door stood open and six people looked like they were in the middle of a gang-bang version of hide-and-seek. Hannah. Jacob. Danni. ML. Noah.

And Brady. I'd know that fine ass sticking out from under the bed skirt anywhere.

Hannah was closest to us and our abrupt appearance scared her so badly she screamed. "Bailey, it's you! Thank goodness, you're back."

Brady's head popped out from under the bed and he rushed over to wrap me up in one of his amazing hugs.

"What happened? Where've you been?" he asked.

I let go of Maria's hand for just a second and wrapped my arms around his waist. His being in the room was exactly what I needed to come back to. He was there. I guessed the kids had called when I disappeared and he'd come for me, and for them.

"Sorry," I said, my forehead against his. "I had to pop out for a minute. Does this mean you've decided to stay, kids and all?"

"I'm staying," he said and he crushed his lips against mine. "Just try to get rid of me."

"I'm so glad."

"Hmmm, hmmm."

I let Brady go to find Maria standing with her arms crossed and her toe tapping. "Aren't you going to introduce me?"

I made introductions all around, amazed at how quickly Maria blended right in to my new phamily. I was glad to be home, to have her with me, but I wondered how long it would be until we were all together again.

I hoped it wouldn't be long. I knew Cooper, Paulo and JoJo wouldn't sit meekly in their cell, waiting on the Queen's pleasure. The buttons I left them might or might not work as an insurance policy if something horrible happened. But it was the only symbolic step I could take to keep them safe until the Queen called and gave me my next assignment.

ABOUT THE AUTHOR

Juliet Nordeen lives on the Kitsap Peninsula of Washington state with her husband and multi-species family. When Juliet is not writing she's training her German Shepherd pup, designing quilts, and baking the best pizza west of the Rockies. You can check on news and story updates at www.JulietNordeen.com.

www.ingramcontent.com/pod-product-compliance
Lightning Source LLC
LaVergne TN
LVHW041106080826
845145LV00007B/1697